About the Author

Mark Hayden is the nom de guerre of Adrian Attwood. He lives in Westmorland, England, with his wife, Anne.

Mark has had a varied career working for a brewery, teaching English and being the Town Clerk in Carnforth. He is now a part-time writer and part-time assistant in Anne's craft projects.

He is also proud to be the Mad Unky to his Great Nieces & Great Nephew.

THE
TWELVE DRAGONS
OF ALBION

The Second Book of the King's Watch

MARK HAYDEN

PAW
PRESS

www.pawpress.co.uk

First Published Worldwide in 2017 by Paw Press
Paperback Edition Published 2018
Reprinted with Corrections, 14 March 2021

Cover Design – Rachel Lawston
Design Copyright © 2017 Lawston Design
www.lawstondesign.com
Cover images © Shutterstock

Paw Press – Independent publishing in Westmorland, UK.
www.pawpress.co.uk

ISBN: 1-9998212-2-X
ISBN-13: 978-1-9998212-2-7

To Chrissy,

Micro-Niece

THE TWELVE DRAGONS OF ALBION

Prologue — Meet the Ancestor

How do you tell the difference between a Ghost and a Spectre?
Give up?

I'll tell you: Spectres are much better looking. Well, that's what my eleven times great grandfather said, and he should know — he's the Spectre haunting my house.

It had been a hell of a weekend, featuring Witches, Gods, Spirits, concussion grenades, talking trees and moles the size of border collies. And that was just the Sunday. After a trip to HMP Cairndale to see my girlfriend, I wanted very much to get back down to the village of Clerkswell in Gloucestershire and drink several pints of Inkwell Bitter — it's good stuff, you know, made with water from the original Clerk's Well at the bottom of our garden. When I say *our* garden, it's really *my* garden, because I own it.

Oh, to be in England in January. It was black, wet, cold and generally miserable as I piloted my Volvo estate through the pool of light from the last street lamp and into the darkness of Elvenham Lane. I swung the car through the gates of Elvenham House, past the ancient yew tree and coasted to a halt.

'I'm back,' I said to the dragon. It's a fearsome beast, is our dragon, carved into a block of limestone that's set into the bricks of our Gothic tower, and which family legend says you must salute when you return from a journey. We all do it, even Rachael.

If you're wondering about the Gothic tower, it's only a little one, three storeys, but it does have pointy windows and doors that look like they were salvaged from a castle. They weren't. Like the rest of Elvenham House, it's all Victorian red brick and bourgeois additions. Maybe the dragon is older. It looks older, but I'm no architectural historian.

I got out of the car and massaged the knots in my spine. When I turned back to the house, there was a man standing on the front step.

'Who the fuck are you?' I snapped.

The apparition flinched with shock. 'You can see me?' By now, my weak and tardy magickal Sight had told me that this was nothing normal.

'Of course I can bloody well see you. Isn't that what you wanted?'

'I...' said the apparition. Then it vanished.

Someone with a real Gift would have done something startling at this point. Someone like my soon-to-be colleague Vicky Robson, for example, would have whipped out her enhanced iPad – her sPad, as I call it – and explored the Sympathetic Echo for traces. Good for them. I got my bags out of the car and limped round to the side entrance. The front doors are only opened for weddings and funerals these days.

Our part-time housekeeper, Mrs Gower, had gone in this morning and put the heating on, but only high enough to stop ice forming on the windows, so I put the kettle on the Aga, whacked up the thermostat, hefted the bags upstairs and made myself a pot of tea. While I waited for the tea to brew (I aim for five minutes), I huddled close to the Aga and grudgingly gave the apparition some head-space.

The man – or facsimile of a man – was weirdly familiar, but I couldn't work out why until I glanced at a family snapshot pinned to the noticeboard. The figure under the dragon had been like a younger, thinner, more handsome and better dressed version of Dad.

I nearly dropped the mug when I heard a cough behind me. I whirled round and there it was again.

'Sorry,' it said. 'I didn't mean to startle you.'

It was like listening to Granddad Enderby. Underneath the Girton College vowels, Mother has the same accent: deepest, darkest rural Lincolnshire.

'Do I know you?' I said.

'Sort-of, but not so well as I know you. I'm Thomas Clarke, your eleven times great grandfather and your brother.'

'I'm not sure which part of that statement is more alarming,' I said. It's a measure of how quickly I've become embedded in the magickal world that I assumed there was some sort of truth in what he'd told me. 'Forgive my manners, Mr Clarke. Would you like a cup of tea? There's plenty.'

'Thank'ee, but no,' he grinned. 'I'm not corporeal at all, really, just enough to talk.'

I took out my cigarettes and sat down at the ancient battle-scarred kitchen table.

'I wish you'd stop smoking,' said the apparition. I'll give him the benefit of the doubt and call him Thomas.

'Not for a while,' I said, 'though it's kind of you to take an interest in my long-term future.' I drank some tea. 'So, Thomas, are you a Ghost or a Spirit?' I had no real idea what either of these truly was, but I didn't want to sound too ignorant in front of my 11xgreat grandfather.

'Neither. I'm a Spectre. Ghosts are involuntary: they gets no choice in what happens to 'em after they die. I chose to stick around, but I'm not a Spirit 'cos I can't go no more than three furlongs from the well.'

'Why?'

He looked down at the flags, and his dark suit got a little paler until I could see the outline of the kitchen sink appearing through him. He looked up and became more solid again. 'It's where I died. Near four hundred years gone, now. I can just go far enough to visit the churchyard. My Alice is waiting there for me.'

That puts my own patience into perspective – I only have to wait until the spring for Mina to get out of prison. Fingers crossed. 'Has Alice been awake…?'

He shook his head. 'Oh, no. Alice is asleep. Deep asleep. Most of the time, I am, too, but I felt you coming back tonight. Something must have happened to you while you was away 'cos you couldn't see me afore, but you can now.'

It was my turn to remember: the cold fingers of the First Sister brushing my wrist, the healing of my hand, the boost in power. 'I was touched by the Goddess.'

'That'll do it,' said Thomas. 'You must have done her good service to have had your Gift enhanced.'

'It wasn't enhanced by much.'

'Take what you can get, my boy. The Gods are very sparing in their favours. Tell me, do you know which aspect of the Goddess was with you?'

I have an idea about that, one which I'm not ready to share with Thomas yet, so I gave him my best shrug. I've been practising my shrugs a lot since I met up with Alain du Pont. The results are about as convincingly French as Somerset Brie, but it did the job.

'I've been watching you on and off since the day you were born, up there in the old nursery,' said Thomas. A wistful, remotely paternal look came over him, and his eyes drifted to the ceiling. This was a good sign, because Thomas had obviously been some sort of Mage, and one of the reasons I've struggled to make progress in the magickal world is the damned *Chymist's Code*.

This "code" has a rule that you don't give away *any* sort of magickal knowledge, no matter how trivial, unless you're either paid for it or you have no choice. Perhaps family ties might afford an exception in this case – there was clearly some sort of personal attachment here.

He was fading again as he reminisced. It seemed that whenever he concentrated on something other than talking to me, his ability to manifest was compromised. Before I could interrupt his reverie, he snapped back to the present. 'I couldn't believe it when you were born,' he said. 'As it was written, it came to pass. A little miracle.'

'Not even my mother thinks I'm a miracle, Thomas,' I said. 'Especially not my mother.'

'You'd be surprised,' he said, with a rather cheesy grin. 'Mary loves you very, very dearly, Conrad. She's just never been good with showing emotions. Doesn't mean she doesn't feel them as much as you or me.'

As the hit of caffeine started to work, all sorts of very, very alarming possibilities opened up. I put down my mug and crushed out my cigarette. 'Just how closely have you been watching us, you immaterial voyeur.'

'Steady on, old chap. Your family is my family, too, and no, I don't hang around the bedrooms. Or the drawing room that night that you and Amelia…'

'…Stop right there, Mr Spectre. No more with the sordid details. Now, what exactly *did* you mean by saying my birth was a miracle? There wasn't a star overhead, or wise men, and though I'm told the midwife was married to a farmer, she didn't bring any sheep with her.'

'You're not the Messiah, you're a very naughty boy,' said Thomas with relish. 'I did enjoy that film.' He held up his hand. 'Seriously, it goes back to what I said about being both your ancestor and your brother.'

'Take it slowly, Thomas. My head is starting to hurt, and I'd planned to go to the pub tonight.'

'It's out of my range, I'm afraid, or I'd join you.'

'Oh, yes, that would cement my reputation perfectly, having a conversation with an empty chair.'

It was his turn to shrug. He did it quite well, considering that he hasn't had shoulder joints for four hundred years.

'I was born in Lincolnshire,' he said, 'but my family came from Clerkswell. My father was a younger son, and he had inherited Elvenham Grange, though he never lived here. When I got married, I decided to move in and become a farmer. There have been Clarkes here ever since.'

'That explains the ancestor part,' I said. Something about the phrase *move here and become a farmer* tickled a memory, but Thomas moved on before I could catch it.

'It helps explain the brother part, as well,' he said. 'Mary – your mother – is from Lincolnshire too and she's a direct maternal descendant of my own mother's sister. As you modern people say, we have the same Y chromosome and the same mitochondrial DNA. I've watched a lot of TV with your family, and read the Sunday papers, Bro.'

'No one gets to call me *Bro*, Thomas. No one except Rachael.' I limped over to the Aga and poured some more tea. I shivered with fatigue, pain and just a little discomfort at having shared my home with a spectral ancestor since the day I was born. Questions? Of course I had questions. Lots of them – huge questions about the true nature of the soul, about free will, divine providence and destiny. What did I actually ask him?

'Tell me, Thomas, how come you've got a beautifully historic Lincolnshire accent but a suit from Saville Row?'

If he'd been expecting something more profound, he was too polite to show it. 'That's another difference,' he said. 'Ghosts have no real choice over their manifestations – hence the gory locks and severed heads. We Spectres can look how we want, with practice. I was never this handsome in the flesh. The accent's harder. In the body, I didn't know I had an accent, so I can't learn to change it without sounding like a broken computer.'

I let the fresh tea warm me enough to loosen my coat. The moment's relaxation took me back to another of Thomas's cryptic utterances. 'You said I was born *As it was written*. What did you mean by that?'

He perked up, and the sheen on his suit got a little brighter. 'You were what I've been waiting for. It was in the Agreement that I could join my Alice *When Thomas Clarke shall be born again by his own mother and father*. I felt it the second you gave your first cry – a wave of magick spread out from the Well like the wind through the reeds. *Thomas is born*, it said.'

I really didn't like the sound of that. 'Why are you still here? Why is Alice still waiting? What's this Agreement thingy?'

Thomas went suddenly and alarmingly transparent. 'I don't know. I used a lot of my Lux before Victoria was crowned, and I've had to let some things go. It scares me, Conrad. I know that my purpose was to keep the Clarkes in Elvenham until you came along, but I can't remember why, or what happens next.' As he spoke, he'd faded completely, and his last words had come out of thin air.

I finished my tea and looked at the clock. There was still plenty of time to get to the pub before they stopped serving food. The mystery of Spectre Thomas could wait.

.

1 — *Peculier by Name…*

L ondon. I really don't like the place very much, I certainly don't know it very well, and I never thought that my career – either in the RAF or out of it – would take me there for the long term. Just goes to show what I know.

The junior tenant in my Notting Hill flat had been sent away suddenly, and the other tenant's rent more than covered the mortgage, so I moved into the second bedroom and prepared myself for a long stay in our capital city.

The weekend's adventures, my encounter with Spectre Thomas and a trip to the Inkwell meant that I was too knackered to travel on Tuesday, and besides, I needed to do some preparation before I came out of hiding.

Thomas Clarke hadn't shown himself, and my Sight isn't good enough to pick him out unless he's watching me, so on Wednesday morning, I left a note for him on the kitchen table with a few lines about my plans, then I drove to Cheltenham and caught the early train to Paddington.

I am about to join a magickal company called the King's Watch, and it's based in the Tower of London, hidden from the world by the efforts of the Royal Occulter. My future workplace, Merlyn's Tower, doesn't even appear on Google Earth. No wonder the magickal world has stayed hidden for millennia.

The King's Watch is led by the Peculier Constable. With Queen Elizabeth II on the throne, why are we called the *King's* Watch? Why does the boss have such a daft title? The world of magick has more anachronisms and historical hangovers than any church, Oxford College or Army regiment, and to explain them all would be a major undertaking. Besides, I know almost none of the answers.

The current holder of the Office – the Peculier Constable herself – is Dame Hannah Rothman. I know very little about her except that she wasn't born a Mage, that she used to be a detective in the Met, and that she lost her husband and part of her skull defeating something called a Revenant. She also packs a mean magickal punch. Oh yes, and she's Jewish. Not that I'm sure what it means to be Jewish in a world where Odin can turn up at your house and the Goddess (?) stands protector to a group of pagan nuns in Lancashire. Not the most pressing issue in my inbox.

To access Merlyn's Tower you don't need to go through the public parts of this great fortress, but I did anyway, paying my fee so that I could pay my respects to the resident ravens. These birds are Odin's creatures in more ways than one, and although he's no longer my Patron, a small sign of our alliance hangs round my neck. It's called a Valknut, three interlocking triangles. Long-term, it might be more trouble than it's worth, but I wouldn't be in the world of magick if it weren't for the Allfather, so there it stays, as does the special

Troth ring he gave me. It's a sort of certificate of honesty that guarantees that *A Clarke's word is Binding*. It makes me very careful what I say.

The front door of Merlyn's Tower isn't locked, and there was no one around on the lower levels. At 09:55 I presented myself to the PC's personal assistant, the larger-than-life Mrs Tennille Haynes. She rushed over to give me a big motherly hug.

'Thank the Lord Jesus, Mr Clarke, for your deliverance. Welcome back. Sit down an' I'll make the tea and tell her you're here.'

Tennille – from Barbados originally – has no magick herself, but she has the ear of the most powerful Mage I've met and her daughter Desirée is apparently a rising star in something called the Invisible College.

Shortly after ten, we were buzzed in to Hannah's ornate and spacious office. Tennille led the way with a tray and I followed, stopping at the edge of the rug and snapping a smart salute. For reasons of history and HR, all Hannah's staff are technically in the Army. She's a colonel.

'Why do you keep doing that?' said Hannah, pointing to my raised hand.

'Officers should salute senior officers on all occasions, ma'am, unless unit policy dictates otherwise.'

She raised her hand in the worst salute I've seen outside the cinema, and I lowered my arm. From the corner of my eye, I could see a very amused expression on Tennille's face.

Hannah turned to her PA. 'Draft a memo, will you? New policy: saluting is only required when in uniform.'

'They won't know what you're talking about,' said Tennille with a chuckle. She left us to it, closing the heavy oak doors behind her.

Hannah was wearing a green bandanna, knotted snugly around her head. It clashed with her conservative outfit of blouse, skirt and boots, but was a much better look than either the wig or the terrible scarring and misshapen repairs underneath. I've got a titanium tibia; she's got a titanium skull.

She came round and offered me a warm handshake, took my arm and guided me to the table in front of the picture window with its view over the Thames.

'How did you do it, Conrad?' she said when we were seated.

This was way too much of an open question with far too many pitfalls to venture an answer. 'Do what, ma'am?'

She closed her blue-green eyes. 'Enough of the *ma'am*, already. You don't even work here yet.'

'Sorry. If you're going to be my CO, and you don't want me to call you ma'am, you'll be fighting against two decades of conditioning.'

'At least while we're sitting down. None of the others do it.'

I thought that it might be a good idea if Li Cheng, the Royal Occulter, showed a bit more respect, but I kept that thought to myself and nodded my understanding.

15

Hannah poured the tea and sat back. 'I wanted to know how you sweet-talked Vicky Robson into joining your personal crusade up North. Strictly against the rules, and a serious matter. For her.'

I fixed my gaze on Tower Bridge. I was going to lie, and Hannah knew that I was going to lie.

'Vicky had decided to spend the weekend walking in the Lake District. It was a complete coincidence that she was nearby after the Battle of Lunar Hall.'

Hannah snorted with laughter. 'Vicky doesn't walk to the Tube if she can get an Uber, she thinks that the Lake District is a shopping mall in Essex, and when I FaceTimed her, she was *wearing a fleece*. I'm surprised it wasn't branded *Team Conrad*. Is this nonsense about a walking holiday what you're going to put in your report?'

I reached into my briefcase and pulled out the first document. 'Already there, ma'am. If there's anything you'd like me to add or amend, please let me know. I have no experience in writing reports with a magickal dimension. Except my expenses – there's always been an element of fantasy there.'

I passed her a second sheet with my claim for nearly £20,000. She passed it straight back.

'You weren't a Watch Captain and you weren't on Queen's Business at Lunar Hall.' She smiled. 'On the upside, I can't discipline you for anything you did wrong.' She took the first document and nodded. 'Thanks for this. I'll read it carefully, Conrad.' She put the papers down. 'Do you trust me enough to talk off the record?'

Everyone else in the King's Watch has come from the magickal establishment. They're all graduates of this Invisible College thing. Hannah and I are outsiders, and I was counting on her support in the future, so, yes, if I didn't trust her now, I might as well quit. 'Of course,' I said.

She nodded again. 'You've had a lot of close shaves. Been in a few sticky situations, and I don't just mean recently.'

There was no point in false modesty: she's read my RAF record. 'You could say that, yes. I've flown helicopters into – and out of – some pretty dangerous places.'

'Teamwork,' she said, more of a statement than a question. 'Tell me honestly, Conrad, does Vicky have what it takes for field assignments?'

I didn't hesitate. 'I'd trust Vicky to have my back 100%. On the record or off it. I know she's struggling to find a role here, so I'd say she has great potential in the field.'

'That's what I hoped you'd say. Good. I also notice you said *potential* and *your* back. She's not ready to go out on her own, and I'm guessing that you couldn't have completed your mission without her. If you pass the test, I'm going to put her with you for a while.'

Her last sentence contained the best and the worst news I'd heard in a while. 'Thanks, Hannah,' I said. 'But I thought that rescuing Abbi Sayer *was* the test.'

She gave what can only be described as an evil grin. I've seen her sad, furious and pissed off in her professional capacity, but this was the first time I'd seen an aspect of the woman underneath. I very much liked what I saw. 'I'm sure you'll pass,' she said. 'I only propose the Watch Captains. Someone else makes the appointment.'

'Eh? And who would that be?'

'It'll be a surprise. Now, down to business. I've never appointed an ex-soldier before.'

'Former airman. Please.' I took out another bundle of papers, and this time her eyes followed my hands.

'That's lovely,' she said, pointing to my briefcase. 'Can I see?'

I handed it over. It's a Victorian adjutant's case, made of soft leather and designed to survive a trip across the battlefield and arrive with its orders intact. Stamped on the front is the fading image of crossed cavalry sabres and, more recently, my initials and a set of RAF wings.

'A present from my Dad, when I passed out of Cranwell,' I said. 'He's an antique dealer. Retired now.'

'Lovely work,' she said, admiring the close stitching.

As Hannah had leaned forward to examine the case, her chest had shifted. I'm not in the habit of staring at women's chests, but I'd never been this close to her before, and I was looking at the briefcase myself, so it was right in my eye-line. I say that her chest shifted – underneath her white silk blouse, her breasts sort of detached themselves and hung loose. Just by a fraction. It was a good job that she was looking down, and couldn't see the alarm on my face. As well as the plate in her skull, it looked like she'd had a double mastectomy. Whatever traumas Hannah Rothman has suffered in her life, she bears them well. Better than I do.

She handed the case back. 'Sorry. What are these papers?'

'I took the liberty of contacting the RAF personnel department. The procedure for resuming a commission is different to giving a new one. I was hoping to get my wings back, too.'

She considered the question, nodded and asked what to do.

'Sign here, here and here. I'll tell Mrs Haynes where to send them.'

She flourished a pen, signed, then tilted her head. 'How do you know her last name?'

It was my turn to smile. 'I've heard about her daughter. Briefly.'

'Hmm. I won't ask. Right, Conrad, you know what to do next in terms of securing your appointment as Watch Captain, don't you?'

'See the Dwarf and claim my reward.'

'Pretty much. Hledjolf has made the badge of office for Watch Captains for generations.'

'I've seen Li Cheng's dagger. Does it have to be like that?'

'It's up to you. The badge of office itself is a small engraving which gets stamped magickally at your appointment. Apart from that, the design is up to you. Some of the Watch prefer full length swords – awkward, but powerful. It depends on your magick and how you use it.'

'And because I have so little?'

'You'll need more Works built in, and it will need a lot of Alchemical Gold to act as a reservoir. Whatever you choose, it takes about a week. I'll arrange the swearing-in for a fortnight tomorrow. You need to wear your uniform for that.'

'I'll get it cleaned, and talking of Works, Vicky will need to get herself one of those Ancile thingies if she's going into the field.'

'Of course. I'll put it in her orders.'

Our business was done, but she hadn't made a move to dismiss me. 'Is there anything else, ma'am?'

She frowned. 'Vicky's coming back from Wray tonight. My Deputy tells me that the case against Keira might be complicated.'

'How come? She murdered that Polish Sister and, what's worse, she tried to kill me. Four times.'

'Mmm. Not sure of the details – Vicky can fill you in. She's taking leave until next week, then she can start your induction. Come back here on Monday and I'll set you off. I think you'll work well together.'

'I hope so. It'll get her away from Li Cheng, too.'

'What?'

'Bad case of unrequited love, I'm afraid. Shall I take the papers?'

Hannah stared at me. 'Vicky? And Cheng? How…'

'Thanks, Hannah,' I said, scooping up the papers. I didn't want her looking at them too closely. 'I'll see you next week.'

I left her shaking her head and smiling.

Outside the formidable oak doors, Tennille accepted the commission papers and my direction to send them to RAF High Wycombe. In return, she took my photograph and got me to fill out a short form while asking about my family. All very friendly.

I was hoping that I never had to account for how I really did meet her daughter and what Desirée was actually up to at the time.

With my Peculier business concluded, it was time for Hledjolf the Dwarf, who lurks in his Hall beneath the vaults of the Bank of England. To get there, I would have to pass through the territory of my oldest magickal ally – His Worship, the Lord Mayor of Moles.

I walked up to Bank tube station, site of Keira's first attempt on my life, and took the service door which allows me to access the Old Network, a series of tunnels under London, of which I've seen about ½ a mile. That could be 10% or 0.001% for all I know. Yet another yawning chasm of ignorance.

The Lord Mayor of Moles was born a perfectly ordinary specimen of *talpa europaea*, the common mole, possibly near Hackney Marshes. Something, or someone, magickally transformed him into a bull-sized bulldozer with magickal skills and the capacity to learn. Later, they tried to chain him for some purpose, and he escaped, eating one of his captors in the process. He now lives as a free creature in his nest under the Mansion House, as befits the first Lord Mayor of Moles.

I gave him that title, and that's not all. Part of my first magickal mission was to avoid becoming Moley's dinner and, rather than risk a fight, I did a deal, providing him with a braille terminal, laptop and phone (hence the huge and hugely unsuccessful claim for expenses). He is one of the very few magickal creatures with an online presence, so I had e-moled him (sorry) in advance, and he was waiting for me when I entered the Old Network, having collected my camping lantern from its niche on the stairs. Unlike in the movies, these tunnels are not illuminated.

What the magickal enhancement hadn't given Mr Mole was the gift of normal vision. Every time we meet, he has to run his squidgy over-sized nose all over me, and every time he does that it grosses me out.

'You are no longer Odin's creature,' he said by way of greeting.

'Hello to you, too.'

'*Ghaagh*,' he said. I think that's Moleish for *Whatever*.

'Are the worms still fat, Your Worship?'

When Moley is distressed, his nose flicks round at twice the normal speed. This was not a happy mole and, for once, it wasn't my fault.

'The best worms have gone. To get Lux, I must do more digging for the Dwarf.'

You'd think that Dwarves would be all for digging, wouldn't you? Not any more, not when they can outsource it. It takes a lot of Lux – magickal energy – as well as a lot of raw meat to sustain a creature of Moley's size and nature. He'd been living off magick worms that crawled out of the basement of various banks in the City. Why are financial institutions infested with glowing worms? No idea.

'What exactly do you dig for the Dwarves?' I asked.

'The human Croshrail is deep,' he said, mangling the sibilants. 'The new tunnel has disrupted the Old Network. I dig to divert and to renew.'

'Here you go,' I said. 'A gift. It's curry paste.' I loosened the lids on two jars and left them for him to nose out. How do I know that moles like curry sauce on their worms? Long story.

He found the jars and his nose flicked round again: he was thinking, and I gave him some space. Mr Mole will never be my friend, as such, because Moles are too territorial, but he is a valuable ally, and I can do things for him that he can't do for himself.

Finally his nose almost stopped moving. 'I have found something,' he said. 'You should examine it.'

I didn't have a fixed appointment with Hledjolf, and the chance of a guided tour was too good to miss. It would help fill that yawning chasm of ignorance. 'Lead on, Your Worship.'

We headed south west, away from the Bank, past the entrance to Moley's nest and into unknown territory for me. These tunnels were obviously ancient, and were lined with stone that was far too well finished to be human handiwork of that period. Definitely Dwarvish.

A little further, the tunnel swung north, then forked. The left fork was full of earth and completely blocked.

Moley nosed it and said, 'That was the old route. The new route is this way.' He found the opening to the right fork and pressed on.

The new tunnel started to descend rapidly, got warmer and became raw dirt. We were now in the New Old Network, as dug by His Worship. He stopped when the tunnel opened into a crossroads. Were we under the Barbican? My sense of direction is one of my strengths, but you have to know the surface to place yourself relative to it, and I just don't know London that well.

Moley's new tunnel continued north and down on the other side of the crossroads, but he had clearly intercepted a *very* old part of the Old Network, because it was lined with long, low bricks. I dimly remembered seeing the like at Pompeii, and the passage was arched in a very suggestive way. Surely this couldn't be Roman, could it?

Mr Mole turned right, along the Romanesque tunnel, stopping at the threshold of a small chamber. 'Here,' he said.

I lifted my camping lantern and unshipped my LED torch. The chamber was about the size and shape of a cathedral side-chapel, minus the altar and artwork. All I could see was unlined brick until I looked down.

'Bugger me,' was my informed, reflective contribution.

At the centre of the chamber was a depression, shaped like a rugby ball but much, much bigger, and seemingly carved from a single piece of smooth black rock, much blacker than any rock should be, especially down here. I've never seen anything like that dug from a British quarry.

The rest of the floor definitely said that we were in Roman territory, because no one else made mosaics quite like these. Great red tongues of fire spread out from the basin, each flame a masterpiece of intricate tiles. The rest of the floor was mostly black, but with a suggestion of roiling smoke. The basin looked to me like some sort of font, some baptismal shrine to a god of fire. I'd have said it was an actual fire-pit, but the roof of the chamber had no chimney or soot stains.

'Have you nosed it out?' I asked Moley.

'I can feel the presence of a Work. You can go in.'

(BTW, a *Work* is what they call a spell down south. The Witches I'd met in Lancashire called them *Charms*. Ghaagh.)

'I think we need an expert opinion,' I said. 'But thanks for the heads-up. Where does the tunnel go in the other direction?'

'It runs 35.36 metres and ends in another Work.'

How did he measure 35.36m? Never mind. I was about to thank him again when a rather obvious thought struck me. 'You dug both of the cross-tunnels, didn't you?'

'Yes. Until I made a way, this tunnel was sealed completely.' He reared up and nosed me again, because that's what he does. I tried not to shudder. 'Mole must dig. Mole must go.' And he went.

I took a last look into the chamber, from a safe distance, and saw nothing new. So, we have a magickally guarded chamber, probably of Roman construction, with possibly some sort of religious function and which was accessed from a tunnel that was completely inaccessible. Hmm.

I took a picture with my digital camera (because I won't have a smartphone), and walked the 35.36m to the other end. Moley had been reluctant to approach the Work at the end, but I soon saw what his blindness and caution had hidden from him: a door.

I took another picture and retraced my steps past Bank Station, on and down, down below the vaults to the antechamber of Hledjolf's Hall.

As far as I can tell, there is one Dwarf called Hledjolf, and it exists in several bodies as a sort of shared consciousness. The instances of Hledjolf have only one thing in common with your average Tolkien dwarf – height. Hledjolfs are about four foot tall, and look like a cross between R2D2 and a Minion. They have diamonds for eyes, no visible ears and a loudspeaker for a mouth. Oh, and they're made of stone. No, I don't understand it either.

If you think that I've got a soft spot for Mr Mole, you'd be right, and if you'd met the Dwarves you'd know one of the reasons. The Hledjolfs are as incapable of emotional interactions as the carvings on their walls, one of which is me.

The antechamber to Hledjolf's Hall is covered with relief carvings of their clients, going back hundreds if not thousands of years, sort of like a visual testimonial. I checked to see if anyone had been added since my last visit, and found images of two women, one in a priestess robe, the other in a mini skirt, further proof that now they'd been given the chance, women were asserting themselves in the magickal world. I took a picture (in case I ever ran across them again), rang the bell and waited.

Seeing the Dwarf again was no less disturbing than the first time. The Lord Mayor of Moles is unique, bizarre and in all senses larger than life, whereas Hledjolf is just plain unnatural. And greedy. Very greedy.

The Dwarf and I got straight down to business when he/it had escorted me to their conference room, the one with the human sized table.

'You made a lot of money out of me,' I said. Best to be clear from the off.

'And we gave you that opportunity. You knew the risks,' said the Dwarf.

'Right. Your risk was only financial – I nearly got killed. Several times.'

'Which is reflected in the bonus paid to you by the Lunar Sisters. A bonus from which we received no commission.'

'You won't starve. What do Dwarves eat, by the way?'

'Lux. Nothing but Lux. Do you have plunder, also?'

I did. Apparently, if you defeat a magickal enemy, you get to keep all their Doodads. *Doodads* is not a technical term by the way, it's just my name for the Artefacts which Mages wear on a chain round their necks to extend and focus their magick. I'd picked up a dozen when I'd killed Deborah Sayer and captured her partner in crime.

I'd been given a Doodad of my own, a personal gift from Mother Julia. It was a *Persona*, a Charm which made it harder, if not impossible, for Mages to use Sorcery to track me.

I spread the plunder on the table – a glass topped stone table that's half mediaeval and half science fiction. Dwarves are pioneers in the science of Quantum Magick, and the tabletop lit up as the built-in sensors assayed the Artefacts placed on it and labels appeared next to each item. Unfortunately, the labels were in Dwarvish.

The little stone monster pointed to four of the medallions and separated them into a pile. 'These are personal, tied to their maker and of no use to anyone else. We can smelt them and release the Lux. You will get 2.7oz Troy.'

Troy ounces are the unit of magickal currency. Lux is stored in Alchemical Gold (real gold with some sort of enhancement), and the Dwarves act as bankers, as well as being the preeminent makers of Artefacts.

The Lunar Sisters had paid the Lord Mayor of Moles a whole 36oz Troy for a special job, and the Sisters had considered it a fortune, so 2.7oz for the useless Doodads was a good price. Things were looking up.

'Done,' I said. 'What about the rest? Can I incorporate them into my new Badge of office?'

The Dwarf pointed to my neck. 'You have a Persona already. A good one. I can incorporate it into your Badge and buy these two spare ones from the table.'

I touched the Artefact through my jacket. 'No, thanks. This was a gift from the first Mage to show me kindness. It can stay there.'

The sentiment was lost on the Dwarf. He just flicked two more medallions towards him. 'Value 0.3oz,' was his only comment. Not so good.

'What about an Ancile?' I asked. The Ancile is an Artefact which can literally divert a bullet. Lots of bullets. There are limits: it won't absorb a concussion grenade, as Debs Sayer discovered when I bowled one at her head.

'There are two,' said Hledjolf. 'This one is burnt out and useless.' That would be Ms Sayer's. 'That one is damaged. We will make you a new one.' He took them off the table. 'Another 0.1oz.'

That left four pieces.

The Dwarf pointed to three of them in turn. 'This is the code for Dodgson's Mirror. It takes much Lux to work, so the Artefact is rare. We offer 1oz. These two are pure gold: they do nothing but store Lux, and both have been much depleted. There is 2.4oz left.'

I nodded my acceptance, and the medallions were removed. That left one.

The Dwarf stared at it for a long time. 'We have not seen a piece like this for many, many years. It is very old, and the Work it contains is folded in on itself, much as you might encrypt a computer program. Without the correct Keyway, not even the gods can use it.' The Dwarf slid it back to me. 'We suggest that you look in the estate of your victims for a clue.' There was a pause. 'We do not recommend that you use this Artefact yourself. The results could be unpredictable.'

'Was that a piece of friendly advice?' I asked. Perhaps underneath that silicate exterior...

'No. It was to cover ourselves if you do anything stupid. We would not want the Peculier Constable to accuse us of negligence.'

Ah well. Never mind.

Hledjolf continued, 'The total for these items is 6.5oz. You are owed 16oz for completion of your contract with the Lunar Sisters. What item do you want us to make for your Watch Captain's Badge of Office?'

When Hannah had admired my briefcase, I was keeping my fingers crossed that she didn't look inside, or if she did, that she didn't unwrap the oilcloth package hidden at the bottom. I took it out myself and peeled back the layers.

'This is what I want,' I told the Dwarf.

It said nothing. For the first time in their presence, I got a magickal tingling of a different sort. It was as if *all* the instances of Hledjolf had stopped what they were doing and were staring through this one Dwarf's diamond eyes.

'We have never done this before,' he finally said.

The only vaguely human trait I'd seen in the Dwarves (other than greed) was pride. 'I can go somewhere else if you're not up to it,' I said.

'Of course we can do it, mortal.'

Ouch. I've never been called that before. It stung.

'Why do you want a handgun?' asked Hledjolf. 'You cannot slash or stab with it. That is how Watch Captains enforce their authority when their magick is insufficient.'

'I don't want any handgun, I want a SIG P226 Elite. Like this one. You can put the Ancile and Badge in the grip, and you can put most of the magick into the bullets. I can't be the first, erm, *Mage* to ask for magickal bullets.'

'No, you are not, but when we explain to Mages how expensive is the targeting rune, and how inefficient is the delivery of Lux, they ask for something else.'

'I don't need a targeting rune. That's one thing I can do on my own.'

'Many claim that.'

What is this? Put Conrad In His Place Day?

'Look, Mr Dwarf, I can shoot an apple off your head at twenty-five metres with this gun.'

'What is the significance of the apple?'

I lowered my head and beat it slowly on the table.

'Just set up a test,' I said when the pain got too much.

'As you wish.'

We did it in a corridor. I insisted on ear defenders, then we argued about the light levels – it's darker in Hledjolf's Hall than in any nightclub. I know that Dwarves are photosensitive, but this was ridiculous. In the end, I did it using my lantern and they watched via video.

Before the Dunblane shootings put an end to live pistol firing as a competitive sport, I was the South West Junior Champion and on the team for the Modern Pentathlon. When the fun stopped, I kept up the riding, and started shooting again in the RAF.

I demolished all five targets and we reconvened for negotiation.

'We will make an exact copy of this weapon,' said the Dwarf. The cost of that will be 12oz, to include your Ancile and the holder for your Badge. We simply cannot incorporate any other Runes or Works in something so mechanical.'

'What do you mean *holder* for my Badge?'

'The actual Badge is stamped onto a socket when you take the oath. As we understand it.'

'Fine. Ammunition?'

'There will be a design fee of 2oz, and each bullet will cost 0.2oz.'

'Rounds. The whole package is called a round. The bullet is what they fire.' I had 22.5oz in the bank. The clip for a P226 holds 12 rounds of 9mm ammunition, so… 'I'll take 30 rounds and two spare clips, and don't forget proving. I'll expect you to provide three rounds and a suitable target for testing.'

'It is agreed,' said Hledjolf.

And that was that. All he said on the way out was that it would be ready in a week.

2 — ...*Invisible by Nature*

Between catching the late train back to Cheltenham on Wednesday, and catching the early one to Paddington on the following Monday, a few things happened that you should know about.

The first – and sweetest – was Thursday morning. I got a text from Vicky Robson, who had obviously just heard the news about working with me: *Howdy Pardner. Not sure if you're Mad or Bad, but you're definitely Dangerous to Know. See you Monday, Uncle Conrad. Vic. X.*

I'm only fourteen years older than her. Truly, the gap between the pre- and post-digital generations is immense. Vicky thinks I'm some sort of psychopathic throwback who doesn't know what he's doing, and knowing Hannah, she probably sold the partnership to Vicky on the basis that Vicky would be looking after me as I blundered round the world of magick like Mr Mole in an art gallery.

Vicky's message arrived while I was supervising the builders who were refurbishing the old stables at Elvenham House into new stables, so that I could get a horse. If that sounds a little extravagant, it's because of my leg.

The titanium tibia came from being a little too close to a rocket propelled grenade in Afghanistan. It hurts after inactivity, then gets easier when I walk, but it's too painful to run very far unless I have to, so the physiotherapist recommended swimming. If you like swimming, skip the next paragraph.

I hate swimming. I loathe it. Swimming is the most boring form of exercise ever invented: who can enjoy thrashing up and down the water with nothing to look at or listen to, and no variety? Sorry. Rant over.

Iyengar yoga is good, and when I'm settled I'm going to find a class, but for a good, whole-body aerobic workout, you can't beat a gallop, and it's perfect for keeping the weight off my leg. What's more, if I hadn't been able to ford the river Roeburn on horseback, I'd never have got to the Battle of Lunar Hall, never mind won it.

The building work was coming on nicely, despite the cold weather, and I left the builders to it while I looked into options for improving the thermal efficiency of Elvenham House, something of a major challenge.

Friday morning saw the second highlight: a letter from my girlfriend. She's only four years older than Vicky (yes, I know, she's too young for me. You're not the first to say that), but Mina Desai is culturally closer in age to me than she is to Vicky, because Mina is not a digital native. If you think that's too much of a coincidence, I'll explain why.

Her family were quite strict when she was a teenager in ways still possible ten years ago, then she was badly injured in an assault and became quite isolated as a result, and now she's in prison and won't use the many illegal phones circulating both because she's a great stickler for the rules and also because she doesn't want to get into debt to one of her fellow prisoners. A wise woman, my Mina.

Mina and Vicky have met, briefly. On Monday morning I had dragged Vicky to HMP Cairndale to explain, and demonstrate, the world of magick to an unbelieving Mina, and I wasn't surprised to receive a letter so soon. Prisoners can send as many letters as they want, but every one is scrutinised. Stuck in her cell for up to twenty-two hours a day, Mina was having trouble digesting the fact that her boyfriend was now hanging out with a bunch of witches and wizards.

As part of agreeing to become an item (as much as we can be an item when one of us in prison), Mina had made me promise not to lie to her, and she has never doubted me since. The net result is that she can't decide which of us has gone mad, a very sensible question in the circumstances.

Saturday was a busy day. It began with a phone call from Mother. I'd been going to ring her, but she normally likes a lie-in now that she's retired. As soon as I answered, I asked her how the finals of the bridge tournament had gone.

'It was close, but we won. Champions again, and we got our revenge for last year.'

'Congratulations. Enjoy it, Mum. You deserve it.'

'I think your father's prouder than I am. A lifetime's hiding my light under a bushel doesn't prepare you for celebration.'

If you're thinking that Dad ever put her down, you're wrong. Mum worked for GCHQ, and I know they're all over the Internet these days trying to recruit people, but in her day it was as secret as my work for Merlyn's Tower.

'I was going to ring you, Mum, but you got in first.'

'That's kind of you, dear, but you've got to get in touch with Rachael. She called me up in a terrible flap this morning and got me out of bed. I can't say any more, but it's about you. Promise?'

I sighed loudly enough for Mother to hear. 'I promise.'

She changed the subject, going back to the bridge club and her determination to get them to merge with a local Spanish group. I congratulated her again and wished her all the best. Before I could lose my nerve, I called Rachael.

'What's up, sis?'

'Has Mother been on the phone?'

'Yes. I take it you didn't drag her out of bed to congratulate her on the bridge championship.'

'The what?'

'Never mind. What's the problem?'

'You are. I was at a function last night and this … woman came up to me. A journalist.'

This didn't sound good. 'Oh?'

'Yes. She'd done her homework. She knew I was your sister, she knew what I did for a living, and she very much wants to get in touch with you. Only a lifetime of being discreet about Mum stopped me saying anything.'

This was not good. It was not good on many levels. 'Did she say what it was about?'

'Sort-of. She dropped all sorts of hints that you've been up to no good, which didn't surprise me, then she said she wants your version of what happened in somewhere called Cairndale. Something about you kidnapping a police officer and hijacking a helicopter.'

That was a relief of sorts. If the woman was only after a story about Operation Rainbow, then I could handle her. If she'd started talking about the world of magick, I'd have become very worried very quickly.

'Did she give a name?'

'I've got her card here. Juliet Porterhouse.'

Aah. I'd once used Ms Porterhouse to get in touch with Chief Inspector Tom Morton, with whom she seemed very friendly. She probably knew more about Operation Rainbow than any other journalist.

'Thanks, Raitch. You did the right thing, and I owe you one. Just tell her you've passed on the message and that I won't be getting in touch.'

'Easy for you to say, Conrad. She was hinting at all kinds of really nasty stuff, and that's how you met Mina, wasn't it?'

There was no point denying it. 'We got out. Both of us. Mina paid a higher price, that's all. Mum and Dad…'

I nearly bit my tongue through. How is it that siblings can do that to you? I knew as soon as the words left my mouth that I'd made a serious blunder.

'You told them? You told them all about it?' Her voice had risen alarmingly.

'Some of it. When I got home at Christmas I'd just been shot and they were worried. Well, Dad was worried. I owed them some sort of explanation. I was a lot better when you turned up.'

'It's not like you to play the sympathy card.'

'I didn't, with you, did I? Probably because I knew I wouldn't get any. You never visited me when I was in rehab with half my leg blown off. Dad did. He came over from Spain on the first flight to see me in hospital.'

'You never sent me the details. I had no idea where you were.'

I stopped myself from saying *You could have rung Dad and asked him*. I had her on the back foot and it was time for some verbal spin. 'Just text Juliet Porterhouse and say I've gone underground. It's literally true, half the time.'

'If that's what you want. Let's hope she can take no for an answer.'

Rachael is basically honourable. I felt confident she'd do what I asked, and felt even more confident that I hadn't heard the last of this. She would give our parents the third degree when she next saw them, and I'd have to face the consequences when she got back.

I'd been trying to build bridges to her, and didn't regret it, but things hadn't gone quite as I'd planned. Oh well.

I turned my thoughts to Project Clerkswell: my plan to stake a claim in village life. Don't forget, I've only been an occasional visitor to the place since I joined the RAF. It's a good job villages have long collective memories or I'd have been forgotten long ago. Perhaps living in the second largest house helps.

To my eternal surprise, not everyone is a cricket enthusiast, so bear with me a moment. I promise not to include much technical stuff, which should make the following story acceptable to the benighted amongst you who don't relish our national game.

Unlike his predecessor, the new captain of the village cricket team is a rather keen sort of chap, which is not always a virtue in village cricket. Part One of Ben Thewlis's winter training regime had been very enjoyable: a lock-in at the Inkwell that he called a "team-building exercise". After that, I now know who the other members of the team are, and whether they can hold their beer.

Part Two was more of a challenge and featured indoor nets at the sports centre in Cheltenham. Remember, I haven't played cricket in any form since well before my leg injury.

No team worth playing for has ever selected me for my batting, as Ben soon remembered when some teenager clean bowled me three times on the trot during the first session.

'I hope you can remember how to bowl, Conrad,' he said, looking worried. The prospect of dropping the man whose ancestor donated the ground can't have been an enticing one.

'We'll see,' I said, taking my coat outside for a smoke, where I found the teenage demon bowler doing something incomprehensible with his phone.

'Well bowled in there,' I said. His mother hadn't allowed him to come to the team-building exercise, so I didn't even know his name.

'Thanks. Your stance is good, sir, but...'

'You're not in the RAF, lad. My name is Conrad Clarke,' I said, sticking out a hand.

He shook it. 'Everyone knows you, erm, Mr Clarke. I'm Ross. Ross Miller.'

'You must be Ed Miller's boy. I went to school with him. Doesn't he play any more?'

The lad developed a sudden interest in the all-weather football pitch. 'Mum and Dad split up three years ago.'

29

Awkward. Why did no one tell me? I changed the subject. 'My stance is good, but…?'

'You're not moving your left foot enough.'

There's a good reason for that, of course, but he doesn't need to know about my scars. I stubbed out my cigarette and said, 'Can you bat?'

He gave me a grin. 'Not as well as I can bowl.'

'Me, too. I hope. It's been a while.'

Back inside, Ben chucked me a ball and pointed to the empty net. He picked up a bat and sauntered down to face me.

My regular deliveries were good, if a little rusty, and certainly adequate for most village games. What I really wanted to try was a little magick. Enhanced spin, you could say.

I can't do very much with my magick, but you don't need to do much to a cricket ball if it's already doing the basics. After half a dozen balls of conventional leg spin, I unleashed a googly with enhanced spin.

Ben stared at his missing leg stump. 'Where did that come from?' he asked, bemused.

'That was an evil delivery,' said Ross.

'Oh, you know, we played a lot of cricket in Afghanistan. Very good spinners the Afghans.'

While we were packing up, Ben gave me a membership form. 'You're already an honorary life-member, aren't you, because of the ground?'

I nodded.

'You need to fill this in for the league, I'm afraid, and I'll have to charge match fees. Sorry. You coming to the Inkwell later?'

'Try and stop me.'

To get it out of the way, I filled in the membership form at the kitchen table before going out to the pub. For some reason, the league wanted to know all sorts of information, and I had to read the damn thing carefully. Rival teams can – and do – go through players' registration details with a fine toothed comb and don't hesitate to report any irregularities or omissions.

At the bottom of the form was a short declaration: *To uphold the laws and spirit of the game and not to seek unfair advantage by whatever means.*

They meant drugs, or bribes, or something commonplace, but what about magick? Working for the Allfather, and dating Mina, had reinforced the importance of making and keeping an oath, so could I sign this and still use enhanced spin on my googly?

'What's the problem?' said Thomas Clarke.

I dropped the pen, banged my leg on the table and fell over, all in one well-executed moment of panic.

'Can't you ring the bloody front door bell?' I said through gritted teeth. I rubbed my leg. 'And what's with the hair?'

My Spectral guest had gone all King Charles with the curls, and sported a lumberjack shirt. He must know I'm sensitive about my bald patch.

'The front door bell doesn't work,' he said, a little disappointed with his welcome.

'The wire's broken, that's all. I'm sure you can summon enough magick to ting the bell. That way I'll know it's you. Sorry. It's nice to see you, Grandfather.'

'And you. Is there something wrong?'

'Can I play cricket and use magick?'

He looked horrified. 'In God's name, no! That would be terrible. Not that I've played cricket, but to use magick in the mundane world is to cross the line. You can never go back.'

This was something I'd have to think about carefully, so I asked the question I'd wondered about since our last meeting. 'Why is our well so important? You drowned in it, and that's where the Allfather appeared to recruit me.'

'It's about the well that I came tonight,' said Thomas. He frowned and became a little transparent. I crossed my fingers, hoping that he could hold it together long enough to have a proper conversation.

'It's getting harder,' he said. 'The effort it takes to materialise means that I can't get at the memories I need to talk about.'

'There's a Catch-22 and no mistake,' I said. 'Is there anything I can do to help?'

'You? No. What you need is a Necromancer.'

'Oh. I killed the last one I came across.'

Thomas raised his eyebrows. 'Go on. You never said what happened when you went away, when you were touched by the Goddess. Why did you kill him?'

'Her. Most Mages are women these days.'

Thomas shook his head. 'Mother Nature never ceases to surprise me.'

'Me neither, but Debs Sayer wasn't being very maternal when she tried to bind her own daughter to the spirit of Helen of Troy.'

'Merciful God, Conrad! Helen? How can she be free? I...'

Thomas faded, and was gone. I waited for a while, thinking about his reaction. The key phrase had been *Helen of Troy*. That was what had disturbed him, and it clearly had some personal significance that was lost in his fading memories. Perhaps I would try to find a more sympathetic Necromancer. Vicky might know one.

I took the unsigned form to the pub and joined the rest of the team (the over-18s, anyway).

When Ben saw me, he said, 'Ross Miller was right. That was a truly evil googly you sent my way.'

31

Don't you just hate irony? I don't think the message could have been clearer: play clean or not at all. I signed the form and handed it over. 'I don't think I'll manage a ball like that again,' I said. 'I nearly dislocated my finger. Too risky.'

'Never mind,' said Ben, clapping me on the shoulder. 'Your bowling definitely has a place, though not on every wicket. Cheers.'

That was good enough for me. I'll save what little magick I have for enemies of the King's Peace, and the batsmen of Winchcombe, Fiddington and Oxenton can sleep easy in their beds.

On Sunday, I went for a long walk around the village, and spent a long time at the well at the bottom of our garden. Since being touched by the Goddess, I could feel the magick radiating from its watery depths, when before it had just been a well to me. The magick was faint, and old, and its flavour too subtle to identify, but it was there. I shrugged, and added it to my inbox, along with the question of Vicky's behaviour in Club Justine.

She and Desirée had gone there wearing Glamours, illusions to make them look even more attractive than they already are. Vicky described it as a game, to see what they could get from the punters. Cricket is a game, too, and if using enhanced spin was crossing the line, what did that say about Vicky and her friend?

Vicky was waiting for me outside Hannah's office on Monday morning. There was no sign of Tennille. Vicky gave me a big grin and shuffled along the sofa. 'Take the weight off your feet, Uncle Conrad.'

I flopped down next to her. 'That would be *Take the weight off your feet, sir.*'

'Howay man, we're both captains. I don't have to call you *sir* because you're older or nothing, do I? Not that I would anyway.'

'Oh, no, Captain Robson, you call me *sir* because I'm a squadron leader and I outrank you. According to regulations, squadron leader is equivalent to major in the army.'

'How did you swing that? You must be on a packet, and you'll get combat allowance.'

'I *swung it* by doing my time on the front line. Or above it. Hannah appointed me on a resumed commission, so I keep my old rank.'

She punched my arm and said, 'You lucky bastard. Again.'

Vicky is a Geordie, in case you hadn't guessed, and is perpetually short of money, mostly because she insists on renting beyond her means. Like most female Mages, she wears her hair very long, and when it's pulled back, it emphasises her slightly heavy jaw and pointy nose. Hers is a striking face, and one that can look very attractive when she smiles. When she's down, she could model for a Victorian workhouse picture.

I'm the last person to pass judgement on women's fashions, but you have a right to know what her wardrobe is like. I think she spends too much money on the wrong things, as if she's trying to express herself in a language she doesn't quite understand. Today it was variations on black and white, with high waisted trousers that I'd last seen on an old Bananarama poster, and a very loose white blouse under a fitted jacket.

Before we could catch up properly, the door opened and Tennille appeared. We both stood up.

'The Constable will see you now. Just you Mr Clarke,' said Tennille with something approaching a frown. 'How is it you can upset her without even being here?'

Oops. What now?

I slipped into the Constable's office and stood to attention at a respectful distance. At our second meeting she'd had a copy of my RAF records, covered with black redactions. She now had the unexpurgated version, and was shaking her head at it.

'You cannot be serious, Clarke.'

I kept my peace.

Hannah looked up. 'How can you apply for a job in law enforcement when you've confessed to money laundering on an industrial scale, grand theft and murder?'

I was going to keep on keeping my peace until I realised that she wasn't being rhetorical.

'I didn't confess to anything, ma'am, I simply provided details of certain activities. I haven't murdered anyone: they were all trying to kill me and I got in first.'

'All? There's only one here.'

Double oops. I examined the ceiling.

'Unbelievable. And then there's this.' She held up a chit of some sort.

'Ma'am?'

'You dragged Vicky to see one of your partners in crime at a prison. Are you trying to corrupt her already?'

Oh. I had hoped that I could keep Mina below the radar, or whatever the magickal equivalent of radar is. *Below the threshold of the Sympathetic Echo*, or something like that. Again, the Constable wanted an answer.

'Captain Robson is her own woman, ma'am, as is Ms Desai. I wouldn't do anything to jeopardise either of them, and on that I give my word.'

'You'd better bloody well not.' She waved at the contents of my file. 'Does Vicky know *any* of this?'

'No, ma'am. Nor will she.'

'Good. Now what about this?' She swapped the file for some more RAF papers. 'You've got more *chutzpah* than my big brother, do you know that? I can't believe you tricked me into appointing you as a major – and I have to pay a bloody fortune out of a small budget for you to get your pilot's licence back.'

'Wings, ma'am. I want my wings back. They're much more than a pilot's licence, and could be an important asset to the Watch.'

'I'm only paying once. Understand? No annual renewals unless you fork out yourself.'

'Yes, ma'am.'

'And none of this will be processed unless you're accepted into the Watch. You are very much on a warning for the next ten days, Clarke, and acceptance is *not* a formality.'

She pressed a button to summon Vicky, then shuffled all the papers off her desk and forced a smile.

'Vicky, Conrad, I'm putting you two together because I think you might complement each other to the benefit of the Watch. Vicky, you've got your orders?'

'Aye,' said Vicky. She looked hurt, like a small child who's being told off for something it didn't do.

'Then get on with it. And don't let me down.'

'Ma'am,' I said quickly, and grabbed Vicky's arm to steer her away before she said something she'd regret.

'What was that all about?' she demanded the second the doors closed behind us. Tennille was thankfully elsewhere.

I pointed to the tray: it was set up with three cups and had most definitely not been used. 'We've been sent to bed with no supper. Sorry, Vic, it was my fault. Nothing whatever to do with you. It will all blow over if I keep my head down for a bit. Let's get a coffee somewhere else, and you can tell me what we're up to.'

We adjourned to the Costa Coffee outside the Tower of London, and Vicky told me that she'd given up smoking again. I took a nicotine minute outside, then we squeezed together in a corner.

Away from Hannah's waves of disapproval, Vicky perked up. 'We're off to the Invisible College,' she said. 'All Watch Captains must be registered, and that's job number one.'

'What is this Invisible College? Where is this Invisible College? And don't tell me you can't see it.'

'You can't. Even with your Talent for penetrating Glamours, you'll need a token to see the place. As to what it is, that's a long story. Where? The front entrance is in Frederick's Place, near Cheapside. We'll get a cab in a minute.'

'We'll walk,' I said firmly. 'It will do us both good, and you can tell me the long story. Before then, you can clear something up for me.'

'Oh, aye?'

'Yes. I know your father was a miner, and that you were sent to some sort of Mage-friendly boarding school, but how did you get from one to the other?'

Vicky looked into her coffee. 'Me Dad *was* a miner – a pitman, but that was years before I was born. I've got two brothers older than you, Conrad, from his first marriage. They split up when he got sacked after the strike.'

The way she said *sacked* clearly struck a nerve. 'He wasn't made redundant?' I asked.

She shook her head. 'He was drunk on shift. Sacked. No payout, nothing. It took him years to get himself straight, apparently, but he did it, and he got married again. They weren't expecting me, and I wasn't expecting this Goth lass to tap us on the shoulder in Eldon Square one day and say, "Can I see your Mam and Dad about putting you in for a scholarship?"'

'A Goth?'

'Aye. Black hair, black nails, black lipstick, black dress: the full Monty. There's quite a few in Newcastle.'

'Right.'

Vicky changed the subject. 'How's Mina?' she asked, with a combination of genuine sympathy and prurient curiosity. Until Monday, Vicky had never been inside a prison.

'She's trying to come to terms with the magickal world,' I said. 'She can't decide if your visit was a figment of her imagination or a practical joke. Unfortunately, I can't get a visiting order to see her for another week.'

'Poor lass.'

'She's been through worse. It'll soon be the first anniversary of her husband's murder.' Before Vicky could ask any further questions, I drained my coffee. 'Come on, let's go.'

'Do we have to walk? It might rain.'

'Won't kill you. You can borrow my woolly hat, if you like.'

'Nah. You need it to cover your bald patch.'

We trod the familiar route up to the Bank of England, and Vicky told me the story of the Invisible College.

'He didn't mean literally invisible,' she began. 'In modern language, it would be *virtual* college – a society to promote knowledge and bring practitioners together.'

'Start again. Who's *he*?'

'Oh. Robert Boyle. Have you heard of Boyle's Law?'

I had, and told her so.

'Well, he was both an alchemist and a scientist; some would say he was the first scientist because he wrote *The Sceptical Chymist*. That's why graduates of the Invisible College are known as *Chymists*. We do our magick slightly differently to other Mages and Witches.'

'I'm with you so far.'

'Robert Boyle was the founding Warden, and he decided it should actually have premises and rules and stuff. He called the building *Salomon's House*, and it got a royal charter. We all have to swear an oath to the Queen. You used to have to be a member of the Church of England, too.'

I thought of the Lunar Sisters. 'I bet that wasn't popular.'

'No. There are Circles all over Britain that have their own apprentices and rules and stuff because they wouldn't swear the oath or join the Church. One of the main roles of the Watch – you and me, in other words – is to keep an eye on the Circles.'

'Mother Julia said something about Glastonbury.'

'The Daughters of the Goddess. It's the biggest Circle in Britain or Ireland, and lots of covens pledge allegiance. They're quite strict and don't give us much trouble.'

'Just daughters? No sons?'

'Not at Glastonbury and the affiliated Circles. Some of the others are mixed, and one or two are all male. I thought of joining a mixed circle in Northumberland after school, but it wasn't for me.'

We had gone up Cheapside, turned into Old Jewry and then into the short dead-end of Frederick's Place. Nothing in this anonymous street looked remotely like a seat of occult power.

'Hold me hand,' said Vicky.

I did, and felt a tingle (no, not that sort of tingle. Vicky is like a niece to me. That's why she calls me Uncle Conrad). I blinked, and there it was. The plain wall next to the Mercers' Company had become the baroque doorway of Salomon's House. Vicky touched the symbolic pickaxe on the chain around her neck, and an invisible hand opened the door.

'After you,' she said.

I stepped over the threshold and into a world of power, privilege and politics. You could tell that just from the walls.

The Receiving Room (as Vicky named it), is about five metres by seven, and covered with exquisitely ornamented dark oak panelling. All across the wood, small animals chased each other. Birds pecked at berries, skulls grinned and carved oak leaves sported acorns.

Most spectacular of all was the painted ceiling, only it wasn't painted. Grey clouds scudded across the sky, moving just like the ones outside, and the whole thing was lit by the sun. You could tell that it was a flat surface, but it was most definitely the piece of sky above us.

'How?' I asked, pointing upwards with a mystified expression on my face.

'Don't ask me. On a clear day, you can even see vapour trails. Clever, though.'

I dragged my eyes away from the canopy above, and only then did I notice the portraits, almost in shadow, along the left hand wall. The first two, a woman and man wearing elaborate Tudor dress, were hanging upside down. I pointed to them and said, 'Who?'

Vicky indicated the inverted woman. 'Mary Tudor, aka Bloody Mary, and next to her is her occult inquisitor, Don José da Logroño. He was a nasty piece of work. Between them, they tried to strangle free magick at birth.'

'Don't tell me: it's a long story.'

'How long have you got? Basically, before the Reformation, all magick used to be controlled by the Church in Rome. You either toed the line and joined a convent or you were killed. I'm no historian, but they reckon that the protestant churches didn't have the centralised infrastructure to contain Mages, and that's when free magick began. And that's when we came in.'

'We?'

'The King's Watch. The first Peculiar Constable was appointed to keep the King's Peace – to stop magick from interfering with everyday life. As you know, James was obsessed with witches, and a lot of the Circles haven't forgiven us for that.'

A twinge in my ears reminded me of Mother Julia's attempt to deafen me, or worse, before we reached an understanding. Memories are long in the world of magick. I noticed that there was no portrait of James here. 'Who are the others?'

'Turn around first, and look up.'

I swivelled and stared up. From above the door, the unsmiling countenance of the Virgin Queen watched over us.

'It's symbolic,' said Vicky. 'Something to do with limited tolerance and Queen Elizabeth watching over us. She's supposed to have inspired this lot.' She turned round and pointed to a series of men, hung the right way up.

'John Dee. He convinced Elizabeth to take hold of Don José's books. Don José did a runner when Mary died because there were a lot of Mages with scores to settle. His books formed the basis of the Queen's Esoteric Library.'

What was it about *Library* that rang a bell? Before I could capture the memory, Vicky moved on.

'Francis Bacon. He was a Mage. He wrote a book called *New Atlantis*, and that's where the name *Salomon's House* comes from. It was supposed to be an ideal house of learning. James I listened to Bacon, but he simply didn't trust Mages enough, so nothing was done until after the Civil War.' She pointed to the final portrait. 'This is Robert Boyle himself. He proposed an *Invisible College* where Chymistry could be studied "for the glory of God." The rest is really boring.'

'Thanks, Vicky. That helps put a lot of things in context.'

The more I looked at the carvings on the panels, the more they intrigued me. If you looked away, then back again, something would have changed. The mouse would eat the nut, and look fatter. The lizard would lift a leg and twist around. The skull would move so that its empty eyes would follow you. Perhaps I should get some for Elvenham House.

'Come on. We're expected,' said Vicky, dragging me away from my contemplation.

I had no idea what to expect beyond the Receiving Room. More of the same? A high-tech homage to Quantum Magick? What we actually got was a staircase – a big one, winding up and down around an atrium. There didn't seem to be floors, as such, just lots of doors and openings at different levels. I peered over the banister and saw another image of the London sky above us. Below, it was a very long way down.

It was only then that I noticed the people, because before then I hadn't heard a thing. I still couldn't hear footsteps or conversations, but I could see them sauntering or scurrying up and down, in and out of the doors. Most of them were young, and most of them were female; higher up the age range, the gender balance shifted towards the male end. The dress code was conservative, but there were no uniforms, capes or pointy hats. Shame.

'Impressive isn't it?' said Vicky, when I'd got the measure of the place. She'd touched my arm before she spoke. 'This is the Junction,' she continued. 'It took me a year to get the hang of it, and beyond here, it's a complete nightmare. We're going to see the Dean, via the Library. There might be another way, but I never found it.'

We climbed the equivalent of two storeys, keeping to the left and attracting little interest. With another two storeys to go before the top, we turned through one of the larger and busier openings.

The noise of people chattering knocked me back after the unnatural silence of the Junction. 'Whoah!' I said. 'It wasn't the carpet keeping things quiet out there.'

'No. It's a large scale Silence. You saw me put a personal one on Keira, remember? Sometimes they take it down, and the whole Junction echoes like St Paul's Cathedral; that's why I touched you – so that you could hear me. This is the Library Rotunda.'

It was round, high ceilinged and thronged with students, but none of them was reading. Drinking coffee, chattering, checking their phones, yes, and usually all three at once. Reading, not so much. I passed my observations on to Vicky.

'It doubles as a common room,' she said, then pointed to a security desk on the right and a series of doors on the left. 'You check out your books there, and take them to the Silent reading rooms there. Only Fellows get to go into the Library itself, and never on your own until you're a Doctor of Chymic.'

I followed her direction as she pointed, and something caught my eye. I immediately developed a coughing fit to distract Vicky, and tried not to look at the portraits.

'Very dusty in here,' I said, turning away and taking a swig of water.

We crossed the Rotunda and into a darker corridor. 'This is the Dean's Secretariat,' said my guide. 'Any other university would call it *Student Services*. The whole shebang at Salomon's House is run by the Warden, and his deputy is known as the Chaplain. Next is the Dean: she's in charge of education. I'll save the rest for later.'

None of the doors along the passage had labels – or none that was visible to me. It ended with imposing double doors which incorporated two blank shields into their carving. I pointed to one of the empty escutcheons. 'Can you see anything?'

'Yes I can. It's changed since I was last here, because the Dean has changed. Soon enough, you'll be able to see them, too.'

She knocked on a smaller door to the right, and we entered a boringly twenty-first century office, where a boringly efficient PA asked us to wait. Then I noticed the view.

'Why can I see rolling green fields out of the window?' I whispered. 'And why is it the middle of summer?'

The Dean's PA must have very good hearing. 'We have no windows in Salomon's House,' she said. 'That's very unhealthy, so we have these Skyways, as they're called. The ones in the ceilings just show the actual sky above us, but wall mounted ones are more flexible. This is the view from my daughter's window in New Zealand. As it was twelve hours ago, of course. Right now, it's the middle of the night. Aah. Dean Hardisty will see you now.'

I was expecting a grand study to match the imposing double doors, but we were shown into a completely bare box with corporate carpeting and no furniture whatsoever. There wasn't even a Skyway – just recessed electric light.

'Just to explain,' said the PA as she prepared to leave us. 'This is the Dean's ten minute room. All meetings of less than ten minutes happen in here. She won't be long.'

I pointed to a second door, opposite the one we'd come through. 'Does that lead to the twenty minute room? Does it have chairs?'

Vicky kept her eye on the second door and whispered, 'This is all new to me. Cora Hardisty was the Oracle when I first came, and she only got Dean last year. The real Dean's study is fantastic.'

The door opened and revealed a professional smile attached to a designer suit and designer hair – no long sweep of loose locks for the Dean. Somewhere underneath the gloss was a woman in her late thirties, which probably made her at least sixty. Senior Mages have ways of defying the clock when it comes to appearance, and I don't mean optical illusions. The smile came forward and offered me her hand. I shook.

'Dean Cora Hardisty,' she said. 'Welcome to Salomon's House, Mr Clarke.' She switched off the smile and turned her attention to my partner. 'Nice to see you again, Vicky. How's life in the Watch? Has Ms Rothman kept her promises?'

Vicky was looking anywhere except at our host, but there was nothing to look at except white walls.

I had once tried to intervene to help Vicky out, and got my shin kicked for my pains – my bad shin – so I wasn't about to intrude on some teacher/student dynamic that went back years. On the other hand, I was being tarred with the same brush here.

'From what I've seen, Dean, everyone in the Watch keeps their promises. Especially Dame Hannah,' I said.

'I'm sure they do, Mr Clarke. Has Victoria explained the procedure?'

I had to concede that one: Vicky is very stingy with her explanations. And she hates being called Victoria. I shook my head. The Dean sighed.

'Rules state that you must be an Aspirant to the Great Work before you can seek an office with the Watch. If you're not already a Fellow, like Victoria is, you have to take the oath and demonstrate your worth. If you survive your induction to the Watch, you can take the test for Master of the Art. It's a fairly easy test, but it does have a requirement that you show progression.'

'That's clear enough,' I said, 'except for the part about demonstrating my worth. How many more tests are there?'

The Dean was unfazed. 'I'm sure the RAF had constant testing during officer training. And pilot training.'

She had a point.

When I'd digested this, she continued, 'All I need to see today is that you can do *some* of the Work. When you're ready, Mr Clarke.'

The only piece of magick I can perform to order is igniting the petrol in my lighter, so that's what I did. The Dean observed me carefully, then gave the most patronising smile I'd seen since I was accosted by a Stop the War activist on Remembrance Day. Up to this point, I'd been giving Dean Hardisty the benefit of the doubt. That smile tipped the balance completely, and now I disliked her intensely.

'That's quite satisfactory, Mr Clarke. I'll fetch the royal arms.'

When she'd turned on her three inch heel and drifted back to her real office, I opened my mouth to say something caustic.

'Don't,' said Vicky. 'Just don't. Not yet.'

'Sorry, Victoria, I'll hold my … Ow!' As soon as I used her Sunday name, she kicked me.

I was hopping on one leg when the Dean returned, a small jewellery box in one hand and a plaque sporting the royal coat of arms in the other.

She ignored my pain, put the box on the floor and held out the heraldic shield. 'We used to swear on the Bible, but sadly that's not an option.' The wooden plaque had a niche from which she removed a card.

I laid my right hand on the shield and read from the card, 'I Conrad Clarke, do solemnly swear my allegiance to Queen Elizabeth, her heirs and successors, and do solemnly swear to use my Gift in accordance with such laws over Nature as she and her ministers may make, and I swear to promote the wellbeing of the Commonwealth.'

'Good,' said Cora, picking up the box to show a tiny Doodad, about the size of a penny. 'This is your Token of Aspiration. It will allow you to see Salomon's House and to get through the front door. After that you'll need help to get beyond the Receiving Room. I'm sure Victoria will oblige, especially with directions for our entrance to Hledjolf's Hall.' She paused until Vicky had given a weak smile. 'Now we come to the Proof of Mastery. I shall recommend to the Inner Council that you be accepted for Master of the Art when you have completed your induction to the Watch, and when you have demonstrated that you can use a Keyway. It should be within your compass, Mr Clarke.'

'No problem,' said Vicky. 'I'll bring him up to scratch.'

My partner was already backing towards the door, but I stood my ground. The Dean of the Invisible College is never going to like me, so I decided to put down a marker. I held out my hand to shake goodbye, forcing the Dean to shuffle the plaque and card. When I'd got her in my grip – lightly – I said, 'It's Squadron Leader Clarke, if you're going to be formal. And Captain Robson. Vicky worked hard to get the Queen's commission. Thank you for admitting me. We'll be back in due course.'

I let go of her hand, nodded, and left, making sure that the Dean heard me thank the office staff for their help, just to prove that it was personal.

'You walk on the right,' I said to Vicky in the corridor.

'Why?'

'That way you can't kick my bad leg. What a horrible woman.'

'She's the Dean of Salomon's House,' said Vicky, hissing in my ear. 'Every Chymist in England is dependent on the good will of the Invisible College. When I leave the Watch, I'm coming back, and it will be up to her to re-admit me. The same goes for every other Officer of the Watch except the Constable. And you.'

We were approaching the Library Rotunda again, and I needed to finish this conversation before we got there. I stopped, leaned against the wall and rubbed my bad leg. I also loosened one of my shoelaces slightly.

'I've got a plan for that,' I said. Vicky looked at me as if I'd gone mad. 'What we need to do is recruit from the Circles.'

She laughed. 'Conrad, five weeks ago you were completely ignorant of the magickal world. You still are. One day you'll find out why you need to build a bridge back to Dean Hardisty. I'll give you this, mind. She's a snotty cow and no mistake.'

41

'Gender based epithets are sexist, Vicky. No calling people *cow* or *bitch*. I learnt that on a course.'

I'd left my flank exposed, and she took full advantage to deliver a whack to the bad shin so painful that I had to lean against the wall to recover. Hands on hips, she surveyed the results of her footwork and nodded with satisfaction. 'Can you make your own way out of the front? I need to pick something up from the Artificers.'

'Vicky, there's something I need to show you first. In the Rotunda.'

'You what?'

'Yes. When I stop to tie my shoelace, look at the portrait next to me and then move on. Don't say anything until we meet up outside. Please. It's important.'

'Why aye, man. You don't need to ask twice.'

I hobbled through the Rotunda, stumbled near the wall and repaired the knot in my bootlace. I could hear the intake of breath from Vicky above me and she shot off towards the Junction at speed.

Back in the genuine daylight of Frederick's Place, while I waited for Vicky, I took the time to thread the Dean's Doodad on to my neck chain, where it nestled against the Persona from Mother Julia. Two more different women in positions of authority you could not get. I turned round and, yes, it worked: I could see the Invisible College in all its glory, and I could see Vicky emerging with a holdall.

'Coffee,' I said. 'And I need a fag.'

Only when we'd put a safe distance between us and Salomon's House did I ask who the subject of the portrait was, the one I'd made her look at in the Library.

'Thomas Clarke, second Keeper of the Queen's Esoteric Library. Also known as the First Rusticant because he walked off with some books. I'm guessing that there's a good reason for all this.'

'There is. He's also my eleven times great grandfather, and his Spectre is haunting my house in Gloucestershire.'

'Well bugger me.'

'Yes, those were my thoughts, too. He's rather faint, I'm afraid, and there's something troubling him. He said that I need to take a Necromancer down there and that's *not* something I'm going to discuss in Salomon's House. Thomas Clarke may have questions to answer about his overdue books, but he's family. We need to keep this on the QT until we know more.'

'Start from the beginning, Conrad.'

So I did, leaving nothing out (except the bit about Amelia and the rug). Like me, Vicky was most worried about Thomas's reaction to Helen of Troy, and she agreed completely that this was a matter for Merlyn's Tower, not Salomon's House.

She sat in silence for a moment. 'If it's definitely a Spectre, I think I could bring him out.'

'Are you sure? I'd rather tell Dean Hardisty than put you at risk.'

'Leave it with me, Conrad. I'll ask around. How much Lux have you got? It'll need at least an ounce.'

'I'm good for that. There's something else.'

'My life, man, you're not even on the books and you're causing trouble.'

'Can you come with me on Wednesday when I go to pick up my piece from Hledjolf?'

'I was gonna show you Hledjolf's front door, via the basement of Salomon's House. What's the problem? I can't help with the Dwarves, you know.'

'Nothing to do with Mr Shorty.'

'Hey. No heightist comments, neither.'

'Hledjolf is not Warwick Davies or Peter Dinklage. Hledjolf isn't human at all, so if I want to call him an overgrown garden gnome, I will do.'

She laughed. 'Fine by me. Just don't call a Gnome a Dwarf. They get very upset.'

'There are Gnomes?'

'Hell, aye, man. They mostly run the Chambers of Occult Commerce, but that's for another day. What were you gonna say about Hledjolf?'

'I wasn't. It's something that Moley came across in the Old Network. It might be nothing, but I'd like your opinion. Anyway, I'm not walking back into Salomon's House until I've got my Badge of Office.'

Vicky looked at the sky, the traffic, the stationery shop across the road and finally at me. 'I don't like tunnels.'

I nodded. Phobias should never be dismissed lightly. 'How bad is it?'

'I can do a few minutes if I take a pill first. Are there any doors?'

'Only one. In the Tube station. The temple-thingy I want your opinion on is about ten minutes' walk from the entrance.'

She tried to pull herself together. 'Temple-thingy? That definitely sounds like a case for the crack team from Merlyn's Tower.'

'Thanks. What now?'

'That's enough for today. I need to go back to the Tower and get a lesson plan ready.'

'Oh? What are you teaching? To whom?'

'To you, and I'm teaching Keyways.' She hefted the holdall she'd brought from Salomon's House. 'It's a practical course. You'll find out tomorrow.' She hesitated. 'Can we go to your flat? If no one's gonna be around.'

'Of course. No problem. I'll text you the address. Do you use the Tube?'

'Aye. The Tube's alright, most of the time. It's busy, it's well lit. You don't notice you're in a tunnel. I'll get an Uber tomorrow. See you about ten?'

43

We stood up and got ready to leave. I had one final thing to say. 'I wasn't being noble about Spectre Thomas. I don't want to put you in a dangerous position just because this is family business.'

'I know. I've had to trust you, Conrad, quite a few times. Starting today, it goes both ways.'

3 — A Magickal Education

After my tenant left for his job at the Air Ministry, I cleaned and aired the flat, then took a stroll to the nearby deli to stretch my leg and get something nice for lunch. And breakfast, in Vicky's case. She was waiting for me on the doorstep, and began by apologising profusely for being early.

'Never apologise for being early,' I said. I stopped with the front door key in mid-air. 'Unless you're a day early. That's pushing it a bit.'

'What's the rent on this?' she asked as we climbed the stairs.

'Do you mean "how much do you charge your tenant"?'

She stopped on the half-landing. 'Your tenant? You mean you own this place? And a house in Gloucestershire? How'd you manage that?'

'That's what Mina would like to know. I haven't told her yet, so you'll have to wait.'

I did tell her about the principle of Clarke's Mess, which she just about accepted. She slowly turned around the living room while I made coffee and warmed her a croissant (she's not good in the mornings).

'Talk about a bachelor pad,' she said. 'I can almost smell the testosterone. It's clean enough, mind.'

'Don't say that to my last tenant. She'd be very upset. And all officers are house-trained – it's drummed into us during basic training.' I pointed to her trousers. 'If I'd turned up on parade with ironing like that, I'd be up on a charge.'

She looked down in alarm, then laughed. 'What's ironing? I've heard of it…' She came over and patted my arm. 'You'll make someone a lovely wife one day. Hopefully Mina.'

Now that there was a bit of distance between us and our encounter with Dean Hardisty, Vicky opened up a little about her student days at Salomon's House.

She had had to complete a four year apprenticeship that was much more hands-on and practical than most university courses. A bit like a medical degree, really. More than anything, I got the feeling that she had been frustrated there, not with her tutor but with herself, because she couldn't find her true strength. Most Chymists – most Mages full stop – have a specialism, and although Vicky said that she was better at Sorcery than anything else, she wasn't good enough. The lead Sorcerer at Salomon's House is known as the Oracle, none other than Cora Hardisty in Vicky's day. The future Dean had told Vicky that she wasn't good enough to study for a doctorate.

'So you joined the King's Watch?'

'Hannah came to speak, like a recruitment session. Unheard of, apparently. She said that she was creating two new posts as general Officers of the Watch to assist and support. I jumped at the chance 'cos I needed the money and the experience is dead useful.'

'So what *do* you do for the Watch? What will I be doing, come to that?'

She started unpacking the bag she'd borrowed from Salomon's House. 'Mine is a new role, and we're still working it out. Some of it is taking the less dangerous work off the Watch Captains.'

'So we can go out and get killed more often. Charming.'

She stopped what she was doing. 'You didn't join for the quiet life and the paperwork, did you, Conrad?'

She had me there. I didn't deny it.

The bag contained all sorts of boxes, which she started to lay out on the coffee table while she expanded on her job. 'I've been doing all sorts of research on the Circles, especially the ones operating in London. I've been updating the records – that helped uncover a trade in stolen Artefacts, and I've been up to Scotland to see how Napier College does things. Napier is pretty much the same as Salomon's House, but Scottish. They don't have their own King's Watch, as such, but Hannah has a Depute (with an E not a Y) who runs his own show north of the border.'

No wonder she was glad to get out of Merlyn's Tower with a job like that. Talk about being a dogsbody. If I hadn't come along, and Li Cheng had continued to mess her around, she'd have been getting in trouble sooner or later. Bigger trouble than I'd rescued her from.

She finished lining up the boxes and patted her thighs as a signal to herself that she was ready. With a deep breath, she said, 'You need to know more about the way that magick actually works. Not the theory, no one knows that, but the practicalities of using Lux to do stuff. Like making and using locks. Not that you'll be making them; that's for Artificers.'

I've thought a lot about the nature of magick since my Enhancement by the Allfather, and I've not got much further than understanding that Lux is a form of power which can directly affect matter and energy, with seemingly no limit on the ways in which you can bend the allegedly fixed laws of nature. Lux is also intimately connected to free will, consciousness and identity in ways that are a mystery to everyone.

There were now seven boxes on the table, made of different woods, ranging from flimsy balsa to dense mahogany.

'We can do this,' said Vicky.

'You're not reassuring me. Is it really so hard?'

'It's a big jump from compressed air, but Hardisty's right: if you can't use Keyways on your own, you'll be at a huge disadvantage.'

'Even bigger than currently?'

'Oh, aye. Definitely.' She tapped her finger on the first box, the one made of balsa wood. 'First question: what's a lock?'

'It's a good job we studied philosophy in the RAF.'

'Are you serious?'

'No. Of course not. That doesn't mean I can't think for myself, though.' I stared at the boxes on the table, the windows and the front door, scratching my chin. I nodded to myself and ventured this definition: 'A lock is any form of device which prevents access to another object and which needs a second device, a key, to release it. A *lock* is not to be confused with a *catch*, which merely holds something in place, like the catch on a window or the magnetic seal on a fridge.'

'Very good,' she said with enthusiasm. 'It took our class nearly an hour to come up with something like that.' She pointed to the first box, physically the flimsiest. 'Try this one. It's as much as I can do myself in terms of lock-making.'

The little box was different from the others in having an actual key sticking out of an ordinary looking lock. All the other boxes had nothing like a keyhole. I tried to turn the key. Nothing. I tried harder and felt the whole thing twist – any harder and it would come apart in my hands.

'All I've done,' she said, 'is to make the mundane lock incredibly sticky. You still need a physical key to open it. Most Mages do this to their front doors when they go out.'

I could see several flaws in that practice, but I'm the student here.

'Take the key out and feel the lock with your eyes closed.'

I did what she asked, turning the box round and round, then feeling the lock using my Sight. It tingled, randomly, with the white noise of magick. I'd been here before, and I knew that it would take patience. I put my finger over the keyhole and rubbed gently. *There*. Like an extension of my finger, I could feel a paddle just inside the lock. If I just flicked it…

'I think I'm nearly there,' I said, remembering the physical key. I put it back and felt for that little paddle with my Sight. *There*. The paddle was now against the business end of the physical key. Turn them both together, and … *click*. Wow. I didn't try to keep the silly grin off my face until I heard the *whoosh* of breath from Vicky.

'C'mon, Vic, it wasn't that unlikely was it?'

'I wasn't sure. Before Lunar Hall, I think you might have struggled.'

'Have I passed, then?'

She shook her head. There was something dangerously like pity in her eyes. 'That wasn't a Keyway, Conrad, that was just basic manipulation. It wasn't even a magickal lock, just a bit of ectoplasmic glue with a reverse trigger. Try locking it again.'

This time, the key turned back and forth with no resistance, and no magickal input from me. Aah well, two steps forward…

Vicky passed me the second box. 'This is a real magickal closure – like you said, a catch. There's no lock or key, but we're getting there.'

The box was made of plywood, of no great age, and had a lock exactly where you'd expect a lock to be, but without a keyhole. I closed my eyes and touched the lock. There was something inside, like a spring pressing two plates together, only it wasn't a spring, it was inside the metal itself…

'Is there magnetism in here? Holding the lock together?'

Her dark eyebrows shot up. 'Now I am impressed. Most Mages, no matter how strong, can only feel the lock, not the force holding it together. I certainly can't.'

'Which way is north?' I said.

'You what? How should I know?'

I pointed to a corner of the room beyond her shoulder, then swivelled to my right. 'That way's north, and Merlyn's Tower is that way, and that's not because I live here. I just know it. I wonder if I've always had a better developed sense of the earth's magnetic field than most people, and it got stronger when the Allfather touched me.'

She gave it some thought. 'You could be on to something, Conrad, but I'd keep it under me hat if I was you. I definitely wouldn't tell the Dean.'

'I wasn't planning to.'

She looked over my shoulder, probably trying to remember something she'd learnt in school, something so basic that she took it for granted. 'A mundane locksmith puts a lot of energy into making a lock. Heating the metal, bashing it, cutting and shaping it. That's what an Artificer does with a magickal lock. Are you with me?'

I nodded.

'You still need energy to *work* the lock – you use the strength in your fingers to turn the key, don't you?'

'Or electricity in the case of my room safe.'

'That's right. Same with magick. There's Lux in the lock, but you need to put more Lux in to flip it. Try to find the magickal switch in this one. Obviously, we're still one step below an actual Keyway.'

I took the box again and probed the lock with my Sight. I felt around the plates, so magnetic that they gripped each other in an unbreakable embrace. Beyond the plates were some little lugs, anchoring the Work to the box. One felt slightly different. I pressed the centre of the lock with my physical finger and channelled Lux to exert magickal pressure on the magickal lug. It was stiff, and I could feel the strain until suddenly the polarity in the bottom plate reversed and the lid flew open.

'Brilliant,' said Vicky. 'Now shut it.'

The lid was now very reluctant to rejoin the base, until I pressed the magickal lug again, and nearly lost a finger when it slammed shut.

'Oops,' said Vicky. 'I should have warned you about that.'

'And I should have seen it coming. Time for coffee and a fag break.'

'I've been looking into your little domestic problem,' said Vicky over coffee.

'Which one? Do you mean the draughts, the drains, the lack of an en-suite bathroom or the phantom book thief of Clerkswell?'

'How old is the house?'

'The house itself only dates back to the 1850s, but the well was definitely there for centuries before that, and there's a stone carving in the house that could be any age. Probably at least Tudor.'

'That helps. I must admit that I'm not keen to fiddle with the well, but if I can anchor Thomas to the house, I think I've got a way to give him a boost.'

'Sounds good. So long as you're sure.'

'I looked him up last night. Don't worry, I didn't go to Salomon's House: it didn't exist when Thomas was in the flesh, so the records are in Merlyn's Tower. I don't agree with you about Dean Hardisty, but I get where you're coming from.'

'Paranoia can be useful, Vicky.'

'Aye, well, I found out the reason that Thomas left Cambridge. He was betrothed to a Witch. Definitely not an option at the time.'

'And he still loves her.'

'Aah. Bless. A sentimental Spectre. How cute.'

'This is my ancestor we're talking about. Show a little respect.'

'Whatever. I looked at the case file on the missing books. They only suspect him because there was a gap in the shelves, and because he re-wrote the index before he left so no one could do a full audit. There's also a suggestion that he bribed his successor to say nothing.'

'A true Clarke then.'

'I couldn't possibly comment,' said Vicky. 'Let's get back to work.'

She picked up the third box, which was very similar to the second except that it was made of light oak and there was what looked like a Doodad set into the top. It was long and narrow rather than circular like the ones Mages hang round their necks.

'This is your first Keyway,' said Vicky. 'The fastening catch is the same as on the one you've just done on Box 2, but this time there's a lock. The polarity will only switch if you apply magickal pressure using a Keyway pattern – that's all it is, a pattern.' She pointed to the Doodad. 'We call these Stamps. They carry a copy of the Keyway pattern.'

'Right. I'm guessing that most magickal locks don't come with the key attached.'

She dug in her pocket and pulled out a little bunch of Artefacts like the Stamp on the box, but smaller. She waved them around to make sure I'd got the message, then put them away and handed me Box 3.

'When Dean Hardisty assesses you for the MA, she'll give you a box and a Stamp. You'll just have to open it. If you can get the principle with this one, you should be good for anything she's likely to throw at you.'

Before touching the Stamp set into the lid, I pushed my Sight into the lock. Instead of a simple catch, the whole of the magnetic plate had little pits along it. I counted eight of them, and tried to press down into a couple at random. It seemed to be the right sort of thing, an impression which was reinforced by examining the Stamp, where I found a series of pits and lands, like the diagram of data on a CD.

I put the box down. 'Is there a binary thing going on here?'

'Mmm. I take it you've found the pattern?'

'Yes. There are only 256 possibilities with this one. I assume things get more complicated.'

'We'll cross that bridge later. I'll save you the bother of messing around: you have to push the right combination simultaneously. That's the hard bit.'

She wasn't wrong. Not only did I have to press pits 1, 4, 6 & 7, I had to *avoid* pressing 2, 3, 5 & 8. After ten minutes, I was sweating and Vicky was checking her emails. I was on the verge of giving up when my phone rang. The ID said *Spain*.

'Excuse me,' I said, heading for the bedroom. 'It's my parents.'

It was my mother to be exact. 'Can you talk?'

'Yes, or I'd have let it go to voicemail. How's things? How's Dad?'

'He's fine, dear.' The line went quiet. I had a good idea why she was calling, and a good idea why she was finding it hard to come to the point.

'Rachael's been on the phone. She wants to know how deeply you got in with that crowd of gangsters.'

'What did you tell her?'

'Nothing, of course. I wish you wouldn't use me as message service, dear. You should talk to her properly.'

'What! That's a bit rich, Mum.'

'Whatever, dear. She was particularly vocal about that girl Mina, and how deeply was she involved with the money laundering. Something to do with the Financial Conduct Authority.'

'I've heard of them.'

'Conrad! Talk to your sister!'

'I will. I promise. Just as soon as I've got myself sorted.'

'I despair of you two, sometimes. How you can both be so successful, and both get into so much trouble amazes me.'

'We get it from Dad. Well, I do anyway. What trouble has Rachael been in? This is news to me.'

'Goodbye, Conrad.'

'Are they OK?' asked Vicky when I returned to the sitting room.

'As much as ever. Honestly, they're fine, but I might have some problems on the horizon with my sister.' I picked up Box 3. 'I've had an idea about this.'

Vicky put down her sPad. 'There really is only way to work the lock.'

'Yes and no,' I said. 'Have you ever flown a helicopter?' She looked at me as if I were insane. 'Just checking. I don't want to be accused of mansplaining.' She snorted. 'It's been said that you need three hands to fly a chopper – and there's some truth in that. Maybe I'll show you one day.'

'Only after a direct order from the Constable will I ever get in a helicopter with you. Or anyone, come to that.'

I let that pass, and put my right hand on the lock, feeling out the pits with my Sight, then did the same with my left hand on the Stamp. Once I'd got the two Artefacts in focus, it was a simple matter to press the one with the pattern of the other. This time the box didn't fly open because instead of reversing the polarity, the lock demagnetised both plates, and that took a lot of Lux. My fingers were aching and my eyes throbbed.

'You've done well,' said Vicky. 'Better than I expected, to be honest. I don't want to tire you out, so we'll leave it there for today.'

I put the box down. There were four more boxes untouched on the table. 'What have I got to look forward to?'

'You're right about the 256 combinations. That makes it a level one lock. Up to level five, you just have to repeat the procedure, and do it in the correct order. I'll let you work out how many combinations that gives.' She smiled and pointed to the boxes in order. 'This one's level two, that one's level three. Then we move on to what's called a non-linear lock by the College, and a natural lock everywhere else.'

The pain in my eyes was turning into a headache. 'It's bad enough having to learn a whole new load of jargon without there being two names for the same thing. Why is a spell called a "Work" in the College but a "Charm" in the Circles?' I pointed to the boxes. 'Why does the College call them "non-linear locks" and everyone else calls them "natural locks"?'

Vicky cheerfully ignored my pain. 'You'll get used to it. Did I see lunch in the kitchen?'

Over food, I gently probed her claustrophobia in anticipation of tomorrow's trip underground. She made the right noises, or enough of them for me to press ahead with the plan. After that, I needed a lie down, and Vicky had to get back to Merlyn's Tower. We agreed to meet at the statue of the Duke of Wellington outside the Royal Exchange, just above Bank station, and the place we'd first been properly introduced.

'Oh, and wear sensible shoes,' I said as she left the flat.

'Yes, Uncle Conrad.'

4 — *Of Moles and Men*

The warning signs were visible before I got to the Royal Exchange – a cloud of smoke was rising above Vicky. She'd started on the fags again.

'Are you sure about this?' I asked, squeezing in next to her and taking the lid off my coffee.

She lifted her legs and waggled her feet. 'Ninety quid I've spent on urban adventure shoes. Not going back now.'

'Good. I was thinking last night – we might run into Mr Mole, and you should know what to expect.'

'I thought you were his pal.'

'I am, but he can get very friendly. He's blind, obviously, and to get to know you, he has to nose you all over.'

'We had a dog like that once, always sniffing.'

'It's more than smell, Vic. His nose is like a ... radar, I suppose. He can't be in the world without touching things. It's like having a thousand giant maggots crawl over your face.'

She went even paler than normal and just flicked her head, not trusting herself to speak.

'Let's get it over with, then,' I said. We picked up our backpacks, dumped our cups and butts, and headed underground.

I led us through the service entrance and pointed to the magickal door. 'Is this a non-linear lock? You have to say *friend* in a silly voice before it opens. See?'

The sound of my Bluebottle impersonation brought the smile back to her face. 'I have absolutely no idea about this, Conrad, and I don't propose to waste my life thinking about it. Let's get down there.'

I walked down the steps and powered up the lantern. I was about to offer her the spare LED torch I'd brought when she took out a stick about two feet long. I had to turn away and blink when the end lit up.

'Sorry,' she said. 'Should have warned you. This is full daylight.'

'Even Moley will see that. How did you do it?'

She shrugged. 'This is the closest we get to a magic wand. It's called a Lightstick, and I'll put it on your curriculum for later. Much later.'

The flood of bright light seemed to calm her further, and we made good progress until we got to the fork into Moley's new diggings. From somewhere, water was getting in, and the tunnel was now both steep and muddy. Vicky had to lean on me to keep her balance.

'This is gonna ruin me new shoes.'

I was going to say something scathing until I saw the Lightstick shake. She was getting worried. 'Not far now. The Roman tunnel should be dry.'

By the time we got to the crossroads with the Roman diggings, Vicky was breathing heavily. She squatted with her back to the dry bricks and told me to put my lantern back on. She put down the Lightstick, which promptly went out, and dropped half the contents of her backpack on the floor. It's a good job her sPad has a rugged housing. She finally found a strip of tablets and a bottle of water.

'I was trying to do without,' she said. 'It's being with you, you great psychopath. Didn't want to look like a girl.'

I gritted my teeth and did something I hope I won't regret: I bent down and snatched the tablets before she could take one.

'Hey! Conrad! Give them back.'

I glanced at the packet: Xanax. I shoved them in my coat and dropped down to her level. I grabbed her hand, partly for reassurance and partly to stop her lashing out – wild magick can be very dangerous.

'It's too late, Vic,' I said. 'Believe me: I've seen it. I've flown lots of reluctant passengers in my time, and Xanax only works in advance. If you take it now, you'll be in all sorts of shit. Trust me: I'm a pilot.'

She managed a laugh. 'If you say so. Give us a minute. And don't let go of me hand just yet.'

We sat next to each other in the gloom for a few minutes while she tried to get control of her breathing. With a big *huff*, she withdrew her hand. 'What would you have done if I'd really freaked out?'

I drew the magickal wirecutters out of my pocket, the ones I use to sever the chain of Artefacts that Mages have around their necks. 'I would have whacked you, cut your chain to stop you hurting yourself, or me, then carried you out as quickly as possible.'

'Do you think of everything?'

'Only when my life's at stake. Or yours. It's called risk management. I'll put it on *your* curriculum, along with strategic advantage and tactical withdrawal.'

'I can wait.'

On her signal, we climbed up, and she re-lit the Lightstick. She looked at the door, and what had taken me half an hour took her ten seconds. 'You're right, it is Roman. There are no traps or Wards, just the back side of a concealment Glamour. We'll do that in a minute after I've got me Focus out.'

I know that Vicky's sPad is a Sorcerer's Focus, sort of like a digital crystal ball, but that's all I know. She juggled the Lightstick and Focus, then scanned the chamber at the other end of the tunnel, walking straight in and examining the well in the floor. She stared closely at her Focus.

'I thought it might be some sort of font. Like in a church,' I ventured.

She looked at me blankly. 'You what?'

53

'Never mind.'

She turned round and looked down towards the door, then back to the chamber. Finally, she took pictures using the mundane features of her sPad.

'This was some sort of repository,' she said. 'Something very powerful was put in that hollow, and it was there for nigh on two thousand years. It was removed less than a year ago.'

I stared at her. 'How did you figure that out?'

'Which way's north, and where's Salomon's House?'

Without thinking, I pointed left, then half-left again.

'Aye,' said Vicky. 'When you can explain how you did that, I'll explain how I know what I saw in there. Let's see what's through that door.'

I grabbed her arm. 'Hang on. We're going to have company.'

The patter of giant paws got louder, and I wondered why Vicky hadn't heard it. When Moley was about to burst into the tunnel, I called out a greeting. I heard him slow down, then he barrelled into view.

'Oh fuck,' said Vicky.

'Your Worship, may I present Officer Robson of the King's Watch?'

He nosed me quickly and turned his attention to Vicky. My partner managed to hold it together until she smelt his breath.

She backed away, gagged and bent double. I thought she was going to deposit her breakfast all over the Roman mosaic.

Mole turned to me. 'The little man has much Lux. What is the matter with him?'

'Nothing, and she's a she. She'll recover. Any news?'

'Mole digs. Mole has been turned down for a credit card. Ghaaeegh.'

Vicky had recovered enough to join in. 'What do you want with a credit card, Your Worship?'

As well as looking whiter than the Snow Queen, a green tinge had appeared on Vicky's neck. One of her Artefacts was obviously working hard. She manoeuvred herself round to Moley's left, away from his mouth.

Moley sniffed. 'I like your stories, human. The Amazon sells such stories with voices. They will not let me listen without a credit card.'

'I can get you one,' I said. 'You can pay me in gold. There must be some around down here somewhere.'

'I trade all things I find to the Dwarf, for Lux. I can get much human currency for gold. Tell me when it is done. Mole must dig.' With a final flick over both our persons, he scuttled away uphill.

Vicky waited until he was out of earshot before saying, 'Uggh. That was disgusting on so many levels, I don't know where to start. For one thing, I could have sworn I smelled curry on his breath. Must be an olfactory illusion.'

'No, that was real. I gave him some curry paste to put on the worms.'

She gazed at the tunnel where he'd disappeared. She looked more wretched than I've ever seen her, more wretched than incipient claustrophobia and exposure to Moley's halitosis could account for. She touched my arm. 'Conrad, I'm really, really sorry. He's not stable.'

I frowned. 'His Worship is a bit of a fruitcake by human standards, but he's quite together in his own Moleish way.'

She shook her head. 'I didn't mean mentally stable, though we could argue about that. Whoever created him didn't do a very good job, I'm afraid. It's his holistic stability that's the issue. Have you noticed any changes since you first met him?'

I reflected on our brief acquaintance. 'Yes. When we first met, he couldn't pronounce "S" sounds at all. He can now, and his nose feels ever-so-slightly different. Less slimy.'

'I thought so. He's still morphing – his Imprint is changing and his body can't keep up. Sooner or later, they'll get so out of kilter that they'll split. He can't sustain himself as a Spirit, so he'll just … die. Sorry.'

Poor Mole. That was just cruel. 'He says a Spirit created him.'

'He's wrong. He probably couldn't tell the difference when he was first metamorphosed. What's been done to Mr Mole has all the hallmarks of Zoogeny. That's the branch of the Work that deals with animals, specifically with tinkering around with their form and fate.'

I was silent, trying to absorb what she was telling me.

Vicky doesn't like silences, much. 'You pretty much have to be born to it,' she continued. 'Even a powerful Chymist like Dean Hardisty wouldn't know the first thing about something like Mr Mole.'

'Is there a … Zoogenist? A Zoogenist at Salomon's House? Could she do anything for Moley?'

'I'm really, really sorry.' She took a deep breath. 'It's a serious offence to create a Particular from an animal, almost as bad as what Deborah Sayer tried to do to her own daughter. Someone has shoved human intelligence on to Moley's natural Imprint and injected Lux to make his body adapt. Is Moleish a word?'

'It is to me.'

'Well, the Moleish part of his DNA is stable, but he's had chunks of homo sapiens grafted on to it. It would be an offence to continue tampering, so the Queen's Zoogenist would just watch over Mr Mole until he became distressed, and then put him down.'

That was harsh. Very harsh. Moley is not an abomination, he's a creature, he is his own Mole. Some human did this to him, and as a species, we owe it to him to put things right.

However, I hadn't missed the warning: if I joined the Watch, I'd have to follow the rules. To avoid the issue, I flicked my lighter – there was enough of a draught to have a smoke and a drink, so we did.

I pointed to the door. 'Is it locked?'

'Aye, but not from this side. The Romans made good locks, and their Keyways are most definitely non-linear. Whoever came for whatever was in that chamber must have had the original Stamp, which is unlikely, or they made one from a schematic. We'll see where it leads in a minute, but I want your thoughts first. Try to think about the Work and what's been done here.'

Was this an official test or an informal piece of staff development from my partner? I suspected the latter. I smoked and speculated. 'Moley was dumped not far from here. Was he created to dig down to this place? Was he abandoned half-finished because they found another way? He's been around since before this door was opened. Too much of a coincidence otherwise.'

'I hadn't thought of that, and I was thinking about the tunnel and chamber, actually.'

I gave her a grin. 'That's why we make such good partners.' I gave it some more thought. 'I've learnt enough to know that magick needs a supply of Lux. The sacred grove at Lunar Hall has a constant presence of Sisters to keep the supply going, but no one's been here since the chamber was sealed. That means it must be drawing a supply from somewhere. And the only protection we know about so far was a Glamour, so probably not that much power.'

'I think so, too,' she said. 'And I'll bet they're connected to the Ley lines. Let's get that door opened – I'll do it.'

'No, Vic. I'll do it. You need to be on guard for whatever's on the other side. Until I get my piece from the Dwarf, you're the one with the firepower, not me.'

'You're the expert.'

Opening the door was very hard. Not only was it physically very heavy, it was stuck with two millennia of dust, and the magickal catch was bloody stiff. I was panting when I drew it back, and Vicky needs to develop more of a sense of danger, because all she did was peer round.

'I've been here,' she exclaimed. 'See?'

Beyond the door was something like a roundhouse: a domed chamber with several exits, well maintained stonework and a series of lines painted on to the floor. I noticed that the thickest line led away from the centre to a large tunnel which could have been built as the continuation of the Roman construction behind us.

Vicky slipped through the door and pointed to the right. 'Salomon's House is two minutes up that way. We were brought down here for a lecture.'

'I'm guessing it wasn't your favourite topic, not with it being underground.'

'You'd be right. I spent most of the lecture hyperventilating and squeezing Desi's hand.' She took a few more steps and stood on the spot where the lines came together. 'I hope there's a simple answer to what was in that chamber, because if there isn't, we're gonna have to talk to the most boring man I've ever met. Even more boring than me Uncle Geoff.'

'Who would that be?'

She sighed. 'The Earth Master. I hate Geomancy. I really, really hate Geomancy. It was the only paper I had to take three times.' She saw me move. 'Stop! Don't close that door or we'll never get back in.'

I remained in post, holding back the heavy timbers.

Vicky scanned them quickly, and said, 'Superb craftsmanship. When that door closes, even you won't see it. Listen, Conrad, I don't think I can take much more down here. If I go up to Salomon's House, through the basement, I can find Desi and ask her to look up what this tunnel and chamber are all about. I've never seen anything like this before. While I'm doing that, you can see the Dwarf. You don't need me for that.'

'Are we allowed to contact Desirée? I don't want to upset Tennille.'

She waved her hand. 'The Invisible College have to help us. It's in their charter and it's in their best interests. It's up to us who we ask. If Desi can't find out, she'll pass it on.'

'Great. Well done, Vicky. And thank you. This morning meant a lot to me.'

'Aye, you're welcome. It's what partners do. I'm just sorry to be the bearer of bad news. I'll be in touch.'

I waved goodbye and retreated to the Roman Tunnel. Poor Moley, caught in the twilight world between human and animal. He is gross, he is unnatural, and he's already killed four people. I just can't help liking him, that's all. We've cleared our debts to each other – if anything, he owes me – but if I can help him by bending the rules but not breaking them, then I'll do it. I took a last look around the tunnel and followed Mole's paw prints uphill for my appointment with Hledjolf.

5 — *Ecce Dwarf*

The Dwarf led me deeper into the Hall than I'd been before: through the conference room, down a passage and into a vast domed space that disappeared into the dark. I could see a table in front of me, at human height, with a portable ramp next to it, like a wheelchair version of the steps to a light aircraft. In the distance, a shadowy scarecrow stood sentry.

Hledjolf climbed the ramp. 'Behold your weapons.'

'No one says *Behold* any more,' I responded, bending to examine the goods. My original Sig P226 was there, now gleaming from a thorough clean, with the clips lined up next to it.

Ear defenders were at the back. Front and centre was an ornate black case made from something like polycarbonate, edged with aluminium. Very professional looking. Even more interesting was the glimmer of Lux.

'Impressive,' I said.

'We thought you would want the same protection as other Watch Captains, even though you did not ask for it.'

You can't say that the little stone robot's customer service isn't first rate. 'Thank you, Hledjolf. I owe you one.'

'You owe us 0.5oz to be precise.'

Fair enough. 'What do I get for that?'

'The case has a lock keyed to your Imprint, and the Forgetting Rune embedded. If you did not know, that rune allows you to deposit the case with any human, and they will forget it's there, and so will their colleagues. They will not seek to examine it. Certain Works will counteract this effect, but they are rare. In addition, only you can discharge the weapon. Please, examine it.'

I touched the lid casually, and felt nothing. I had to give it a magickal nudge before the lock clicked open – no magnets, just a sturdy pair of latches.

Inside, the handgun was snug in its black foam and looked exactly like the original on the table next to it, except that it seemed somehow *perfect*. I couldn't tell you how, or why, but Dwarven crafting is just flawless. There were differences – the grip had two insets, one empty and one with an Ancile. I was staring at it in admiration, unwilling to spoil the moment. Hledjolf thought I must be unsure.

'We have made the case over-sized,' he said. 'In the lid is a compartment for magickal rounds, with room for your human badges. ID cards you call them.'

'Useful.' I pointed to the stock. 'I thought the Ancile only worked if you touched it. I can't carry a gun in my hand all the time.'

'Nor a sword, nor an axe. This is the finest Ancile: you activate it by touch, and so long as it remains on your person, you are protected. You should deactivate it unless you are at risk, because it puts a drain on your Lux.'

'Right.'

'Let us perform the test. We have placed an Ancile on the mannequin. You should verify that with your mundane weapon before using the enhanced bullets. You may begin when the lights come up.'

The Dwarf trundled away and I heard a door closing. Seconds later, the room was filled with light. 'Wow,' I said out loud. It was huge.

The target had been placed at 25m, I guessed, but it wasn't even in the middle. The walls had columns, rising to a vaulted ceiling with stone facings between. All over the walls, I could see pictures, too far away to make out the details. What was this space? What on earth did the Dwarves want with such a vast cathedral?

I took a few more seconds to soak up the atmosphere, and from somewhere, I got a sense of *emptiness*, that this hall should be filled with tables, benches, chests and cabinets. There should be laughter. There should be song, and there should be dancing. Had it all been and gone, or had it never existed?

'Mr Clarke. When you're ready,' came the familiar voice. Whatever ghosts had been whispering in my ear shut up and vanished.

The target was a human sized and shaped mannequin, fixed to a stand. There was a chain round its neck with a single Doodad hanging from it, presumably the Ancile. I donned the ear defenders, checked the mundane pistol, inserted a clip and took aim.

I fired three rounds at different points on the target. All three were diverted to ricochet around the hall, as expected. It was time to really examine Hledjolf's handiwork.

I've met quite a few soldiers – not all of them American – for whom guns have some sort of sexual attraction. I mention this because I want you to understand the difference between an appreciation of power and precision on the one hand, and drooling on the other. I do not drool over guns. We'll leave it there.

I fired one shot. There was a rainbow flash around the target and smoke poured off its chest where the Ancile had, literally, burnt out. I put the gun down and went to see what had happened to the bullet.

'Impressive, Mr Clarke,' came Hledjolf's voice.

I'd aimed for the head, and there was a hole in the target's face. I raised my voice. 'No point in shooting again.'

'Then join us in the conference room.'

I packed everything away and stowed it all in my backpack, well out of sight. Hannah and I are going to have an interesting conversation about carrying firearms in the near future, and I don't want to get arrested before then.

The Dwarf was waiting for me, and for the first time in our relationship, there was refreshment available in the form of a Nespresso machine and choice of capsules. Customer service means thinking what the customer needs before they know they want it, even when you're made of stone and the customer is mostly made of water. My eyes nearly popped out of their sockets when I saw an ashtray.

There were some packets and boxes on the table, which Hledjolf talked me through – cleaning and oiling products which had been adapted for the Dwarven gun. Talking of which, 'This weapon needs a name,' said Hledjolf.

'Fair point,' I agreed. 'For one thing, I need to distinguish between the two guns. Any suggestions?'

'Yes. We showed our work to another Dwarf. When doing something so new, we always seek an outside opinion we trust. Our cousin said that it should be called The Hammer. This is a play on words, because the weapon has a hammer.'

'Thank you for explaining. I wouldn't have got it otherwise.' I've said before that sarcasm is lost on Hledjolf, but I couldn't help myself. Even so, *The Hammer* is a good name. I'll keep it.

'We have one more thing to say,' said the Dwarf. 'You should recover your shell casings. Not only are they easily identifiable, they are specially made. We will discount further purchases if they are returned.'

'Thank you, Hledjolf, for such a fine piece of work. It is worthy of your name.' I lifted my cup in a toast. 'If you don't mind, I've got a couple of things to discuss.'

'Yes?'

'Do you remember a mobile phone you traded with Mr Mole? The one he recovered from that man who tried to chain him?'

Hledjolf reached down and pulled out a dumb phone, which he placed on the table. A gang had been sent to capture Moley for some unspeakable purpose. He had chased them off, killing and snacking on their leader. That was a while ago, before I'd introduced him to the world of electronic devices, and he'd dumped the phone on Hledjolf not understanding what it was. The Dwarf had tried, and failed, to identify the owner.

I pointed to the phone. 'This is worth nothing to you. Give it to me and I might find something. I'll owe you a favour. Look on it as a speculative investment.'

The Dwarf slid the phone to me. 'Agreed. It is fully charged and we have removed the passcode.'

I stowed it away. 'One last thing. Why didn't you tell me that Mr Mole is unstable. Why didn't you tell *him*?'

Hledjolf went still, talking to his other selves. 'We did not know this. The biology of water based creatures is unknown to us. Thank you for informing us. We will accelerate the digging programme before he expires.'

Charming.

We were done, and I left the Dwarves to their labours. I'd learnt something today – not only are there definitely other Dwarves somewhere, the other Dwarves make puns. Interesting.

Before I left his Hall, I had one final question. 'Your bullets deliver a lot of Lux. Isn't that like putting petrol on a fire? Doesn't the target get a boost of Lux?'

'This was asked before, in the time of Robert Boyle himself. The Work in the bullet disrupts the patterns of Lux. Mr Boyle said that being hit on the head with a leg of lamb does not constitute a meal. Humans seem to find this explanation useful. There is something else you might not know.'

'Oh?'

'If you shoot a mundane human anywhere closer to its spinal cord than its elbow or its knees, the Lux will destroy their Imprint completely and instantaneously. There is no surviving a wound from these bullets. Goodbye Mr Clarke.'

There was a lot to think about as I climbed the stairs from Hledjolf's Hall towards Bank Station. I'd barely started when I got a message from Vicky. Before the Battle of Lunar Hall, she did something to my phone which entangled it with hers and allows me to communicate with her in all sorts of unlikely places, such as underneath the biggest gold vault in Europe. I had been thinking about Moley, but I put that aside when I read this: *Conrad, we have a problem. Urgent appointment with Hannah at 2. Vic. X.*

6 — *Enter the Dragon*

'Can you take that?' said Tennille when I arrived at the Constable's office. She was pointing to the tea tray, so Hannah must have calmed down a bit since Monday.

'Of course. Do you know what's going on? And whose is the fourth cup?'

'My girl's come with Vicky. All I know is that there's a big to-do.'

She opened the door for me, shooing me through as if I were late. Hannah, Vicky and Desirée were already seated at the larger of the tables. The first and only time I'd met Desirée was at Club Justine, an encounter that had officially never happened. Both young women looked at the floor when Hannah said, 'I believe you've heard of Ms Haynes, Conrad.'

The young Chymist and I shook hands without making eye contact. Desirée isn't quite as dark as her mother, and she's certainly a lot taller – strikingly tall, in fact. She's one of the few female Mages I've met who doesn't grow her hair long, preferring to wear it cropped close, curled and streaked with vermilion. There are layers of racial, gender and cultural issues going on with that haircut which I couldn't possibly untangle.

I was going to be mother until Vicky beat me to the teapot, so I sat down and waited.

'Are you 100% sure?' said Hannah to Desirée.

'Completely. I showed Vicky the sample in our museum and she compared it to the Echo in the tunnel. It's a perfect match.'

'Why me?' said Hannah. She stared out of the window, her hands making little fists in her lap. 'This was supposed to be a quiet job, you know.'

Vicky and Desirée looked at each other in the way that only close friends can do, seeking and receiving confirmation and support with just a glance. Vicky turned to me and raised her eyebrows. I gave the smallest shake of my head: the Boss would be back in the room when she was ready.

A deep breath from Hannah, and we were off. 'Conrad, there could be a Dragon on the loose.'

I've met Helen of Troy in the guise of Cindy Crawford c.1995. I've bought a gun from a Dwarf. Of course there's a Dragon on the loose.

'Please tell me this is a test,' I said to Hannah.

'I wish.' She scratched her head by sticking a finger under the back of her headscarf (a bright green today). 'Now I know why I put you two together. Well done, Vicky. Good work, Conrad. That's the only good thing about today.' Having given her head a good scratch, she leaned forward and took both chocolate digestives off the tray. 'Over to you Ms Haynes.'

Desirée took out a book, the sort of book you'd expect to find in an occult library: thick and dumpy, with cracked leather bindings, yellow vellum pages and a gold dragon stamped on the cover.

She placed her hands on the book and stared at them for a second. 'None of us knows anything about Dragons because the last one to fly over Britain was killed by the Romans, but not before it had laid its eggs in Londinium. I only recognised what had been in that chamber because Vicky had taken a picture of the mosaic, and I looked it up in the Codex Ignis – the Book of Fire. I didn't believe it either, but it's right. There was a dormant egg in that chamber, and now it's gone. All I know is what I've read in this book since lunchtime.'

With a deliberate gesture, she passed the book to Hannah, who promptly passed it back. 'I don't understand Alchemical Latin. Treat this as an official request for a summary translation. For now, tell us what you know. First of all, are we talking sixty foot long fire breathing monsters?'

'At least sixty feet long, Constable Rothman. If fully grown.'

'Hannah, please. What else?'

'According to the book, there are two types of Dragon – Chinese and European. The Chinese ones don't have wings. Our egg belongs to the species Draco borealis albionis. The Dragon of Albion. British, if you like, but definitely not English. Apparently the Midgard Serpent was some sort of Dragon, and the followers of Woden/Odin didn't much care for them. The book even says that it was because the Romans had destroyed the Dragons that the British tribes were unprotected from the Angles and Saxons.'

Hannah waved a hand. 'Fine, but what about the eggs? Could they be viable after two thousand years?'

I wouldn't have been so quick to dismiss the history, but she's the Boss.

Desirée squirmed a little. 'I think so. Vicky said that the egg had been preserved off a Ley line, so yes, it should be viable. I think. I haven't got very far.'

'Good, but let us know as soon as you've finished. Thank you, Desirée.'

It took the Chymist a second to realise that she'd been dismissed. She scrambled her things together and left us to it. Vicky looked very put out on her friend's behalf, and didn't realise that Hannah shares my ambivalence about Salomon's House. In this instance, the Constable wanted the planning to stay firmly within the King's Watch.

The Constable rubbed her headscarf, tracing the outline of her titanium insert. 'I need you two on this asap. We can't wait until next week for your induction, Conrad, which is a shame because I wanted to get everyone together. We'll do it at eleven o'clock on Friday, so 10:45 in my office. Some of the team will be here. At least you don't have to go to Sandhurst.'

'But I do need to go to Odiham. You'll have no end of bureaucratic hassle if 7 Squadron find themselves listed as hosting an officer they thought they'd seen the back of.'

'Fine.'

'And there's this,' I said, pulling out the phone I'd collected from Hledjolf. I explained where I'd got it from, and why its owner might be linked to Moley and an attempt to dig the egg out of the tunnel. 'I believe that the Watch has a liaison officer at Scotland Yard,' I continued. 'Could you put me in touch with them to pursue the data trail on this phone?'

Hannah pulled her lip. 'Also fine, but not until after your induction. I don't mind messing the RAF around, but the City Police is a different matter. Vicky? Can you open the door?'

With the door open, Hannah shouted some instructions. 'Bring Conrad's commission papers to sign, and put a fast track on them. Invite everyone to his induction on Friday, parade at eleven thirty, order lunch for those coming. And make an appointment for him with Chief Inspector Kaplan for Friday afternoon. Tell her it might be cancelled.'

Hannah turned to me, a smile and a frown struggling over her face. The smile won. 'Listen, Mr Pilot, this story is *not* going to end with you flying a helicopter into battle with a Dragon. Is that clear?'

I stood up. 'Yes, ma'am!' I also saluted, just to annoy her.

Outside the Constable's office, Vicky had one more thing to say before she dashed off to catch up with Desirée. 'If I give you the evil eye on Friday, it's because of what you've made me do.'

'And what would that be?'

'The one thing in my wardrobe that I hate above everything else is me uniform, understand? If you ever win a medal, I may have to kill you.'

'I wouldn't do that. You'd have to wear it to my funeral.'

'Not if I'm Below Blackfriars.' She gave me a look that, for once, I couldn't fathom. 'It's where Mages are imprisoned. Keira's the only occupant at the minute.'

I'll spare you most of my trip to RAF Odiham on Thursday afternoon because it was boringly pleasant. The CO of 7 Squadron was new since my time there, and it was nice to have a meeting which didn't pick over the scabs of my chequered career. The guy assumed that I'd been brought out of retirement because of my experience with special forces missions, and that I was being seconded to the SAS in some capacity, so there were no awkward questions to dodge about what I was going to be doing.

He handed over my ID and logbook, then asked me to let him know when I'd been to RAF Shawbury to get my pilot's accreditation back. 'I'll fix you up some time in the heavy brigade whenever you like,' was his generous offer.

What a nice man. He almost made me wish I were re-joining properly.

Far less pleasant was a return visit to Salomon's House. Vicky had summoned me to the Receiving Room for 19:00, and I was beginning to think that she didn't want me to see the inside of her flat.

She was waiting for me in the Receiving Room, which was even creepier at night: only the magickally rendered sodium glow lit up the scampering mice and … was that an owl? Yes.

The daytime carvings had been replaced by creatures of the night, and I didn't fancy the mouse's chances against that lot. Vicky looked no happier than the doomed rodent. 'Let's get out of here. The sooner you get your MA the better. Then you can come and go without an escort.'

The Junction was no brighter overall, but ankle lights had been fitted to pick out the stairs. This time we went down.

Vicky touched my arm to break the Silence. 'The Watch has a couple of rooms here, and it seemed easier for Desi to work there so that we can come and go without attracting too much attention.'

We descended two sides of the square, where a passage led away, much better illuminated and almost normal. Before entering, Vicky touched me again. 'I forgot to show you these last time, I was that mithered. Touch that panel to the left of the entry.'

A piece of glass had been mounted on the wall, like the ones you see outside the different rooms of a museum, only this one was blank until I touched it.

WYVERN CHAMBERS
1-2 The King's Watch
3-7 Office of the Provost and Proctor
8 Proctor of the Invisible College
9 Provost of the Invisible College

Rooms 10-16 were occupied by various occult academics, whose names meant nothing to me. 'Who or what are the Proctor and the Provost?'

'The Proctor is in charge of student discipline. You don't want to upset her. In fact, you don't want to meet her full stop. The Provost deals with all the Fellows – every qualified Chymist in England has to keep the Statutes.' She grinned. 'Except me. Officers of the Watch are excused compliance. Good job, too. If we're not eaten by a Dragon in the near future, I'll introduce you. The Provost and the Watch don't always see eye to eye about what Mages get up to. Come on, Desi's been working flat out all day and most of last night.'

I followed her down the passage. 'Shouldn't the Boss know this first?'

'She does; we emailed her. You're getting the *Dragons for Dummies* version with no long words. In here.'

There was a small plate on the door, the first I'd seen that wasn't powered by magick. It informed the visitor that *This room is under the jurisdiction of the Peculier Constable*. Vicky took out her bunch of Keyway Stamps and waggled one at me. 'I'd get you a copy, but it's level 3.'

It's bad news when you can't even get into your own office, I know, and I also know that being locked out of here is at the bottom of my Bad News feed. Vicky worked the Keyway and pushed open the door.

A pair of cast-off civil service tables had been pushed together in the centre of a windowless bunker, a prospect made even more depressing by the threadbare carpet and assortment of mismatched chairs. I felt sorry for the Queen, marooned in portrait on the far wall.

'Please tell me we're not responsible for the decoration,' I said.

'Unfortunately we are. It was on Hannah's to-do list when she became Constable. It's still there.'

Further wallowing in institutional misery was postponed by Desirée's arrival, and by an injection of colour from her outfit – a tropical green dress covered by a rich purple wrap-around cardigan which she promptly dumped on a chair. Salomon's House is warm enough once you get past the Junction, which seems to have draughts coming up from the Old Network, or somewhere even colder.

Desirée was avoiding me in a subtle way that I didn't like. She's Vicky's best friend – the only one Vicky's mentioned by name so far – and I'm sure that my partner has said a lot about me to her. All I know about Desirée Haynes is that she's on the fast-track in Salomon's House and that she likes going out. I even know her mother far better.

I am a long way from seeing the Invisible College as the enemy of the Watch, but there's definitely something out of kilter in the relationship. I had to trust Vicky, and I needed to know sooner rather than later if I could trust her friend.

'I'm glad you arranged this meeting,' I said to Desirée, forcing her look at me. She was about to deny it when I pressed on. 'It was really awkward yesterday. For both of us. We don't have to pretend any more that we'd never met.'

'Yeah, well, I wish we hadn't. No offence.'

Vicky went bright red. 'Pack it in, Desi. Conrad did us a favour by keeping his mouth shut about Club Justine, you know.'

Desirée looked at me but spoke to her friend. 'The jury's still out on that one, Vic. If he hadn't gone spying on us, you wouldn't be about to chase round the country after a flaming Dragon, would you?'

Vicky held her ground. 'Aye, and you'd be up before the Proctor an'all. Did you get the glasses?'

Desirée reached into her bag and pulled out two wine glasses while Vicky opened one of the many boxes lying around and pulled out a bottle of wine. She looked at her friend. 'Two glasses? Howay, man.'

Before they could start a tug-of-war over who got the glasses, I spoke up. 'Any chance of a cup of tea? I haven't eaten, and I'm the one who needs a clear head.'

There was a scuffed sideboard in the corner, c1950, with one door missing. A grubby tray on top held a kettle and the makings. Vicky shook the kettle and found it wanting. She couldn't ask Desirée to go, and I'm not allowed out on my own, so, reluctantly, she left us alone while she went in search of water.

'You should know something, Mr Clarke,' said Desirée. 'There is absolutely nothing about you that I like or respect.'

'Not my problem, Ms Haynes. I don't need you to like me, I just need you to understand that I've got Vicky's back, and I trust that she's got mine.'

'Of course she has. She won't let you down, but no matter how much you've *got her back*, that won't do no good against a mature Dragon unless you know what you're doing, and you don't.'

Vicky reappeared with the kettle. She didn't need her Sorcerer's talents to sense the atmosphere. She turned to me. 'What have you said?'

Why me? Oh, well… 'I was just saying how grateful I am to Ms Haynes for giving up her time.'

'Yeah, right, Conrad. Never mind, I'll find out later.'

She put the kettle on while Desirée poured two large glasses of wine and tried to stay as far away from me as possible.

I get it that Desirée isn't happy that I'd put a stop to their gallivanting around the fleshpots of Chelsea, and I could see that the King's Watch wasn't Desirée's choice for her friend's career, but that couldn't be the whole story behind her anger towards me. It had evidently got worse since yesterday, because in Hannah's office, she had been embarrassed rather than hostile.

I watched her hand over the glass of wine, when she could have just left it on the table, and I realised that she was just being very solicitous about her friend. What could Vicky have said that made things worse? Aah – Desirée had left the room when Hannah gave her parting shot about aerial combat. Vicky must have said something that tipped Desirée's concern into serious worry.

I gestured toward the laptop. 'Ms Haynes, could you Google *Prince Harry* and *Apache Helicopter*?'

Desirée clearly didn't want to, but couldn't find a good reason to say no, and tapped at the keys. I pointed at one of the images. 'Look. Green uniform. These things are flown by the Army, not the RAF. I will not be flying any form of chopper anywhere near any Dragons, mature or otherwise.'

The kettle boiled, and I made my tea. Vicky busied herself tidying up the papers while Desirée read through the search results to see if I were lying. She grunted and put the lid down. It wouldn't change her overall opinion of me, but it might buy me a few days' grace.

'Right. Dragons,' said Desirée. 'Like the Dwarves, they're supposed to be "As old as the gods," which is another way of saying that no one knows where they come from, and obviously there have been limited opportunities to study them.'

I picked up on something. 'Excuse me, but you said *limited* – have there been *any* Dragons around since Roman times? Anywhere in Europe?'

'Two. The Dragon of Bohemia in 1627 and the Wyrm of Moscow in 1943. We've got nothing on either of them, and I'm not sure the Mages who dealt with them found out much either. Most of what we have is in this fifteenth century compendium of reports.' She lifted the book she'd brought to the Constable's office. 'What it boils down to is this: the sooner you find that egg, the better. If it hatches, in less than a year there could be an apocalypse somewhere in Britain. Almost everything in here is rumour and speculation. I wouldn't rely on it as a guidebook – you're better off not knowing because it might be very dangerous if you make an assumption on false information.'

Vicky looked a little crestfallen on her friend's behalf. She clearly hoped that the Queen's Esoteric Library would be able to furnish something more substantial. I took a slightly different view.

'That's good, Ms Haynes.' I turned to Vicky. 'Knowing the reliability of intelligence is as important as the intel itself. Your friend is doing the right thing.' To Desirée, I said, 'Is there anything you're certain of?'

Desirée nodded to acknowledge my appreciation of her strategy. 'I've picked up a couple of things that are corroborated across all the sources. First, that all dragons are female. Second, that to hatch an egg needs two things: milt from a Dæmon and a special nest.'

I tried not to look at either woman when I asked what a *Dæmon* was. After an exchange of glances, it was Desirée who said, 'You tell him. You're better attuned to Mr Clarke's level of … knowledge.'

'You mean my level of ignorance,' I said.

Desirée looked at the book and muttered something.

Vicky cleared her throat and said, 'You know what a Spirit is, yeah?'

'A Mage who has left their body behind and only exists as Lux.'

'A Creature of Light. That's right. Well, a Dæmon is exactly the same, but they've never been human, or not since the dawn of time, as they say. It gets a bit political as to whether some Dæmons are also Angels or demi-gods or whatever. If you stick to the idea that Dæmons are the warlords of the spirit world, you won't go far wrong.'

'I see.' I could also see that Desirée thought the explanation was reductive, oversimplified and suspect on several levels. That's academics for you. 'Can any Dæmon fertilise a Dragon's egg?'

Desirée couldn't contain herself and took over. 'The expression is to *quicken* an egg, and no. The sources are quite clear that only the Brythonic gods and two specific Dæmons can quicken the eggs of an Albion Dragon.' She paused. 'This is where it gets difficult. We can't ask the gods what they've been up to, and if someone did, I doubt we'd get a straight answer. What I am sure of is that no library I know of has a record of *which* Dæmons have the power to quicken them, still less do they have a clue about how to summon them. Remember, I've only had a day. I'll keep on it.'

'Thank you. And what about the nests?'

'We know that there were twelve of them. We also know that Britain had a complete network of Ley lines before the Romans, and that all twelve nests were hooked into the grid. Without that energy, even a quickened egg won't develop. After that, the Hatchlings are kept underground until they mature. The Romans destroyed or decommissioned all the nests, and that was one of the reasons they pushed north of Hadrian's Wall for a time – to finish the job.'

'Mmm. That's given us a lot of food for thought. Can we go back to the timescales? If I'm right, and Mr Mole was created to help them, they can't have recovered the egg before August, at the earliest. It's now the end of January...'

Vicky spoke first. 'I'm not sure about where Moley fits in, but I reckon that egg was still sitting in the chamber six months ago. I've done some comparative readings.'

Desirée looked back through some of the notes. 'If they had immediate access to a nest, and their Dæmon lined up ready, then we've got until April to find it, May if we're lucky.'

'Thanks,' I said. 'That helps a lot.'

Desirée started packing away. Vicky started clearing up.

'Penny for them?' said Vicky.

'What? Sorry. Do you need a hand?'

'Nah. All done.'

Desirée was standing by the door, bags in hand. She looked like she was sucking a lemon when she said, 'Good luck with your induction, Mr Clarke.'

'Thank you. And thanks again for all this.'

Desirée nodded the barest of nods, and left Vicky to escort me back to the Receiving Room. I waited until we were climbing the Junction before touching her arm and asking my first question. 'Who are the Brythonic gods?'

Vicky gave a generalised wave of her hand. 'Welsh, basically. With a bit of Cornish and Breton thrown in. Not to be confused with the *Tuatha Dé Danann* of Ireland.'

I don't spend all my evenings in the Inkwell, you know. I can't read real books about magick because they're all in the library my 11xgreat grandfather once ruled, so I've been trying to read around the mythology, where the gods have interacted with the mundane world.

'Some people say they're one and the same,' I suggested. 'Have you any inside info?'

Vicky gave me a dirty look, and paused to stare over the banisters. Salomon's House was quieter in the evenings, but not deserted. 'How should I know? Some people have asked them. None of them got a straight answer, and some of them really did get struck by lightning.' She turned back to me, a look of real conflict on her face. 'Thank you for trying so hard with Desi. I don't like being caught in the middle.'

We had to keep touching to continue the conversation, which was not how I normally talk to people. 'Is there anything I should or shouldn't say in her presence?'

'Whatever you do, don't mention the Allfather. Desi's mam is a committed Christian, and so is she.'

I'd been wondering about that ever since I'd first met Tennille and seen her faith in action. How does faith in Jesus co-exist with a knowledge that the Allfather walks around the world? Now is not the time.

'Do you fancy a drink?' I asked.

'Not tonight. I think we've both got a lot to sleep on.' She stood on tiptoe to give me a kiss on the cheek. 'Good luck tomorrow. You'll pass, Conrad. I know you will. See you at the parade.'

We let go of each other and left Salomon's House in natural silence, waving goodbye outside. If Desirée is right, and a mature Dragon could cause destruction not seen in Britain since the Blitz, then a few things were obvious to me that probably hadn't crossed the young Chymists' minds.

The biggest issue is *Why*? I can see why Keira and Deborah did what they did, expending enormous resources, committing murder and offering Abigail as a sacrifice. They did it to get the Bowl of Cassandra. What they did was evil to you and me. Evil but understandable, given that the potential rewards were huge. But who benefits from an apocalypse?

7 — *The Sword in the Well*

Tennille was dressed for a graduation when I arrived on Friday morning, talking to the Constable through the open doors. She announced my presence and stepped aside.

I marched into Hannah's office and gave my smartest salute. She made an effort to respond in kind, then said, 'Squadron Leader Clarke. Do you wish a commission in the King's Watch?'

'Yes, ma'am.'

'And have you brought suitable arms with which to discharge your commission?'

'Yes, ma'am.'

'Good, then let's sit down. These shoes are killing me.'

The RAF dress uniform does nothing for women. The RMP dress uniform does even less, especially when it was bought some time ago and hasn't been altered… I kept my eyes firmly on Hannah's cap badge as she lowered herself into the easy chair. When she was settled, she took the cap off. Today's headscarf matched the bright red of the RMP headgear – they don't call them redcaps for nothing, you know.

'I know it's early, but open that cupboard, will you?' she said, pointing to the elaborately carved Jacobean piece I'd admired on previous visits. 'Get the black bottle and two glasses.'

I gestured at the sideboard. 'My dad would give you a good price for this. There's still demand for pre-Colonial furniture in America.' Inside, I found two antique glasses and a dark bottle with a stubby cork. I put the glasses on the table and glanced at the label on the bottle. It was in Gaelic.

'A gift from the Master of Napier College,' she said. '*Dawn's Blessing*, they call it, and don't ask me how they make it, or even who makes it. They don't tell. Just a little finger.'

I poured two splashes and returned the bottle to the cupboard.

'Your father would sell his soul for a case of this,' she grinned, raising her glass. 'Comrades in arms.'

'Comrades in arms,' I echoed. I sipped, and I was sipping a measure of Heaven. The smell of spring heather floated through my nose, while autumn mist and the peat fires of winter flooded my tongue. 'Ma'am, for a whole case of this, my father would sell his soul and offer the rest of the family's, too.'

'I wonder what I'll do when the first teetotal officer joins us.' She looked into her glass. 'I didn't have to nominate you, Conrad. Why do you think I did? And no jokes please.'

'Because of my experience, I presume. I didn't know you had a choice.'

'I did, and it wasn't just your track record. It was because you don't think you know it all. Because you're not afraid to ask for help. Or scheme for it. And despite everything, I think I can trust you.'

'Thank you.'

'You could have petitioned over my head if I'd refused, but I'm glad you're here.' She fished in her pocket, and produced a bright disk of gold. 'I put your name to the Vicar of London Stone, and by some backstairs process, your name goes to Buckingham Palace, and back comes a golden guinea, touched by the sovereign. It's your bounty, and part of it will become your Badge of Office, stamped onto your sword. Every magickal human and most of the Creatures of Light will know what it is and the authority it represents. Use it wisely.'

'Ma'am.'

'Where's your sword?'

'Here,' I said, and took the case containing the Hammer out of my adjutant's bag.

Hannah blinked. 'What on earth?'

I opened the case, flipped it round, and presented it for her inspection.

'Oy vey, Conrad, you cannot be serious. A gun!'

'It seemed the best fit for my talents, or lack of them.'

She stared at the weapon. '*A terrible beauty*. Was that what Oppenheimer called the Bomb?'

'No, ma'am, that was what Yeats called the Easter rising, I believe. Oppenheimer said something like, "I am become the destroyer of worlds."'

'You know, I've never fired a gun. Ever.' She closed the lid. 'Time for the last warning. If you fail the induction, your weapon is forfeit.'

I breathed a sigh of relief. 'Is that all? I wrote a letter for my parents last night in case I didn't come home.'

She looked at me as if she didn't quite believe me. 'Let's go.' We stood up, and Hannah led me to a door at the far side of her office. I had thought it led to a private bathroom, and it did, but it also revealed a tight spiral staircase. She flicked on the lights. 'It's a long way down.'

There were no windows to punctuate the descent, and only one other door, just below Hannah's floor. 'Back entrance to the Watch Room,' she said in passing. 'Only Watch Captains and the Clerk can use it. If you need to see me, it's best to make an appointment. Unless I call you for a private chat, of course. And there's one other reason I'll tell you about later.'

After that, we went down a long way, until damp oozed out of the stones because we were at river level, below the foundations of all of the Tower of London buildings.

'One more turn,' said Hannah, and then we got to the oldest door I've ever seen. I know what fungus does to damp timber, and there must be magick all through this door because it was both dry and unblemished. 'Don't bother coming back here without me. Only the Constable or the True King can open this door.'

There was no handle, lock or bolt to keep it closed, and all it took from Hannah was a steady pressure. As the door swung back, a rush of cold air and cold magick escaped up the staircase. I shivered, and I'll swear my cap rose half an inch as what's left of my hair prickled.

Hannah leaned inside and touched something that flooded the room with light. She went through, and I followed, pausing on the threshold. The room was circular, about half the diameter of the tower above. In the centre was a well, standing about four feet above the floor. There was no winch to lower a bucket. Opposite the door was a workbench with a small crucible and burner on top. The only sign of modernity in the whole room was the propane cylinder on the floor next to it.

The Constable had made her way to the bench and was busy lighting the burner. That gave me a chance to look at the rest of the fixtures. We had come in at the east, and the bench was to the west. In the south was a Dickensian writing desk – high, with a sloped top, designed to be used standing up. To the north was a monumental picture, so big that it must have been carried down rolled up and the gilded frame built around it down here.

The burner roared into life, and Hannah turned to face me. 'Shut the door and come in.' I did so, and she pointed to the picture. We converged on it from either side of the well.

With the door closed, and as I got deeper into the room, I could smell flowers. Nothing obvious, like jasmine or roses, more like the distillation of an English water-meadow in spring. We stood before the painting, and I could now make out the subject. In the midst of a classical landscape, ruined columns scattered around, sat a throne, and on the throne sat James the Sixth and First, as regal as you like. Before him knelt a gentleman in half-armour, his face turned to the king, and between them, being dispensed by James, was an elaborate sword, covered in symbols and glowing with a light that didn't come from the cloudy sky. The well was there, in shadow, behind the kneeling figure.

'Horrible, isn't it?' said Hannah. 'Not van Dyke's finest hour, though it might have helped if he'd seen any of the subjects, or the sword, or been allowed to enter the Water Room. This is James appointing the first Constable, in case the moody looks hadn't given it away.'

'Does the sword still exist?'

'It does, and you'll soon see why it's kept down here most of the time. Two more little jobs first – the crucible should be hot enough by now.' She led me round to the bench and dropped the guinea in the vessel. 'It took me ages to learn how to do this without getting molten metal everywhere. And setting fire to my uniform. Come on.'

We reached the writing desk. There was a great ledger sitting on the slope, closed and with no markings on the cover. I could see gold lettering on the spine, too faint to read. 'Can you open it to the bookmark?' said Hannah. 'I'm too short to reach up, and this jacket's too tight.'

A red silk ribbon marked the place, and I carefully opened the volume to reveal a page ruled with columns headed for name, date, DOB and signature. The page was about half filled but unreadable. I sensed magick – sort of like the occult version of pixilation, I suppose. There was a final column, unheaded and filled with red splodges.

'This is the Annex of Westphalia,' said Hannah. 'You've heard of the Thirty Years' War?'

'Proportionately the most deadly conflict in Europe, World Wars I & II notwithstanding. According to some.'

'That's the one. It was the first time that magick was militarised, and all sides used it. When they negotiated the Peace of Westphalia in 1648, a separate treaty was appended as the Annex. It forbids any Mage from fighting *In the Wars of Popes or Princes*. The responsibility is on the Mage, and every Mage who serves any government has to sign. It worked very well until the Cold War came along and blurred the boundaries. Even the Nazis stuck to it, which I'm sure was a great comfort to my relatives in Theresienstadt.'

'I'm sorry.'

There was a short pause, then Hannah reached into her jacket and pulled out a Mont Blanc fountain pen strapped to a short plastic tube with a rubber band. She unwrapped the bundle and gave me the pen. 'Fill it in.'

I added my name to the roll. When I gave her the pen back, she put it on the ledge and showed me the small tube. 'Sorry about this – we need blood. Give me your left hand.'

She swabbed my finger and took the top off the needle kit, the sort used by health professionals. 'You can't do this to yourself,' she said. 'So I had to practise on my sister when I got the job. Tennille refused, for some reason.' She held my finger, jabbed and squeezed until the blood flowed. 'Just squidge it next to your signature.'

The Annex of Westphalia isn't just a register, it's a magickal register. I felt the book stick to my finger like a sucker, pulling out blood until it knew who I was. There was an audible *pop* when it let me go. Hannah opened a drawer and offered me a selection of sticking plasters, all with cartoon characters. She held them up in turn.

'Mr Bump? Donald Duck? How about a Minion? They're new.'

'Looks too much like Hledjolf the Dwarf.'

'It does, doesn't it? I wish you hadn't said that – I won't be able to watch *Despicable Me* with the nieces and nephews again now. I know. Mr Happy. That's you all over.'

Rather more blood than necessary had run down my finger. She wiped it off with maternal efficiency before applying the plaster, and I wondered again whether Hannah had had any children before her husband's death. Her kids might be too old for *Despicable Me*.

She smiled and stepped back. 'I'm going to stand behind the water. When I summon you, approach from the opposite side, kneel and place your weapon on the ledge. Stay kneeling until I tell you to get up. Are you ready?'

I nodded, and she took up a position in the west. I moved to stand by the door. I took the Hammer out of its case and waited for the command.

Hannah took a deep breath. 'My lady. Squadron Leader Clarke seeks a commission in the Watch. Will you hear him?'

Blue light appeared in the well, and I could see the surface of the water for the first time. Bubbles rose, ripples spread, and the room started to sing. Stones rang out with a choir of women's voices, an ancient hymn in a lost language. From the water, a hand came up, a hand clutching a short, broad and glowing sword. Hannah leaned awkwardly down and took the sword. She held it in parade grip and said, 'This is *Caledfwlch*, the sword of Albion. Approach and submit your petition.'

I marched forward, saluted, and assumed the position, placing the Hammer on the lip of the well. The water bubbled, then boiled up into a fountain which hit the ceiling before collapsing into the seated form of a woman, naked, watery locks flowing in a stream down her back and her legs in the well. There was nothing below her calves because her whole form emerged from, was made from, and returned constantly to the water. In the deluge of the fountain and the ripples of running hair, not a drop had spilt beyond the stone rim.

The voice of the stones fell silent, and the woman spoke. 'I am Nimue of the Water, keeper of Caledfwlch and Guardian of Albion. Drink of me.'

She offered a hand which was also a vessel. I drank from her fingers and tasted water which had flowed melting from the retreating glaciers to form the first lake, shocking and cold, fresh and ancient.

Nimue returned her hands to her lap. 'Constable, how fares the realm?'

'Troubled, my Lady, as it ever was. Shall we admit this man to the ranks of the King's Watch, to preserve the King's Peace?'

The water laughed, a full throated gurgle. 'Would I refuse one who has been touched by the Goddess? Receive him, Constable.' There was a pause, filled with a waterfall. 'Receive him, Constable, because he has more to offer you than you know. Farewell.'

Nimue collapsed back into the well, and its light dimmed a little. Having drunk from her hand, I could sense her close by, her presence in and under the surface.

The sound of parade shoes scraping on the flags snatched my attention back to Hannah. She placed Caledfwlch on the rim, opposite the Hammer,

75

and moved to the workbench. She dipped a long-handled bowl into the crucible and moved swiftly across to me, picking up Caledfwlch on the way. With one move, she poured a drop of liquid gold on to the stock of the gun and stamped it with the pommel of her sword.

Hannah let out a sigh of relief and carried the bowl back to the bench. She fiddled with the crucible for a moment, and while her back was turned, I took the chance to ease my aching knee and peer at my gun. A perfectly formed image of Caledfwlch now adorned the Hammer.

There was a *hiss* of metal meeting water and another sigh of relief. She returned to the well, holding a gold coin in her left hand, slightly smaller than the guinea she'd dropped into the crucible. Her right hand carried the sword.

'Do you solemnly swear…'

She recited the oath that I'd made when I became a commissioned officer in the RAF, with the minor variant of *Keeping the King's Peace according to Nature's Law.*

'I swear.'

She placed the sword on the surface of the water, which instantly formed a hand to receive it and draw it back down to the depths of the well. As the ripples died, so did the light.

'Do you want a hand? That floor's hard when you get to our age.' I found myself staring at Hannah's knees, as if I'd woken from a dream. She held out her hand. 'Don't pull too hard. I'm not as strong as you.' With her help, and a groan, I got to my feet.

'Congratulations, Conrad. You're now a Captain of the King's Watch. How does it feel?'

'I've never felt so old and so young at the same time.'

'That's one way of putting it.' She stared at the well. 'That sword is the original Excalibur. Looks nothing like the films, does it? Now, hold out your hand.' She placed the gold coin in my palm and wrapped my fingers closed around it. 'Take this home and put it in a safe place. It will protect you, your home and your family in unexpected ways.' She let go of my hand and cast a farewell glance at the well. 'She was unusually talkative today. She hasn't made a personal comment since I was inducted. Oh well. Let's tidy up, then I've got one more surprise for you upstairs.'

When we came to leave, Hannah told me to go first. It was a long climb back, and I set as slow a pace as possible, for my sake as much as hers. Outside her office, she showed me a tiny door which had been hidden by the angle of the staircase. 'Roof access. You can smoke up there, but no littering. I'll see you in a minute.'

I could just about squeeze through the hatch without ruining my trousers, and found a narrow walkway round the battlements. Merlyn's Tower is lower than most of the complex, so the landward view isn't brilliant. I walked round to the river side and leaned out to get a good look before lighting up.

Sometimes you reflect and consider what's happened and sometimes you just need a moment. Today was a day for moments.

Judging by the half-full coffee jar near the hatch, there was at least one other smoker on the Watch. I stowed my butt and headed down.

8 — Meet the Gang

Hannah had just finished wiping a stain off her uniform jacket when I returned. As per standing orders, I saluted.

'Must you?'

'Yes, ma'am. May I ask a question?'

'Just the one. They're waiting downstairs.'

'How long have you been in the Watch?'

She struggled into her jacket. 'I've been Constable for a year and a half. I was Deputy six months before that, and two years a Captain before that. I spent a year in hospital between the police and the Watch, more or less. It's the fifth anniversary of my husband's murder this May. Have I missed any creases?'

She moved to look in the full-length mirror pinned to the outside of her bathroom door, and I treated her question as rhetorical. She gave herself a final smooth down and picked up her cap. 'As your CO, I'm giving you a direct order, Clarke.'

'Ma'am?'

'If I reach for one of the strawberry tarts, you are to say, "A lifetime on the hips." Is that clear?'

'Yes, ma'am.'

'Good. I'll be knocking on the door, it will be opened, and I'll take the salute. I'll introduce you to everyone, then it's a free for all, hats off and feet up. Let's go.'

The spiral stairs to the Water Room and the induction ceremony had taken their toll on Hannah. She leaned heavily on the handrail as we descended. Outside the double doors on the next floor, she paused to catch herself.

'This is the Watch Room. It's a combination of office, mess room and laboratory. The electronic keypad is one of Cheng's innovations – digital magick he calls it. You key in your date of birth and it does a limited scan of your Imprint. Next floor down is the Officers Room. Cheng, Vicky and the others work there and socialise up here. Toilets, I'm afraid, are in the basement, though there are decent showers and a bunk room, too.'

She knocked three times on the doors, and they were drawn open by a young woman in civilian dress. Through the doors, a semi-circle of uniformed and non-uniformed members of the King's Watch waited. The ones with the red hats all saluted when Hannah came to a stop.

While she made a speech of introduction and welcome, I cast my eyes along the line-up of my new colleagues, looking first for Vicky. She gave me a grin and a wink; I nodded back. Eight of the crowd were in uniform, with a lieutenant colonel at the left hand end. He was a man in his fifties, with sharp eyes, worry lines and a body that wouldn't pass the current Armed Services Physical Test. Next to him was Major Li Cheng, the Royal Occulter. He's a powerful and clever Chymist with ambition and arrogance in equal measure who's in the process of breaking Vicky's heart, something for which I may never forgive him.

I visually skipped over four captains, all male and all notably younger than me, which left two women in uniform. One was Vicky, and the other must be the one recruited at the same time as her, who I only know about by deduction, because Vicky has never mentioned her once. The other Officer was physically most of the things that Vicky is not: tall, athletic, well-proportioned and blond.

I had expected Tennille to be next in the pecking order, but there was one civilian ahead of her, another woman, and probably the oldest person in the room. Her suit was neat and well fitted, her greying hair pulled back from a lined face. Before I could consider the final three, Hannah finished her speech, and I was given three cheers, followed by a round of applause. I rather enjoyed that.

Hannah led me to the lieutenant colonel, clearly her deputy. I saluted, noting the MC and bar on his medal ribbons. Hannah introduced him as Iain Drummond and we shook hands.

'You did excellent work at Lunar Hall,' he said cheerfully. 'Cleaning up afterwards is proving to be a bit of a nightmare, but that's for another day and not your responsibility. My job here is to put together prosecutions, negotiate with the Circles and keep the peace with Salomon's House.'

'Ian does a lot more than that, believe me,' said Hannah. Her tone was respectful rather than warm. Clearly Iain Drummond did not see his role as mentor and confidante to the relatively new Constable. Why he himself was not in the top job is also a question for another day.

Next in line was Li Cheng, who gave me a formal welcome that was like polished glass, all smooth and cold. Hannah moved swiftly on to the four Watch Captains here today, telling me that there were another eight scattered around England.

She had to cough to the first one as a reminder for him to salute me. He didn't seem to take it personally. All four Watch Captains were pursuing the same trajectory: graduation from Salomon's House followed by a stint in the Watch, followed by a return to the Invisible College. As we went down the line, they got younger, less lined, and had fewer creases in their uniform. I'll tell you their names if it becomes relevant.

Vicky made a real effort to salute smartly. 'Congratulations, sir. I knew you'd do it. Now for level 2 Keyways,' she said with a grin.

'One step at a time,' I said, feeling Hannah's touch on my elbow. I moved to the final member of the Watch in uniform.

'This is Annelise van Kampen,' said Hannah as the young woman saluted. 'She's from the Netherlands.'

'Not so much any more,' said Annelise with the sort of sunny smile that would have her playing the newlywed in an IKEA commercial. Vicky had riveted her eyes to the ceiling.

'Annelise is a qualified solicitor,' said Hannah. 'The CPS don't know we exist, and we've had to rely on a very small pool of lawyers to put prosecutions together. Annelise is helping change that.'

We moved to the first of the civilians, the older woman. She stepped forward to shake hands without waiting for Hannah. 'Congratulations, Conrad. I'm Maxine Lambert, Clerk to the King's Watch.'

'Maxine used to do everything,' said Hannah, 'until Tennille took over the HR side. Maxine will be booking you in for the *real* induction.' Her tone was almost deferential, and definitely flattering. This would be another interesting relationship to untangle.

Tennille broke ranks to give me a hug. Before her arms wrapped round me, I noticed that Maxine was not amused. Tennille spoke straight into my ear. 'When I prayed to Jesus this morning, I told Him you were trouble, and I told Him that you had a lot more trouble left in you.'

Hannah was getting twitchy. The three other women were quickly introduced as the Assistant Clerk and two interns. She said that Maxine would explain everything, then she returned to the centre of the room. I took my new place in the pecking order, above Vicky but below the most junior of the Watch Captains. I may outrank them, but as Hannah said in her speech, I'm the baby of the Watch.

'Hats off, time for lunch,' said Hannah. I saluted, Vicky followed my lead, and the others joined in slowly. Then, the four Watch Captains all threw their caps at a baroque hat-stand by the door. I could feel the trail of magick as the caps arced perfectly through the air and nestled on their pegs. All of a sudden, everyone was looking at me.

Should I try for a googly? No. I had a better idea. I turned and presented my cap to Vicky. Making sure that my voice carried, I said, 'As the one with all the magick in our partnership, would you like to do the honours?'

Vicky's eyes widened in surprise. I didn't know whether or not this was a good thing. Maybe she couldn't do it, maybe I'd committed a gross faux pas. For all I know, in the weird world of the Watch, it might have counted as a marriage proposal.

She tested the weight of the cap, closed one eye and sent it flying towards the hat-stand. It accelerated from her hand like a rocket. It shot past Hannah far too closely, causing her to lurch into Iain Drummond before it crashed into the hat-stand, slamming it into the wall and snapping it in half.

The only noise in the stunned silence was a quiet whimper from Vicky. To save the moment, I said, 'You need a course in ballistics, Captain Robson.'

Two of the Watch Captains burst out laughing, and Maxine coughed loudly to stop herself joining in.

I also heard a snort of superior derision from Annelise, something that took her down at least two notches in my estimation.

Everyone else started moving furniture in a well-drilled manoeuvre, leaving Vicky to approach the pile of firewood by the door in a daze. She contemplated the wreckage and said, 'Oh fuck.'

I bent down to collect the other caps, stacking them neatly out of the way. I tidied the wood, retrieved the crumpled mess of RAF blue and stood up. 'Listen, Vicky, I'll sort out the hat-stand. Don't worry, all right?'

'I've made a right div of meself, haven't I?'

She had. There was no getting round it, so I didn't try. If I'd been Desirée, I might have something more consoling to say, but I'm not, so I passed her my cap. All the stiffening in the top had been smashed, and there were several tears.

She looked down guiltily. 'I'm so sorry, Conrad. I'll get you a new one.'

'Not you. Put in a claim – Damaged on Exercises. That's what we always did. Oh look, food. I'm starving.'

For the first time, I concentrated on the room, not the people in it. It was big, with no less than three windows, and the centre was now filled with three pairs of tables. A selection of office chairs was being wheeled out of nooks and crannies between bookcases, cupboards and a sink unit. There were no desks as such, and the only other furniture was a trio of battered sofas. A large map of England (MOD issue) and a portrait of HM (ditto) completed the inventory.

Platters of food were being set out, glasses lined up and bottles retrieved from a fridge (handy). Hannah wandered over, and Vicky excused herself rapidly.

'You do like to make a scene, don't you?' said Hannah.

'Me? Not guilty, ma'am. It's just the effect I have on people.'

'Come over here.' I followed her to a cupboard. 'Can you get that holdall – this skirt's a bit tight for bending.'

I retrieved a black sports bag, nearly overbalancing with the unexpected weight. Hannah pointed at the bulging contents: it was stuffed with lever arch files and ring binders. I took out a blue file at random, and read the cover out loud. '*Orders of the Occult Council relating to Divination. Volume III.*' I looked at Hannah. 'It's the *Volume III* that's killing me.'

She leaned down to whisper. 'Maxine's monument – all the law and principles of the King's Peace, digitised.' She straightened up and I did the same. 'After this afternoon's trip to the City Police, you've got an appointment with the Earth Master tomorrow morning. I know it's Saturday, but we need to get moving on that Dragon. When you've seen him, take your homework to Clerkswell and stay away from London until I call you back. I read Desirée Haynes' report, and we've got time before the Dragon becomes a threat. I definitely don't want you going into the field again until you've absorbed the two red files at the bottom, and the blue staff handbook. You can skim the rest for now.'

Lunch was good, if rather frustrating. Vicky had told me about the *Chymists' Code* – a semi-formal set of rules, and the first attempt to govern magick outside the Catholic Church. As far as I can tell, the only principle to be followed religiously is the one which says *Tell no one anything for nothing*. I tried to spark up several conversations with my new colleagues, and every time I asked something useful like, *Who are the Fleet Witches, and why are they scary?* my interlocutor would change the subject.

The most difficult part was trying to keep a whole table between me and Annelise whilst simultaneously watching the (divine) strawberry tarts in case Hannah approached them. The crunch moment came when I had to interpose myself between the Constable and the desserts, allowing Annelise to corner me for what amounted to an interrogation by flattery and flirting.

'It's such a change to have a *real* soldier on the team,' was her opening salvo.

'I'm an Airman, not a soldier, but thanks for the welcome.'

'Why did you leave the air force? It can't be because you're too old.'

Vicky was standing by the sink, giving me daggers and chewing on a sausage roll like it was her last meal. If Annelise really was ignorant of my history, it shows that the others can't have been talking to her very much.

I put down my plate and twirled my glass. 'It was time to move on. Time to find a life where I didn't have to live a lie. Somewhere that wouldn't be prejudiced against my partner. Somewhere we could live openly.'

I could hear Annelise's mental gears crashing as she changed course. 'That's even better! The Watch needs to have so many of its prejudices challenged.'

'Thanks, Annelise. That's good to know.'

She touched her hand to my back and went to talk to one of the interns.

As Hannah approached, I stood my ground.

'You're not going to move from in front of those tarts, are you?' she said.

'I'd rather stand here than be forced to shout a warning.'

'Then I'd better go back to work.'

'One more thing. How do you get deliveries here?'

'It's in the staff handbook. Oh, and you've got a locker and a pigeonhole in the basement. I'll be in touch.'

As soon as the Boss left, the party started to break up. I picked up my other holdall, the one with the change of clothes, and collected the Hammer from Tennille's desk before venturing into the basement. It was pretty much what you'd expect a mediæval basement to look like after a twenty-first century refurbishment.

Half an hour later, I was changed, packed and waiting for Vicky by the Ravens in the Tower proper. She bustled along in a rush, also changed from her uniform.

'I cannot believe you,' she said. 'The whole building, apart from the Boss, Desi's mam and me think that you're gay. What was that all about?'

'I had heard that Holland is full of dykes, but clearly that isn't true.'

She stopped moving to work out whether or not to be offended on behalf of the sisterhood. She shook her head, trying to dislodge the memory of what I'd said. 'Are you completely immune to flattery?'

'Of course not, when it's done by an expert. Ms van Kampen is a rank amateur. Odin only knows what she's like to work with.'

'Aye, well you'd better ask Iain Drummond about that. She clings to him like a leech.'

'Don't put images like that in my head. Where are we going?'

'How should I know? You're the navigator. I reckon Scotland Yard would be favourite.'

'Wrong force. Hannah said it was the City Police, in which case I do know where we're going.'

She looked forlorn. 'Please tell me we're taking a cab. I had too much to eat.'

'Then you need to walk it off. I see you've made a commitment to comfortable footwear.'

'Only on days when you're around.'

It was a miserable day for walking, until Vicky burst out laughing. 'I was just thinking about your hat,' she said.

'I'm glad you found it funny. What happened, by the way?'

'Not all the Watch Captains are personally chosen by the gods, you know. If your name's not Conrad Clarke, you have to take an aptitude test, which includes projectile magick. They all practise like crazy, but I never bothered 'cos I didn't have to take the test.' A thought scootered across her brow. 'Anyway, how are you gonna use your sword if you can't project it?'

'Oy!' shouted a cyclist when I stopped dead with one foot in the road.

So that's how the Watch Captains use their swords in a fight – they "project" them towards the enemy rather than get up close and personal. Or perhaps both.

'It's a good job there's more than one form of projectile magick,' I said.

'No there isn't,' said Vicky, dragging me back on to the pavement.

'You'll see. Tell me something: how did you get your Badge of Office without going through … induction?' I had been going to say *without meeting Nimue*, but a taste of iced water stopped me.

'I took me pickaxe to Hannah's office one day, and the next day it was there. Don't forget, I only have powers of arrest. I can't dispense summary justice.'

'I can't forget that because I didn't know until you just told me. Is that all in the red files?'

'Aye.'

'Come on, then. The sooner we meet CI Kaplan, the sooner I can start on my homework.'

'Is that all you've got for a Friday night?'

'I asked Mina out, but she's washing her hair tonight, and every night until May. If you've got Annelise's number, I could try her.'

'Shut up. Is this it?'

The large sign saying City of London Police was a bit of a giveaway. Five minutes later, we were collected from reception by an admin assistant who promised coffee. She took us up, around, down, and along the building until even I was getting unsure about our location. She knocked on Chief Inspector Kaplan's door and left us to it.

I pushed open the door, and thought I'd gone through a time-warp, back to before the day Hannah had had her near death experience with the Revenant.

'Hi,' said our host. 'I'm Ruth Kaplan, and yes, I am Hannah's sister. Younger sister, I hasten to add.' She came from behind a desk which sported an impressive array of computer monitors. It was a day for uniforms, one way and another, and CI Kaplan was wearing hers.

'Guess how much younger?' she said after we'd shaken hands.

Now that was a minefield I wasn't going to step into. It was time to start getting my revenge on Vicky for ruining my hat. 'I always think that women are the best at answering that question, don't you, Vicky?'

'Err...' said Vicky, going red, almost as red as the scarf which she pulled off in the warmth of Ruth's office. Sometimes Vicky can't help herself. She looked at the Chief Inspector in a different way, and a grin broke out. 'You think you're younger, but you're not.'

'I'm sorry,' said Ruth. 'How's that?'

Vicky does tend to forget her audience sometimes: this is her boss's sister, a senior(ish) police officer, and someone we might need a lot of favours from. She steamed straight in: 'You think you're half an hour younger – give or take – am I right?'

It was Ruth's turn to blush. 'Yes. I don't think our mother or the midwife lied about that.'

'They didn't. You were born second, but conceived first. You're actually one day older than Constable Rothman, if you count from the moment when...'

'Stop there. Stop right there. TMI, as the kids say.' She took a breath. 'It's Conrad, isn't it, unless we're being formal?'

'What?' It was my turn to look foolish. I'd been trying to digest several bites of discovery. First, that if Ruth were Hannah's twin, then my estimate of their age had to drop several years: Ruth doesn't look much over forty, if that. And then, how did Vicky do that? Tell someone's age to the moment of conception? I got my focus back. 'Sorry. Yes. It's Conrad.'

Ruth tilted her head to the side in a gesture I'd never seen from Hannah. Ruth has her sister's blue eyes, but her colouring is darker, her mouth a little fuller. I could tell from the way she looked at me that the sisters were close, and that Hannah had already been talking about me. Having given me the study, Ruth nodded her head. 'Hannah said you were tall. How did you fit in the cockpit?'

'There's more room in a helicopter. We don't get the ejector seats, for one thing.'

Coffee arrived, and we squeezed around a small table. Ruth dispensed with the small talk and said, 'Growing up, I had a bit more magick than Hannah, but neither of us had very much, and neither of us knew it. We both joined the Met on the same day, as graduate entry applicants. Hannah made CID before me, and was an inspector before me. When things went pear-shaped, and she joined the Watch, I was on maternity leave. The Watch used to have their own access to the national databases, but all that changed. The last Home Secretary but one insisted that all data requests be handled by the regular force. Hannah agreed, so long as there was only one contact – me. I got promoted, too.'

I picked up on the timeline. 'Hannah wasn't the Constable when the last Home Secretary but one was in office.'

Ruth blinked. These girls needed to get their stories straight. 'No,' she said. 'She was Deputy, and it was delegated to her.' She flicked her eyes to Vicky, to see if my partner were on the same trail, then back to me. Vic was oblivious.

Ruth continued. 'I can do anything that's legal for a police officer and that can be done from here. Some things will need Hannah's direct approval.' She focused properly on Vicky. 'I'm afraid the Protocols haven't been amended yet, so I can only deal with requests from Watch Captains. Sorry.' Vicky shrugged. 'Conrad, I believe that you've got a phone for me.'

I took out the mobile from the Old Network. 'How much do you know about the world of Magick?' I asked.

'Enough. I don't live in it, but I pay frequent visits.'

I passed over the phone, and gave her the story. She seemed most alarmed when I said that Hledjolf had already been looking into the network provider.

'Thanks for that, Conrad. I dread to think what the Camelot Committee will say when I tell them.'

Vicky leaned forwards. 'Conrad's never heard of them. Not even the official title.'

'Oh,' said Ruth. 'There's a committee of non-Mages in Whitehall who consider the impact of magick on the mundane world. The nickname tells you how highly regarded they are.'

'Is it in the red file?' I asked Vicky.

'Nah. One of the green ones. It's not that important. Normally.'

Ruth stood up to put the phone on her desk. 'I'll make a start today, but don't hold your breath.' She turned to face us, leaning back on her desk. I couldn't help noticing that Hannah has nicer ankles. Ruth made up her mind and said, 'Vicky, could you excuse us a moment?'

Vicky frowned at me. 'Aye. I'll be outside. I don't trust meself to get out of this rabbit warren without a native guide. Or Conrad.'

I had to stand up to let my partner to the door. Ruth stayed on her feet when the door was closed. Before she could speak, I said, 'Did you know DS Morton when he worked here?'

She *tsked*. 'Of course I did. And I read the Operation Jigsaw files when Hannah told me about you.'

'How is he?'

'He's doing well, Chief Inspector and all that. He's on a high profile case in Cheshire at the moment.' She waved Tom Morton away with her hand. 'I'm not bothered about the past, Conrad. Hannah's too by-the-book to ask this, but I will: what are your plans? What are you doing in the Watch, and who are you doing it for, if not yourself?'

She was probably the only person in the world who had the right to ask those questions, and she deserved an honest answer. 'I'm my own man, Ruth, make no mistake about that. I'm in the Watch because I've got nothing better to do until Mina Desai gets out of prison. If I'm still alive when that happens, I'll think again.' I opened my palms to show that this was all I'd got.

She nodded slowly. 'Thank you.'

'Tell me,' I said. 'Where did Hannah get her magick from? She evidently didn't have it when you were teenagers.'

Ruth looked very awkward. You can't ask a question like hers and not expect to get one back. She blew out her cheeks. 'Can't. If you'd asked me my favourite sexual position, I'd have told you, but I can't tell Hannah's story.'

I wondered whether Rachael would be as discreet about me. Actually, she probably would, which thought cheered me up. 'Fair enough,' I said. 'Now, about that other question…'

She laughed. 'Go. You missed your chance.'

I went.

Mr & Mrs Robson did a good job bringing up their daughter – Vicky was too polite to ask what Ruth had wanted. I waited until we were outside before I said, 'Ruth's worried about her sister.'

'Oh, aye? In what way?'

'That's the problem. I don't know. All she did was ask about my long term plans in the Watch.'

'Funny question to ask. What did you tell her?'

'The truth: I haven't got any. Or none beyond Mina's release date. A lot can happen before then.' The rain was getting worse. 'I've got mountains of stuff to take to Notting Hill. Do you want to share a cab to Merlyn's Tower? I'm going straight off after.'

'Please.'

'While we wait, you can tell me how you know when Hannah's mother conceived. That must take serious magick, Vicky.'

'You dropped me right in it, there, you bastard. I was that put out, I couldn't help meself.'

'So how did you do it?'

She gave me a strange look. 'It's not something to boast about, Conrad. They call it *Imprimation* at the College, and it's how I knew that Mr Mole is unstable, and how I found Abi Sayer's biological father. It's an aspect of Sorcery, but a pretty useless one. I don't know … it's like wanting to be a pilot, but only being able to land, not take off or fly.'

A cab appeared, and answered my wave. I held the door closed a second. 'Landing's the hardest part, Vicky. I should know. You're letting them sell you short. Don't do that.'

She leaned up and kissed me. 'Thanks, Uncle Conrad. And well done with the induction.'

'Hurry up,' said the cabbie. 'You can snog all you like when the meter's running.'

Vicky laughed. 'He's me uncle, and he's not getting another kiss until me birthday or we find a Dragon. Whichever comes first.' The cabbie looked like saying something. Vicky pointed a finger at him. 'And no cracks about your wife being a Dragon.'

He lifted his hands. 'You're the boss. Where to?'

'The Tower of London,' I said. 'The tradesmen's entrance.'

9 — *Master of the Earth*

I was way too tired to read the red files on Friday night, but I did glance at the staff handbook and learnt that the Deputy Constable has his office without Merlyn's Tower, in a small apartment next to the main admin block for the Tower proper. All post and deliveries for the King's Watch are addressed to *The Curator of Heraldic Law*, which is Iain Drummond's cover name. Now there's a job title that sounds impressive without meaning anything.

I needed the address so that I could make a phone call to Spain. Dad answered, and couldn't believe his ears when I asked him to source an antique coat stand with at least six hooks.

'That's a bit of a tall order, son,' he said. 'I've never seen one with that many. What on earth do you need that for?'

'Bit of an accident at the initiation ceremony for my new job. You know what it's like.'

'No I don't, and I don't suppose you're going to tell me.'

'Sorry, Dad. Look, if you can't find one, just fake a couple of extra hooks. You've had enough practice.'

'How dare you! When do you want it?'

'Soon as. I'll text you the address. Love to Mum.'

My tenant had just broken up with his girlfriend, so we had a couple of pints in the nearest pub, and I had an early night. My last act was to burn the letter I'd written to Mum and Dad in the event of my not returning from induction.

The meeting with the Earth Master wasn't until eleven o'clock, so I got a proper lie-in for a change. Now that I've been commissioned into the Watch, it was safe to take the Hammer with me on duty. Given the cost of magickal bullets, it seemed a shame not to take the SIG, too, in case of attack by mundane opponents. There's no point in carrying a weapon if you can't get to it, and I stashed each gun in an OWB (Outside the Waistband) holster, put on a hip-length waxed jacket and looked in the mirror. Oh dear.

The Great British Public would think that I was going to a fancy dress party; the Great British Policeman would think that I was an assassin/terrorist and summon reinforcements. I sent a quick text to Hledjolf: *How much to build a Glamour into the Hammer to stop me looking like a poor man's John Wayne?*

Would the Dwarf need someone to explain the cultural references? Do Dwarves work Saturdays? I was still trying to find something more concealing when I got an answer to both questions: *Your weapon will not take an extra*

Artefact. We did tell you. We can make a personal amulet for 4oz. You have 3.5oz on deposit.

And I would need at least an ounce for Vicky to summon the Spectre of Thomas Clarke. Great. With a sigh, I unclipped the holsters, leaving the belt in place, and stowed weapons and holsters in my backpack, where they would be of no use whatsoever if I were attacked on the street. It's a good job I don't stand out in a crowd. Oh, hang on, that's exactly what I do do.

I don't often dwell on my schooldays, but I'll never forget the Deputy Head stopping on the way out of assembly one day to announce in a very loud voice, 'Clarke! You are far too tall and distinctive to get away with talking in assembly. Don't do it again.' I looked over my shoulder three times on the way to the Tube, and strapped the holsters back in place as soon as I entered the Old Network.

Because of the fearsome lock on the Roman door, I had to access the tunnel from Moley's diggings, and then open the door from the inside. Hopefully, Vicky and the Earth Master would be waiting for me in the roundhouse junction outside.

As I strode down the tunnels, I wondered if Moley had become human enough to have a concept of the working week, or was it always *Mole must dig*? I suspect the latter. I didn't see him on the journey, but I did notice that the new down tunnel had been re-dug, by Mole or others, and that drainage had been installed.

Nothing in the Roman tunnel or the egg chamber had changed since Wednesday, so I heaved on the door and looked out.

My partner and the Chymist were present and correct, standing a few feet beyond the door. From Vicky's description of his character, I was expecting a funny little man in a bow tie. Wrong. That Deputy Head from my old school had another life lesson for me: *Never forget, Clarke, that there will always be someone taller and stronger than you just round the corner.* I'm not sure about *stronger*, but the Earth Master of Salomon's House is definitely *taller*, at about six-six, and probably two stone lighter.

If the height/weight ratio didn't make him stand out, the many fluorescent patches on his running gear would do the job nicely, as would the glow from his shaved head.

I propped open the door, and Vicky made the formal introductions.

'Chris Kelly,' he said when we shook hands.

'Conrad Clarke. Thanks for coming out on a Saturday.'

'I wasn't going to miss this. D'you know, I've been teaching students, including young Victoria here, in this spot for nearly twenty years, and in all that time, not one of them, or me, had a sniff of that tunnel. Even now the door's been opened a few times, you can't see a thing from this side.'

Vicky was standing slightly behind him, and her mouth turned down when he used her Sunday name. It turned down further when I asked my next question.

'Did no one notice the drain of Lux down to the egg?'

'I always tell my students to look on the Network as like the public water supply, and this is a major junction.' He paused to wave his arms around, encompassing the many tunnels leading from the roundhouse. Vicky had anticipated this and stepped out of reach. 'Try to imagine this as a great lake,' he continued. 'Lux is flowing *in* from there and there, and it's flowing *out* down there and there, and mostly it's flowing that way down to Salomon's House. If you were standing in five feet of rushing water, would you notice a half-inch pipe below the surface?'

Vicky was making signs behind his back. I think she wanted to move on before he got completely carried away.

'So, Chris, what can you tell us about the egg chamber?'

'Let's have a look.'

I stood aside and gestured down the tunnel.

'What in Nimue's name are you doing with that?' asked Vicky, pointing to my belt, now visible because I'd raised my arm.

'It's my Badge of Office,' I said. 'Hledjolf named it the Hammer. Do you want to see?'

She looked outraged. 'No, I do not, thank you. What is it? A laser?'

I took out the Hammer anyway, because Kelly looked interested. 'No, it's just a gun. The bullets are charged with Lux, that's all. I'm working on an idea for a concealed-carry amulet.'

'Two!' she squeaked. 'What are you planning with *two* guns?'

'The SIG? That's just a mundane weapon. Magickal rounds are very expensive. Shame to waste them.'

'Howay, man, you can't walk around with two guns. If Hannah finds out, she'll go ballistic.'

'Ha ha.' I pulled my coat shut. 'Have you ever met a pro rugby player?'

The look in her eyes said that she'd done more than meet one. As I've said, Vicky had quite an exotic social life, until I put a stop to it.

'How would you fancy playing an actual game against them?' I said. 'All fifteen of them. On your own.'

'You what? That would be suicide.'

'Now you know how I feel in the magickal world. I'm just doing what I can to level the playing field, though I take your point about subtlety.'

'If we could move on … ?' said Kelly.

'Sorry,' said Vicky and I together.

The Earth Master took off his stringy backpack and unshipped a dowsing rod like none I'd ever seen before. Forget hazel or copper, this was the gnarled fork of some ancient tree, blackened with age, inlaid with gold chasing and fizzing with Lux. He balanced the rod in his hands and stood in the entrance to the tunnel, then moved slowly from left to right until he picked up the scent. 'Here we go,' he said with great enthusiasm, and moved swiftly down towards the egg chamber. He reached the scooped-out hollow and circled it before squatting down and feeling the blackened stone lining with his fingertips. 'Do you know what this rock is?' he asked.

'I know it's not local,' I said. 'Did the Dragon bring it with her, do you think?'

He shook his head. 'You're half right in both cases. It's local in origin, but not natural. The Dragon scrapes a mound of earth together, then incinerates it – hotter than lava – before dropping the egg. She chooses a spot with a connection to the Network and leaves the rest up to fate.

I looked around the chamber with new eyes. 'If the Romans killed the last Dragon, why did they preserve its eggs?'

He nodded his approval at a good question. 'When is a Roman not a Roman? When they're Romano-British.'

Vicky sighed and rolled her eyes, channelling an inner teenager who's never far from the surface.

Kelly continued, oblivious of Vicky's attitude. 'The builder and mosaic maker had learnt their craft from the Romans, but they were still British, and the giveaway is the powerline.' He gestured back towards the roundhouse. 'There's a powerline running back that's braided, three strands thick. No Roman Earth Master would do that. Their method was two channels, exactly 4' 8½" apart.'

Vicky spoke up, 'Which, as I'm sure you know, Conrad, is the same size as the standard gauge on railways.'

I didn't, as it happens.

Kelly arched his eyebrows. 'So you do remember something, Victoria.'

She gave him a grin. 'Only the useless stuff, sir: I can't remember *why* the Romans used a twin channel and the Brits braided. It all somehow slipped out of me head the minute I found that I'd finally passed the exam.'

I stepped in between them. 'Tell me, Chris, when you look at these networks, do you see them as water or electricity?'

He was putting his dowsing rod away, which was not a good sign to me. 'A bit of both,' he said. 'Lux flows and swirls like water, but the physics is more like electricity – there has to be a potential difference between two points for it to flow. Then again, like water, there doesn't have to be a circuit: it can all flow one way.' He paused. 'Vicky tells me you don't find it easy to sense magick.'

'That's a polite way of putting it,' I said. 'It doesn't stop me wanting to learn what everyone else is up to, though. For example, I thought you'd be able to track our egg, but you seem to have finished.'

91

'I don't know what gave you that idea,' he said, glancing accusingly at Vicky. 'The Constable and the Warden wanted me to check two things as discreetly as possible, hence the Saturday shift. First, has anyone been maintaining the powerline, and second, did they leave any traces.' He moved to where Moley's diggings transected the tunnel. 'This new route damaged the braid, but otherwise it hasn't been touched since the first century. As for traces, Vicky didn't find any, and she's much better at that sort of thing than I am.' He gave my partner a big smile.

She blushed and dived to check her phone. 'It's the Boss. She wants to see us in her office at Salomon's House.'

'Does she want me?' asked Kelly.

'Erm, no. Sir, would you mind escorting Conrad to Wyvern Chambers while I answer a call of nature?'

'A pleasure. Nice to see you again, Victoria.'

She scurried off, leaving me to secure the tunnel and pack my guns away. I gestured to the roundhouse and the sound of Vicky's footsteps. 'I know that passage leads to Salomon's House. What about the rest?'

He started in the north west, and worked his way anti-clockwise. 'That's the deep route to the West End and Knightsbridge. Next is a down channel from some of the Collectors – a good illustration that Lux flows uphill. Next is the main highway — it goes to the Old Temple and the Undercroft, then carries on West.' He swivelled to point due south. 'That one, as my in-laws would say, goes *sarf of the river*. There are two routes down there, one is a tunnel to Lambeth Palace and the other leads to the Free Borough.'

'I might sign up for one of your lectures. This is all fascinating stuff.'

He gave me a sideways look. 'You actually mean that, don't you?'

'I do.'

'Then I'd love to have you as a student if it wasn't for the practical element. I've wittered on today because I can't just show you what's here. If you can't sense the Lux flowing, it's a bit meaningless.'

We set off on Vicky's trail.

'Is Lux really like electricity?'

'Yes and no. This gets very complicated because no one truly knows. It flows, it can be stored, but no one knows how it's generated or where it goes. It's everywhere at some level, but gets concentrated by human mental activity. Have you heard of JANET?'

'Something to do with the Internet, isn't it?'

'It's the Joint Academic NETwork, running between universities, and yes, the British Internet grew out of it. There's one for magick, and it concentrates Lux as a by-product of students' work. Oxford and Cambridge have been powering Salomon's House for centuries, and now we have Collectors under UCL, Imperial, King's, the LSE. If you've wondered why Mages choose the disciplines of the Invisible College over the freedom of the Circles, that's often the answer: access to lots of Lux. Obviously there's a Collector at every Locus Lucis, too, but nothing like the Network of Albion. I know how to build Collectors, service them and lay powerlines, but I have no idea how they work.'

We came to another junction. Steps led down to the right, another passage to the left, and an impressive arch was straight ahead. Around the arch was carved something in Hebrew. Kelly pointed to the inscription. 'It says *Salomon's House*, that's all. Those steps down will connect with that new tunnel the Dwarves are creating. It's mostly used by visitors to Hledjolf's Hall who don't have access to Salomon's House, but it does go on to the Water Margin.'

'It's not the Dwarves' doing. His Worship the Lord Mayor of Moles is digging that tunnel.'

'Of course. Yes.' He pointed left. 'That way to Newton's House.'

The staff handbook had already told me that Newton's House was the meeting place and office of the Occult Council. I'd have to wait until I'd got to the red files before I found out what the OC actually was.

Through the arch to Salomon's House, the stonework was shaped into smaller inset arches, like the west front of a cathedral. At the end was a small but stout door which Kelly opened using magick.

'This is the South Basement,' he said.

It wasn't so much of a basement, more of a concrete box with stairs up and down, the sort of thing you'd expect to find in the nether regions of an abandoned nuclear power plant. He pointed down. 'That leads to Hledjolf's Hall, and only Hledjolf's Hall. We're going up.'

He started up the stairs, and a thought struck him. 'You must know a bit about clouds.'

'My passengers would be rather alarmed if I didn't.'

'Quite. You'll know all about thunderclouds, then.'

'*All* is a bit strong, but yes, they're generally bad news if you're in a helicopter. Not as bad as a twister, but not something you fly into.'

'Have you ever wondered why so many of the gods had power over thunder?'

I shrugged. 'Not top of my inbox.'

'We think the gods have a knack of combining Lux and the Earth's magnetic flow to raise or lower electrical charge.'

He was pushing me, ever so gently, but pushing me. Vicky had told me not to mention my ability to sense direction to anyone else, so I just made an interested face and waited for Kelly to open the institutional fire door at the top of the stairs.

We were now at the very bottom of the Junction, and the bare concrete of the stairwell gave way to the baroque fripperies of Salomon's House. He touched my arm lightly to break the Silence. 'Over there is the North

Basement. It goes much lower than the South one, and leads to most points North and East.'

We started climbing the Junction staircase, but hadn't gone far before Kelly nudged me into a corridor. 'Hang on a sec,' he said, and disappeared.

Kelly's whistlestop orientation to the Old Network had been very useful, but left me with a lot of places I could name but about which I had no idea. I mentally re-ran the list. *The Free Borough. The Old Temple. The Water Margin.* And all that was assuming that "Lambeth Palace" actually meant the Archbishop's residence, and not some Invisible College in-joke.

I leaned out into the Junction to touch the glass plate and see where we were.

Gaia Hall
Earth Studies 1-3
The Earth Master

Kelly returned with a poster sized tube. 'Here. This is a student's dowsing rod, a map of the Network of Albion and a few suggestions for field work. Try it outdoors some time – you never know, you might get something. Right. Your boss will be wondering where we've got to.'

The King's Watch's other room in Salomon's House is a big step up from the conference room next door where I'd been briefed (and insulted) by Desirée.

Room 2, Wyvern Chambers, is a courtesy office for the Constable, and it certainly projects the Watch as an ancient and formidable organisation. Hannah's desk had a large shield behind it, with an image of Caledfwlch being held by a woman's hand, an image I'd not seen before. Given the gender of the current Constable, it's an image I thought she'd have made more of.

The wall opposite the door had a Skyway showing the exact prospect of the Thames from Hannah's office in Merlyn's Tower. There was a bookcase full of familiar green, blue and red files, a hospitality sideboard with a boiling kettle, and just enough room for four chairs in front of the desk. Of the five total seats, three were occupied.

Hannah was behind the desk in a grey sweater dress and blue headscarf; Vicky was in front, and had got changed in the time I'd climbed up from the roundhouse, but we'll come back to that. She was a little out of breath, you could almost say that she was panting, and that was down to the guy standing up to shake my hand.

'Conrad, this is Richard James,' said Hannah. 'He's the senior Watch Captain – and a major, if you're counting, which I know you are.' Hannah did not sound full of good news this morning.

'How d'you do,' I said, returning the firm handshake. Richard James is black and older than me, both of which marked him out as different amongst the other Watch Captains. He had grey appearing at his temples and a patch of white skin on his jaw that looked like well healed scar tissue. He said hello, told me to call him Rick and sat down without further comment.

Hannah spoke again. 'While you're standing up, you can be Shabbos-goy, Conrad.'

That stumped me. Rick gave me a sympathetic grin and said, 'Hannah pretends to keep kosher when it suits her. A *Shabbos-goy* is one of us who does the dirty work on Saturdays.'

'Shut up, Rick, and let Vicky finish her report.'

I started to make the tea, and had a proper look at Vicky, especially the short red skirt and tight black top that was just *too* tight. Aah – the message Vicky had received underground hadn't just said that Hannah wanted to see us, she'd also learnt about Rick, and had raced off to raid Desirée's locker, which was why everything was too small for her, except the heels, which were two sizes too big.

Vicky spoke to Hannah but looked at Rick. 'There's nothing else to say. The Earth Master came up empty on where the egg might be now.'

I started fixing the tea and said, conversationally, 'Is he going to look for the other eggs?'

'What other eggs?' said Hannah.

'I can't believe that something with a Dragon's life-cycle would only lay one egg. Perhaps Desirée hasn't got that far in her translation yet.'

'Ask her, will you, Vicky, though how we find them if there are any out there is anyone's guess.'

I had an idea about how to find the eggs, but now was not the time. Hannah accepted a weak cup of tea gratefully. I hung on for the strong stuff.

She continued, 'Rick is your local Watch Captain, Conrad, when you're in Cheltenham. His personal patch covers all of Wessex, the Severn Valley and Cornwall. All the Watch Captains outside the south east report to him, and he's the liaison officer with the Daughters of the Goddess at Glastonbury, because he has inside knowledge.'

Rick gave a wry smile. 'What our boss is trying to say is that I married a witch. I left London to be with her, and I'm still there because of the kids. We split up a while ago.'

I wonder how that sits with Iain Drummond's declaration that liaison with the Circles was his responsibility. Our Deputy was conspicuous by his absence this morning.

Hannah gave me a shrewd look, as if she'd read the thought that had just passed through my head. 'A lot of Rick's work would normally be done by a Deputy Constable. As you know, I only have one, and Rick declined to apply for the other vacancy.'

Rick tried to make light of what Hannah had said, but I could see this was a recurring argument. 'I can't take a job in Chester when my kids are in Glastonbury, can I?'

'So you've said. And what did the Daughters of the Goddess say about Dragons?'

Rick shook his head. 'That they're an abomination against nature, the work of men and utterly repugnant to the Goddess, unless they're doing the Goddess's work, in which case they are a symbol of triumphant femininity.'

'Are they always so decisive?' I asked.

'Tell me about it,' said Rick. 'Bottom line: they're clueless. None of the ones I've spoken to have seen so much as a wisp of smoke.' He turned in his chair to face me fully. 'Bear in mind, Conrad, that I only get to speak to the ones who will talk to the Watch. That's very much a minority.'

'So I discovered at Lunar Hall,' I said, sitting down with my tea. Vicky did not look happy at facing Rick's back.

'Should we go national with this?' said Hannah, looking at each of us in turn.

'I think we need all the help we can get,' said Rick.

'I agree,' said Vicky.

'We've got nothing at the moment,' said Hannah, 'and the clock on that incubator is ticking. What do you think, Conrad?'

I stirred my tea. Hannah had shown more trust in Rick than anyone else on her team, so I was loath to go against him, but… 'Speaking as the only one with inside knowledge of a criminal conspiracy, I think you're wrong.'

'What?' said Rick. 'Have you done undercover work?'

'You could say that.'

Hannah looked appalled and amused in equal measure; Vicky looked confused.

Having got their attention, I said, 'We haven't given enough thought to what they want the egg for, and it has to be a group of them.'

'Go on,' said Hannah.

'I can see three possibilities: criminal, magickal or ideological.'

'What do you mean by *criminal*?' said Rick, putting down his tea.

'Who's the richest single Mage you know? Human not Dwarf.'

Glances were exchanged. Vicky looked keen to get back in the conversation, and said, 'Lady Kirsten. I met her in Scotland.'

Rick turned round. 'Isn't she the one with the castle? Have you been?'

Vicky's eyes lit up. 'Never mind the castle, you should see her place in Edinburgh: it's like a palace. She threw the best party I've ever been to.'

'You should see where Milton lives,' said Rick. 'Owns half a valley in Cornwall.'

'Oy, you lot,' said Hannah. 'Conrad, get on with it, already.'

'How much would the richest Mage you know pay for a Dragon's egg? More than enough to compensate for the risks, I'll bet.'

'It's a thought,' said Rick.

'And a valid one,' said Hannah, 'but where does that get us, and what did you mean by *magickal or ideological?*'

'Dragon's eggs are unique,' I said. 'I've seen enough Mages to know that there will be a Mage somewhere who would break any laws to get their hands on one. Even so, if that egg was taken for a collector or for experiment, they'll have covered their tracks, and if we never find them, I don't see a great threat to the King's Peace.'

'Why's that?' said Vicky.

Hannah was one step ahead of her. 'Because they know what they're doing.'

'That's right,' I agreed. 'No one wants an apocalypse unless you're a fanatic. Which magickal groups would unleash mass destruction to further their cause?'

This time they really were stumped. Finally, Rick spoke. 'There's no such thing.' Hannah nodded in agreement.

The office wasn't very big, which made the elephant in the room even more uncomfortable. 'Hannah, does Islamic State subscribe to the Annex of Westphalia? What's the Islamic view of magick in general?'

You'd have thought I'd dropped my pants, such was the response. All of a sudden, everyone was staring at Hannah.

She drew a breath. 'The Islamic view of magick isn't dissimilar to the Christian one as it was a few centuries ago. Progressive Islam embraces it; mainstream Islam suppresses it as a weakness afflicting women; extremists consider it the work of Satan. If this was India, or some African countries, I'd say you were spot on, Conrad, but not in Britain. Not yet. Not again.'

'Fair enough. I still think that, whatever the motive for the misappropriation of the egg, widespread publicity will only give away our hand. At the moment, almost no one knows we've even found the egg chamber.'

I'd said my piece, and if the Boss still thought that an appeal was the best option, I'd keep quiet and follow orders.

'Let's leave it for now,' she said. 'Ruth may yet get something on that phone, and there might be some mileage in sniffing round some of the known collectors. I'll get Iain to draw up a list. Thanks, everyone. Rick? Can I have a word?'

Vicky and I stood up. She failed to hide her displeasure at being sent out.

Hannah had one last thing to say. 'You've disappointed me, Conrad. I had a joke ready about you being pleased to see me.'

'Ma'am, I'm always pleased to see you, even when I haven't got a gun in my pocket.'

She blushed and pointed to the door. 'Go. I now have to explain that to Rick.'

'Explain what?' said Vicky outside the office. When I'd told her about Mae West, she grinned. 'Will you two just get a room? Mina might have to worry if you carry on flirting like that.'

'You can talk.'

'What do you mean?'

'You've got a difficult decision to make, Vic. When I've gone, are you going to give Desi her outfit back, or are you going to hang around waiting for Rick? You didn't mention him when you told me you'd been to Glastonbury.'

She waited until we were out of Wyvern Chambers and into the Junction. She took my arm and kicked my bad leg so hard that I cried out in pain.

Still clinging to my arm, she said, 'I wanted you to suffer in Silence.'

10 — *All Work and no Play*

The old pubs in the City of London used to close in the evenings and at weekends, or so I'm told, because their customers all caught the train to the suburbs at five thirty. The arrival of 24/7 global capitalism changed all that, which was why the Churchill Arms was doing good business on a Saturday afternoon. My lunch companion was less enthusiastic.

Alain du Pont is a French postgrad, currently completing a low-wage placement at Praed's Bank. He is also my occasional private detective and consultant, as well as being my role model for the Gallic Shrug.

'In France, this would be illegal,' he said, taking a healthy knock of the bottle of wine I'd bought. 'Not only do I 'ave to work over the Working Time Directive, I 'ave to do it on a Saturday and get no extra money. Pfft.'

'Any sign of a permanent job?'

'Yes. If I want one, but there's something else I'd like first.'

Alain covets my sister — or at least a placement at her firm. 'Don't hold your breath. Rachael and I have some family stuff to work through before I ask any favours. I promised I'd do my best, and I will. A Clarke's word is binding, and all that.'

He grunted. ''Ow is your application coming along? 'Ave you got your new job?'

I raised my glass. 'I have, thanks to your help. I took the oath yesterday, and I was hard at work this morning. I really am grateful for what you've done for me, Alain.'

'Thank you. 'Ave you got any more jobs? I could use the money.'

'Later. After lunch. They've given me a partner, you know. Vicky.'

'The one 'oo looks like a 'orse, or 'er sister 'oo looks like a 'Ollywood star?'

Alain and Vicky have met, and Alain's seen photos of Vicky out clubbing, wearing a Glamour. He doesn't believe they're the same person, which is sort of the point.

'She's good at disguises,' I said. 'That's all. The real Vicky Robson is a lovely girl. I think you could do a lot worse.'

He gave me one of his most eloquent shrugs. Alain knew me before I discovered magick, and I'd like to wait as long as I can before he finds out. This means he looks at Vicky as a someone in administration, and Vicky only has eyes for Mages when it comes to serious relationships. Never mind: they're young, and I'll persevere.

''Ow is your girlfriend?' he asked. He does know about Mina.

'Fine, as far as I can tell. I'm seeing her on Wednesday.'

The food arrived, and Alain embarked on a long story about his efforts to get the girl at work who he really fancies to go to the Valentine's dinner they have at his house-share in West London. I wished him luck (and mentally wished the poor girl luck, too. I've seen their kitchen).

We went for a smoke, and I passed him an envelope with some cash and two names. I'd only decided to do this on the walk down from Salomon's House, and I'd had to stop at the ATM to get some money, and a tourist tat shop to buy a card with an envelope. 'Find out all you can about these two names. They might be completely invisible. Nothing at all back to me electronically, OK? And cover your tracks.'

He nodded, glanced in the envelope and frowned. 'What is this? *Lady Kirsten — Scotland* and *Milton — Cornwall*? 'Ow can I work with this?'

I clapped him on the back. 'You're good, Alain. Give it your best shot.'

If you're wondering why I would spend my own money on this project, when I could find out a lot more from Vicky or Hannah, it's because I wanted to see what sort of footprint in the mundane world would be left by two of the richest Mages in Britain (or Albion, as everyone seemed keen to call it).

I spent the next eight nights at Elvenham House, and I began to wonder what was going on in Merlyn's Tower that Hannah wanted to keep me at arm's length – *rusticated*, as they say in the Invisible College. Apparently.

The first thing I did was to place my King's Bounty – the gold coin from the Water Room – under the floorboards on the little landing of the tower, just behind where the carving of the dragon is fixed into the wall. I must admit I looked askance at the dragon when I got back (after saying hello, of course). 'What sort of dragon are you?' I'd said, but got no reply. It's a good job I live in the country. Not only can no one hear you talking to a stone dragon, if they could they'd assume you were a harmless eccentric.

After that, there was a certain amount of sitting in front of a log fire while the rain beat on the windows, and a couple of trips to the Inkwell, but I was far from idle. I read the staff handbook. I read the red files (twice), and I dipped into a good number of the green binders. The blue ones defeated me. If/when I am called back to duty, at least I'll have a good idea of what I can and can't do as a Captain of the King's Watch.

The essence of the King's Peace is this, and I quote from that riveting legal landmark *The Peculier Constable vs the St Peter's Merchants*:

All the King's subjects, whether or not they have been blessed with the gift of magick, have the right to enjoy their lives in peace without the interruption of unnatural forces.

What this boils down to is that my use of enhanced spin in a cricket match would be against the magickal law, as would the unleashing of a Dragon. Everything is built on the St Peter's Principle (as it's known), and all the Orders of the Occult Council, all the Statutes of the Invisible College and all the case law from the Cloister Court are just elaborations of that judgement.

After reading that, I could see why Vicky's use of a Glamour at Club Justine was embarrassing rather than illegal. She wasn't trying to profit from her deception, and no one got hurt. It was very, very different for Desirée because her entire career was based on membership of the Invisible College, and she could easily have been expelled for what she'd done.

The red files also covered my rights as an officer of the law, which are quite alarming in their scope. I'll just say that a Captain of the Watch is part bounty hunter, part judge, and only partly a policeman (or woman). We are a long way from the Police and Criminal Evidence Act.

When I'd finished my homework, the Occult Council was also less of a mystery, though not by much. In its current form, the Council functions like a magickal parliament with an in-built plurality for the Crown in the shape of royal appointments. Hannah is a member ex-officio, as are the Warden and Dean of Salomon's House. Some of the seats are even elected by voters in the Circles, and Creatures of Light have the right of audience. Then there were several curious references to the Vicar of London Stone, who may or may not be Hannah's boss. What I didn't find out was any detail – no reports of actual missions or what the Watch Captains did on them.

The green folders had the statutes, and the blue folders had case law from the Cloister Court, written by lawyers and full of things like, *As Dickon said in Richmond vs Glastonbury, the principle of* non tangere *does not apply in cases of consent...*

When it wasn't raining too hard, I did a lot of walking, I went for a couple of gallops near Worcester, and I made a trip to a secret location in Staffordshire.

In the grounds of an Army base is a tract of woodland surrounded by MOD Keep Out notices because they use it for live firing exercises. It also includes the crossing point of two Ley lines – a junction in the Network of Albion, as it said in the Earth Master's notes. My RAF ID badge got me access one miserable morning when all sensible squaddies were asleep.

Feeling a complete div (as Vicky would say), I stood next to a stone marker and held my dowsing rod lightly between my fingers. The idea was to circle the stone until I got a response from the twig, then follow the track.

I spiralled slowly away from the marker and felt absolutely nothing. Both times. I'd come too far to give up that easily, so I went right out to the treeline and worked in – and without realising what I'd done, I moved anti-clockwise. Half way towards the stone, I felt it. *There*. Just a twinge. Just enough to know that Lux was flowing under my feet, and that it was flowing north north west.

It took half an hour, and a thorough soaking, before I got the lie of the Leys. The powerlines ran much further under my feet than they were in the Old Network under London, and I could only find one of them with any certainty.

101

I did discover that when following a Ley line, I could feel the difference between True North and Magnetic North. How this worked, whether it's any use, and why there is a Ley line between Stratford-on-Avon and Chester are all mysteries that remained unsolved, even after a full English breakfast.

My new colleagues and old allies did not desert me completely. I took delivery of a pre-paid debit card for Moley; I got a text from Alain inviting me for a drink (= *I've found something*); Vicky kept me posted on what she was up to – a trip home to Newcastle and a visit to the Shield Wall (?) with the regional Watch Captain.

The highlight of the week was of course on Wednesday. It's a long way to HMP Cairndale for an hour's visit, but worth every mile of the drive. Not that you feel like that in the holding room, knowing that you're going to be searched intimately, and surrounded by children who shouldn't be exposed to despair on that scale.

I feel embarrassed when I look at the other visitors, because my life is nothing like theirs, and they know it instinctively. A lot of them smoke, but none of them make small talk with me while we're waiting outside.

Most of the adults are the prisoners' mothers, ashamed or defiant, bringing their daughters' children to visit, and there's a sprinkling of male partners doing the same job. It's a sweeping generalisation, but the men are either emaciated from addiction or bulked up with muscle, probably from steroids, and that's the worst thing about prison: it denies the women inside their individual stories and pours them all into the same mould, to be stamped with a criminal record they'll never erase.

Then you slow down and watch more carefully. A little boy carries a work of art to the desk to be inspected: shells, pipe cleaners and felt shapes glued to sugar paper. 'It's me house,' he says. 'I put me mam in it. And a dog. We haven't got a dog, though.'

Next in the queue, a middle aged woman dumps a pile of books in front of the Prison Officer – the PO – 'Bleedin' Open University. Nearly pulled me shoulder out carrying that lot.'

I waited until last before I handed over my form, because I wanted to conduct an experiment. I got my chit for the items I was taking through security, then I put the Hammer in its case on the counter. 'Look after that, will you?' I said, as casually as I could.

If he put that case anywhere near the X-Ray machine, I'd be face down on the concrete with a Taser in my back before I could say *King's Watch*. He picked it up and put it under the counter without even looking.

The visiting room was nearly full today, and I had to use my height to spot the splash of colour in the corner that was Mina Desai. The love of my life is not very tall, and used to be too thin. Now that she can eat properly, she's put on a few pounds, and she doesn't look like she might break if I picked her up.

If being a Witch was just a matter of having long hair, Mina would be a Coven leader by now. She spent years using a great black curtain to hide the damage to her jaw, and I was only half joking when I told Vicky that she spends every night washing it.

Mina has never liked me staring at her face, for obvious reasons. In a letter the other week, she told me that she was going to celebrate her freedom by having a nose job. She also wrote that she was going to start a campaign to have segregated areas on the Tube for people under five foot four who have to stand.

She was standing when I reached her corner. I bent down to enjoy the Minimal Physical Contact which we're allowed, then she did what she usually does and started crying.

'I promised myself I wouldn't cry. I promised. Ten times an hour all morning, I promised. Shit. See the effect you have on me? Get the tea.'

Prisoners have to remain seated and can't visit the refreshment hatch. It gives her time to stem the tears.

'I have to know, Conrad. I have to know if I dreamt it. Can you really do magic?'

'It's not *do magic*, it's *use magick*. With a "k". Yes, I can, but I'm totally rubbish, as Vicky told you. She sends her love by the way.'

'Do you see much of her? Should I be worried?'

'Yes and no. It's me that should be worried: Vicky keeps telling me you're out of my league.'

'That's because she wants you for herself.'

I had to laugh at that. Mina looked slightly offended. 'She actually calls me *Uncle Conrad*, you know. She's got terrible taste in men, too. She only goes for the ones with big … Talents. My Talent is very small.'

'I hope nothing about you is small. That would be a terrible disappointment.'

'Erm. Right. Moving on… I've discovered that I can sense Magnetic and True North,' I said, with some pride.

'What are they?'

'They're … never mind.' Does no one appreciate navigation any more? GPS will be the end of civilisation. 'And I've been set a challenge. Look at this.'

I'd submitted the level 1 Keyway box for inspection, saying that it was a gift. Prisoners are not allowed to have lockable boxes, so it passed muster. Mina turned it over and looked inside.

'What's this?'

I took it back and worked the Keyway. She spent nearly five minutes trying to find a hidden catch to open it before giving up. I unlocked the box and said, 'It's a gift. You can keep stuff in it, and you'll be the only woman in here with a magickal Artefact.'

She stared at it again, then cradled it in her lap. When she looked up, her eyes flicked first to someone behind me, for the third time. I turned to look.

'Don't!' she said in alarm.

I locked eyes with a shaven-headed thug who was visiting a beefy woman I'd not seen before. Two chubby children were looking bored, their thumbs moving to play with phones that they'd had to leave in the lockers outside.

I leaned as close to Mina as I could and said, 'What's the matter?'

'Nothing.'

'Mina, you've got no one else to talk to, so tell me.'

'It's Sonia. She's new.'

Mina turned her body so that none of Sonia's table could see her face. 'They put me back to work as a literacy tutor after I sorted out the Governor's budget spreadsheets. Sonia got in the group even though she can read well enough. Keeps her off outside work. No one wants outside work in winter. Anyway, in the first session, the PO sat in the corner facing away from us. Sonia made one of the other girls hand over a phone, then spent the whole time texting.'

'Oh.' That was bad enough, but I could see that it wasn't the end.

Mina looked at Sonia's table again, and drummed her bright red nails on the table. I took a moment to admire her gorgeous hands.

'Promise me you won't get involved,' she said. 'If I tell you what happened, you have to promise not to get involved.'

'I am involved. I love you. That makes me involved.'

'And I love you. Does that make me involved in your King's Watch?'

'Yes. You just can't do much about it. Yet.'

That stopped her. She spent one of our precious minutes winding her hair into a twist. I didn't complain because I love watching her move, and at the end, I could see all of her face, nose, scars and shining brown eyes.

'Let me sort it out,' she said. 'You have to promise not to do anything about Sonia. No phone calls to friends in high places. No interfering with the POs.'

'I promise not to do anything about Sonia. Now, tell me.'

She clenched her fists. 'At the second session, yesterday, there was a PO right in the middle of the room. I asked Sonia to read something. She said, in a very loud voice, that I was a brown nosed grass, and that I should go back to Pakistan.' Mina looked as if she wanted to throw up. 'Do you know what the screw did? She said *Leave it out, Sonia.* The rest of the class are now scared of Sonia: two of them refused to read anything to show that they are on Sonia's side.'

'You've never called a PO a *screw* before.'

'It gets to us all, Conrad. No one is innocent in here. Not for long.'

'What are you going to do?'

'I don't know. I could ask for a transfer down south now that my jaw and teeth are fixed. I could just keep out of the way. I don't know.'

We sat back, away from each other, for a moment. Mina has fought back from much, much worse. Perhaps it's the illusion of normality that's made her worried. She now has a normal face, she eats normal food and she clings to the promise of a normal life to come.

I leaned forward. 'You're a Desai from Gujarat. You're not going to let her get away with calling you a Pakistani, are you? Not that there's anything wrong with Pakistan.'

'Would you rather I shanked her?'

'Only if you didn't get caught. Sonia isn't worth doing extra time for.'

She laughed. 'Listen to us. I'm not sure which of us is further from the real world, you or me.

'You'll think of something. You've got more fight in you than all this lot put together.'

'I used to. I'm not so sure any more.'

'You know what I'd do?'

'As long as it doesn't involve guns, magick with a "k" or being six feet tall, then yes, I'd like to know.'

'Why did the PO do nothing? Figure that out and you'll know the source of her power, or your lack of it. You're not alone in here. Some of the girls really like you. You've said as much in those epic letters. Have a think. It'll take your mind off magick.'

'No. I don't want to think about Sonia while you're here. You have forty minutes to tell me what you were doing in Lancashire with Vicky, and what you're up to now.'

I spent the next thirty-eight and a half minutes telling her. Do you know what bothered her most? 'You can't leave Mr Mole to die like that. You owe him, and what is it you're always saying? *A Clarke always pays his debts.*'

'That's the Lannisters' motto. You're confusing me with a young Charles Dance.'

'Not so young.'

'Whatever. My Dad didn't always pay his debts, but he never broke his word.' She didn't notice the pause when I remembered that I still hadn't had a straight answer about whether he'd always been faithful to Mum. 'I've never broken my word, either, and I have never promised to be Moley's keeper.' She gave me the grim expression, the one that makes her look like a hungry eagle. 'Okay, okay. If I can help His Worship without getting into serious trouble, I will.'

'Good.' She looked at the clock. The POs were starting to move. 'Now for the hard part.'

That was a surprise. I sat up, suddenly worried.

Mark Hayden

'I don't want you to send me a Valentine on Saturday. I don't want the day that Miles died to be remembered for anything else. If he hadn't loved me and married me, I would be dead.'

It was a bit melodramatic, but broadly true, I suppose.

She put her hands on mine. They were cold. 'If we have a future, Conrad, I want that future to be remembered from the day I get out of here. It can be our private Valentine.'

'Time!'

Chairs scraped, mouths kissed, women and children cried, and men stiffened their lips.

I lingered at the exit to see whether an armed response squad was waiting for me in the holding area. No. I just collected my case and walked out. For all his weirdness, Hledjolf certainly knows his magick. And have you noticed that it's easier to say *him* when I'm not actually with him. It. Whatever.

You'll have noticed, I hope, that my promise to leave Sonia alone was not extended to her family. Her pet gorilla was holding open the door to a white van with the name of a Liverpool building contractor on the side. I took a note of the numbers and let them drive away in peace. For now.

On Saturday morning, I went into Cheltenham and did a bit of shopping. Back home, I did a bit of searching on the Internet to find out what an old acquaintance was up to.

Mine and Mina's nemesis, DCI Tom Morton, was up north, not a million miles from HMP Cairndale, and he'd been given his first solo command of a murder enquiry. On a very cold, snowy and wet Valentine 's Day last year, Tom Morton had turned up just in time to arrest Mina, but too late to catch me. Later, we'd shared a near-death experience in a helicopter. I gave him a call for auld lang syne. He was a bit mystified to hear from me, but didn't threaten me with an injunction for getting in touch. It never hurts to have a contact in the police. He even said he'd do his bit to keep Juliet Porterhouse off mine and Rachael's backs.

And Spectre Thomas? One whole week of using magick in the house, and he never showed his ghostly face once. I'd have to move Vicky's seance up the agenda or he might re-join his Alice before we could find out what the problem was.

Monday Morning. I stood outside the Watch Room in Merlyn's Tower and squared my shoulders ready for the day's new beginnings.

Inside, I found Maxine Lambert doing some filing and no one else. Perhaps they were all out slaying Dragons or conjuring Dæmons. As it happens, Maxine would do nicely…

'Good morning, Conrad,' she said brightly. 'I'm not going to salute you, so don't stand around waiting for it.'

'It's me who should salute you. From what I've been reading, the Watch would fall apart without an efficient Clerk.'

She searched my face for irony and found none. 'The kettle's just boiled. Tea, one sugar. And not syrup like Tennille makes.'

I dumped my bag and moved to follow her instructions. When I'd poured water into two mugs, I said, 'I'm afraid I'm with Mrs Haynes on the tea, if nothing else.'

Maxine shoved a folder into a bookcase with an air of finality. 'We get on very well, do Tennille and I.' I listened hard, and I could hear her thinking, *so long as she stays upstairs.*

Maxine's tea was ready and I put it on the table. She pointed to my bag. 'Have you brought your laptop?' I nodded. 'Leave it out, and I'll get Mr Li to put his program on it. You can access all these files online with that.'

'Will I find out what the King's Watch actually does if I read them?'

She thought that was hilarious. 'Were you that naive when you joined the RAF?'

'No one tells you the truth before you join up. Go on, I met Rick James last week. Tell me what he got up to in January.'

'All right,' she said, and picked out the folder she'd slammed home a few minutes ago. 'In January, Watch Captain James escorted a coven of Lithuanian Witches to an Esbat in the Lake District on the orders of the Constable. Don't ask me why. He also visited Dunster in Somerset at the request of the Daughters to investigate an 038.' She looked up. 'Have you got your card?'

I took out a laminated card and looked down the list. 'Code 038 — performing Necromancy on designated holy ground. Not to be confused with 039 — performing Necromancy without consent of the next of kin.'

'Correct. Rick convened a Badge Court and fined two ladies called Summer and Hazel the sum of 2.4oz Troy between them. He keeps half. These Witches do love to ditch their birth names. There's a fully cross-referenced index of names in the database.' She replaced the file. 'Not quite like what you got up to at Lunar Hall, is it?'

'There's a lot to be said for the quiet life and simple pleasures, such as my cup of tea. Are you going to join me on the roof? I've got time before I'm due upstairs.'

'How do you know…? Never mind. You get the door, I'll get my coat.'

While she pulled on her rather striking red waterproof, I gazed at the door leading to the Water Room stairs. 'How do I open it?'

'Just pull. It's not locked.'

I carried both mugs and handed Maxine through the hatch.

'You're a real gentleman, Conrad. I like that. Makes a change.'

We shared a light and gravitated to the river side of the battlements. 'You've been here a while, I take it?'

'It only feels like forever, but yes, thirty-eight years, believe it or not. I failed to get into Salomon's House by a country mile and took a job here. The Boss has just about found her feet now, so I'll be thinking of retiring before you know it. I would have gone three years ago if hubby hadn't taken up golf.'

'Filthy habit.'

'I know. My daughter got married last year, and they're trying for a baby. I can't wait to be a proper granny.'

'Is your daughter…?'

'No chance. Neither her, nor the boys, nor my husband or any in-laws has any Gift whatsoever. My family all think I work for MI5.'

'How much do you know about me?'

'I haven't read your un-redacted file because Tennille keeps the HR records. Virtually everything else comes across my desk. People talk, as well, and I for one didn't think you were gay for a single second. Not that it would have made a difference.'

'Quite. You might not know that my girlfriend is currently serving a sentence for GBH with intent.'

She gave me a sharp look. 'No, I didn't.'

'She's coming out in the spring, and she's very bright. She'd be a chartered accountant if it wasn't for the money-laundering conviction.'

That got a full-on laugh. 'I can't wait to meet her.'

'That's what I was leading up to. Just hypothetically, could she work here?'

'Short answer: yes. Long answer: it would be an uphill struggle. You'd better go. Don't forget to leave your laptop out.'

I twisted my way back down, past Hannah's back door, through the Watch Office and up to Tennille's lair. There was no sign of Vicky.

Hannah's PA stared at me. 'You've been talking to Maxine. I heard you go past.'

That was worth knowing. 'You'll always be my first love in Merlyn's Tower,' I said.

'Hah. And don't you forget it.'

'I won't – you check my expenses, remember?'

'Get in. She's waiting.'

There was still no sign of Vicky when Hannah waved me to the chair in front of her desk rather than the comfy seats by the window. 'Busy week?' she asked.

I offered a printout. 'I didn't know if there was an official time-sheet for when we're away from here, so I prepared this to show that I was being productive.'

She waved it away. 'I don't doubt your capacity for hard work, Conrad. That's not the problem.'

I crossed my legs. 'Let me guess: the problem isn't a *what*, it's a *who*.'

She had a folder in front of her which she stared at. 'I took a risk in nominating you, not a risk to the Watch, but to my way of doing things. There's been a complaint.'

'A complaint, ma'am? I've only been here five minutes. Even I can't get in trouble that quickly.'

'We've been ambushed, I'm afraid. The Vicar of London Stone has decided that carrying firearms is not compatible with the aims and values of the King's Watch.'

She was holding up her hands to ward off my outrage. I could see that she was deeply unhappy, but not nearly as unhappy as me. 'I'd be a sitting duck without my weapon! I wouldn't even have my Badge. This is…'

'…I know, I know. Hear me out. Please.'

I folded my arms to show how receptive I was going to be.

She placed her palms on the desk. 'The Vicar of London Stone has refused to pursue my request to authorise your weapon. I've taken advice, and none of the Orders of the Occult Council will allow me to designate you as a firearms officer. According to the Vicar, this would represent *an unwarranted escalation of institutional violence.*'

I pointed at the damage to her head. 'Tell that to the enemy.'

'Don't push your luck, Conrad.'

'Seems like I've run out of luck. Ma'am – Hannah – you survived terrible injuries. The last time we had this conversation, you passed the buck to the Allfather, and blamed him for me blundering around with no protection. I'm *your* officer now, and so's Vicky. Are you going to send us after a Revenant with no shield and no sword?'

'Of course not.'

'Then how much do you need me? I can go and set up on my own.'

She swallowed hard. 'Don't even think that. I need you inside the tent, but I can't just click my fingers and make it right. With the Vicar's help, this could have been sorted by now. With her opposition, I'll have to go the Occult Council on my own and get a new Order. That won't happen until St David's Day, and it's not a done deal. For one thing, I need Salomon's House on board, and you haven't exactly made a friend of Dean Hardisty, have you?'

'When Dean Hardisty goes chasing Dragons, I'll be her BFF, ma'am. Until then, what?'

'Keep a low profile. It's not all doom and gloom. I did reach a compromise with the Vicar. You can keep the Hammer, and use the Ancile and Badge. However, I've promised to hang on to all the ammunition until the Council can debate my motion.'

'You're joking. Ma'am.'

Her irritation was starting to spill in my direction. 'Take it or leave it. Literally. You can keep the Hammer and your status, or I'll take it off you and rusticate you until the vote. Without pay.'

It was the proposal of rustication that swung it. I didn't want to get out of the loop so soon after being brought in. 'Very well, but if you put me to counting paperclips, I reserve the right to change my mind.'

'I'm not having you under my feet, or Maxine's.' She opened the folder she'd been staring at and took out a note. 'I've been on to Hledjolf. He says that he sold you thirty rounds.' She put it down and stared at me. 'Did you live fire any last week? I want the truth.'

'No, ma'am. I still have all the rounds. Some are in my locker. I'll go and get them.'

'Thank you.' She pressed the intercom. 'Tennille? Can you get Vicky now, and put the kettle on.'

I had a brain-wave, and lifted my case while Hannah was busy signing papers. I shot out of her office and down the stairs as quickly as I could so that I was waiting for Vicky when she emerged from the ground floor rooms. I put my finger on my lips when she saw me and motioned for her to close the doors.

She came over and whispered, 'What's gan' on?'

I took out the Hammer, removed the clip and thumbed out two rounds. Hledjolf had given me three for testing, and I was now very glad that I'd only used one. Had the Dwarf deliberately misled Hannah when he said that he'd sold thirty, not mentioning the other two? Or was he just being literal because two were freebies? Don't look a gift horse in the mouth, Conrad.

I pressed the rounds into Vicky's hand, as Hannah had pressed the King's Bounty into mine. 'These are a gift. Feel free to use them as you see fit. Especially if I'm about to be eaten by a Dragon. And don't say a word, obviously. Get upstairs and I'll explain later.' Before she could speak, I was on my way down to the basement.

Back in Hannah's office, in front of Vicky, I made a great show of counting out twenty-nine rounds then emptying the chamber of the thirtieth. 'Ma'am, I have no further magickal rounds.'

She passed me a receipt and moved the meeting to the comfy chairs. 'How was Northumberland?' she said to Vicky.

'Cold. I was actually glad that Conrad made me buy all that outdoor gear.'

'Where've you been?' I asked.

'Up in the Cheviots with the Shield Wall.' She shook her head. 'And to think I nearly asked to join them. Mad as a box of frogs, all of them. The only time they listened to me was when I said that Odin had once been your patron.' She grinned at me. 'On behalf of the Northumberland Shield Wall, Conrad, you are invited to their Hall as a guest of Honour. Do us a favour, will you?'

'What?'

'If you're mad enough to go, make sure it's when I'm in Tenerife, OK?'

'This should be a bit more congenial,' said Hannah, pointing to a folder. 'It's…'

She was interrupted by Tennille knocking on the half-open door and bringing in a sheaf of papers. 'I just got this from Ruth Kaplan. It's the report on that phone. You said it was urgent. I've emailed a copy, too.' She put it on the table in front of us and went back outside.

Hannah looked at the door, the folder, and finally at me. She traced her finger round the plate in her skull and sat back. 'I literally don't have anyone else to pursue this, and it's your case by right of discovery. I can't stop you chasing it up, but I can order you not to approach any potentially dangerous situations. Is that clear?'

'Yes, ma'am. Message understood.'

She turned to my partner. 'Vicky, you are to keep him out of trouble. OK?'

'Yes, ma'am.'

'Don't you start with the *ma'ams*, already.' She picked up the papers which Tennille had brought in and gave them as much time as it took to eat a biscuit. 'There's not much to go on. Should keep you both out of trouble for a while.' She put them on the table. 'I'll forward the email. Good luck.'

Vicky looked at me. 'You take the paper copy. I can read it on me tablet.'

'Thanks everyone,' said Hannah, rising to end the meeting. We did the same and were on our way out when Hannah held up a flimsy, yellowing piece of paper. 'I had a good laugh this morning. I asked Maxine to check out the archives to see if the Watch had anything on Dragons, and this is what she came up with. It's dated 1967 and is the official protocol for dealing with the event of a Dragon attack. You'll appreciate this, Conrad, in view of the Vicar's views on the aims and values of the Watch.'

She held the paper up for me to read. 'Very droll, ma'am. I promise not to put it into action without your permission. Unless I've had a very bad day.'

She hesitated, the antique memorandum fluttering in the draught. 'You mean that, don't you?'

I smiled by way of an answer and bowed my head in farewell. Vicky had been craning her neck to see the protocol, and couldn't wait to pester me for details. I made a point of thanking Tennille for the refreshments and waiting until we were on the stairs before answering her question with a question. 'Have you ever been on a tiger hunt?'

Vicky went to kick me, but she was on the wrong side. 'Howay, man. You ask the most weirdest questions ever. "Have I flown a helicopter?" "Have I fired a Kalashnikov?" "Have I been on a tiger hunt?" No, Conrad, I have not been on a tiger hunt, and I sincerely hope that haven't either, and what has that got to do with killing Dragons?'

'Tiger hunting was a big thing in the Raj.'

'Where's the Raj?'

'Not *where*, *what*. The Raj was the name for the British Empire in India. And Pakistan, Bangladesh, Sri Lanka, Burma … all those bits. To kill a tiger, you tie a goat to a tree, climb the tree and wait.'

She stared at me. 'I don't somehow think that'll work with a Mature Dragon.'

'Granted, but I think the guy who wrote the protocol might have been an old colonial hand. For a Dragon, he says we evacuate all the livestock in a thirty mile radius of the Dragon's lair, deploy fighter aircraft to discourage it from flying further afield and wait until it gets hungry. Then, while it's sleeping, we truck in a herd of beef cattle and pen them up.'

'Great. Then what? We all hide in nearby trees?'

'No. We wait until it attacks the beasts and use a tactical nuclear warhead.'

'Man, that's brilliant! Devastate half the country and give the rest radiation poisoning. Why didn't I think of that?'

'You haven't heard the best bit yet.'

'It gets better?'

'Oh, definitely. There was also advice for the Royal Occulter. It said, *It is difficult to conceal an atomic explosion or to blame a foreign power. The bomb should be admitted as an accident.*'

We'd had this conversation standing half way down the stairs. Vicky laughed, and moved to continue our journey. I touched her sleeve.

'It's still the best idea, Vic. A small tactical nuke wouldn't destroy much more than the farm it was used on. Mind you, it wouldn't do much for local property prices.'

She blinked. 'You lived with stuff like this every day in the RAF, didn't you? No wonder you're mad.'

I started down the stairs. 'It takes a President or Prime Minister to start a nuclear war. Round here, any two-bit Zoogenist can create a giant talking mole. You tell me who's mad.'

12 — On the Scent

We set up camp in the Watch Room and started on Ruth Kaplan's report. It turned out that Hledjolf's capacity for accessing phone data wasn't as big as he liked to make out. The Dwarf clearly had access to some of the masts, but not to the network providers' data sets. I'm sure the Camelot Committee will be reassured.

The police, on the other hand, can get everywhere. Ruth's report showed that our phone had been bought from a London shop in June last year, not long before the guy using it was killed by Moley. And that was our enemy's first mistake: if you're going to be a criminal, never buy your phones retail. Even though they'd paid cash and given a false name, the purchaser's image had been captured by the store's CCTV. I showed the picture to Vicky.

'Ever seen him before?'

'Nah. Was he the guy underground?'

'He's got the same build. Don't forget, Mr Mole ate his head, so a positive ID is difficult.'

'Eurgh. Bet that did wonders for his halitosis.'

We turned to the detailed call logs. Our phone had been used in a cut-out pairing: all its calls had been made to one other number, and that number had only been used to call ours. This is basic stuff, but you need to be truly paranoid to get the next level right.

People are so attached to their phones now, that they can't live without them. The dead guy had called his contact, but his contact needed to talk to other people. The late Sir Stephen Jennings had numerous phones for the Jigsaw empire, but he never used them in the same place. He would take a call on one, then drive somewhere else to use one of the others. And he never travelled with them switched on. Our enemy hadn't been so clever.

On several occasions, the second phone had been used in a remote area, and immediately after, from the same mast, further calls had been made from a third number to a fourth number (both, alas, a dead end). This gave us two locations to start with: the whole of Newport, Wales, and the middle of a field in Buckinghamshire. We looked up at each other. 'Spot the Occulter,' I said.

'Not a very good one,' said Vicky. 'A halfway decent Occulter would never allow their phone to ping off the nearest mast.'

'Assuming our target didn't actually stand in the middle of a field, they might have been visiting someone, and relied on that someone's camouflage. There might be an entire community there. Can we check?'

Vicky tapped her tablet for a while. 'There's nothing showing for that location. According to Cheng, less than ten per cent of magickally occulted properties are known to us, so I'm not surprised.'

'I brought the car up last night. Fancy a field trip?'

She put her tablet down. 'Aye. Of course. But, Conrad, the Boss was serious. We don't get into any situations. No stupid heroics.'

I met her eyes for a second. 'Hurry up, Vic. If we leave before twelve thirty, we can claim lunch on expenses.'

'You're such a romantic, Conrad. No wonder Mina fell for you.'

During the drive, Vicky gave me a bit more background on Occulting – the magickal art of hiding things from the mundane world. 'Most Mages don't live in completely Occluded houses, Conrad.'

'Hang on, Vic, so far I've seen Lunar Hall, Merlyn's Tower and Salomon's House, all of which are completely Occluded, to say nothing of Hledjolf's Hall. I doubt that Mark Carney knows that there's a Dwarf living under the Bank of England.'

'He does, actually.'

'Oh.'

'Honestly, it's very rare. None of the Mages from Salomon's House that I know of live in total Occlusion. Not even Dean Hardisty.'

'Are you speaking from personal experience?'

'Aye. Christmas party at her place. Very nice it is too, even if it is South of the River.'

I could see that. Hardisty would definitely go out of her way to get her students in an informal setting to see what they were like. She's the sort of woman who picks winners and plays the long game. 'Does she have a family.'

'She does. Her husband is a builder/developer. Nice bloke.'

'He has my sympathies.'

If we'd been going to Whitchurch, Shropshire, or Whitchurch, Cardiff, I would have had time to pursue the private lives of noted Mages, but we were headed for Whitchurch, Bucks. It was time to put a plan together.

As the one with the Badge, I had to speak first. When we arrived at the village, we were still arguing about what should happen next. I pulled up next to a grass verge and we got out to look around.

'That's clever,' said Vicky. She pointed to a compact bungalow at the end of a track. Beyond the building, the land dipped out of view.

'What's clever?'

'I think that our guy must own the bungalow and use it as cover to keep a foothold in the village. I can see a Work anchored to the bungalow that spreads backwards and out of sight. Best of both worlds.'

'Let's see if there's anyone at home.'

I drove up the track and parked behind a compact hatchback. We took a note of the number plate (or *Index* as Ruth Kaplan insisted on calling it), as well as the house name. Vicky said she'd do a search of some local records to see who was registered as living here.

The bungalow was empty but not deserted: an oil fired boiler was ticking over to keep it warm and lights were showing from a back room. My impression of the owner, based on the soft furnishings, was definitely female, but not a Witch.

'Why not?' said Vicky.

'No chintz. Let's see what's round the back.' There was no road, but there was a covered area at the side of the house under a canopy. 'See that? It's an electric charging point. I bet she uses a golf buggy. We'll have to walk.'

'At least I'm dressed for it today.'

It took us less than two minutes to find a Ward built into a gate and its surrounding hedge. Vicky examined it magickally and said, 'I can't see any defences. This is a simple Glamour and Compulsion to keep the mundane world out and make them carry on the path round this hedge.'

She was about to unhitch the gate when I spotted something in the grass. 'Hang on.'

'What?'

The path to the gate, and a few metres further along, was chipped stone. I'd gone to check where it led. I beckoned Vicky and pointed to tyre tracks in the grass. 'You don't take your buggy along here if there's a nice dry gate to go through. I think that Glamour is a well concealed trap.'

She looked at the boggy puddles and the gate. She wasn't going to get wet without a good reason. I decided that it was time to raise my Ancile: if Vicky was going to tamper with a potential booby trap, I wanted protection. I hadn't raised it before because I'd discovered when practising at home that it gave me a bad headache after a couple of hours.

She stood well back and stared at the gate. Finally, she got out her tablet and looked something up. 'That's really clever,' she said in disgust. Without explaining, she splashed off round the hedge. I caught up with her at a second gate, and even I could sense the Glamour around it.

Vicky raised her hands. The metal bars of the gate began to shimmer with rainbow colours, finally coalescing into a green which matched the grass. The steel structure sparked green for a few seconds, grew brighter, and then grass, gate and field all disappeared, leaving us with tyre tracks and view of a stand of trees. 'I didn't think she'd want to get off the buggy to open the gate,' said Vicky. She gave me a smile. 'I'm starting to think like you, see? Come on.'

The path led through the trees at an angle, and we were soon in sight of our target. Our woman was standing on the steps in front of a log cabin, the golf buggy parked on slabs to the side. This was not the sort of log cabin you see on Swiss postcards, more the sort you find on a holiday lodge park. The building was wooden, yes, but it had come here straight from the factory in sections, as had the double-glazed windows and door. The owner was standing with her arms folded, a frown clearly visible.

The rest of her came into focus as we approached, and was very ordinary by magickal standards – a fleece, a sweater, jeans and slippers. She looked about sixty, and the only feature you wouldn't see on the dozens of similar women in Clerkswell was the long ponytail.

'Who the hell are you?' she said when we got closer.

The red file had a section on formal introductions, and so for the first time in my new career I took a deep breath and said, 'Good afternoon, ma'am. I'm Conrad Clarke, captain of the King's Watch, and this is Watch Officer Victoria Robson. Could we…'

'No,' said the woman. 'I do not recognise your law or accept your authority. You are nothing to me.'

That wasn't in the red file. I looked at Vicky, who was clearly annoyed but not surprised. I took a half step back to let her take over.

'Your statement is noted, ma'am. Could we enter and speak as equals before Nature's law?'

'No.'

Vicky wasn't expecting that. I stepped forward. 'Aren't those slippers a bit cold?' I said conversationally. 'Surely it's warmer inside, for all of us?'

'No. I am not extending hospitality or its protection to those without need. Say your piece and continue on your way.'

Vicky touched my arm, and the same muffling I felt in the Junction at Salomon's House fell over us. We were in a Silence. Vicky turned her lips away from the woman and said, 'She's what we call a non-juror. They refuse to acknowledge all forms of state authority in magick. So do most of the Circles, actually, but that's not usually a problem because they adopt the Occult Council's Orders without accepting its authority. If you see what I mean.'

She had spoken clearly, in a normal voice. I couldn't help whispering. Speaking at that volume with our target only feet away is just *wrong*. 'So what do we do?'

'I don't know. This hasn't happened before. Not to me. Let me look it up.'

Vicky started to pull out her tablet. The woman looked scornfully at us and stepped back towards the door of her lodge. It was time to finish my introduction.

I took the Hammer out of its holster and touched the Badge. Magick flashed. I made sure that she could see what the Badge was attached to. 'This is…'

The woman burst out laughing. 'A no-Talent man with no bullets and a third-rate Sorcerer. Who do you two think you are? Don Quixote and Sancho Panza? Please go away and leave me alone.'

Vicky looked crushed, and the woman had made a big mistake: no one gets to insult my partner except me. I leaned close and hissed in Vicky's ear, 'I've got an idea. Get back to the car and leave me to it.'

'Oh, no, Conrad. We're in this together. Besides, I'm completely stumped, so whatever you come up with is bound to be a learning experience.'

The woman grasped the handle. She was about to leave us outside like unwanted cold callers.

'Nice lodge,' I said. 'The only problem with wood – even treated wood – is that it burns very easily.'

She let go of the door and gave me a strange look before turning to Vicky. 'He does know that I've captured an image of this whole conversation.'

Vicky grinned. 'He doesn't, actually, not that it would bother him. Unless you've caught his bald patch.'

The woman turned back to me. 'Your law would put you in that hell-hole under Blackfriars for arson, to say nothing of you not having the Talent to start a fire.'

I looked at the lodge, bending down to check for a gap where the walls met the foundations. Having found what I wanted, I straightened up and lit a cigarette. Magickally. 'You're right. I have no talent for Pyromancy, but I do have the skills to make an IID, and that's not a crime under Occult law. I might get a slap on the wrist from the Constable. That's all.'

For the first time, she looked something other than annoyed. 'An IID?'

'Improvised Incendiary Device.'

Vicky followed straight on. 'And as you know, ma'am, you can't sue in the Cloister Court unless you acknowledge its authority and unless there's magick involved.'

The woman blinked. 'I'm going to call your bluff.' And she did, turning her back and walking through the door, leaving us in the cold.

'Nice try,' said Vicky. 'What do we do now?'

I gestured at the door. 'Does this sort of thing happen often?'

'No. They usually agree to talk as equals. We could arrest her, but we've got absolutely no evidence. We'd get more than a slap on the wrist for that.'

'Come on, then.'

I led us round to the buggy. Being used to complete privacy, the woman had left the key in it. 'You drive. I'll keep watch.'

'You're gonna steal her buggy?'

'Borrow. If she attacks magickally, we can arrest her.'

We climbed in, and Vicky broke into a grin. 'Hold on tight. I've always wanted to play with one of these.'

We shot off the hardstanding and across the grass. I twisted round to watch the lodge, but the woman held her nerve and stayed inside.

Despite Vicky nearly toppling the buggy on a sharp bend, we were back at the bungalow in seconds. I could see why the woman used it. 'What now?' asked Vicky. 'We've pissed her off, but we're no nearer getting an answer.'

'You know the old saying? A threat's not a threat unless you're willing to carry it out.' I clambered down and pointed to the shed behind the bungalow. 'Can you get the padlock off that?'

Her eyes widened. 'Seriously?'

'Seriously, Vic. We're in this together, so which do you fancy? Robson's Raiders or Clarke's Commandos?'

'Does it have to alliterate?'

'No.'

She went up to the shed and fiddled with the lock. I spotted a water butt. Handy. I tipped out a winter's worth of water and rolled it up to the heating oil tank. I was busy disconnecting the pipe when Vicky offered me the padlock like a prize. 'How about the Merlyn's Tower Irregulars?' she said.

I took the padlock. 'Thank you. We can think of Irregular code names later.'

'Not so fast this time,' I said. 'I don't want oil on my trousers.'

I was sitting in the back of the buggy, holding on to a half-full butt of heating oil. The front passenger seat was now occupied by a sledgehammer from the burgled shed. Vicky drove us carefully back to the lodge, pausing to remove the Glamour for a second time.

'She must have thought we'd gone for good,' she commented. 'It takes effort to rebuild something like that from scratch. Quite a bit of effort. Where shall I stop?'

'The lodge is built on a slope, so pull up on the right. There'll be a bigger gap under the floor.'

The woman held her nerve as we approached, and there was still no sign of her when everything was in place. Vicky stood guard in front of the lodge. I took off my coat and lifted the sledgehammer.

The bricks crumbled after the fourth blow. She appeared after the fifth, white with fury and carrying a five foot wooden staff, glowing with inlaid magick. 'Get off my land. Get off now.'

I rested my hand on the sledgehammer. 'Or what?'

'You would start a feud over this? You would risk the lives of your family after burning all the evidence you came looking for?'

That stopped me. I wasn't going to put my family – or Vicky's – on the line over this. Rule Number One in Alfred Clarke's rulebook is: never start a fight unless you can afford to lose. However, we hadn't *quite* got to that point yet. I turned to my partner. 'Vic? Do Dragons burn?'

'No. If it's still here, it'll survive the fire.'

The woman lowered the staff. 'Are you insane? What Dragon?'

'That's what we're here for,' said Vicky. 'We just want to find the egg. Or the Hatchling.'

The woman looked at me. 'A Dragon hunt? Is this the truth?'

'Yes.'

'Are you willing to swear that this wild goose chase is all of your business?'

'Of course. As the Allfather is my witness, I swear that there is a Dragon's egg in circulation, and that finding it is all of our business here.'

She stepped away from her door and pushed her staff carefully into the bare ground, watched closely by Vicky. The woman clasped the staff and said, 'On my staff, I swear that I have no knowledge of Dragons or their eggs save what I learnt at school. I have heard no word of Dragons these thirty years.'

I put the sledgehammer by the wall and walked up to stand on the opposite side of the woman to Vicky. I took out my notebook. 'Have you ever used these mobile numbers, or made calls to them from this location?' I rattled off the digits.

'What's that got to do with Dragons?'

I noticed that she was still wearing slippers, and that she was starting to sink into the mud. It was my turn to say nothing.

She sighed loudly. 'I swear that I have never owned or called from those numbers, or to my knowledge called them. I swear that I have never called them from here because I never bring my phone to the lodge. Ever.'

That was interesting. 'Then who visited you on the 7th July last year, and what was your business with them?'

She looked disgusted, with what I couldn't tell. 'Are you sure about the date?'

'I can get the Vodafone printouts. They're in the car.'

'Henry Octavius.'

I jotted down the name. Before I could ask who this might be, Vicky spoke. 'The chief of Clan Octavius himself?' The woman nodded. 'He's a Gnome, Conrad. We can get hold of him.'

I wrote *Gnome!!!* in my book and said, 'Thank you, ma'am. What was your business with him?'

'Nothing to do with Dragons. That's all I will answer to.'

She had a point. I held up my hands in apology. 'Did your guest leave the lodge to make or receive calls?'

'Yes, he did. He answered one phone inside, and it didn't look like good news. He went out, finished the call on the first phone and took out a different one to make a second call. All of this I swear, and I think we're done here.'

She took her hand off the staff and was about to pull it up when Vicky stepped forward and said, 'Not yet. You need to say the words. We will, too.'

The two women locked eyes for a moment. Vicky was not the first to look down.

'Go in peace, our business done,' said the woman.

'We leave in peace, our business done,' echoed Vicky. 'You too, Conrad.'

I repeated the formula, then picked up my coat. The emotional temperature plummeted from flash-point to cold fury as the woman surveyed the damage I'd done to her lodge.

'Careful with that barrel,' I said. 'It's full of heating oil. And you'll need someone to fix the pipe at the bungalow.'

She curled her lip. 'You're nothing but a thug with a badge. Nothing but an ignorant Witchfinder.' She turned her scorn to Vicky. 'Traitor. You should know better than to pander to him. I'm going to call my handyman and call an estate agent. You won't find me so easily again.'

It was starting to get dark as we walked back to the car. 'Did you find her online?' I asked.

'Oh, aye,' said Vicky. 'The registered owner of the bungalow and surrounding land is Ms Stella Newborn. I'll get Ruth Kaplan to check the DVLA and the Passport Office. We'll find her again if we need to.' She walked in silence for a moment, replaying the scene in her head. 'I've heard of Don Quixote, I think. Who's Sancho Panza when he's at home?'

'Don Quixote is a foolish old man, and Sancho Panza is the loyal sidekick who gets him out of trouble.'

'That sounds about right. I still prefer the Merlyn's Tower Irregulars, though.'

'Me too. Where do we find that Gnome?'

'The Octavius Clan is based at the Olympic Park in London. They moved there in 2012.'

'Tomorrow, I think.'

'Definitely.'

13 — *Gnome from Gnome*

Protocol dictated a briefing from the Watch Captain whose patch covered East London, which Vicky volunteered to handle because I had business underground first. I paid a quick visit to Hledjolf, who agreed to top up Moley's pre-paid debit card on an as-and-when basis. I left the Dwarven Halls and stood in the antechamber, gazing into the blackness of the tunnel which led south-east towards the Fleet Witches and other parts of the Old Network that no one wanted to tell me about. Chris Kelly had mentioned somewhere called the *Water Margin*. It must be down there, too.

It was tempting. Very tempting. I could just wander down and see whether it branched. With a sigh, I turned my back and climbed the stairs. I have too many responsibilities these days to be wandering off.

One of the responsibilities is Mina. I had paid for a first class return so that Mr Joshi could visit her tomorrow, and told him some of the pressures she was facing. As Vicky would say, he's a canny auld fella, and I trust him to do what's best.

Less enticing was a supper invitation from Rachael to *have a proper talk*. She wouldn't let me put it off any later than Thursday.

I got to the top of the stairs and took a moment, then it was off to Mr Mole's nest. The first odd thing was the light attached to the wall above his pile of gadgets, because moles don't need lights. I suppose it could be for Hledjolf's benefit. It was dim enough to be Dwarf-friendly, and Hledjolf had said he'd delivered and set up a sound system. Very nice it was, too. I wish I had speakers that big.

His Worship was resting on his bed of straw, and only got up slowly to nose me. 'Are you OK, old chap?' I said.

'Mole digs long hours. The Dwarf pays well, but Mole must rest. Have you got the card?'

I explained how the debit card worked, and used his laptop to register it with Amazon. When he came over to examine what I'd done, he moved slightly differently. Yes, he nosed forward, but he was using the light as a beacon, aiming towards it and slightly to the right of his actual destination. There was no doubt: Moley was acquiring vision.

I found it hard to swallow, harder still to speak. He was anxious to buy some audio books, and didn't notice that I left rather abruptly. If I'm going to save him, I'll have to work faster.

'Vicky! You look…'

'Don't. All right? Just don't.'

'If you say so, yes.' I'd been moved to speak when she appeared at the Tube station in quite a short dress with a vivid red geometrical pattern, something quite at odds with her normal work wardrobe. As far as I know, we aren't meeting Rick James today, so…?

On the train to the Olympic Park, she told me that Gnomes look human, have a stable Imprint and often lead completely human lives, apart from the fact that their life-expectancy is somewhere north of three hundred years. According to the Watch Captain, Henry Octavius was definitely around during the French Revolution, and now leads his Clan from a base in East London having moved up from Bristol after the Second World War.

'Listen carefully,' she said as we approached Stratford Station. 'Under no circumstances can you make Gnome jokes. No "This place is very Gnomely" or "Gnome is where the heart is". Got that?'

'More than my life's worth.'

'Don't you forget it.'

Henry Octavius & Sons LLP occupied the whole of a two storey new build office a couple of streets from the Tube. They even had their own parking. We were offered coffee by a very attractive young receptionist in killer heels who had her nose in a stack of bridal magazines when we arrived, and to which she returned with relish.

We got the call before we'd finished our coffee, and the receptionist took us upstairs in a lift. We were shown into a spacious man-cave of an office, and the receptionist took us all the way to Henry's desk before announcing our names.

Octavius shook hands, blatantly watching the woman's arse as she walked back to the door. He seated us at a low table, making sure that he got a good view of Vicky. Aah. Now I understood the dress, and she went even higher in my estimation. Knowing what she would face, this can't have been easy for her.

If I'd met Henry Octavius in the pub, I wouldn't have guessed that he was anything but a successful small businessman (emphasis on small: I towered over him). Underneath the well-cut suit, he was in late middle age, well-padded and affable.

'What can I do for the Watch?' he asked, after providing fresh coffee (it was very good. I wouldn't have had the second cup otherwise).

I began. 'What can you tell us about your client, Stella Newborn of Whitchurch, Buckinghamshire?'

'I can tell you that she's been on the phone, reminding me of the confidentiality clause in our contract.'

Vicky slowly crossed her legs and brushed some fluff off her tights. I turned slightly, so that I didn't have to watch her flaunt herself.

'Did you tell her that clause doesn't apply to the Watch?' I said mildly.

'I did. She wasn't happy.' He went to get an envelope from his desk. 'I acted as agent for the sale of a unique manuscript, well over fifteen hundred years' old. She bought it from my client, and don't ask what was in it because I only know the title: *Of the Lady of the Fountain, and her adventure with Owain ap Urien.*'

'Welsh?' I said, mostly to Vicky.

'Cumberland,' said Octavius. 'The ancient Brythonic kingdom of Rheged, I believe. I delivered it in a sealed tube. She paid half, broke the seal, examined it and paid the balance. She seemed happy enough.'

'How much?'

'Seven thousand Troy ounces.'

'Seven *thousand*?' said Vicky.

Henry smiled. 'One of our biggest transactions this century. And why do you think I'm telling you?'

'Because it's better to co-operate with the Watch?' I suggested.

'Usually, I'd just lie,' said Octavius. 'Usually, you'd have no idea what I was up to.' He snorted. 'Stupid woman. That Stella Newborn spends a fortune occluding her shed, then she doesn't bother to mask the mobile signals. If she didn't want me talking to the Watch, she shouldn't have hung up a big neon sign saying *Secret Location*.'

I made a point of not looking at Vicky when I said, 'One day, the magickal world will fully enter the digital age. Until then, I'll take what I can get. Now, about those phone calls.'

Henry Octavius fidgeted in his chair. When he'd made himself comfortable, he spoke directly to Vicky, finally acknowledging her as a person. 'Gnomes have a conscience, you know. I've been wrestling with this since last summer.'

'But not enough to actually pick up the phone,' said Vicky.

He turned back to me. 'When the Allfather and Hledjolf got involved, I decided to step back.'

'Go on.'

'Your young colleague will tell you, if you didn't know already, that we – the Gnomes – started underground, like the Dwarves, but we prefer the surface now. That doesn't stop us having an affinity with the Old Network.'

'And doing a lot of business there,' added Vicky with a smile. 'Or so I've heard.'

'Not everyone likes to deal directly with the Dwarves,' said Octavius. 'Last spring, I was approached by a group calling themselves the Lions of Carthage.'

'Where?' said Vicky.

I offered the military perspective. 'A North African city. They lost the Punic Wars to Rome. Lost badly.'

'They did a bit more than that,' said Octavius. 'I promise that I know nothing more of the modern-day Lions than this: that there are at least two women involved, and that they are both Welsh.'

'What did they want?'

'The Lions said that they wanted to get into a sealed tunnel. They had a clue to the Keyway, and could I find someone to crack it? I went to the Dwarves, and they quoted a sum that the Lions said was too high. I thought Hledjolf was being reasonable, but there you go.'

'A code?' I said. 'Shame I wasn't around. My mother loves a challenge.'

Octavius paused. 'Really? I'll bear that in mind. The Lions came up with plan B – they would create a Particular and I would provide a team to harness it. Then we'd dig our way in.'

'Harness? I think you mean *enslave*. And Mr Mole is a *he*, not an *it*.' I gave the Gnome my best parade ground stare. Behind the closely shaved and well-moisturised cheeks, I detected a blush. Perhaps Gnomes do have something resembling a conscience.

'Point taken,' said Octavius, looking down. 'We harness the horse to the plough, and that's what I planned for their Particular. I chose my best journeyman Warlock and three lads from security.'

Vicky got the picture from the phone shop and leaned forward to show it to the Gnome. He studied Vicky's chest carefully, then glanced at the picture.

'That's him.'

'What happened?'

'The Lions came down, created their Particular, and gave us the location.'

'Didn't you meet them?' asked Vicky sceptically.

'No. Their Zoogenist is one powerful Witch. She picked up a natural mole, doubled him in size, put him in the Old Network and did the rest from her hotel room.'

Vicky sat up straight. 'She created Moley when she was Discorporeal? That's incredible.'

'And a mistake. She bungled it. I'm no Zoogenist, but I believe she got too close. It can happen when you Discorporate. She left the Transformation open, so when my boys went down there...'

'Moley killed your Warlock and absorbed some of his Imprint,' said Vicky, finishing his sentence for my benefit. 'What happened to the others?'

'When they saw Mr Mole for the first time, the Warlock realised that they were in deep trouble. There was no way that they could attempt the mission, so the Warlock covered a fighting retreat. He got eaten giving the others a chance to leg it.'

Vicky went slightly pale, so I took over. 'If I'd been in your shoes, I'd have been pretty mad. Mad with Moley and mad with the Lions.'

Vicky cleared her throat. 'You were also a witness to a serious crime by their Zoogenist.'

Octavius kept his face neutral. 'That's where the Allfather comes in. In a manner of speaking. I went to see for myself, and I could see that the creature – sorry. I could see that the mole was not going to live long, and that he'd acted in what he saw as self-defence. There was no point in taking it out on him; he was dying. Shortly after, Hledjolf sent me a message saying that the Allfather had stepped in. Something to do with his debts, and something to do with you, Watch Captain.'

'Me?' I said.

'The Allfather arranged for the tunnel to be blocked, although he didn't know about Mr Mole. Odin asked Hledjolf to arrange for an extra obstacle, and that's when the Dwarf and the Mole got together. Mr Mole's nest was originally further east – Hledjolf got him to move to the Mansion House and block the access tunnel. The Allfather wanted his … aspirants to face a substantial challenge before they got to Hledjolf's Hall and won the contract to help the Lunar Sisters. Sort of a preliminary interview. You were the first to pass the test, and did it with no magickal resources whatsoever.'

He said it with a smile. A very dangerous smile. I'd seen the headless corpses of three young women who'd tried to get past Moley's blockade, and those girls had nothing to smile about. This was a different sort of test: could I deal with the realpolitik of magickal business or not? I smiled back. 'The RAF selection process could do with toughening up. I'll suggest single combat with giant moles as a good eliminator.'

There was a lot to digest in that. Henry Octavius sensed it too, and suggested that we take a break. Outside with a fag, I wondered again at the gods and how they deal with us. Vicky joined me, but declined a smoke.

'I just wanted a break from Henry,' she said.

'Are all Gnomes as lecherous, or is it just him? That was awful for me, I dread to think what it was like for you.'

She shuddered, both from the thought of the Gnome and from the wind blowing around her legs. 'They don't touch you unless you want it. They just look, and the younger ones hide it much better.' She wrapped her coat tighter. 'No one has ever seen a female Gnome, you know. If a Gnome has a child with a human, the first seven of his offspring are human. Only the eighth is a Gnome, and a male gnome at that. They can spread the load over more than one woman, believe it or not. Henry is rumoured to have had seven sons with Gnome blood, and according to legend, the sixty-fourth child will be a female Gnome … I would not like to be that receptionist in a couple of years' time.' She shivered again. 'Let's get this over with.'

I opted for tea when we got back upstairs; Henry had poured himself a scotch. I picked up the thread from where the Gnome had changed the subject. 'So, your Warlock was dead, you'd seen a horrendous crime, and you still didn't report it.'

Octavius stared at me for a second, just to let me know that I'd overstepped the mark, and that he would forgive me. This time. 'I was thinking of the Warlock's family. The Lions paid the Wergild. The blood-price. There was no crime under the Old Law.'

'Mmm,' said Vicky, to let Octavius know what she thought of the Old Law. Being completely ignorant, I reserved judgement.

'Excuse me, Henry,' I said. 'Those last phone calls were made on the same day that you sold the manuscript.'

'Another reason I'm talking to you. The Lions must have known what they'd done with Mole, and they still let my boys go down there, so that pretty much ended any obligation I had to them. I was sent the manuscript along with the location of Mr Mole. They told me to line up a buyer in case they needed the money. I went to see Stella Newborn on the day that my team went underground, and the Warlock had put me on speakerphone when they opened the doors. I heard him die.'

'So, you rang the Lions, demanded the Wergild, and said you'd take it out of the proceeds of selling the manuscript.'

'It was business. That Warlock was the first man I've lost in twenty years.'

Vicky stepped in to move things along. 'You sold the scroll, paid off the family and got Hledjolf to crack that code. Did you have any idea what they were looking for?'

'No. I'd forgotten about it until Stella rang me last night and said something about Dragons. She's a bit flaky, sometimes, but there's nothing wrong with her hearing. What's going on here? There can't be Dragons, surely? Horrible things, apparently.'

'So I believe,' said Vicky, standing up. 'Thank you for your time, Father Octavius. If you hear anything at all that may help us, I'm putting you under an obligation to inform the Watch.'

'Accepted gladly. Nice to meet you both.'

The wind is stronger and colder out of the City and we both shivered on the way to the Tube. 'That's another one to tick off,' I said.

'Another one what?'

'I've met two gods, Dwarves, a Spirit, talking trees, a giant Mole and now a Gnome. What's next? Trolls?'

'Extinct. We hope. A bit like Dragons. The last one in Britain was killed on Dartmoor in 1805, by Henry Octavius himself, would you believe. He's got the morality of the Mob, Conrad, but he's no coward. As for other Creatures of Light … sooner or later, you're going to meet the Fae. There's a lot more of them than there are Gnomes.'

'Fairies?'

'The Fae. They've never liked being called Fairies.'

We paused to swipe our Oyster Cards at the turnstiles, and found a sheltered spot on the platform.

'If Gnomes are the shady side of magickal commerce, what do the Fae specialise in?' I asked.

'Dreams. They're into entertainment in a big way.' She peered down the track in search of a train. 'And drugs. After all, what's more entertaining than a big high?' She pulled a face. 'You'll find the best and the worst of magick in the Fae.'

I remembered a lecture from the anti-narcotics officers before my first posting in Afghanistan, a long time ago, now. *The Algebra of Misery*, he'd called it. This was the equation: $\Sigma V = (AP \times C)/S$, where the sum of Violence (in all forms) is equal to Addictive Power times the Cost, divided by Supply. It stuck in the memory.

'Let's find our Dragon first, before we meet the Fae. If that's all right with you, Vicky.'

'That's fine by me.'

A train rattled towards us. 'Tell you what, Conrad, I'll go and talk to Desi if you'll write up today's report.'

'Deal. Text me if you learn anything.'

14 — *Cream Cakes and Red Wine*

There is a wonderfully retro dial telephone in the Watch Room at Merlyn's Tower. The King's Watch jumped straight from the 1950s to the new Millennium when they installed a VOIP telephone system, and instead of ripping out the old switchboard, they just cut the external lines and left it to carry on connecting internally. Much of this may have been because there was a direct line to the Deputy's office that way.

I took one cream cake from the box and put it on a plate, leaving the other one in the fridge. I filled the kettle and dialled 101 for Maxine. She arrived just as I was squeezing out the teabag and eyed the cake with suspicion.

'What do you want, Conrad? I only met you ten days ago, and it's a bit soon in our relationship for bribes.'

'Call it an investment. If you have a preference for pastries, cakes, bottles of gin…'

'Fresh cream cakes will do nicely, but not on Mondays, Fridays or in the week when there's an office birthday. Where's Vicky?'

'At Salomon's House looking into something we discovered today. There's one thing you can help me with while you enjoy your cake.'

She sat down and tucked in with relish. 'What?'

'You'll see it in my report – when I've written it – but someone paid 7,000oz for a manuscript. Is that unusual?'

Her reaction was pretty much the same as Vicky's. 'Are you sure?'

'Henry Octavius has no reason to lie. If anything, he probably understated the price.'

'Goodness me. Seven thousand. Mmm.' She demolished the rest of her cake and waved her fork in the air. 'Most Mages turn their Lux into Artefacts of one sort or another, like most people turn their cash into assets – property, cars, pensions, investments. Of course, many Mages pool their Lux in covens, brotherhoods and so on, like some people are partners in businesses.'

I mulled it over. 'I think I see what you mean.'

She took her cup and plate to the sink. 'Quite a few individuals and businesses in the mundane world have assets of seven million pounds, don't they? But how many have seven million in the bank? That was a serious purchase; I'll look forward to that report. Thanks for the cake.'

'You're welcome.' There was an awful lot going on here: Stella Newborn's access to vast quantities of Lux; the nature of that manuscript; the real agenda of Clan Octavius. However, none of those would lead us to the Dragon. Only the Lions of Carthage could do that. Everything else could go in our report to Hannah, and she could worry about it. That is her job, after all.

I wrote the report and printed a copy after emailing it to Hannah and Vicky. I took the printed copy and the other cream cake upstairs to Tennille, who accepted both with a smile.

'That's very good of you, Conrad. You shouldn't be buying these for a woman on a diet.' She tapped the box. 'I ain't joking. No more, unless it's a very special occasion. Promise?'

'I promise.'

She lifted the lid. 'There were two cakes in here. What have you done with the other one?'

Blimey. I didn't think her rivalry with Maxine extended to jealousy over cakes. 'I had to eat it,' I lied. 'I couldn't face writing that report on an empty stomach.'

'That's all right, then. Thank you.'

My phone rang as I was heading to the battlements for a smoke. It was Vicky, who said that she had some news.

'Do you fancy telling me over a well-earned drink?' I suggested.

'Yes, but not until a bit later.'

'I'll see you in the Churchill Arms at half past five. It's not far from Salomon's House.'

She hesitated, assuming that I was trying to trick her into a long walk. I even think she was Googling the pub while she kept me on hold. 'Fine,' she said. 'See you at five thirty.'

What I didn't tell her was that I was meeting Alain at a quarter past.

Walking up from Merlyn's Tower, I noticed that it wasn't quite dark. There had been plenty of snowdrops at the Tower, too, and the daffs weren't far behind. A little thing, perhaps, and not a big deal to most Londoners, but it made me feel a lot better. I don't know if Alain felt spring in the air, too, or whether he felt guilty for not getting his round in, but there was a very nice red on the table when I arrived. We swapped envelopes surreptitiously and raised a glass.

'What did you find?' I asked.

'There are lots of Miltons in Cornwall, but none of them are rich. I looked as 'ard as I could, but without a full name, nothing. The other one was easy. Lady Kirsten of Lotch Ulfa is very rich, very beautiful and very 'igh profile.'

It took me a second to realise what he'd said: Loch Ulfa. 'It's pronounced *Lock Ulfa*, not *Lotch Ulfa*.' Alain nodded to show that he'd understood. 'Tell me, in one sentence, where she gets her money from.'

'Land. And 'ospitalité. She 'as a big 'oliday park on 'er big estate by the lochhhhhh.'

'Very good. Thanks, Alain. I'm seeing Rachael tomorrow, and if we haven't murdered each other, I promise that I'll ask her about a placement for you. Hang on, I'm just going to get another glass.'

Vicky had arrived, and was giving me a serious frown. We had a brief whispered conversation in the middle of the bar while Alain looked on.

'What's he doing here?' she hissed.

'He's a Merlyn's Tower Irregular but he just doesn't know it yet. Can I mention Merlyn's Tower? We could say that it's a nickname.'

'No. Everything with a capital letter has to stay secret.'

'Sit down, Vic. Have a drink. Relax.'

She looked at the bottle and licked her lips. 'Go on then.'

She took her coat off, causing Alain to check out the red and black dress, and recalibrate his opinion of her. He stood up to make room for her and poured her a glass of wine.

'Nice to see you again, Vicky,' he said. 'Is this just social, or do you two 'ave a job for me.'

'I've got some news for Conrad,' she said, emphasising my name and Alain's status as an outsider.

He looked a little put out, as well he might – he'd bought the wine. He gave one of his master-shrugs, the one that said *You can play your games, it does not bother me*. He got up and said, 'I am going for a cigarette. You 'ave to wait, Conrad.'

Vicky leaned forwards and took a small book and printout from her bag. She passed them to me and said, 'The Lions of Carthage isn't a random name. You can read about it in these, but basically, it's down to the Romans. When they conquered Britain, they had to deal with the Dragons. To do that, they brought these hybrid creatures and sealed a group of them in each Dragon's nest. No nest, no Dragon, see?' I saw. 'There was a nest in South Wales near the Roman garrison of Caerleon, and now there's an order of Druids based there. Caerleon is near Newport, where all the mobile phone signals led to.'

I was digesting this when Alain sauntered back. Vicky didn't see him coming, so I slid out to go for a smoke, leaving the two of them alone. When I got back, Vicky had disappeared.

Alain shrugged one of his many *women!* Shrugs. 'I know less about 'er now than when I first met 'er. She is a "closed book", and she is very quiet.'

'She can be quiet. Sometimes.'

He poured the last of the wine into our glasses. 'Forget about work, Conrad, and let's talk about your sister.'

For the first time in my life, I thought this was a good idea, and sat back to tell him about Rachael Clarke.

I did my homework, Vicky wrote her report, and Hannah read it. She agreed that it was a top priority for someone to visit the Most Ancient Druidic Order of Caerleon (MADOC), but who? When we gathered in her office to discuss it, I could see that she was sorely tempted to give the job to someone else, and that was because of the Lions. Not the Welsh people calling themselves The Lions of Carthage, but the original Roman ones.

Try to imagine that you have seen your god, that he pays regular visits to your city, that he demands frequent child sacrifices, and that his priests are Mages of great power. That was life under the watchful eye of Ba'al Hamman in ancient Carthage. According to the Romans, anyway.

Whether the Romans' version is truth or malice, we may never know for certain because history is written by the winners, and the Carthaginians lost big time. When the triumphant legions of Scipio Aemilianus marched their thousands of slaves and bags of treasure out of the ruined city, the Builders of Light brought up the rear, leading their own captives in covered wagons: the Lions of Carthage. If you're expecting the Latin names for all this stuff, I'll spare you. I'm going to call the Roman Mages *Builders of Light*, and that's that.

These Lions, I discovered, are a form of Spirit, the sort that can be Incorporated and messed around with. The short version is that the Carthaginians kept them as guards in their sacred places, and the Builders of Light found a way of shutting them up in the Dragon nests to keep out the natives. As Vicky said, no nest, no Dragons.

Because the nests were linked to the Ley lines, the Lions continued to draw Lux long after the Builders of Light disappeared from the scene (which is a story for another day). As far as we know, some of the Lions are still in place. Of the original twelve nests, four have been opened and explored. In all cases, the Ley lines had been destroyed, killing the Lions and deleting the nests as places of magick. In the case of Caerleon, the nest was identified in the Victorian era but the seals were left untouched. The Druids of MADOC planted a sacred grove on top of the hill where the nest was located and left the Spirit beasts untouched. Evidence from the tunnel under London would suggest that this is no longer the case, a conclusion that Hannah couldn't avoid.

'I'm delegating this,' she said after we'd tossed around some scenarios. 'I appointed Rick James as Senior Watch Captain to supervise activity outside the south east, and he can decide what happens. You can see him on Monday.'

'Not tomorrow?' I asked hopefully.

'Why the rush?'

'Anything to avoid dinner with my sister.'

Hannah and Vicky both gave me that look, the one which says *Stop it Now, Conrad*. Sometimes, I think they've both been to Spain to take lessons off my mother.

'No,' said Hannah, 'because you're going to be busy tomorrow, Conrad. I've had Dean Hardisty on the phone, and the Invisible College wants you to demonstrate your expertise in the opening of locks tomorrow. Is he ready, Vicky?'

'So long as he practises tonight, he should pass.'

'I'm still here, you know.'

'What for?' said Hannah. 'Get out, both of you, and take this.'

I accepted a stiff invitation card and we left the Constable in peace.

We had been squeezing in the odd lesson in Keyways since my induction, and I was fairly sure that I had enough Lux in me to manage a level 3. The locks didn't get more complex with additional levels, you just had to find the right sequence of bits from the Stamp. The problem came from having less than half a second to activate all the components of the sequence in the right order. I just don't have enough Gift to do it easily, but I'd done it several times already. It wasn't impossible.

Life got more complicated when I read the details on the invitation card and saw that I'd been summoned to a meeting of the Inner Council of the Invisible College to take my test. Alone.

I showed the card to Vicky on the way back to the Watch Room. 'I don't know whether to feel relieved or guilty for leaving you on your own,' she said. 'Probably both. Put it this way, I'd give a lot to avoid appearing before the Inner Council. At least you'll get to see the Dome.'

'Should I be worried?'

'If you've got any sense, yes.'

'Right. Alain was disappointed you left so suddenly last night.'

We stopped outside the Watch Room doors. 'I nearly walked out of the pub when I saw him,' she said. 'That was mortifying. He's seen what I look like under Glamour. He'll think … The gods alone know what he thinks.'

'He thinks you're an attractive…'

'…Stop. Stop right there, Conrad.' She jabbed me in the chest. 'If you want to risk your Badge involving mundane civilians, that's your choice. Don't get me involved, OK?'

I held up my hands. 'Sorry. Won't happen like that again. Promise.'

'Good. Now go home and practise your locks like a good boy.'

The plan had been to practise on Wednesday evening and Thursday morning before going in to Merlyn's Tower to get changed. The plan suffered badly when Mr Joshi sent me a text asking to be picked up from the Cairndale train.

I forked out for the Congestion Charge and collected the old priest from as close as I could get to Euston Station. He used to be a mid-ranking civil servant before taking early retirement to become the (Hindu) priest of a small temple which we'd used as a safe meeting place when Mina was on bail and I was trying to keep my face out of surveillance photos. He lives in the leafier part of Clapham with his grown-up daughter and her family. He's very good at chess, or at least he's much, much better than me.

Although he looked tired when he got into the car, there was still a sense of calm around him that I've always found contagious. If good things can be contagious.

'Thank you for the lift, Conrad, and for the first class tickets. I'm not sure that these old bones could have done that trip twice in one day without your help.'

'How is she?'

'She is well, but she is very worried.'

I tried to stay as calm as the London traffic would let me. Mr Joshi would tell me in his own time and in his own way.

'That horrible woman – what's her name?'

'Sonia.'

'Yes. Sonia. I saw her, and she saw me. When she saw me, you'd think that she'd seen something on her shoe. I haven't come across that for a long time.'

'I'm sorry.'

'I walked out at the end. Mina can't.'

'Are things worse?'

'Yes. This Sonia woman was convicted of racially aggravated assault. She was drunk, and attacked a waiter in Manchester after he asked her to leave his restaurant.'

This did not sound good. On behalf of the silent majority of Englishmen and women, I felt very embarrassed.

'This would be bad for Mina,' he continued, 'but what makes it worse is the number of Prison Officers who sympathise with this woman. Not many, but enough for Sonia to know who her friends are.'

We got over the river and things moved a little more freely. 'Does Mina have a plan?'

'Sonia will be out in three months. Mina says that she can cope so long as the bullying stays inside the classroom. I think that what worries Mina the most is that the bullying might spread, that she might get marked down as a victim.'

I drove in silence, turning this nightmare scenario over in my head. Mina has a core of steel, I know, but it's wrapped in a very small, very vulnerable package. Statistically, the biggest risk to women in prison is themselves – self-harming is endemic, apparently. Actual prisoner-on-prisoner violence, especially at Cairndale, is quite rare, but knowing that Mina is at a very low risk is of no comfort whatsoever. It only takes one incident…

'What can I do? What can we do?' I said.

'Nothing, Conrad, except be there for her. She made me promise not to call the Justice Department, and I know that she would never forgive you if you interfered. I will pray for her to Ganesha, and the best thing that you can do is to visit her every week if you can.'

'I think that doing nothing is the hardest thing anyone's ever asked me to do, you know.'

'You may be right. Turn left here.'

I pulled up outside his house and we turned to face each other. 'The prison officers wouldn't let Mina give me a note for you,' he said, a smile creeping into his voice, 'so I had to learn this by heart: *You fight your Dragons, Conrad, and I'll fight mine. One day, we'll fight them together.*' He paused. 'I got the impression that there was more to that message than a metaphor. Good night, Conrad. I shall pray for her every day until she is released.'

15 — Master of the Art

The Inner Council of the Invisible College did at least let Vicky escort me to their lair. She collected me from the Receiving Room at two o'clock, and even though she wasn't allowed to remain during the meeting, she had put on a severely tailored black suit with trousers and a silk blouse. This was a step up from most days, but was nothing next to what she had on top. Technically it was an academic gown, but…

'Do I call you Josephine, as in…'

'A coat of many colours. I know. Your jokes get worse when you're nervous, and they're bad enough when you're in a good mood.'

The gown was truly spectacular. All the colours of the rainbow moved like waves as the material swirled with her movements. If you looked closely, they became seven individual shades; together, they were a dance of hues from blood-red at the neck to blackest violet at the bottom.

'Do I get one of those if I pass?'

''Fraid not. You need to be a Fellow to get this. All you get is a hood over a black gown, but I wouldn't bother: you look better in that uniform. Oh – should I have saluted you?'

'Erm, yes. I think so. Hannah's new Order didn't specify whether both officers had to be in uniform or just one.'

She saluted, then moved her hand to her mouth. 'I forgot about wrecking your cap. Did you get a new one on expenses?'

'Yes. Let's get going.'

She escorted me up the Junction, past the Esoteric Library and Cora's Den, and all the way to the top landing, just below the big Skyway that lit the whole space. Today it was showing thin cloud with some blue sky peeking through.

There was only one exit at the top, a big pair of double doors in black oak, unmarked by the phantom sculptor who'd made the Receiving Room so creepy. Vicky touched them with magick and they opened towards us.

'This is the Warden's Parlour,' she said, pointing inside. 'They use it for functions and stuff.'

Beyond the threshold was a lightly furnished open space with a bar to the left, a platform to the right and dead ahead an intricately embellished wrought iron spiral staircase that glowed a faint green in the gloom. Vicky led me towards a group of chairs near the bottom of the spiral. I wasn't that keen to get close because there's something about phosphorescent green that makes me think of decay and radioactivity.

'Why so dark?' I asked.

'The whole room's panelled in Skyways, but they darken them when there's not a function.'

'Have you been to any?'

'Oh aye. A few. One year we were stood in the middle of Stonehenge, and someone even supplied the smell of grass. Another year they showed a 360 view from the top of the Empire State Building. Visitors are very impressed, which is the point, I suppose.'

We sat down and waited, Vicky's gown the brightest thing in the room. 'What's in the bag?' she asked.

My adjutant's case was bulging more than normal. 'The Hammer. Chris Kelly's dowsing rod. Bits and pieces.'

The air moved behind me. I started to turn before Vicky noticed, and saw the walls parting to reveal a lift with a woman in it. 'They're ready for you,' she announced.

'What about the stairs?' I whispered to Vicky.

'Special occasions. You're not special.'

The woman was in her fifties, smartly turned out and had the easy politeness of an experienced functionary. 'I'm the Council Recorder,' she said. 'When we get upstairs, I'll walk slowly back to my desk, then announce Ms Robson. She will then present you to the Council.'

'Why slowly?'

Before answering, she gestured at the doors. They closed silently, and the lift began to rise in equal silence. Very impressive all round. The Recorder smiled at me. 'The dome can be quite unnerving the first time you see it. It certainly was to me. Oh, and don't worry about damaging the floor. It's not as delicate as it looks.'

'Is there somewhere I can stash my case?'

'Just leave it outside the dome.'

The lift stopped, the doors opened, and I was very grateful to the Recorder for her thoughtfulness. Every time I see something new in Salomon's House, it blows me away.

The rooftop was rectangular with the lift housing in one corner and the top of the spiral staircase in another. Filling most of the space was the Dome – twelve slender columns holding up a circular roof. The wind cut through my uniform as I stashed my case, and both women shivered until we stepped across the border into the dome. Inside the columns, despite the complete lack of walls, there was no wind, no traffic noise and no puddles from the earlier rain.

My eye followed the pillars upwards, about four metres, to the domed ceiling. Black, a night sky, stars…

'Do you recognise it?' said Vicky.

I sought out north. 'There's Polaris. Where's Ursa Major… oh.' I double checked. 'That's what the sky would look like if the sun didn't shine during the day. Like now, in fact.'

'Full marks, partner. Now check out the floor.'

It was polished jet, gleaming and covered in golden designs. Around the edge, a metre wide, was a border marking the divisions of the Zodiac. Each segment had a picture of the astrological symbol. A picture that moved. Under my feet, an angry goat was chasing a woman with a pitcher of water. Behind the goat, a bearded centaur notched an arrow and fired at the animal, who turned to face his antagonist. Inside the astrological border, a spider's web of lines pulsed and faded, connecting nodes and forming a pattern. Were these the stars of the Zodiacal constellations? No, they were something else.

'Warden, I have Watch Officer Robson, a Fellow of the Great Work,' came the Recorder's voice from across the floor.

My head snapped up to look at the human population of the dome. They were in the middle, seated at a round table and all staring at me.

'Approach,' said an elderly man who faced us directly.

Vicky set off, crossing the gleaming web and trailing me in her wake. She'd tried to brief me as much as she could, but the Inner Council hadn't made it easy for her because they weren't wearing name-tags.

The guy facing us was clearly the Warden of Salomon's House, the CEO and vice-chancellor of the Invisible College. He was small, white of hair and long of nose. His eyes were blue, as blue as my father's and twice as sharp as my mother's. The same blue swirled in his gown, and if Vicky's gown was a rainbow, the Warden's was a supernova. The colours were so bright and morphed so quickly that I had to look away.

With a round table, the senior posts are opposite the boss. Directly opposite the Warden was an empty chair. On either side, turning to face us, were two women, with my sparring partner, Dean Cora Hardisty on the left. The other woman was Cora's stylistic opposite. Where the Dean was pressed creases and pointed elbows, this woman was a rumpled smock and meaty fists. Before I could take in the others, we had arrived at the table. Vicky cleared her throat.

'I have the honour of presenting Watch Captain Conrad Clarke, Aspirant to the Great Work, for his examination.' She bowed and blinked.

'Thank you,' said the Warden, nodding his acknowledgement. 'The Council is grateful for your contribution. Aren't we?'

At the Warden's prompt, some of the Council voiced a clear *Hear, hear*, some muttered, and some lowered their heads a fraction, hiding their lips. The Warden turned to his left and said, 'Unanimous,' to a woman who was making notes. The woman nodded and turned round to a table near the far edge of the dome where the Recorder was doing just that: recording.

Vicky bowed, took a step back and turned to walk away. I came to attention and saluted.

A grumpy man on Cora's left said, 'Warden, why is he in uniform?'

Of all the assembled Chymists, only the Warden had a gown, though one of the men on my right was wearing uniform of a sort – a clerical collar and pectoral cross. The Warden turned to the man who'd objected to my uniform. 'I imagine that he's proud of it and that it's a mark of respect to Salomon's House and this Council. Is that right Mr Clarke?'

Cora Hardisty gave a thin smile. 'I imagine he'd prefer you to use his rank. It's Squadron Leader Clarke.'

The Warden pointed to the empty chair. 'Sit down and take your cap off. Then we can call you Conrad.'

I did as he requested. This was definitely one of those occasions when one does not speak unless one is spoken to. Now that I was seated, I could see properly around the table, though for the moment I restricted myself to noticing the Belisha Beacon bald head of the Earth Master, Chris Kelly. He gave me an encouraging smile and a nod.

The Warden spoke again. 'You're going to be tested, Conrad, not as a Watch Captain or decorated RAF officer, but as an Aspirant Chymist, which is why I'm using your first name. As an Aspirant, you should know who's judging you, so if we could just introduce ourselves by title? I'm the Warden, as you know, and this is…'

He turned to his right and smiled at a woman in her sixties who was wearing a green twin-set. Her chair was a little closer to the Warden's than was necessary. 'Keeper of the Queen's Esoteric Library,' she said.

The introductions continued, moving anti-clockwise from the Keeper.

'Senior Fellow of the Great Work,' said a man in his forties, keeping his expression neutral.

'Master of Synthesis.' An Afro-Caribbean woman in an expensively subdued floral dress. She was notable for having the only non-white face in the room.

'Occult Physician.' Another woman, the only one apart from Cora Hardisty to have short hair. She looked a lot like my GP in Clerkswell.

'Proctor,' said a bulky woman in a black suit jacket. She frowned, and I knew why the undergrads were so afraid of her.

'Provost,' said the man with the attitude about my uniform. That would be the guy that Vicky says doesn't like the King's Watch.

'Dean,' said Cora.

I was next, and after Cora had spoken, the Warden said, 'We are missing two Members. Our Rector, Her Grace the Duke of Albion does not often attend meetings. We should also have a Guardian, but the position is vacant.' He nodded to the woman on my right, the one in the smock.

She immediately broke protocol by shaking hands and earning a sniff of rebuke from the Warden. She made no secret of trying to nose out my Talent when she touched me. 'Custodian of the Great Work and Master Artificer,' she said.

Next was the priest, who opted not to attempt a handshake and bowed his head instead. 'Chaplain to Salomon's House and Deputy Warden,' he intoned.

Everyone else had been watching everyone else, except the next man, who had been annotating a pile of documents until it was his turn. He stuck his finger in the middle of a paragraph and said, 'Steward of the Great Work.' He nodded and resumed reading.

'Oracle,' said the young redheaded woman next to the Steward. I knew that Vicky liked her, and that she'd been appointed over a lot of older heads. Did I detect an Irish accent? I think I did.

The woman next to her was wearing her hair in the distinctive Goddess Braid, something I associated with the Circles rather than with the Invisible College. She was mature, aristocratic and had nothing in front of her on the table. 'Mistress of Revels and Masques,' she said. Despite the odd title, I knew that she was a very powerful Occulter. Vicky had said, pointedly, that this woman was the only one who'd changed her title from *Master* to *Mistress*. No, me neither.

Chris Kelly was next, announcing his title and repeating the encouraging grin.

An old man, probably older than the Warden, announced, 'Senior Doctor of Chymic,' as if reporting for duty. There was something about his attitude which suggested that he might be ex-King's Watch.

We were now back to the woman on the Warden's left. She was pale, thin, flicked her eyes around a lot and constantly fidgeted with her pen, book, spectacles and glass of water. She stopped moving and gave me a smile. 'Clerk to the Great Work. I'm a non-voting member. Just so you know.'

'Thank you,' said the Warden. 'Let us begin Conrad's test. Custodian, are you ready?'

The woman in the smock, the Custodian of the Great Work, reached into a bag on the floor and produced a wooden box. It was the same size as the ones I'd been practising on, but all similarity ended there. This piece was not for the classroom. This piece was a work of art.

'Silver on Black,' said the Custodian. 'Level 3.'

I took the box and ran my hand over it. The surface was lacquered black and inlaid with silver tracings. Inlaid so smoothly that I couldn't feel where the metal ended and the lacquer began. I tried to follow the silver lines, to make sense of the shapes they formed, but all I got was endless crossings and repeats, intersections and branchings that moved over all six faces.

'It's Dwarven,' she said.

I couldn't take my eyes off the box. 'I didn't know Hledjolf had it in him.'

She laughed, a big chested laugh. 'He doesn't now, if he ever did. This was made by Niði up in the Black Country. He called it *Ragnarok*.'

I forced myself to look up. 'Thank you for letting me handle this. It's a privilege.' This seemed a good moment for humility, so I turned to face Cora Hardisty. 'I've learnt a lot about the Great Work after you set me this challenge. It's already made me a better Captain of the Watch.'

The Dean smiled, because that's what she had to do. Behind the smile, her internal abacus was trying to work out why I'd been nice.

'The Stamp,' said the Custodian, passing me the encoded metal. As much care had gone into this as into the box – bright green and red enamel instead of plain brass.

There might be a catch in the catch, so I took it slowly. My fingers ached, but opening *Ragnarok* was no more difficult than the plain oak box that I'd been practising on. I opened the lid and looked inside, where a diamond nestled in black silk. It was flawed and uncut, but still the biggest gemstone I've seen outside the Crown Jewels display at the Tower of London. 'I take it the diamond is not a prize.'

'No,' said the Custodian. 'It's part of the box. It's meant to symbolise the heart of a Dwarf.'

This whole piece was creative, symbolic and as much a work of art as any human artefact, even if I didn't understand it. How could this Niði be of the same species as Hledjolf? I closed the box, locking away the diamond and my curiosity about the nature of Dwarves.

Dean Hardisty sat up straight to say something, but the Provost beat her to the punch.

'Could I ask if the Custodian has brought the other box?' he said.

'Yes, but why?' she answered.

Having gained the initiative, the Provost pressed on. 'Warden, before we accept Mr Clarke as a Master of the Art, we can't ignore Item 9 on the agenda – do we support Hannah Rothman's bid to arm the Watch?'

With sixteen people around the table, it was impossible to capture all the responses. The Dean and the Warden were too good to give anything away. Some of the others were annoyed (at what?) and some were anxious. The only one who played her hand openly was the Proctor, who nodded vigorously in support of the Provost.

The Warden pursed his lips and said, 'And how do you think this is relevant?'

The Provost folded his hands. He'd been waiting for this moment. 'With all due respect to Mr Clarke, if it weren't for him, the Constable would not be seeking to obtain an Order of the Occult Council. By admitting him as a Master of the Art, the Invisible College is giving him access to Salomon's House and acknowledgement of his authority. Without that acknowledgement, I believe that the Constable would withdraw her proposal to arm the Watch. I propose that we should set the bar higher, to show that anyone who might carry guns has sufficient Talent to be part of our community, not just an instrument of oppression from outside. We've had good governance in magick in the past because Merlyn's Tower and Salomon's House have been close. Let's keep it that way.'

Several hands went up to speak. The Warden chose the Chaplain to go first.

'The Provost has raised a number of issues, and I think we should avoid discussing Item 9 while poor Conrad is sitting here. I propose that we postpone a final decision on his admission as Master of the Art until the Occult Council has met. If they authorise firearms, we can think again.'

The Custodian was next. 'That's hardly fair on Conrad. We shouldn't leave him in limbo. Could I ask how high the Provost wants to set the bar?'

'Provost?' said the Warden.

'I asked the Custodian to bring the Lock of Knossos, something I would expect any Chymist worth the name to be able to undo.'

I didn't like the sound of that at all. *Knossos* meant the Minotaur's labyrinth, and that sounded suspiciously non-linear. I'd failed dismally at non-linear locks, something the Council could probably see in my face.

'Dean?' said the Warden.

Cora Hardisty placed her hands on the table. 'I set Conrad a task in good faith, and he has learnt a lot, relatively speaking. However, that was before I knew he'd commissioned his own magickal artillery. I am happy to be guided by Council.'

That seemed to be the end of it – and me. The Provost made a proposal setting the bar higher, the Proctor seconded it and the Warden asked for a vote. Six voted in favour, none against and nine abstained. I didn't know whether to be disappointed that Chris hadn't stuck up for me, or encouraged that Cora had abstained.

'Over to you, Conrad,' said the Warden. He kept his voice as neutral as his vote: he had also been an abstainer.

'Point of order, Warden,' said an unexpected voice. Chris Kelly drew all eyes to him, and when the Warden signed for him to continue, he said, 'The resolution does not specify the actual test, and I for one would not have been able to tackle the Lock of Knossos until after my Fellowship.' He paused, and several of the abstainers nodded in agreement. Kelly pointed beyond the boundary of the dome and said to me, 'Conrad, is that the dowsing rod I lent you?' I nodded. 'Could you get it?'

I stood up. The Provost started to speak until the Warden silenced him with a raised hand. I collected the tube with the dowsing rod and returned to the table.

'What do you think the floor represents?' asked the Earth Master.

141

The lines were still glowing and fading, but unlike the stars above, they hadn't rotated since the start of the meeting. Given who was asking the question, the lines in the floor must be a map, and the obvious answer was Ley lines. I followed a few and they mostly converged on a bright spot in the opposite quadrant. I pointed to the glowing nexus and said, 'Ley lines. That's London, and this table is in the North Sea.'

'Very clever,' muttered the Provost with some sarcasm.

Kelly turned back to the Warden. 'I propose that the illuminations on the map are dimmed and that I randomly rotate it. If Conrad can find London using his Sight, then he's met the higher level.'

The Warden lifted a finger to silence the Provost before he could interrupt, then said, 'Conrad, are you willing to try?' I nodded, and the Warden turned to the Clerk. 'Could you verify this test for us?'

The Earth Master stood up, as did the Clerk, who walked up to him and placed her hand on his shoulder. 'I see what you see,' she said.

He spread his hands, and the glowing lines went completely blank. He looked at his watch, made more gestures, and then offered me the floor. I got out the dowsing rod and dried my hands on my uniform.

I stumbled when I tried to move, my bad leg going into spasm. Of all people, it was Cora who reached out to steady me. When the pain had subsided, I walked to the edge of the dome, raising my senses and the rod. Nothing. *Don't Panic*, I told myself. *You've got plenty of time.* I started to move anti-clockwise, slowly and carefully. Still nothing.

By now, I had a feel for the curvature of the dome, and there was a slight chill near the open sides to guide me, so I closed my eyes and continued my slow progress. *There.* I'd found it – the first line.

I turned left and tracked the line to a small nexus, keeping my eyes closed. From here I chose a dead end, nearly losing the trail completely. The next line was stronger, and I got a sense of size as well as direction of flow, and then I was on a highway of Lux that either led to London, Oxford or Cambridge. I chased down the highway until I heard gasps of breath, very close. I stopped moving, but kept my eyes closed.

'Should we move the table?' asked the Warden.

'Let me know if I'm going to hit something,' I said, and set off again. The highway led to a bigger nexus, but not big enough to be the capital. I circled round it and found a magickal motorway to the right, away from the crowd. Five steps later, I hit the jackpot and stopped. 'Here,' I said and opened my eyes.

The Earth Master gestured, and the floor lit up. Bingo. I was standing plumb in the middle of the brightest spot under the dome.

Murmurs of appreciation broke out in the Council, most of whom were now standing. I got a full-on wink from Chris Kelly. The Clerk took her hand off his shoulder and said, 'I certify that this Work was completed fairly by both parties.' She returned to her seat and said something to the Recorder.

The Dean was not about to let the Provost upstage her again. While I was still walking back to the table, she said, 'Warden, I propose that the candidate has more than demonstrated the level required for admission as Master of the Art.'

It was a clever call on her part. She'd probably been watching the others while I completed my task and knew that she would win, but the Provost wasn't finished yet.

'Perhaps we should take this opportunity to formalise things and pass the issue to the Academic Sub-Committee,' he said.

Oh no. Death by sub-committee. I'm not joking – I think a good percentage of the names on our national war memorials are only there because of some sub-committee somewhere. I did not want to join them (there's an Honour Board in Merlyn's Tower, I believe. Haven't seen it yet).

'You do it,' said a new voice. It was the Senior Doctor of Chymic, addressing the Provost directly. 'If you think that what this fellow did wasn't good enough, you should show us how easy it is.'

The Provost burned a deep red, a nuclear fusion of anger and embarrassment. Cora turned her most patronising smile on him and lifted an eyebrow. The Provost gritted his teeth and said, 'Warden, this isn't a personal matter. We must consider the principle of admission, or rather, the Academic Sub-Committee should consider it.'

The Warden seemed to be enjoying himself. He signed for the Senior Doctor to continue.

'It's very personal,' said the old Chymist. 'Conrad Clarke is here in person, and our Dean has proposed that we admit him. I second that proposal. Let's vote and move on before I formally propose that you repeat the Earth Master's test.'

The Provost waved a hand to the Warden. It was an admission of defeat.

'Anyone else have anything to say?' asked the Warden. No one did. 'As is traditional, the vote is Unanimous. Congratulations, Conrad. Dean, would you like to do the honours?'

Everyone stood. Cora reminded me of my oath, formally awarded me the honour and handed over a new medallion to go on my chain. I was now allowed to come and go in Salomon's House without an escort. It felt good.

The Recorder had disappeared during the ceremony and emerged from the lift with a hospitality trolley. I was invited to stay for a cup of tea while they had a break. The first thing I did was offer the dowsing rod back to Chris Kelly.

'Keep it for now,' he said. 'You must get your own. Really.'

'I will. When funds permit.'

'If you can get wood from a sacred grove – legitimately – I know a guy who can do a much better job than any Dwarf. There's no creature better than a Dwarf at working gold, but they're pretty poor when it comes to wood.'

I raised my coffee cup in salute. 'Thanks for what you did, Chris. I don't know if you've made an enemy of the Provost, but you've made a friend out of me.'

He waved it away. 'No one here considers me important enough to be a friend or an enemy. You can buy me a pint some time though.'

'I look forward to it. What do you think will happen when Item 9 comes up for discussion?'

He pointed to an intense conversation between the Dean and the Senior Doctor. 'I think the answer is over there. Whenever those two get together and reach an agreement, they usually get their way. Hang on, here comes Cora. I'll leave you to it.'

The Dean approached and congratulated me again.

'Thank you, Dean. Your intervention was timely.'

'Cora, please. Unlike the Senior Doctor, I'm not a member of the King's Watch fan club. Nor am I its enemy. You earned your MA, and I shall be backing the proposal to support Hannah.'

'That's good to hear.'

'You're not going to get a licence to kill: you'll have to follow the rules. That's why I agreed to support the Doctor, you know. You respected the rules, and you listened.' I think that's as close as I'm going to get to a compliment. She even added to it by saying, 'The RAF trusted you and decorated you. Who are we to disagree?'

It's a good job they don't have access to my unredacted file, that's all I can say.

'Council, two minutes,' said the Clerk in a loud voice.

I slipped quietly away. I'd got what I came for and I could find out who the rest were later, if I needed to know. I was collecting my case when the Keeper of the Esoteric Library emerged from a previously hidden door. I caught a glimpse of sinks and mirrors before it closed behind her. I thought the Keeper would hurry back to the meeting, but she stopped to shake my hand.

'I'm Francesca Somerton. I'm sure you remember my title.'

'Yes, ma'am. Or Madam Keeper. Or…'

'Dr Somerton, or Keeper, but I do prefer Francesca.' She looked at the Council table where cups were being cleared back to the trolley.

'Tell me, Conrad, is a Clarke's word still binding?'

'Still? Have you met one of us before?'

'Your father. You remind me of him a lot.'

'Oh?'

She patted my arm. 'He was very nice, considering that I was casing the joint.'

'Oh.'

'I'm not the first Keeper to visit Elvenham House incognito in search of the lost books, and I'd be very surprised if you didn't know what I'm talking about.'

'I have been made aware, yes. And I promise you that I have no idea where they are.' As I said that, I wondered if my 11xGGFather had kept an especially low profile during the Keeper's visit.

'I bought a hideous chair from your father because I felt guilty,' she said. 'One day, someone needs to have a good look at that well in your garden, to say nothing of the dragon stone.'

'It's on my agenda. My long-term agenda.'

'Good. You were away at boarding school when I visited. If any Clarke were going to be here, I'd have bet on your sister. She saw straight through my story, even though she was only six.'

'Count yourselves lucky. Salomon's House is not ready for Rachael Clarke.'

The Warden's voice carried over from the table. 'Hurry up, Franny.'

'Good luck with the Dragon hunt, Conrad.'

'Where in Nimue's name have you been?' said Vicky when I emerged into the Warden's Parlour. The new Doodad had given me the ability to see a set of glowing buttons in the lift. Unlike the Recorder, I had to reach out and touch them.

'You could have warned me, Vic.'

'About what?'

'That the Inner Council is a nest of vipers. Let's go somewhere we can get a drink and I can get a smoke.'

'I've got a surprise for you. I shouldn't, but I will. This way.'

One floor down from the Warden's Parlour was a small door that led to a balcony with a view down Ironmonger's Lane and a big ashtray. Vicky stood upwind of me while I told her the story.

She rubbed her jaw when I'd finished. 'You might get your bullets back, then.'

'Eventually. So long as it's not too late. Thanks for your lessons, Vicky. I didn't realise just how important this was at the beginning. It's not much, but here you are.' I passed her a bottle of Champagne from my case.

'Taittinger Reserve. Good choice, Conrad. Gods, is that the time?'

'Have you got a date?'

Her reaction told me that she had, and that she was planning to spend a long time getting ready. 'You need to get back to the Tower,' she said, ignoring my question about her date completely.

'Why?'

'Hannah wants a word. Pass or fail, she wants to see you. I think she's worried about who you might have upset.'

'It could have been a lot worse,' sighed Hannah when I'd finished telling the story. 'The Provost didn't like us anyway, so no loss there. You've built bridges with Cora, so that's good, and you're the only Watch Captain I've met who's got to first name terms with the Earth Master, so that's definitely progress. Well done.'

We were sitting by the windows in her office. I cast a longing glance at the cupboard where she kept the bottle of Dawn's Blessing, and by some miracle of Odin she saw my gaze. 'You're not having the best stuff, but you might like this. Vicky brought it back last week.'

Now that Hannah wasn't in uniform, she could move more freely. She hid the cupboard with her body and fiddled with the bottles, turned round and gave me a tumbler with a generous shot of something yellow. 'What do you reckon?'

I sniffed. Not Scotch, not by a long shot. It was something sweet. I took a sip. 'Wow. That's the best mead I've ever tasted. Not that I've had much. Is this from the Northumberland Shield Wall?'

'It is. To you, Conrad. Master of the Art today, Master of Arms to come.'

'Ma'am.'

Tennille knocked and came in. 'Rick wants to rearrange the meeting with Vicky and Conrad for tomorrow. Is there any chance?'

'Yes please!' I said.

'Why the rush?' said Hannah. 'Not that I object.'

'It gets me out of seeing my sister. Vicky might not be so happy, though. She's got a date tonight.'

Tennille *tsked* very loudly. 'You'll be saving her from herself,' she said to me.

Hannah and I shared a look. 'Bit late for that,' said Hannah, 'but tell Rick to go ahead.'

16 — Croeso I Gymru

My partner in magickal crime fighting is not a morning person. We nearly had our first proper fight on Friday when I arrived at her flat in Islington and she was still on her way back from Fulham. Fulham!

I had to threaten her with the train to Bristol before she agreed to a) get her flatmate to run down with a residents' parking permit, b) pay for a full English round the corner and, c) tell me what she was doing in Fulham.

The first excitement was the flatmate, whose very existence had been a secret until five minutes ago, and Vicky had made it very clear that her co-tenant was from the mundane world. The flatmate (Nicola) emerged wearing a pink hoodie, black running tights and white trainers, and her face glowed with the aftermath of a visit to the gym. She high-stepped up to the Volvo and stood holding the permit out of my reach. I leaned back on the car and smiled. Nicola was older than Vicky, probably thirty, and although she had a healthy figure, her face was a little pinched, her skin a little rough.

'So,' she said. 'You're Conrad Bloody Clarke. You're older than I expected. Smoking does that.'

'So does being shot. And blown up. I'm afraid you have the advantage of me. For some reason, Vicky never mentioned you, so I don't have a suitable epithet.'

Confusion spread over her face, clearly an unusual phenomenon. It was quickly replaced by suspicion. 'What's an epithet?'

'*Bloody Clarke* is an epithet. I don't know whether that's frustration with my humour on Vicky's part or simply a factual comment. I could call you *Sporty Spice*, but that's a bit lame.'

She moved the permit to her left hand and stepped forward to shake hands. 'Nicola Rowley. I'm a trainee oncologist at Barts.' She handed me the permit. 'And what is it you do, exactly?'

'I work with Vicky, so whatever she told you she does, I do it too, but differently.'

We stared at each other. I mentally christened her *Dr Nicola*, and if she'd been more sympathetic, I might have felt more guilty about stonewalling.

She nodded, and took a step back. 'Vic said you were dangerous. I thought she meant emotionally dangerous. Now that I've met you, I'm not so sure.'

'Me? Dangerous? I'm just a semi-retired helicopter pilot, and I'm in a relationship.'

Dr Nicola didn't want to leave on a sour note, so she made the effort to smile. 'I hope the job goes well, whatever it is. And look after her.'

'Always. Nice to meet you.'

'Twelve quid for breakfast?' said Vicky when she'd tried the door and couldn't get in the car.

'It was organic. I had to walk for ages until I found somewhere that wasn't vegetarian. Pay up if you want a lift.'

She handed over a twenty, grumbled and said, 'You can get the coffees when we stop.'

I unlocked the car and we set off for a village near Wells in Somerset, about four hours away. I waited five minutes before asking what she was doing in Fulham.

'How come you're not married?' she said.

'What! I have every intention of getting married.'

'I know. And I hope you do, but how come it's never happened before? If you're standing by Mina while she's in prison, you're hardly commitment-phobic, are you?'

'No.' It was a long drive, and we had to talk about something, so I told her about Amelia Jennings refusing my proposal, about Carole Thewlis, about the spy who loved me, about several doomed relationships with civilians. 'Eventually,' I concluded, 'it was easier to take more tours in Afghanistan and pile up the cash. I'd got my post-RAF plan all worked out and ready to put into action when I was in that chopper crash. I met Mina when I was in physical rehab, and all my plans changed. Now, what were you up to in Fulham, and who with?'

'Li Cheng. He's got a house on Topping Street. All Arts & Crafts. It's beautiful.'

'I didn't know that there was a Work that allowed you to have intimate relations with a building.'

'Oh yes, there is, but it only works on the first day of the fourth month.'

'And … oh. The first of April. Very good. You almost had me there.'

Vicky gave a happy smile. 'For the sake of full disclosure, there are some sacred places that you *can* have intimate relations with. And Dæmons. And before you say another word, I haven't tried either of them.'

'But you did try Li Cheng last night, and not for the first time.'

She looked out of the window, watching the headache-inducing red and blue livery of a Home Bargains trailer slip behind us. She was still watching the wagons when she started speaking. 'It's weird, having this conversation with me Uncle Conrad. I wouldn't talk to me brothers about it, that's for certain.'

If she'd looked back at me, I'd have apologised and promised to mind my own business, but she didn't. She carried on studying the stream of HGVs as if there were a test coming up. 'It's gotten complicated,' she said. 'I normally tell Desi everything, but I can't any more, and you've met Nicola.'

This was getting serious. Time to lighten the mood. 'Oh yes, I've got the measure of Dr Nicola. I can see she wouldn't be happy with half a story, and I'm guessing there's a magickal element to these complications.'

Vicky turned round, a half-smile returning to her face. 'Are you gonna call her *Dr Nicola* for ever more?'

'Absolutely. Probably to her face as well.'

'Well, don't, OK? I need her rent, and I need you two to be on speaking terms.'

'Deal. So long as you tell me your cover story, so I don't mess it up.'

'Yeah. She thinks we all work for the Military Investigation Bureau, and that we keep tabs on the RMP.'

'But that doesn't exist.'

'It didn't, until Cheng created it, and now we have a go-to cover story. I should have told you before. Look, Conrad, can I ask you a favour?'

'Well, aye, pet.'

'Stop there. That's the worst Geordie accent, ever. Hmph. Look, Conrad, yes I slept with Cheng last night, OK? Can you wait until we're finished in Wales before I tell you the full story?'

That, I was not expecting. 'Yeah, of course. I'll keep it to myself completely. Time for me to buy that coffee.'

'See? No Occulting necessary,' said Vicky as I pulled off the lane and drove up to the Old Rectory without encountering any magickal barriers or dissembling Glamours. Vic had done her share of the driving, but I was still stiff and sore when we arrived. We got out and shivered: it was a good eight degrees colder than London, more with wind chill.

'Isn't it beautiful?' she continued, sweeping her arm to encompass the house and well-kept garden. She smiled as if we'd passed through the gates of Paradise.

'It's lovely,' I said, rubbing my leg.

'You're jealous!'

'Eh? What? No. It's … Georgian. My house is Victorian. You prefer what you know.'

She tipped her head. 'Just how big is Clarke's Castle?'

'It's called Elvenham House, and you'll get to see it soon enough when we go in search of Spectre Thomas. Here's Rick.'

I wasn't just stiff, I was hungry, and Rick had the decency to provide sandwiches before business. Besides, we couldn't do anything until the other Watch Captain turned up. Rick left us alone in the kitchen. Vicky explained that it used to be a library, the original kitchen having been designed for servants. I'd guessed that already, but kept quiet.

'This kitchen is much bigger and better appointed than Elvenham,' I said. Truthfully.

Vicky looked thoughtful. 'They did it up together. Before the divorce. Rick's only given the house a lick of paint since then.'

'Even the bedroom?'

'Yeah ... Conrad! Shut up and mind your business.'

The doorbell sounded before Vicky could take offensive action. Rick brought the new arrival into the kitchen and introduced him as Iestyn Pryce, Watch Captain for Wales. I could sense Vicky's libido rising from across the table.

Iestyn had *second row forward* written all over him – literally in the case of his off-centre nose. He was tall, muscular and carried himself with both confidence and the sunny smile of youth. While Rick made coffee, Iestyn said, 'I'm based at Machynlleth, so it's a bit of a trek to see the boss. Do either of you know Wales?'

Vicky coughed and shook herself. If she was smitten by Iestyn, I don't blame her. She was also professional and swallowed her interest before saying, 'I've never been. When I visited Rick last year, he said he wanted to give you some space so we stuck to the West Country. I did meet the Druid of Blaenau-Gwydir when he came to the Invisible College.' She shuddered at the memory. 'Creepy isn't in it.'

'You're not wrong,' said Iestyn. 'What about you, Conrad?'

'My first posting was at RAF Valley on Anglesey. I got to see a lot of Wales from the air.'

'Oh, really? What did you do?'

'Learnt how to fly rescue helicopters, then flew sorties, mostly rescuing climbers in the Lake District. When they realised that I was in for the long haul, they sent me to Odiham, then Iraq.'

'Okay,' said Iestyn, unsure how to follow that.

Rick came to his rescue by taking us and the coffee through to a drawing room that can only be described as tasteful. I hate tasteful. Vicky loved it. I actually heard her sigh with contentment when she settled into the sofa, though that could have been at the prospect of Iestyn, facing us on the opposite couch.

'We've read the reports,' said Rick. 'Conrad, what do you think the chances of there being a Dragon in Caerleon are?'

I glanced at Vicky. She didn't look put out, but she should have been. I turned back to Rick. 'That's a magickal question. Vicky knows much more than I do.'

'Fair enough. Vicky?'

'I – we – don't think the Dragon will be there now, but it must have been hatched there, and to be honest, there's nowhere else to start looking.'

'So we're going softly-softly to begin with?' said Rick. We nodded. 'Then I've got no choice, I'm afraid. I know that this is your case, and you're definitely going with him, but Iestyn's taking the lead.'

That sounded perfectly sensible to me, and I'd have thought that Vicky would have been pleased to get to know the young Welshman better, but no: she looked rather narked. When she saw me nodding to Rick in agreement, she squirmed in the cushions and frowned. 'What is it, Vic?' I asked.

She looked from me to Rick. 'Sir. Rick. With all due respect, we didn't pick up this case because we were at the front of the queue, it's been ours since Conrad made friends with Mr Mole. Every step has been ours.'

'Mmm,' said Rick. 'Conrad?'

'I agree with everything my partner said, sir, but I also think you're about to tell us something more about why you made your decision.'

'Don't call me *sir*. Iestyn, tell Conrad about the Welsh Petition.'

Iestyn gave an apologetic smile. 'Two years ago, the Druid Gathering voted to submit a petition to the Prince of Wales. Basically, they want parity with Scotland. They want the College of Druids to have a royal charter, like Salomon's House and Napier, and they want an independent Deputy Constable for Wales appointed to the King's Watch.'

Politics. I hadn't expected to land in a political swamp only twenty-four hours after crawling out of the mire of the Inner Council.

'There's more,' said Rick. 'They didn't just petition, they've got a campaign going, and one of their first decisions was only to communicate with the King's Watch in Welsh.'

'Welsh,' I said.

'I'm afraid so,' said Rick, 'and Iestyn was recruited from the College of Druids to show good faith on our part.'

'I had to cut my ties with the Druids and take the oath in Merlyn's Tower,' said Iestyn, a little defensively. 'I'm as loyal to the King's Watch as anyone.'

'More than many,' said Rick.

'It's your show,' I said. 'I'd much rather you led, Iestyn, than that we worked with an interpreter. What do you think, Vicky?'

'Aye, well, I suppose so. What do you know about this lot, the Most Ancient Druidic Order of Caerleon?'

'MADOC. Not much. I know the Pennaeth – the leader – but I've not been involved much. They don't have any apprentices yet, so I've had no regular visits, and there's been no breaches of the King's Peace to investigate.'

'Forgive me,' I interrupted, 'but is that normal? To have no breaches of the King's Peace in over a year?'

Rick scratched his stubble. 'You could have a point there, Conrad. It is unusual. Did you get that appointment sorted, Iestyn?'

'Yes. Tomorrow at eleven. I've booked you both into a lovely hotel in the Usk Valley. We don't need to go anywhere near Newport. It's not my favourite part of Wales.'

Vicky wasn't sulking, but she wasn't exactly engaging, either, so I tried to lighten the mood. 'Will Tennille stump up for a "nice hotel" do you think?' I asked her.

Iestyn didn't give her a chance to answer. 'No, no, this is on me. You're guests in Wales. I'd join you for dinner, but I need to be somewhere else.'

'Then we'll see you tomorrow for breakfast,' I said. 'We can plan our strategy over a full Welsh.'

'Right. Yes. I'll message you the hotel details. See you tomorrow.'

Something about the way that he looked at the fireplace wasn't quite right. I would have said something to Vicky, but I was trying to be positive so I left Rick to smooth her feathers while I went for a walk.

She looked a bit happier when I got back, so we mounted the Volvo and rode north to the Severn Bridge. By this point we'd run out of conversation and I had to resort to Classic FM to keep my focus on the road. Both of us jumped when my phone rang at full volume through the car's sound system. It was an unknown number.

'Hello?'

'Conrad! I was worried I might get voicemail.'

'Mina, I'm in the car, with Vicky, on the motorway.'

'Oh.' She went quiet.

'It's great to hear your voice. Is everything OK?'

'Yes. It is. I've come to a decision.'

'About what, love?'

'I had to decide whether the problem was racism or Sonia, and I decided that it was Sonia. I can't fight racism on my own, but I can fight Sonia. Not literally, of course.'

'Glad to hear it. Sonia would come off worse. Definitely.'

'I know.'

I risked a glance at Vicky, who looked alarmed in all sorts of ways. If she could have jumped out of the window, I think she would.

'What's your plan?'

'I don't have one yet.'

Something in her voice said that she most definitely had a plan, and that her denial was for the benefit of eavesdroppers. I painted a mental picture: small, she had probably been forced to stand on her toes to dial the number. Her hair had now fallen over her face and covered her hand. Perhaps she was sweeping it back while she waited for me to speak. What did this woman need from me right now? Not the predictable: her life was full of the predictable.

'You know what, love?' I said. 'Go for it. Give her what she deserves. We can start a new saying.'

Her voice dropped an octave – that meant she was smiling. 'What do you mean?'

'As you know, "A Clarke's word is binding".'

'I do.'

'How about, "If you push a Desai, we push back"?'

'I like that. "We push back". It's a shorter than "The wise tiger fears the shepherd".'

'Okay...'

'I shall explain one day. Hi, Vicky.'

'Erm. Hi, Mina.'

'Is he behaving himself?'

'Why no, pet. He's always getting himself into bother. Good job he's got me to get him out of it.'

'Glad to hear. I have to go now. Block your ears, Vicky.'

'I can go one better. I'll put a Silence on meself.'

'Is that a thing? Really?'

I sensed the change in the atmosphere around the passenger seat. 'She's gone, love. Just you and me now. I love you, Mina, and I can't wait to spend all night kissing you.'

'Conrad! The PO will hear you!'

'I don't care. You need to know that my arms are open and waiting for you.'

'I love you...' Bleep. Call ended.

I tapped Vicky on the shoulder and pointed to the message on the display. She removed the Silence.

'That was all kinds of embarrassing,' she said.

'Not for me. For me it was worrying.'

'Who the hell's Sonia? And no, you can't tell me to mind me own business, not after you've been sticking your neb in all day.'

The speculation about what Mina might do to Sonia continued all the way to Llanhennock and the Usk View Hotel. When I reminded Vic that Mina had shot and killed someone, and shown no remorse whatsoever, things went quiet until Vicky said, 'I reckon she's a secret Ninja.'

'They're Japanese. Try *Thagee*. Thugs. They're devotees of the goddess Kali.'

'Definitely.'

We got the biggest laugh of the day when the owner of the hotel asked us if we wouldn't prefer a double room to two twins, arching her eyebrows suggestively as she did so.

'No,' said Vicky, beating me to it. 'I am not sharing a room with me Uncle Conrad ever again. Not after Marbella.'

The owner looked both shocked and baffled. I played along. 'You shouldn't have drunk so much sangria, Victoria.'

'I was only twelve. You shouldn't have given it to me.'

'Well,' said the owner. 'I look forward to hearing more stories over dinner. We eat together when there's only four people.'

'Can we keep it up over dinner?' I whispered to Vic as the owner disappeared up the stairs holding a key in each hand.

'Better not,' said Vicky. She raised her voice. 'He's not really me uncle, but we definitely want two rooms.'

The room was comfy, the food was wholesome and the company was pleasant, but I was shattered. I headed upstairs very early and I was almost asleep when Vicky sent me a text: *Mina's a Survivor. She'll be fine. G'night. X.*

17 — The Pennaeth of MADOC

The day started badly and got worse. Vicky was a no-show at breakfast, predictably, but so was Iestyn. He sent a text to say that he was running late and would meet us at the Old Chapel in Uskpont.

Vicky took it philosophically when she finally emerged. She gave a French shrug and said, 'I thought he was on a promise last night. She's a lucky lass, whoever she is.'

'Never mind his love life, we've got a mission here. We don't know the first thing about this bunch, and our leader's AWOL.'

She sat back from the table. 'It's not like you to get antsy.'

'That's because I've been in charge before, and you need to believe that I know what I'm doing.'

'You just don't like taking orders, do you?'

'You don't last five minutes in the RAF if you can't take orders, and if Iestyn had orders to give, I'd follow them. This is just *turn up and wing it*. That rarely goes well.'

I'd been expecting a conference over breakfast, so I was up well ahead of time, and now I had time to kill. I took a long walk down to the river to loosen my leg and clear my head. In the sunnier spots, the daffodils were well on their way, and it was a much calmer Conrad who checked out of the hotel and drove up the valley. I left the car up the hill from the Old Chapel in the tiny village of Uskpont and we walked down to scope it out.

'How did they get permission for that?' she asked.

I looked at the modern brick extension behind the dreary barn of the chapel and had to agree with her. The original building had little merit, and the congregation can't have had much money. The extension looked much classier and more luxurious, though I had to agree that it wasn't in keeping.

'Are there any Wards or Glamours?' I asked

While Vicky walked slowly past, scanning for Lux, I noticed something more obvious: a brass plate in Welsh and English. The Old Chapel, Uskpont, was the registered address of MADOC Music Ltd.

'Nothing out here,' said Vicky.

'Look at this plate,' I said. 'They've got change of use planning permission for commercial purposes. That'll keep the general public off their backs. Doesn't solve the mystery of the extension, though. That looks distinctly residential.'

The sound of a hot hatch engine signalled Iestyn's arrival and a round of apologies.

'No problem,' I concluded. 'What's the plan now we're here?'

'Just follow my lead. I'll get my Badge of Office and we'll go in.'

I was not happy. Vicky shook her head: *Leave it.* I left it.

Iestyn opened the boot and pulled out a sword. Not the dagger favoured by English Watch Captains, or a short sword like Caledfwlch, this was a bloody great big sabre. Even Vicky raised her eyebrows.

'Embarrassing, isn't it?' said Iestyn. 'My Dad was in the Royal Marines and I told them to make me one like his. By the time I'd seen Rick's natty little dagger, it was too late.'

It was, of course, sheathed, and I wasn't going to suggest he took it out in public. The swords carried with dress uniform in the services are stainless steel and thin. They look good, but they'd shatter if you hit someone with them. 'What's it made of?' I asked.

'I couldn't afford Dwarven steel. Clan Farchnadd, the Gnomes of Harlech, they made it. They used Atlantean steel, which is pretty good.'

'Can you use it? As a sword?'

He looked at me as if I were mad. 'Don't be daft. I don't normally unsheathe more than the top twenty centimetres. Too sharp. Might cut myself.' He checked that no civilians were near, took the hilt in his right hand and scabbard in his left. He pulled out the blade, and it glistened and glowed. A good half dozen runes were etched into the metal. The only one I recognised was the mark of Caledfwlch, his Badge of Office.

'Let's get going,' I said, before he could ask what my Badge was attached to.

Iestyn led the way, and we were soon admiring what the Druids of Caerleon had done with the Old Chapel. 'There was a big Ward on the Door,' whispered Vicky.

'I'm not surprised,' I responded. 'They wouldn't want Dai Public in here, would they?'

The interior of the chapel had been left open. No new walls broke the space, but no trace of its original purpose remained either. Purple banners hung between the windows, embellished with golden dragons. More dragons adorned the back of a stage, chasing each other in a Chinese/Welsh fusion. The stage was empty, apart from two stacks of speakers, as was most of the floor. Stowed neatly against the south wall were chairs, folding tables and several piles of purple cushions. Was that a rolled up carpet? Yes.

The north wall had new oak panelling behind a chair of honour. The panelling had a list of names and dates, but don't ask me what they commemorated, because the headings were in Welsh. There was no mistaking the man in the chair, though. He was the boss.

'*Croeso i...*' I only recognised the first two words. This was going to be a long meeting.

Iestyn thanked him (I presume), then said to us, 'The Pennaeth of MADOC bids us welcome and offers us hospitality.'

This was an honour and guarantee of sorts, and a lot more than we'd got from Stella Newborn.

The Pennaeth got up from his chair of honour with some difficulty. He was old, much older than the Warden of Salomon's House, and frail in body. He'd never been a big man, and now he was tiny next to Iestyn and me. He was wearing white robes that hung off him, and a golden torc around his neck.

Sharp eyes surveyed the English contingent, then the Pennaeth beckoned us forward to shake hands. 'Harry Evans,' he said. Clearly the vogue for surrendering birth names had passed him by.

The Pennaeth offered his arm to Vicky, and leant on her as he took us through a concealed door to a room at the far end of the old building. The function of the space was obvious from the table, chairs and cupboards: this was the committee room. If I were a Druid of MADOC, I'd find it very hard to concentrate during a discussion of the budget on account of the murals.

The Pennaeth was still leaning on Vicky, so she had the unenviable task of responding to the art first. 'Stone me, sir, these are very ... striking.'

The Pennaeth spoke, and Iestyn translated. 'He says that's one way of putting it.'

The room was long and thin, with windows at either end and two murals covering the longer east and west walls, both clearly by the same hand. On the east wall, there was a composite picture featuring the same characters in different scenes – Druids healing the sick, Druids cooking, Druids singing, Druids tending a flock of sheep, Druids at work in a forge. All the activities were outside, staged along the banks of a river, with no sign of a house or coal tip anywhere.

The artist did have some strengths. The composition of groups was good, as were the inanimate objects. The figures were OK, given that Druidic robes cover a multitude of crimes against the human form, but the perspective was all over the place, and as for the faces...

'...' said Harry.

'The Pennaeth wonders if you recognise him,' said Iestyn.

There weren't many male Druids on show, and I identified Harry mostly by eliminating the tall ones. Vicky was lost, so I moved over and pointed to a figure directing work in some sort of modern scriptorium. I looked Harry in the eye. 'You were a handsome chap in your youth.'

It was a risk, but I'd seen the glint in his eye when Vicky helped him through the door. He burst out laughing. 'Still am,' he said. He moved slowly to an orthopaedic chair with its back to the west wall and sat down. This meant that we had to confront the other mural.

The same Druids were gathered in a sacred grove at night, the full moon providing illumination. Harry was shown seated on a throne of raw logs, and everyone was listening to a woman singing and playing the harp. This woman had featured more prominently than any other Druid in the other mural, and was clearly a star of some sort. She was painted with very long black hair and a generous figure. There was something about her that seemed familiar, but it was hard to be sure, and I didn't want to stare because all the Druids in the western mural were naked.

Iestyn found it amusing. Vicky found it embarrassing. She didn't know where to look, and after she'd settled Harry, she offered to pour the tea from flasks on a sideboard.

'The artist made a mistake in using acrylics for the flesh tones,' I said.

'Very diplomatic,' translated Iestyn.

'Who's the singer?'

The Pennaeth broke into a beatific smile. 'Adaryn, the high-flying eagle,' he said, then he switched back to Welsh. 'She is the Bard of MADOC. She has a Gift of Song like no other. In the mundane world, she would be a ... mega-star.' Harry went misty eyed for a second. 'Adaryn Owain. She worked with the greatest Bard of the twentieth century and took his name. She won the Druidic Eisteddfod hands down three times running – the first to do so since Owain himself. We're very lucky to have her. The Old Chapel and MADOC Music are her project completely.' His tone changed, back to business. 'Obviously we're meeting here because it's our nearest property to the Grove, and Iestyn said that your business was with the Grove.'

'Obviously?' I said.

Iestyn spoke in his own voice. 'Another article of the Welsh Petition bars everyone but Druids from the sacred groves without authorisation from the Archdruid.'

The Pennaeth nodded in agreement. If you're expecting me to be annoyed with this farce of translating a man for whom English was probably his first language, I'm sorry to disappoint you. I spent too long with Afghanis of various stripes not to understand where the Druids were coming from. The Druids wanted their distinctive magickal identity recognised, and that was a perfectly reasonable thing to ask for. If I were the Prince of Wales, I'm not sure I'd grant their petition, but that's for him to decide. I'm not sure that unleashing a Dragon was going to help, either.

Harry enjoyed his cup of tea after repeating his statement of welcome and hospitality. He took two big gulps, using both hands to hold the cup, then pushed it aside and stared at me. He blinked, glanced at Iestyn and Vicky, then looked at me again. 'The Constable either likes you or she's desperate,' he said, in English, 'because she didn't choose you for your magick. Why have you come all the way from London, Mr Clarke?'

Vicky and Iestyn were stunned. I took a stab in the dark. 'If we speak in English, it's off the record, isn't it?'

He grinned. 'Now I know why she chose you. There's a whiff of Loki about you, Mr Clarke. Just a trace. I can smell the Old Enemy, of course. You reek of Odin. And tobacco. Get on with it before I ask you for a cigarette.'

I half turned to point at the east mural. High above the too-blue river, a Dragon flew towards the sun. 'We have evidence that some of your Druids have acquired, quickened and hatched a Dragon's egg.'

The silence stretched out. Harry blinked a couple of times and ran his hand unsteadily over his face. He looked behind us at the mural. Iestyn moved to speak, until I gestured him into silence.

The Pennaeth finished his art appreciation and stared at me again. 'I can tell you're not lying, but this can't be true. None of my children would actually do this. It must be a trick.'

'A trick, sir?'

'Either there really is an egg, and someone's framed us, or one of the youngsters has played you. Pulled a fast one.'

I looked at Vicky and raised my eyebrows. The Pennaeth needed to hear this from a proper Mage.

With some effort, she plucked up the courage to say, 'There was definitely an egg, sir. That's indisputable.'

'I can see that,' said Harry. He turned back to me. 'It seems you've been a bit premature with the rest, though. Having an egg doesn't mean it was quickened or hatched. We know a bit about Dragons, Mr Clarke, probably more than you'll find in Salomon's House, and nowhere in our lore is there anything that says which Dæmon can do this, or how to get into a nest. Besides, raising a Dragon is a huge undertaking. Do you know how much they eat? And how much Lux they consume?'

'Would 7,000oz cover it?'

Vicky and Iestyn both drew a breath, both thinking I'd overplayed our hand. That's what happens when you don't plan things. Harry said something, clearly a curse because Iestyn didn't translate it. Then he asked for fresh tea and said nothing until Vicky had put a new cup in front of him.

He took his two gulps and rested for a second. 'Say that again, Mr Clarke.'

'Someone from Newport sold a manuscript called *Of the Lady of the Fountain, and her adventure with Owain ap Urien*. They sold it to a buyer in England for 7,000oz Troy.'

As soon as I named the scroll, his eyes closed with pain. 'Sold? To an Englishman?' His voice was shrinking to match his body.

'Englishwoman, but yes. Last summer.'

Suddenly, I heard a door slam outside the committee room, the noise coming from the new extension. Then I heard footsteps crossing gravel. Someone had made the flasks of tea before we arrived, and that someone had just left in a hurry. Vicky heard it, too, but the footsteps had gone before we could even stand up.

159

The Pennaeth's right hand was shaking. Over the last few moments he had aged terribly. I looked at Vicky.

She leaned towards me. 'He was getting help from a *Deuxième Mère*. I've only realised now that she's gone.'

'And she heard every word?'

'Oh, aye.'

'I can still hear as well,' said Harry, much more faintly. 'And she wasn't helping me think.' He swallowed loudly. Several times. Then he switched back to Welsh.

Iestyn strained to hear the words, then said, 'You must do what you must do, but the grove is sacred.'

Harry was still looking at me, so I spoke for all three of us. 'I understand. We won't desecrate the grove. We're going underneath. To the Nest.'

He shook his head. I had no idea what he meant, but it wasn't a prohibition. He waved us towards the door, and we stood up.

'Will you be okay?' asked Vicky, placing her hand on his shoulder.

His shaking hand reached into his robes. He pulled out a big phone with huge buttons and a tiny screen. He placed it on the table and waved us off again. I had to wait a second because my leg was stiff, and I don't think he knew I was still there when he next spoke. Or maybe he did, and that was the point, because he spoke in English.

'From Cardiff docks to Champion Bard,' he whispered. 'And now this.' He was staring at a picture of Adaryn Owain singing to children, and I knew where I'd seen her before and what her name used to be. I whispered my thanks to the Pennaeth of MADOC and left him to make his phone call.

Vicky was holding open the door to the Old Chapel. 'Iestyn's gone up the hill to turn his car round. He'll stop in front of us, then lead the way.'

We set off to the Volvo, walking past the empty space where a rusty green Volkswagen Golf had sat when we arrived. 'What's a *Deuxième Mère*?' I asked. 'I can guess, but it's all useful knowledge.'

'You saw me help Li Cheng do his stuff at Bank Station, yeah?'

'You put your hand on his shoulder. The Clerk to Salomon's House did the same during my test on Thursday.'

'That's called Subordination. It's not difficult if both parties have a good supply of Lux.'

'So you couldn't help me, for example.'

'I couldn't, but an Occult Physician could. Being a "Second Mother" is harder because you have to enhance your partner's faculties. To do it from another room means that there must have been another link active – probably the two chairs he sat in.'

'Which was why he needed your help to walk.'

She nodded to confirm my suggestion, and we reached our car. Iestyn's was in front, engine growling. I unlocked the Volvo so that Vicky could get in, then I went round to Iestyn's window. He saw me coming and lowered it.

'Is it far?' I asked.

'Other side of the Usk. About twenty minutes.'

'You did well in there, Iestyn, but I think the next step could be dangerous now that they know we're coming.'

'Don't patronise me, Conrad. I let you take over because Harry said he wanted to keep me out of it for the sake of my future in Wales.'

I doubted that. I doubted it very much, but not quite enough to challenge him about it. 'Fine. Is there a safe place to leave the cars before we approach the Nest?'

'Secure car park at the bottom of the hill, on private land. The grove is on top of the hill, the Nest is underneath. We'll sort things there.'

I stepped back, he raised the window, and I got in the Volvo. On the drive over, I repeated his comments.

Vicky frowned. 'You did patronise him a bit. Not in the Chapel, but just now. On the other hand, I'm no linguist, but I didn't spot any bits of Harry's speech that weren't translated.'

'Me neither, and I don't think they cooked it up in advance. I think Captain Pryce's nose got put out of joint a little in there. I hope he doesn't do something stupid to prove himself.'

'He's a young lad,' said Vicky. 'Of course he'll do something stupid. Don't tell me you didn't at his age.'

'That's why we have two years of officer training. To stop us doing something stupid.'

18 — The Nesting Instinct

'They chose a nice spot,' said Vicky.

The sun was getting stronger, and unlike winter rays, these were actually warming my bones. We were leaning with our backs to the Volvo, looking up at a densely wooded hillside. From the road, half a mile away, it was just a plantation. Up close, you could see how generations of woodsmen and women had shaped the trees to screen whatever was happening at the top.

The Druids, said Iestyn, had a hall up above, and mostly used it as a changing room, conducting their business under an open sky. The path to the grove was hidden behind a dry stone wall and was invisible unless you knew where to look. The Nest, on the other hand, was much easier to find because a short track led from the car park to a public footpath. Apparently.

'You can't lock something as big as the entrance to a Dragon's nest,' said Vicky. 'I reckon it will be set away from the footpath and have a Xanadu Portal.' She turned to me. 'A Xanadu Portal is the best way to conceal an opening. It folds back on itself, so you can't see it at all from the outside. You just have to know it's there and walk backwards. You walk into a lot of walls that way.'

'Tell me there's a better plan,' I said.

'You used to be good at seeing through Glamours,' said Vicky.

I'd been thinking about that. I'd had to rely on her a lot at Stella's place, but I'd got through the defences at Lunar Hall on my own. Either one of the gods had been helping me up there, or I was getting lazy. 'Only one way to find out. If we do get in, what do we do?'

'I'll lead,' said Iestyn emphatically.

I waited. 'And?'

'If there's a Dragon, we run.'

'I'm on board with that, Iestyn.' The lad did have a point. We had no way of knowing what was in there at all. We really couldn't do much more without further intelligence. 'Which way?'

We walked down a bank to meet the public footpath. I looked back, and the car park was already out of sight.

The footpath followed the course of a brook which had cut a notch through the hill, making the land on which the Grove and Nest stood something of a promontory. It was a lovely walk up the path, and only a totally mad Rambler would want to stray off to the right and hack their way through the brambles to climb the steep slope which would lead to the grove.

Even without the Wards which Vicky told me were there, the grove was well defended.

We'd gone a third of the way up the gully, and I was shivering. Out of the sun, it was almost freezing here, and the full-flowing beck seemed to take even more heat out of the air. I slowed right down and tried to sense anything off to the right. I got nothing, and neither did the others. Two thirds up and the path switchbacked. For a moment, we were in the sun, and I stopped to warm up and light a fag. We all looked around, up and down the gully.

'I think we've missed it. We're too high,' said Iestyn.

'I agree,' said Vicky.

So did I. As I smoked, I let my mind wander and I let my eyes follow the stream down its rocky channel, past the stepping stones, round the rock and out into the flat meadows of the Usk floodplain.

Stepping stones.

Why could I see stepping stones now when we hadn't passed them on the way up? I put out my cigarette in a puddle and stowed the butt in my pocket ashtray. 'Come on, you two. I've got it.'

'Really?' said Iestyn.

'Looks like it,' said Vicky.

I'd taken a mental note of the big rock, and when a twist in the path brought me back to it, all signs of the stepping stones were gone. To all intents and purposes, this was a deep, fast-flowing stream with big drops. 'Over there,' I said. 'The Xanadu Portal is over there.'

'Wrong side,' said Iestyn. 'The Grove and Nest are on this side of the stream.'

I grabbed Vicky's hand and willed myself to see the steps. I felt a tingle from her palm, and I could see three perfectly placed rocks to guide us across.

'Bugger me,' said Vicky, letting go of my hand.

'There must be a tunnel under the stream,' I said.

'What are you looking at?' said Iestyn.

I wasn't going to hold his hand, so I stepped confidently into mid-air and felt solid rock under my foot. I didn't let them see my sigh of relief.

We helped each other across the beck and I soon spotted footprints beyond the short strand of rock. 'Who's going to walk backwards into the lion's den?' I said.

'Well, me,' said Iestyn.

'Wrong,' I said. 'I'm the only one with no offensive firepower, but I do have an Ancile. I need to go first, you two need to be ready to fight back.'

Vicky looked away because she knew I was right. Iestyn took a moment to think it through. 'If you're sure,' he said.

'I am, but I want my comfort blanket.'

While Iestyn looked mystified, I took off my rucksack and got out the components of my AK47.

'What use is that?' he asked.

'It has a number of uses. If you think I'm going to fire, put up a Silence. Or wear these.' I offered them some ear defenders, which they declined. I put mine in place, fastened the Hammer to my belt, activated the Ancile and switched on my torch. Vicky worked a Lightstick, and Iestyn gripped his sword.

I turned my back to the rock. 'Ready?'

They nodded. To stop me worrying, I closed my eyes, gritted my teeth and parade-marched backwards towards a large lump of rock.

In mid step, someone took my good leg and whacked it on the heel with a hammer, or that's what it felt like. I pushed hard with my foot, threw my back into it and took another step. Everything went cold. I took another step, eyes still screwed shut.

'Conrad! Stop!' shouted Vicky. 'Don't move. Open your eyes and turn round slowly.'

I opened my eyes. I was already inside a tunnel, and the others were standing on the threshold. Gripping the torch, I turned on my throbbing heel and gasped. I was half a step from falling down a stone staircase so deep I couldn't see the bottom.

'Good job I left one earplug half way out,' I said. 'Thanks, Vic. You keep saving my life, and I never buy you flowers.'

You'll have noticed that Iestyn hadn't shouted a warning. Maybe Vicky beat him to it by a fraction of a second. I don't know – my eyes had been closed, so I couldn't see his face.

'There's a big difference this time,' said Vicky. 'This is our mission together, not yours on your own.'

'True. After you, Iestyn.'

He led us down the stairs, and the reason I couldn't see the bottom is that they curved to the right, under the stream and down towards the Nest. We'd dropped about half the height to the car park when the steps levelled out.

'We're approaching a point underneath the footprint of the grove,' I said.

'How do you know that?' said Iestyn.

'It's his party trick,' said Vicky. 'He'll be right, though.'

From here, the tunnel ran at a slight tangent to the centre of the hill. I looked down at Vicky and she was starting to shake. Oh dear.

'Did you take a Xanax?' I whispered.

'No. Hold me hand for a bit, will you?'

I moved to her left. Vicky is right-handed and I wanted her free to act. I'm just the pilot here. I squeezed her hand and coaxed her forward. Iestyn moved ahead, and in the glow from my torch and Vicky's Lightstick, I could see the tunnel turn sharply to the left, which would point it back at the centre. Now would be a good time to regroup.

'Iestyn,' I hissed.

He waved a hand to show he'd heard me, then carried on round the corner. Up till now, the tunnel had been rough-hewn and uneven. Beyond the turn, it became smooth and finished. I moved closer to the wall and peered round.

A short way ahead, the tunnel opened to a huge cave with its own lighting. Iestyn was already half way there. I figured that Vicky might prefer the bigger space, so I led her forward. We approached the entrance, and I couldn't take it all in at once.

The cave – chamber – was huge, at least 30m in diameter, and lit throughout with Lightsticks fastened to the walls. Even I could feel the magick in here, and it was the most Lux I'd sensed since gatecrashing the grove at Lunar Hall. I scanned round quickly, spotting a small opening diametrically opposite us, and a large, presumably Dragon-sized tunnel leading away to the right, towards the car park. When I saw that it was full of Roman concrete, my heart sank.

'Shit, Vicky, we've been set up. Get ready to run.'

'What? Why?'

I looked frantically for Iestyn, and saw him behind the chamber's central feature – a stone plinth (altar, I suppose). Above the altar, high in the roof was a chimney, its opening blackened with soot.

Iestyn called something down the opening, then did it again louder – a name. 'Surwen! It's Iestyn.' He heard something and started walking back.

'Fuck. You're right,' said Vicky.

It was my call – should we leg it or stand our ground and play it by ear? I looked down at Vicky: the open space, bright lights and adrenalin had perked her up a bit. I grabbed her shoulder and leaned in to whisper, 'If it goes tits-up, run like fuck. That's an order. Clear?'

She heard my tone, saw the look in my face and said, 'Aye. Sir.'

I eased myself in front of her as we heard footsteps coming into the chamber. Four figures emerged into the light, and only one was human. The other three were lions, if you can have tabby lions. They were the size and shape of lions, the male had a mane like a lion, and they had lions' feet and muzzles, but they were striped like the tabby cat your next door neighbour once had.

'Iestyn?' said the human. Two steps further in, and I could see a tall woman in a green boiler suit. Given the custom, figure-hugging tailoring, I should probably say *jumpsuit*, but this was a practical garment. You could tell that by the bloodstains.

Iestyn, by now on our side of the altar, said something in Welsh. I could tell from his tone that he was apologising, then he waved at us and said something that included the words *Watch Captain*.

165

The woman snapped at him, then took a deep breath. She turned round and gave an order to the lions, also in Welsh. They growled and lay down by the opposite tunnel. The woman sashayed round the altar and stopped in front of us, planting her hands on her hips.

'This is Surwen,' said Iestyn to us. He was going to say more, but she cut him off and they started an argument in Welsh. I watched closely at first, checking their body language to see if we were at risk. Iestyn seemed to be putting his foot down about something, and Surwen was backing off, metaphorically speaking.

I widened my gaze to see what I might have missed before. I noticed a dagger tucked into Surwen's belt, I noticed air moving between our tunnel and the chimney and I noticed the art – old art on the walls, too far away to see, and more art on the floor. Not Roman mosaic this time, but vivid dyes applied in bold strokes. There was no avoiding the circling, twisting, flying and swooping Dragons. The floor gleamed a little, and despite two thousand years of neglect, the images were as powerful as the day they'd been laid down. At the foot of the walls, balls of brown fur had gathered.

'I know her,' said Vicky to herself.

'Where from?'

She snapped back to the present and pointed a finger. 'She's the Zoogenist.'

Surwen had style and presence. The combat-chic jumpsuit, the wavy hair, the way she thrust out her hip and the laced up DM boots all combined to present a woman who was both powerful and dominating, and who had created Mr Mole. I would never, ever forgive her for that.

'Out of curiosity,' I mouthed. 'How old is she? She doesn't look a day over my age. And no jokes.'

Vicky was looking puzzled when Iestyn turned to face us and interrupted her study.

'Conrad, Vicky, there's something we need to discuss,' said Iestyn.

'Oh?' I said. I could have mentioned his treachery, but I was underground with three magickal lions, two potential enemies and a partner with claustrophobia. In these circumstances, discussion is good.

'The Dragon is a demonstration,' said Iestyn. 'A demonstration of our ability to make magick at the highest level. There was never any intention to release it, only to show it could be done.'

'That sounds dangerous. A mature Dragon is a dangerous thing, Iestyn.'

'Once it has fire, we can show the world what we've done before we put it down. It won't mature fully. You're right, that would be too dangerous.'

He actually believed it. Iestyn Pryce truly believed what he was telling us. 'What about you, Iestyn? What's your future?'

'I hope to be the first Constable of the Prince's Watch. It might take a few years, but Wales has to grow up and run its own magickal affairs. After all, you've become a Watch Captain despite your record.'

Vicky gave me a raised eyebrow, but only for a second.

'Maybe,' I said. 'Perhaps you're right, but that's not my concern. When did they drag you into this?'

'When they brought the egg here to the Nest. I was here when VOLAC was summoned to quicken the egg. I was here when the egg hatched.'

Surwen had been watching closely and interrupted Iestyn's youthful enthusiasm. 'You do know that nothing we've done is illegal. Dragons are native to Albion. VOLAC was confined according to natural law. We'll surrender the Hatchling. I'm a bit narked that you got here first, but Iestyn said he couldn't stop you. He's done his job perfectly.'

'Vic? Is she right about the law?'

Vicky looked at me, willing me to understand something under her words. 'About the Dragon, yes, that's true. And the Dæmon.'

I nodded to show I'd got her drift and turned back to Surwen. I had one more question. 'What about Harry Evans?'

'He's as passionate about Welsh magick as we are, but his campaigning days are long over. He'll be thrilled when he hears what we've done, but we did it without him.'

Harry had been anything but thrilled, and her words confirmed that he was innocent of any involvement. It was time to act.

I let the sling on my shoulder take the weight of the Kalashnikov and touched my Badge of Office. 'Surwen of MADOC, by the authority of the Constable I am arresting you for breaching Article 19 of the Code by creating a Particular with Conscience, namely the creature known as His Worship, Lord Mayor of Moles.'

'What?' said Iestyn, aghast.

'What mole?' said Surwen.

Vicky got her badge from around her neck. 'There's a reason that Mary Shelley was allowed to publish *Frankenstein*.'

'Is there?' I said. That was news to me.

'Aye, Conrad. It was mostly a true story, only a lot more people died in real life. The book was a warning.'

'That book was a travesty,' said Surwen. 'But that's beside the point. What is this mole you're talking about?'

I stared at her, letting her see in my face what I thought of her. 'He's a friend of mine. If I thought you could stabilise him, I'd resign my commission and offer you a deal, but you botched the job so badly that he's beyond help. All I can offer him is justice.'

'Surwen? What's this about?' said Iestyn. All of a sudden, he wasn't so keen on talking in Welsh. Perhaps he was coming to his senses.

Vicky stepped to the side. 'I'm a qualified Imprimatist. I never thought it would be any use, but I've examined Mr Mole, and you, and your Imprint is clearly visible in his Enhancement.'

Surwen pointed to us, speaking to Iestyn in quick-fire Welsh. So quick he didn't get it. She said it again, jabbing her finger at Vicky.

'No,' said Iestyn. 'You can answer that in the Cloister Court. I'll speak up for you.'

She spoke again.

Iestyn looked at us, fear in his eyes. I stepped further away from Vicky.

'No, Surwen,' said Iestyn. 'Let them take you in before Vicky gets out a recorder and translates what you're saying.'

That was the moment. That was the moment the talking stopped.

Surwen screamed at the lions, then jumped on the altar, scattering ashes. She gestured at me, and I braced myself for an attack like the ones I'd endured from Keira. I needn't have worried – Surwen had no power with blast magick, and it barely troubled my Ancile. What she did have was three lions.

The beasts spread out and we each got one. When the big male headed for Iestyn, he finally realised which side he was on. The male approached him first, the females hanging back for moment. Iestyn took a blast at the lion and drew his sword.

The blast blew over the lion's mane like wind rippling the fur. It took two more steps, then pounced.

We were all protected by Anciles. An Ancile will deflect a magickal blast, a mundane bullet, an arrow or a spear. A lion doesn't need any of those, and the Ancile is powerless in your personal space. The lion jumped on to Iestyn, and he tried to roundhouse it with his sword, using it like a club. He missed, and the lion knocked him over, taking great gouts of flesh from his chest with its claws.

Iestyn didn't scream as the lion bit his neck. He gripped his sword and discharged all his Lux into the beast in a flash of light. They died together.

All five survivors blinked. The lionesses shook their heads, dazed. Surwen had stumbled and fallen in the ashes. Vicky was staring at the bloody mess of Iestyn's throat. I had half a second to come up with a plan, and I saw it sticking out from underneath Iestyn's body.

I grabbed the hunting knife from my belt and jerked Vicky's shoulder. 'Vic! Wake up!'

'I…'

I jammed the knife's handle into her chest. 'Take this.'

She swayed on her feet, but she gripped the knife.

'Silence. Hat-stand,' I said, and slipped the AK47 from my shoulder.

Surwen stood up and spoke to the beasts. I took four steps away from Vicky and tried to keep both my opponent and my partner in sight. When the other lioness stepped forward, Vicky finally swept her hand and brought up a

Silence. I jammed home my ear defender and emptied a full magazine on auto, aiming at the lions.

Aiming at the lions was pretty pointless – you can't aim an AK47 on auto, and the few mundane bullets that were on target just bounced off their protection. Hitting them wasn't my objective: scaring them was. Both beasts were terrified by the noise and backed away. Even Surwen clapped her hands over her ears. I threw the rifle at Surwen and made a grab for Iestyn's sword. If I was right, the protective rune which bound it to his Imprint would have been discharged when he emptied his magickal magazine into the dead lion.

Then my leg gave way. Instead of giving me support, my bad leg gave me pain. I staggered to a halt in front of the two corpses as the lion recovered from her fright, egged on by shouts from Surwen. I put my weight on my good leg and poured all my willpower into an Olympic grade triple-jump hop over the dead beast, landing on Iestyn's body. The lioness helped me out by skirting the remains of her dead mate.

I was grabbing the sword, my lioness was coming round for the kill and Vicky was remembering what she'd done with my cap in the Watch Room. With poor control, she set the hunting knife dancing in front of her and moved slowly backwards. It was enough, just, to discourage her opponent for a moment. I got a good hold of the sword and climbed on to my good knee to wait for the lioness to pounce.

You have to train animals to be frightened of knives – that's half the point of a bullfight: the bull isn't frightened of the sword. To a lion, three feet of Atlantean steel is just a big stick. There was no magick in the sword, but the edge was good and the blade strong. I brought my right hand down just as the lion grabbed my left arm. I felt her teeth hit my bone as the sword hit skin, flesh and spinal cord. The lion's last gasp opened her jaw and freed my arm.

I checked the wound. No arteries had been severed, but the pain…

I stood up as Vicky backed away from the remaining lioness. Should I go for Surwen or the beast? A red glow rose up from the altar, swirling around the Druid. I'd take the lioness first.

Surwen fired a blast before she disappeared behind the red curtain, enough to knock away the dancing dagger. I shouted to grab the beast's attention and was limping forwards when something changed in its eyes.

'She's inside it,' said Vicky. 'Surwen's inside the lion.'

On its own, the beast would have seen me as the bigger threat. With Surwen on board, it turned back to Vicky.

'Get behind me. Quick.'

There was enough adrenalin in her for Vicky to move on autopilot, and she dashed out of the way before Surwen could fully control the animal. The problem now was that the lion was between us and the exit, and my plan for a fighting retreat was up the Swanney.

Mark Hayden

The lion moved from side to side, testing its reflexes. Sooner or later she'd get the hang of this, and we'd be in serious trouble.

Vicky used her broadest Geordie. 'D'ya want owt for ya Hamma?'

She was offering me a bullet. Unfortunately, there was blood dripping down my left arm and a sword in my right. 'Listen, Vic, you need to do this carefully. Step up, take the Hammer and do it yourself. Don't let her see what you're doing. I can only put this sword down once.'

'Gotcha.'

I took a step forward and slashed at the lion. When I stepped back, Vicky pulled out the gun. Our lives now depended on her doing something she'd only see me do once.

I pretended to go on the offensive, to keep the Surwen/lion focused on me. It feinted left, then right, coming at my damaged arm. I only got my guard up just in time to stop it pouncing. A clang from behind me, and a curse, said that Vicky was struggling.

'I'm going to open a path to the tunnel, Vic. Get ready to run.'

If Vicky didn't get the round in soon, I was going to have to open that path by sacrificing myself.

'Right,' said Vicky. What did that mean?

The Surwen/lion stepped aside, offering a path. If Vicky ran now, she wouldn't be fast enough. I needed a bigger gap, but Vicky just legged it.

'No, Vic…'

The lion crouched, ready to pounce, then Vicky turned and tossed the gun to me. I dropped the sword, caught the gun and prayed to Odin that Vicky had remembered to chamber the round. If she hadn't…

I had to fire over her shoulder, and do it one handed. The blast echoed round the Nest, and I saw something I hope I never have to see again: two spirits flowed, merged, swirled and blew apart into infinite fragments.

'I think we're quits on the flowers,' said Vicky from the floor.

'No need to shout.'

'I didn't have a Silence. I'm half deaf. I mean deaf.'

I holstered the gun and offered my hand. She got up and we turned to the altar. The red curtain was gone, and Surwen's human form lay in a heap. I went to pick up the sword, alert to any danger.

'The shock will have killed her,' said Vicky. I checked for a pulse. She was right.

'What now?' she asked.

'First aid kit.'

170

19 — *Brotherhoods and Other Family*

V icky looked at my arm. 'Step closer to the altar.'

'Why? The first aid kit's in my rucksack, and the light's better near the walls.'

'I'm gonna try healing you. There's enough Lux in here to make up for the fact that I'm rubbish at it.'

'You can heal? Why didn't you say?'

'All Mages can heal, but most are rubbish. Hurry up before the scar tissue starts to form.'

We stood by the body of Surwen, now filthy from the ashes as well as being dead. I took my coat and shirt off. There were deep punctures on both sides, as well as gashes. The more I looked at them, the more they hurt.

Vicky closed her eyes and gripped my arm in both hands. Lux flowed, and the pain hit the roof and flew out the chimney. I shoved my sleeve in my mouth and bit down hard. Really hard. Then I passed out.

She caught me before my head hit the altar, and managed a controlled collapse. I took a moment to mime drinking, then closed my eyes until she returned with water. She joined me in resting against the altar.

'You could have warned me.'

'Sorry. I honestly forgot. Unless you're really, really good, all the pain of getting better comes at once. I'm not gonna try that again for a while.'

'I'll try not to get bitten by a lion until you're ready.'

'Good. Now break out the tabs and don't tell Nicola.'

We smoked in silence for a while, trying not to look at the bodies around us.

'How did you know Iestyn was working for the opposition?' said Vicky.

'When I saw the entrance blocked up with concrete. That's why Harry shook his head when we said we were coming here: he thought it was sealed off and inaccessible. If Harry didn't know about the back door, Iestyn could only have found out from the Dragon crew. Come on, we'd better look down the other tunnel while we're here.'

We collected our gear and I led us down the tunnel. First on the right was an empty pen that stank of lion. Second on the right was another pen, but this one wasn't empty. We stopped and stared. Four lions stared back.

'Shit.'

'Aye,' said Vicky. 'Hang on. These are different. By the gods, Conrad, these are the original lions from Africa. Surwen must have made the others herself.'

'I'd guessed that. Even the Romans wouldn't have made tabby lions. I'm guessing she wanted something she could control.'

I looked around and saw an open door on the left. Through the gap I saw benches and cages. Surwen's place of work, no doubt.

Vicky was still staring at the lions. They were still staring back. The ones we'd killed were lionish enough – the same size as safari park lions, but these were altogether more *real*. Bigger, sleeker and prouder. These guys knew they were the king of any jungle. 'Do you see that gate?' said Vicky.

'Yes.'

'I hate to say this, Conrad, but she'd keyed the lock to her Imprint. It failed when she died.'

'So they're not locked in?'

'No. And the gate opens outward. I'm betting they know that.'

'Vic? How much more can you cope with?'

'Why?'

'I'm going to stand guard. I want you to run into the lab and grab any scrolls you see lying about. And anything else of interest.'

She moved before her courage failed, sliding along the wall and through the door. I took two steps toward the lions. They took two steps toward the gate. We stared at each other until the male took two more steps toward the gate.

'Vic. Come out.'

She appeared at the door, stuffing something in her pack. We backed away until we reached the chamber.

'What now?'

'You watch the tunnel.'

I quickly laid out Surwen's body on the altar and checked the pockets of her jumpsuit, finding nothing of interest except a phone. I took my pliers to her neck chain, tipping the amulets into my bag. The dagger I ignored because it could easily be booby-trapped.

'Conrad, the first one's out of the cage. It's starting to come down the passage.'

I checked the phone: it was locked. Vicky's phone has a magickal key, but that was put on by Li Cheng, a leading expert in the field. I gambled that Wales was behind the times in electro-magick and gingerly pressed the Home button to Surwen's thumb. It unlocked.

'Vicky, I'm ready. You take the sword and the AK47. And keep this phone unlocked, whatever you do.'

She jogged back to the altar. 'What?'

'I can't carry them and Iestyn.'

She glanced at the tunnel. Shadows were getting closer to the entrance. 'Why?'

'Iestyn was one of us in the end. I'm not going to let him end up as cat food.'

I couldn't have done it without the altar to help me get Iestyn's body into a fireman's lift. We headed for the exit as a roar came from the tunnel.

'What if they follow us?'

'They won't. There was lion hair all over the Nest, but none in the tunnel.'

I carried Iestyn down the tunnel, around the corner and laid him at the foot of the stairs. 'I could probably get him up, but there's no point,' I said. 'We certainly couldn't get him across the beck. Let's go up a bit and take stock.'

We ascended until the curve of the stairs had hidden Iestyn from view, then settled down to sort things out. Vicky was two steps ahead of me on the technology front, as you'd expect. While I was still dismantling the AK47 and re-packing my rucksack, she'd gone through Surwen's phone.

'Got it,' she said. 'I've found an encrypted message group called ...' She showed me the screen: *Brawdoliaeth y Draig*. 'Draig is Dragon,' she observed. 'I can't look the other word up because there's no signal. Doesn't really matter — the names are here.'

'Go on.'

'There's Surwen, Adaryn, Gwyddno, Iorwen, Rhein and Myfanwy.'

'But no Iestyn.'

'No. He's in a different group set up not long ago.'

'What else is on there?'

While Vicky worked her magic on the phone, I took a moment to close my eyes and let the stress drain away. This was the fourth time in less than a year that I'd had to defend myself against a violent attack and killed someone in the process. In the moment, you don't think. In the moment, all you want to do is survive. How long I can keep putting myself in that moment is another matter, and it wouldn't get any easier when Mina was released.

'This is complicated,' said Vic.

'How so?'

'I've looked at the general messages, calendar and photos. As far as I can tell, Surwen is married to Gwyddno and they have twin girls aged eleven. See?'

She showed me a snap of a much older man — in his fifties at least — and two rather intense girls, all wearing Druid robes. The twins were not identical. One was taller and looked more mature than the other. 'Are you sure that's Gwyddno?' I asked.

'Aye. It's their fifteenth wedding anniversary in May.'

'Then we've got real problems.'

'More real than a Dragon on the loose?'

'Much more real. If the Dragon goes on the rampage, we have a plan.'

She gave me that look again. 'The plan with the atomic bomb in it.'

'I prefer to call them *tactical thermo-nuclear warheads*. Much less apocalyptic.'

'Makes all the difference, that.'

'Yes it does, and it's someone else's problem. Our problem is a dead wife and mother. I do not want a grieving husband after us, or two screwed up kids in a few years' time.'

Vicky looked over her shoulder. I don't even think she knew she was doing it. 'You reckon?'

'Vic, I was only granted access to the Esoteric Library two days ago, so I've got a lot of catching up to do on magickal history. Can you put your hand on your heart and tell me that the library isn't full of feuds, score-settling and revenge served cold?'

This time she caught herself glancing up the staircase. 'You've got a point.' Her eyes moved to the tunnel, towards the altar and Surwen's body. 'Please tell me you're not planning to "take out" those girls.'

It was time for a reality check. 'Only if I have to.' I let that hang in the air for a second. 'Vicky, would you rather that they killed you or you killed them? If it came down to it.'

She looked away. 'I'm not sure I want to be in a job with choices like that.'

'Me neither, which is why we need to make more choices. It's time to recruit more members for the Merlyn's Tower Irregulars.'

I got off the stairs, partly to move things on, and partly because I was getting very stiff. 'Are there any clues in the phone as to what sort of Druid Gwyddno might be?'

While she returned to the phone, I returned to Iestyn. I collected his car keys and said, 'Congratulations, old boy. You've just been promoted from traitor to hero.'

Vicky was standing up ready to go, too. 'It would have been a lot easier if the messages hadn't been in Welsh, but looking at Gwyddno's chain of Artefacts in the pictures, he's definitely a Sorcerer and Necromancer. He'll be the one who summoned the Dæmon to quicken the egg. And Myfanwy's a Herbalist/Healer. I have no idea what Rhein does – from the hardware, you'd think he was some sort of mediaeval guerrilla, all swords, spears and bows. New to me.'

'Great. Let's get going.' We started the long climb. 'You never got to tell me how old Surwen was.'

'I must be losing me touch. I thought she was sixty at least, closer to seventy. All that protection magick must have confused me.'

In death, Surwen had looked as she had in life: a trim woman in her mid-thirties. 'Trust your instincts, Vicky. I do.'

We saved our breath until we emerged from the Xanadu Portal to an empty stretch of rock and the rushing stream. I shivered and fastened my coat.

Before I could start my plan, Vicky bent down to the water and dipped her handkerchief in the raging brook. 'I'm gonna wipe the blood off your face,' she said.

It was freezing, and at first I flinched away, but she persisted, and her delicate touch, along with the mountain water, washed way more than a layer of gore.

'Thank you.'

'Thank you, Conrad. You were going to sacrifice yourself in there. I won't forget that.'

'I...'

'Shh.' She put her finger on my lips. 'This time, I get the last word.'

When the moment had passed, I helped Vicky over the beck and took out my phone. There was a signal. Good. 'We need to make some calls, then leg it down to the car park. I want you to ring Rick James.'

'Why me?'

'You need practice in lying.'

She managed a smile. 'Really? There was no mention of that being a Development Need in my last appraisal.'

'We have appraisals?'

'This is the twenty-first century Watch. Of course we have appraisals. What do you want me to say?'

'Keep it simple. Tell him that Iestyn had been working to gain their trust, but that he'd got too close. Right? Now, this is important: in the firefight, say that *he* killed Surwen when she was inside the lion, and that he died in the act. Don't mention my gun. Say we finished off the other lions with Iestyn's sword and your magick. That's not so far from the truth is it?'

'No, but why not tell Rick everything?'

'We need the official story to be that Iestyn killed Surwen. That's crucial for our long-term safety, and we need Rick to believe it when he tells the Council of Druids. We'll tell the real story to Hannah. OK?'

'I like that, Conrad. I can definitely sell that one.'

'Good. And tell him to get over here asap. There may be prisoners before we're finished. Now, give me Surwen's phone. I'm going to call Harry.'

We moved a few feet apart, walking slowly down the hill as we made our calls. The Pennaeth of MADOC answered on the first ring.

'Surwen? Is that you?' He sounded both shocked and angry. He also sounded strong of voice.

'No, Harry, it's Conrad Clarke. Who's with you?'

'Gareth and Bridget. They're good people, Conrad.'

And they weren't in Surwen's phone. Good. 'Are you sure, Harry?'

'I know who it was who did it. All six of them. Gareth and Bridget are not their friends. In fact, Bridget hates Adaryn, though she won't thank me for telling you.'

'Fine. Things have gone badly wrong, and I want to stop them getting worse.'

'In the name of the gods, Conrad, so do I.'

'Tell Bridget and Gareth to get sandwiches, flasks of coffee and a wheelchair. Bring them, and you, to the grove car park. We'll see you in half an hour. Don't talk to anyone else. Anyone.'

'I understand. We'll be with you soon.'

I disconnected, and saw that Vicky was still talking to Rick James. I liked her style – short and factual, no great embellishments. We'd make an officer of her yet. When she'd finished, we were nearly at the bottom of the hill.

'Can you sneak up to the car park and see if there's anyone there?'

'No.'

Oh. I scratched *stealth* from our options and shrugged. 'Fair enough. Let's front it out.'

We climbed the grassy bank and found a white Mercedes 4x4 sitting next to Iestyn's red Fiesta. There were two shadows in the back, and Gwyddno was getting out of the driver's seat.

'Get the kids,' I said. 'Keep them away and say nothing to them. Literally.'

'Right.'

Gwyddno took two steps towards us, his grey hair blowing in the gathering breeze. I engaged my parade ground gear and marched up to him. The look on his face was mostly terror.

In one move, I grabbed his arm, swung him away from his car and dragged him to a low wall. He barely struggled, but Vicky had to use both arms to keep the twins confined.

'Where is she?' said Gwyddno. 'Have you been in the Nest? Is she there?'

I took out the Hammer. 'Do you want to see your girls again, Gwyddno?'

'What do you mean?' Anger was starting to surface. Good. It would come out sooner or later, and the sooner it came out, the sooner I could knock it on the head.

'Iestyn and Surwen are with the gods, Gwyddno.'

'What have you done to them?'

'Me? Nothing. Iestyn was a Watch Captain, not a Druid.'

'He was one of us!'

'Part of him, yes, but most of him knew what was right, and creating Mr Mole was very, very wrong.'

'How did you…?' His anger blew away in a blast of fear.

'Iestyn tried to arrest her, Gwyddno. She could have surrendered, but she fought back. Her and the lions.'

'He was a boy. He couldn't have taken them on.'

'He died a man. He died killing the lion with Surwen's Spirit inside it. They died together.'

I'd got through to him, and I could see just how much he loved her by the light dimming in his eyes. I gave him as long as I could to sink into grief, then it was time to yank him back again. I touched my Badge of Office. 'Do you want to see your girls again?'

'The girls.' He looked at the Mercedes. Vicky was standing with her back to us. Beyond her were two frightened children. The taller, darker one was wearing a thick coat, jeans and walking boots, her black hair whipping round her face unnoticed as she stared at her father and me. The other girl was focused on Vicky and visibly shivering, her pink leggings and denim jacket not offering the same protection, though she did have a matching woolly hat and scarf. As we watched, she leaned in and put her arm around her sister.

Gwyddno stood up. 'How can I tell the girls?'

I took his arm. 'You can't. That's our job. The only question is whether you get to see them again before they're grown up. If you help us now, there's a chance.'

'You can't do that.' He started to pull against me. It didn't take much effort to hold him in place.

At that moment, Vicky reached out her arm to touch the shorter girl, then took two steps back, turned and ran towards us, her face set in a thin-lipped fury. Gwyddno stopped struggling. The girls stayed where they were.

Vicky arrived and steamed into Gwyddno, punching his left arm with a sharp jab. Ow. That must have hurt.

She thrust her finger into his face. 'When were you going to tell your son what you did to him?'

It's not often I'm gobsmacked, but today was one of those days. I stared at the girls until Gwyddno pulled on my arm again. This time, it wasn't to run over to the twins, it was to collapse on to the wall.

Vicky mastered her anger enough to speak. She spoke to me, but in a loud enough voice for Gwyddno to know it was for his benefit as well. 'The one on the left, the little one with the pink hat, that one has a Y chromosome but no … reproductive organs. On the outside, she's physically a little girl, but she won't be hitting puberty any time soon.'

Gwynno's shoulders were starting to shake. I clenched and unclenched my fist a couple of times until I'd controlled the urge to smear his sick face across the hillside. Vicky looked like she was working up to do the same thing.

'Vic? Were the keys in the ignition?' She nodded. I leaned in to whisper. 'Lunar Hall.' She nodded again, and I spoke up. 'Take their phones off them, get them in the car and don't stop until you're out of Wales.'

'When shall I tell them about their mother?'

'When they're safe. Stay over tonight, and we'll meet up tomorrow.'

She gave me a quick hug and a peck on the cheek. 'Unlock the Volvo, Conrad. I need me bag.'

Gwyddno and I watched them leave. He didn't speak until Vicky, his car and his girls were half way to the main road. 'We joined the Brotherhood for her, you know.'

'What Brotherhood?'

'*Brawdoliaeth y Draig*. The Brotherhood of the Dragon. We joined it to get the chance for Surwen to get in the Nest. To find a way of giving Guinevere what Surwen had taken away when she was in the womb. Where have they gone?'

'Somewhere safe. Why, Gwynno? Why did Surwen experiment on her unborn child?'

'To give her a chance of magick. She didn't get the right genes.'

'And you went along with it?'

'She said she'd abort him if I didn't.'

If there was a Charm to raise Surwen from the dead, I would have marched back up that hill, down to the Nest, through the Lions of Carthage and performed it, just to have the pleasure of strangling that woman with my bare hands. What is it with Witches and their children? First Deborah tries to get her daughter joined to the Spirit of Helen of Troy, then Surwen does this. I got out my cigarettes.

'Time to talk, Gwynno. Where's the Dragon?'

He wiped some tears away. 'I don't know. We were always going to move it, because the Nest is sealed with concrete. Bloody Romans. We got a shift on when that Mole broke into the egg chamber. We knew someone would come calling after that. We didn't expect it to be so soon. That's when Adaryn started to bring Iestyn on board.'

'I don't believe you. Where's the Dragon?'

'I'm telling you. I don't know. Adaryn said that some of us should stay here and negotiate while the others looked after the Hatchling.'

'Negotiate what?'

'The Welsh Petition. Magickal independence for Wales. It's what we all wanted.'

'Talk me through the end-game, Gwyddno. How was this going to work?'

The look on his face said it all. The plan didn't sound so good now. 'Iorwen, Rhein and Myfanwy are looking after Welshfire. That's the name of the Dragon. Adaryn was going to release a statement through Iestyn. He was going to take it to your boss.'

'Or what?'

'The threat was London. To release Welshfire on London.'

'You must know that the government never gives in to terrorists.'

'Yes, they do. They did in Belfast.'

Oh … that was a can of worms I couldn't afford to open today.

Gwyddno spoke over my hesitation. 'We knew we wouldn't get it all straight away. Our fallback position was to get a royal commission. That would give the government an excuse to overrule the Invisible College.'

When he put it like that, it almost sounded reasonable. I'll tell you something else that sounded reasonable: the decision to occupy Basra with two men and a dog. Look how that turned out.

He looked at the hillside that covered the Dragon's Nest, and which would now be his wife's tomb. 'If only she'd stayed up top, Myfanwy could have told her you were coming.'

I kept my counsel. A people carrier turned off the main road. 'Hand over your Artefacts, Gwyddno. My CO is on his way to take you into custody.'

His eyes glazed over as he unhooked his chain of Artefacts. I got some rope and a blanket from the Volvo and tied him to a gate before formally arresting him and placing him under a Silence (I can only use a Silence if I'm arresting someone).

When I'd finished, a burly couple were standing by the people carrier watching me. The female – Bridget – lifted a flask and waggled it in the air. I left Gwyddno to his memories and limped over to the warmth of their vehicle and a difficult conversation with the Pennaeth of MADOC.

They let me get warm and fed me before the serious business started. The back seat of Bridget's MPV was no enchanted chair, and she had to sit next to Harry to lend him magickal support. Gareth, a lifelong devotee of the oval ball, sat next to me in the front. Although very much a Druid, Gareth himself had no magick.

Bridget had offered me a box of wet-wipes for me to clean my hands before we ate, and I took another when I'd finished to wipe off the mayonnaise, which for some reason was stickier than blood. When I dumped the wipe in the rubbish bag, everyone knew it was time.

'Thank you for your hospitality, Pennaeth,' I said. I'd already complimented the chef, so my thanks to Harry were protocol. 'You are not my enemy, nor I yours, but I have a problem. I nearly died up there, and I tend to bear grudges when that happens.'

Gareth moved in his seat and stared at me. I let him.

'I accept that you didn't know about the Dragon, Harry, but what did you think was going on? You must have suspected that they were up to *something*.'

Harry looked out of the window towards Gwyddno, hunched under his blanket. 'You tell him, Gareth,' he said, without taking his eyes off Surwen's husband.

'Not my place,' growled Gareth.

'Then I'll say it,' said Bridget. She let go of Harry's hand, and the old man slumped a fraction. 'Harry was a fool,' she continued. 'He let his head get turned by a song on the lips of a pretty girl. He's not the first man to do that.'

'Adaryn is no girl,' I said.

'No, and that makes it worse, so does the fact that it wasn't her body she was offering him. Lust has never been Harry's weakness, has it?'

The old man smiled. 'You make me sound like a monk. There *was* a bit of lust, you know.'

'That's as maybe, but it was mostly pride, wasn't it?'

Harry's hand moved a fraction. I had to strain my ears to hear his whisper. 'An old man's dream of glory.'

We all waited until Harry had moved his hand to Bridget. When she had accepted it, and become his *Deuxième Mère* again, he told me the story.

In Druidic magick, the Bard has a special role as the spiritual and artistic leader of the Order, and their power can multiply the effects of others' efforts in ways not fully understood. Adaryn had come to Newport, to Caerleon, as an up-and-coming Bard, and had taken the Order to the top of the Premier League in two seasons – if you'll forgive the footballing metaphor.

She had almost doubled the size of the Order, and set up a second centre of power in the Old Chapel, away from Newport. Then, after the Eisteddfod a couple of years ago, she had come up with a plan: a lost manuscript was coming on to the market, and she wanted the Order to buy it.

'What manuscript?' I interrupted.

'*The Palace of Rhiannon*. One of the texts on which the *Mabinogion* is based. It would tell us where the Great Queen's palace was built. MADOC would be the richest and most powerful Order in Wales.' Harry had been talking to the hillside. He turned to face me. 'It doesn't exist, does it?'

'The manuscript she sold was real enough.'

'What manuscript?' interrupted Gareth. He was starting to look very alarmed.

'The one the Brotherhood sold for 7,000oz to that Englishwoman. The one about Urien and the Lady of the Fountain.'

Gareth and Bridget started an intense argument with Harry. In Welsh. When I'd dragged them back to English, and calmed them down, a completely new crime had emerged. Harry had avoided telling them about the sale of the manuscript, and Gareth was the Order's Treasurer.

It seems that Adaryn had not only embezzled thousands of Troy Ounces of Lux, she had convinced the Order to borrow thousands more from some Gnomes in Belfast, thousands which had disappeared.

'We're finished,' said Gareth. 'We've got no option but to go to the Council and ask the Order in Cardiff to take over.'

Bridget looked at Harry, hoping for a show of defiance. He looked down and said nothing.

'I think I can help,' I said.

'How?' they chorused.

'No promises, but if you tell me about the rest of the Brotherhood, and grant me a boon, I may have an idea. As I said, no guarantees, but you don't have to throw in the towel just yet.'

'How?' they said again.

'Trust me. I know that's what Adaryn said, but it's that or get on the phone to the Archdruid.'

'What do you want?' said Harry.

'Let me make a couple of calls first.'

I'd told Vicky not to stop until she was out of Wales. By now, the call of nature would be pressing, so I messaged her to ring me when she'd stopped. Then I called Mother Julia at Lunar Hall, and told her to expect Vicky and the girls.

'Of course we'll take them in tonight,' she said, 'but why are you shipping them so far from home, like parcels?'

'Two reasons. First, I think they could be at risk of harm in Wales, and second, I can think of no one better to look after them when they find out their mother's dead, their father's in jail and that Guinevere should be a boy.'

'What?'

When I explained, Mother Julia was as furious with Surwen as I'd been. 'The poor child. I don't know what we can do, Conrad, but yes, Lunar Hall can be their sanctuary.'

Vicky was trying to get through, so I thanked Mother Julia and switched calls. 'How are they?'

'In bits, the poor bairns. Elowen – the taller one – tried to use magick on me while I was driving. I've just locked them in the disabled toilet to stop them running away. I may have to put a Silence on her.'

'Whatever it takes. I trust you, Vic.'

'We'll get there.'

'You will, and Mother Julia's waiting to help you.'

'Good. I need it. How's your end?'

I gave her the ten second version, then said, 'There's something I haven't told you because there wasn't the right moment. Do you remember our conversation about my romantic history?'

'Aye. Where in Nimue's name is this headed, Conrad?'

'Back to school. My first crush was Adaryn Owain, only she was called Imogen Jones then.'

'What!'

'I know. She's changed a bit since, and those murals were quite an eye opener. I didn't get to see that much of her when I was seventeen.'

'OMG, Conrad. Stop it.'

'Quite. Did you find anything valuable in Surwen's lab?'

'I haven't had a chance to look. Hang on. I'll get the twins out of the toilet and call you back.'

It took her longer than I expected, but it was worth the wait. 'There was a sealed Egyptian Tube,' she said. 'It's what the most powerful scrolls are kept in. On the label, it says *The Lions of Carthage, by Quintus Julius Lucis, Autograph manuscript*. If that's true, we're talking 20,000oz, easily.'

'I take it we don't get to keep it.'

'You're joking, aren't you? A find like this goes straight to the Constable. We'll get a reward eventually. Perhaps as much as 50oz.'

'I've got a plan, Vicky, but I haven't got time to explain it now. If you're willing to trust me, we should be able to eat our cake and have it after.'

She hesitated. 'I've got to go. I'll keep quiet about the manuscript until you can explain it properly. See you later.'

I pocketed my phone and got back into the MPV. 'We're good to go,' I said. 'Bridget, can you keep an eye on Gwyddno? Until my CO arrives?'

'I can. Why me?'

'You have magick, and I need Gareth to help me push Harry's wheelchair up the hill.'

The Druids of MADOC had invested in an electric wheelchair for their Pennaeth, so Gareth and I had an easy job until we got to the Wards protecting the sacred grove. Beyond them no electric device functioned properly. We left the chair, and Gareth carried Harry on his shoulders. As we approached the final turn before the grove, Harry started to whisper a song. Gareth joined in, a deep bass that thundered in Welsh to an ancient tune.

The grove itself was the reality on which the mural had been based, and was more dramatic than its image pretended because the image had ignored the central feature – literally at the centre was the chimney outlet which led down to the Dragon's Nest.

The mural had misrepresented the layout of the grove to emphasise the stage, which was actually a side feature, no more than an awning to keep the harpist dry. This was a magickal place of ancient power, and that power radiated from the ring of stones surrounding the chimney. I could imagine the ancient Druids laying their Ley lines to the nest and making sure that the surplus power was discharged into the grove when there was no Dragon hatching underneath.

A cinder track had been laid around the stones and at the northpoint was the wooden throne. Still singing, Gareth carried the Pennaeth to his chair and placed him in it. Harry drew power and sat up straight.

He gave an instruction to Gareth, who walked gingerly between the stones then lit up like he'd been drawn by an enthusiastic animator. If Vicky's academic gown had been a rainbow, Gareth's workaday fleece had just transformed itself into the love child of a glitterball and a lava lamp. He did not look at all comfortable.

Slowly, he worked his way to the slabs that edged the chimney. Bending down, he knelt to approach the void in a crawl. Keeping his head well back, he reached out and grabbed at the empty air. Like the blaze of a lighthouse, a white glow swept round the stones, and Gareth's hand wasn't empty. No, he had hold of a thick staff of aged, yellow wood, and he was straining every muscle to pull it out of the chimney. With an audible pop, he dragged it up and staggered backwards.

Relief made his return to the throne a quick one. He bent the knee again, in honour not fear, and offered the Staff to his Pennaeth. Harry took it, pronounced a blessing and became the Druid he had once been. The woollen robes glowed green, the hair was black, and the hand was as steady as the logs it rested on.

Gareth straightened with a wince and stepped aside. The Pennaeth stood up, strong and resolute in front of his throne, and beckoned me forward. I think Vicky would have knelt, but I'm not Vicky. I came to attention, saluted, then bowed my head.

'Welcome, in peace,' said Harry.

'In peace, I thank you,' I responded, as expected. Beyond Harry's shoulder, Gareth was heading to a low cabin in the trees.

'Is Surwen really on the altar?' asked Harry. I nodded. 'Then in four days, there will be a storm. Lightning will strike, and she will become ashes. Will Gwyddno be able to attend the rite?'

'No, sir.'

He looked round and saw Gareth returning, his red face made redder by the setting sun. We waited until Gareth had laid a steel tray on the path and poured three measures of clear liquid from a clear bottle into stemless silver vessels about the size and shape of a shot glass. Gareth picked up the tray and offered it to the Pennaeth.

'Water,' said Harry. 'From the spring above the grove. The gift of life.' He gripped his staff, looked up and passed his hand over the tray. Green sparks fell from his fingers and winked out as they hit the water.

Gareth took a vessel and intoned, 'The gift of life,' before downing it and offering me the tray.

The folklore of Europe has all sorts of warnings about accepting hospitality in magickal company. According to Vicky, these are all rubbish. Not only is it beyond rude to refuse, it is the most dangerous act possible for any kind of Mage to turn on a guest. I raised the vessel and said the words.

It didn't have the power of Odin's draught, the one that had healed my broken collar bone, but it filled my head with suppressed energy – the sort that you can sense in the woods at this time of year, just waiting for a little more sun to burst into spring. Harry drained the last measure, and Gareth disappeared back to the hut.

'It'll be dark soon,' said Harry. 'What's this deal?'

'It's simple, sir. I have a plan to … leverage some of the people in play here. I think I can leave MADOC out of pocket, but not bankrupt. The risk is mine – if I screw up, you'll be no worse off than you are now, and I'll make that a promise. As any Chymist will tell you, a Clarke's word is binding.'

'Is it now?' He studied me closely. 'There's more to you than I thought, Mr Clarke. What do you want from us?'

'Three things. First, pronounce all six rogue Druids anathema. Expel them from MADOC and petition the Druid Council to put them beyond the pale. Hold the funeral for Surwen, but make sure that MADOC know you're burning her reputation as well as her remains.'

'I can do that. It won't make me popular in many places, but I can do it. Next?'

'I need some paperwork. Gareth can sort it.'

'Fine. What's the third thing. Neither of those counts as a boon.'

'Help me find the Dragon. Nothing can be resolved while that creature's out there.'

'How?'

'How old is the oldest tree in this Grove?'

He pointed west, towards a substantial yew which was leaning over, and although still vibrantly green, had clearly seen better days. 'That yew was old when the infernal Romans sealed the Nest.'

That was just about perfect. That tree's roots would be very familiar with the essence of Dragon. I know that yew isn't the best for dowsing, but this was no ordinary tree. I like to keep things simple when I'm making a pitch, and simple is usually good. However, this is Wales. They like butter on their bread round here, and if that's not a proverb, it should be.

I raised my voice a little. 'Pennaeth. As the bowmen of Wales did great service in a noble cause at Agincourt, let the Welsh yew do service again.' I could see a sparkle in Harry's eye. 'As the yew made great bows, cut me a length to take into battle with the Dragon, a standard to bear.'

The Pennaeth responded in kind. 'That tree gave me my staff, and all the Druids before me. I see you have Iestyn's sword with you. He fell in the service of the Prince of Wales. Take his sword and take what you need. Bring it to me.'

I had to choose carefully. The branch couldn't be too long or too short, and had to be old enough to have both sapwood on the outside and heartwood in the core. I looked at the tree carefully, then realised I was going about this the wrong way. I closed my eyes and span round three times on the spot. I raised the sword and let the tree draw me towards it. Keeping my eyes closed, I swung the sword down and hoped for the best.

A quarter of the way into the swing, the blade bit wood with a crack as loud as the Hammer firing a shot. On the ground in front of me was a metre of branch. I looked back to the circle as the last rays of the sun struck Harry's face. He smiled, nodded and sat down.

Rick James was pacing up and down the car park when we returned with the branch firmly strapped to my rucksack. Harry had added his own blessing to the yew rod before we left. Gareth said it was something to do with passing safely through Welsh lands.

Reluctantly, Rick agreed to take charge of Gwyddno on one condition: I did the death knock for Iestyn's parents.

'If it can wait until tomorrow, then yes, I'll do it.'

From the way his shoulders slumped, I'm guessing it was his first time, and that he hadn't fancied it. He put Gwyddno in his car and we sat in the Volvo with the engine running as night fell. I repeated the story Vicky had told him.

'I still can't believe it,' he said. 'I thought Iestyn was King's Watch through and through.'

'He was naïve, sir. He was a good man, but he hadn't the experience to know where to draw the line.' I could have added that he should have been taught where to draw the line, but Rick James was still Senior Watch Captain. If he didn't know, it would do me no good to tell him.

Rick nodded absently. 'This is a real mess, and no mistake. Well done, Conrad. It wasn't your fault you lost Iestyn.'

'With all due respect, sir, I've never lost a man or woman in my command. This was Iestyn Pryce's command, not mine. I didn't lose him.'

I heard the sharp intake of breath. 'Is that…'

Whatever Rick's first thought was, he kept it to himself. Eventually he said, 'I should see his parents.'

'No. You should get back to London and lock Gwyddno away before anyone tries to rescue him. Ever since Harry and his lieutenants left this car park, we've been vulnerable to attack by the Brotherhood. They'll have sympathisers in MADOC who'll tell them what's going on soon enough.'

'Right. One last thing: why did you send those kids up north?'

'The same reason, sir. They need a safe, neutral space to recover, and so long as only the Watch knows where that is, they might be useful as bargaining counters.'

He gave a short laugh. 'I bet you didn't tell Vicky that.'

'She's not stupid, sir. She'll work it out.'

'Stop calling me *sir*.'

There was a list of things to work out: recovering Iestyn's body, removing his car, when to contact the Archdruid and so on. By the time all that had been arranged, I was very grateful to find that the hotel where we'd stayed last night had a vacancy. I treated myself to a bath before dinner, and had nearly fallen asleep in the soothing water when Vicky made contact.

'How are you? How are the girls?'

'We made it in the end. Elowen finally realised that her sister needed her more than she needed to get at me. The further we got from Wales, the more they clung to each other. They actually fell asleep near Stoke on Trent.'

'It has the same effect on me. Did you get a warm welcome?'

'We did. It freaked me out a bit to see Mother Julia with only one arm, but she's made her peace with Theresa and they took the twins down to their grove for me to break the news about their parents. They're still down there now. I left them to it as soon as I'd done the deed. Their Healer is going to use the grove's power to have a discreet look at Gwen's condition, see if there's anything legal they can do to help. I'm going to tell her about what her mother did to her tomorrow.'

'Good luck. I'm not sure I'd swap jobs with you. I think I'd rather tell Mr & Mrs Pryce about their son than tell Guinevere about what her mother did to her.'

'Why are you going?'

I told her about Rick. I said I'd tell her my plan for MADOC and the Dragon when we were face to face.

'Excuse me,' said Vicky in the middle of a yawn. 'You can tell how tired I am because I'm not gonna pester you about how you met Adaryn, or whatever her name was.'

'Imogen – Immy to her friend. She only had one. Definitely a story to be told over a drink. Goodnight, Vicky.'

At least Hannah waited until after dinner before calling me. It probably took her that long to get the report from Rick after she'd turned her phone back on, it being Shabbos today and all that.

'I assume you didn't tell Rick the truth,' she said. 'And don't bother arguing.'

'No, ma'am. Honestly, he has all the important parts. I only kept back the bits that will help me find the Dragon.'

'Really?'

'Really.'

'Then it can wait until Monday morning. Have a safe journey tomorrow, Conrad.'

'Thanks.'

I was asleep by ten o'clock. At eleven, Hledjolf the Dwarf rang me. For Mr Shorty to make a voice call, it must be important.

'We hear that you are away.'

'I am, but I'll be back tomorrow.'

'We thought you should know that the Mole has begun to disintegrate. We do not understand the chemistry, but he can no longer move out of his nest.'

I sat up straight away. Poor Moley. 'Is he in distress?'

'We owe him a portion of Lux in back pay. We are feeding it to him in a sufficient dose to keep him alive and subdue the pain.'

You'll notice that Hledjolf had answered a different question to the one I asked. Dwarves are good at that. 'How long?' I said.

'He will exhaust his supply on Monday.'

'Then take 0.2oz from it and make a bullet. I'll pick it up tomorrow.'

I didn't get back to sleep until nearly dawn.

20 — A Time to Dig, A Time to Die

The only consolation was that he couldn't smell it. I had to stop and gag half way down the tunnel to his nest. It was truly awful. I took a deep breath to get over the worst and pressed on. From the nest itself, I could hear a woman's voice as I got closer.

'Miss Bennet, you ought to know that I am not to be trifled with, but however insincere *you* choose to be, you shall not find *me* so.'

'Your Worship?' The woman's voice stopped in mid-word, and I entered the nest.

Vicky had explained over the phone this morning that Moley's mitochondria were going on strike. All over his body, newly human bits of DNA were refusing to take orders from Moleish enzymes. It sounded bad. When I got to see him, believe me it looked a lot worse.

Most of his hair had fallen out. His back leg was clearly broken and stuck out at a grossly unnatural angle. His left digging paw was twitching randomly, and the other would have done if he hadn't rolled on to it. Worst of all, even worse than the fluid oozing from sores on his back, was his nose. Half of the tendrils had withered, the rest were limp. Only his eyes looked alive, and that was wrong. So wrong.

'Hello, old friend,' I said, trying to keep the emotion out of my voice. 'What are you listening to?'

'*Pride and Prejudice*. The Dwarf told me you were coming. Thank you.'

'I didn't have you down as a Jane Austen fan.'

'Neither did I, until I found myself with so much time on my hands. What have you brought me?'

There was an edge to his question, but I took it at face value. I'd actually brought a chicken curry, but I didn't think that was a good idea. 'Can you eat?'

'No. The Dwarf's potion takes away hunger, but Mole must drink.'

'Then try this.' I placed a dish in front of him and poured neat 15yr old Macallan malt whisky to cover the bottom. 'I've got water if it's too strong.'

He was just about able to lap up the scotch with his tongue. 'Aaah. So that's what Mole has been missing. More.'

I poured more. I also unfolded the camp stool I'd brought and made myself as comfortable as possible. I took a measure of scotch for myself and lit a cigarette. 'It wasn't a Spirit who created you, Your Worship, it was a human person.'

'Have you found him? If you bring him here, I can use what's left of my magick to punish him.'

'She did other things, too, just as bad as what she did to you. I shot her.'

'Good.'

He rested for a second, then lapped up some more whisky. 'Thank you for this gift. I'm also still wearing your first gift to me.'

It was a bit of tat, a fake chain of office to go with the title I'd given him. He'd taken it seriously and added a Dwarf-made medallion. 'So I can see.'

'It is my only Artefact,' he said. 'I name it to you.' Before I could say anything, he rushed on. 'Will you listen with me to the end of the story?'

'Of course.'

The sound of Rosamund Pike's voice filled the nest. We sat quietly as we listened to Jane Austen giving Lizzie Bennet the happy ending that had been denied to Mr Mole by Surwen's incompetence and by the brutal reality of magick. When the music played at the end, we both had tears in our eyes.

I activated my Ancile, just in case, and stood up, moving to a spot behind his head.

'Will it hurt?' said Moley.

I slipped on the ear defenders, took aim and fired.

'No,' I said. 'You didn't feel a thing.'

I took his chain of office and left everything else for Hledjolf to sell or use in exchange for giving a dignified cremation to the first – and last – Lord Mayor of Moles.

21 — Overture and Beginners

I looked like shit. I know this because people kept telling me so when I arrived at Merlyn's Tower on Monday morning for my debrief with Hannah. Here's a sample:

'Who's died?' — Maxine.

'Oh. You look ... I'll come back later.' — Annelise van Kampen

'Your soul carries a heavy burden today.' — Tennille

And finally, from Hannah, 'You look like shit. Where's Vicky?'

Well, I didn't join the Watch for a hug, did I?

'She's at the City Police with your sister, tracking down Adaryn Owain aka Imogen Jones. After that, she's going to Salomon's House.'

She gave me that evil grin. It's a special grin, only available to siblings. 'You mean with my *older* sister. That was neat work by Vicky. Have a comfy chair.'

Things have come a long way since I had first set foot in Merlyn's Tower. Hannah now trusted me enough to dispense with Vicky's version of events, which is a good job because Vicky needs a lot more practice in lying. I was about to confess to Hannah that I'd used magickal bullets twice over the weekend, and the reason I was doing so was to divert attention from our possession of the Quintus Julius manuscript. If Hannah got a sniff of that, we'd have to hand it over.

When we'd sat down, she surprised me by leaning forward and saying, 'Hledjolf's been in touch. I'm sorry about Mr Mole.'

'Thanks. He's out of pain, poor sod. Surwen's other victim – her own daughter, for goodness' sake – has only just found out that she's got a lifetime of pain to come.'

Hannah rubbed the wound under her scalp and pointed to my bad leg. 'You, me, Mother Julia, Guinevere. At least we're alive.'

I managed a smile. 'That should be my line. Thanks, Boss. Is the Senior Watch Captain coming?'

She stared at the Thames. 'I thought Rick was a safe pair of hands. He as good as offered his resignation last night.'

That put me in an awkward place. What I said next could have an impact on the future of the whole Watch, including me. And Vicky. Mina, even. 'Has he let you down before?'

'No.'

'But he's never had to deal with a Dragon and a terrorist operation before, has he?'

It was her turn to smile. 'No.'

'Then leave him to do what he does best. The other stuff hasn't gone away, Hannah, nor will it. Let Vicky and I track down the Dragon and make it very clear to the Occult Council that the Welsh Petition needs to be at the top of their agenda.'

'Perhaps. First, tell me what really happened under the grove.'

I told her, and I told her why I'd put out a different version straight after the event. She went pale when she realised just how deep Iestyn had got with the Brotherhood, and paler still when I got to the magickal bullets.

'It's a good job you can think on your feet,' she said at the end. 'Get more coffee and have a cigarette while I think this over.'

I met Maxine on the roof, round the side, catching a few rays, and I told her about Mr Mole. She squeezed my arm and changed the subject. Maxine Lambert is growing on me very quickly.

'You do realise that Annelise is scared of you?'

'Me? Why?'

'Because she can't get her claws into you, for one thing, and you're Vicky's friend for another.'

'If being faithful to my girlfriend and my partner makes me scary, she must have a very limited range of interpersonal skills. What did she do with all the women at Salomon's House?'

'Why do you think she came here? Anyway, she needs to see you about Keira. It's important. Try to be nice, and don't say you're always nice, because you're not.'

'Keira? Has she escaped?'

'No. The Undercroft isn't hermetically sealed, but no one's escaped in five hundred years. They used to keep magickal prisoners in Merlyn's Tower, you know, before the Dissolution.'

'No, I didn't know. Keira can wait. One mad bitch at a time, thank you. I'd better get back to the Boss and learn my fate.'

Rick was sitting with Hannah when I got back. I noticed that she'd put him in the third chair, leaving the one opposite her for me to sit in. These things do matter. He looked tired and drawn, white flakes of skin coming off his black scalp, but he still looked better than I felt.

Hannah passed me a note in her handwriting: *Vicky's going to surrender the spare bullet to Maxine tonight. If you procure or use another one without my permission, you're finished. Otherwise, well done. H.*

And if I didn't use one, I might be dead. I tapped the paper against my fingers as Hannah waited patiently and Rick looked confused. 'No problem, ma'am. You have my word.'

'Good. That's what I hoped you'd say. Now, sit down and pour the coffee.'

They discussed Gwyddno's appearance this morning at the Cloister court, and I kept quiet, even though both the Court and Blackfriars Undercroft are still a complete mystery to me.

When they'd finished, Hannah put her cup carefully on the saucer. Rick and I sat up straight. 'I've been thinking,' she said. 'Conrad's a major, in RAF terms, and we should look at his strengths. For a trial period, I'm going to designate him Watch Captain at Large, reporting directly to me. He can lead on situations where the local Captain might need help. If it works, I'll ask the Vicar of London Stone to make it permanent.'

That was a shock. A nice one for me; not so nice for Rick. He pursed his lips, looked at Hannah, then looked at me. He blinked, and I think he remembered then what I'd said about Iestyn being in command of the Nest operation, and that I'd done the death knock yesterday morning. He looked back at Hannah and jerked his head in a nod.

'Good,' said Hannah. 'What's your plan to find the Dragon, Conrad?'

'Find Adaryn.' I turned to Rick. 'It would really help if you give me covering fire, Rick.'

'What do you mean?'

'Go back to Newport straight away and tell everyone you've taken over the search. Be visible. Ask questions. Tell them that Vicky and I have been seconded to Aldermaston to make plans.'

'Aldermaston? The nuclear bomb place?'

'That's the one.'

'There's something else you can tell them,' added Hannah. 'Iestyn Pryce is getting a posthumous Military Cross.'

'Right. That message won't endear the Watch to the Druid community.'

'But it lets them know where we're coming from.'

'I presume it's still down to me to find Iestyn's replacement?'

'Eventually. Let's find the Dragon first.'

On the way out, Rick said, 'Do I have to call you *sir* now?'

'I'm not your commanding officer, Rick. We both work for Hannah. She needs us both, and we need each other. This isn't office politics – it's war, or something like it.'

He stuck out his hand. I was impressed. 'Thanks for seeing the Pryces, Conrad. That should have been my call, and I know that now.' Tennille appeared up the stairs. 'It never used to be like this, you know.'

I smiled at him, but I didn't get to reply, because Tennille held up my expenses form.

'Mr Clarke. A word, if you please.'

We didn't leave London until Tuesday afternoon. I had to collect my upgraded yew rod from Chris Kelly, and we wanted to give Rick some time to start distracting the Druids. Chris said that he'd done the work on my yew branch himself, and that it was only a quick fix. He'd also told me that he'd never seen a dowsing rod quite like it, and that I should invest in getting it fully worked up. Vicky came into the City and picked me up in Surwen's Mercedes.

I ate my lunch and let her concentrate on the unfamiliar traffic in a very unfamiliar vehicle. She didn't relax until we got to the Hammersmith Flyover.

'Seriously. I cannot keep this car in London,' she said.

'Just relax and enjoy the drive.'

'I'm enjoying it, right enough, I just can't afford it. Do you know how much the insurance is on this thing? To keep it, I'd have to pay two grand. Two grand, man, and don't get me started on fuel consumption – I nearly fainted this morning when I had to fill the tank. Howay, Conrad, why don't *you* keep it?'

I was tempted. Surwen had treated herself to a top spec Mercedes GLX 4x4, and by the rules of plunder, it was now ours. The passenger seat was much more comfortable than the Volvo, and it was faster, quieter, newer and much better equipped. It was also incredibly vulgar: no Clarke, not even my upwardly mobile sister would ever own one of these things.

'I'll tell you what, Vicky, if we find this blasted Dragon, and you still don't want the car, we'll put it up for auction in Chipping Norton. There's plenty of incomers who'll snap it up.'

'Where's Chipping Norton? Never mind. If you know somewhere to flog it, then fine. Anyway, I believe that congratulations are in order, Watch Captain at Large.'

'Thank you. Shame there's no promotion to go with it.'

She looked over to me. 'It sends a few messages, that's for certain. I'm not sure you're gonna win any popularity contests outside the top floor, but Hannah clearly trusts you.'

'Us, Vicky. I couldn't do this without you, and Hannah knows that. In fact, it's you that should be worried about the popularity contests. You can get reassigned after Wales, if you want, and I can take some of the less demanding assignments.'

'Nah. I'll stick with me Uncle Conrad for now. So, go on then, tell us again about Immy.'

'No.'

'Go on, Uncle C. Tell us about your first girlfriend again. I'll let you smoke in the car if you do.'

'No.'

'Howay man. All you've told us is that she's a year younger than you, that she went to a girls' school in Gloucester and that she grew up in a rough part of Cardiff.'

'Which was enough to find her bolt-hole in Llandeilo.' I went to turn on the radio as a distraction, but Vicky slapped my hand.

'No Classic FM while I'm driving. What makes you think she'll be sitting at home waiting for us?'

'One day soon, we'll be up against a Mage who truly understands the mundane world and gives a false name to the Land Registry, and when that day comes, we'll be in trouble. Adaryn will be there because she's spent half a million quid refurbishing it, and because Rick James is running interference miles away in Newport telling everyone confidentially that we're in Aldermaston.'

I had another reason for thinking that Adaryn would be there waiting. If I remembered her, I was fairly sure she'd remember me, and from the way that Surwen had gone behind her back to create Mr Mole, I reckoned that Adaryn Owain / Immy Jones would be looking for a way out of the Brotherhood, and that she'd see me as that way out. However, if I'd said all that to Vicky, she'd have accused me of having an ego the size of a Dragon's nest, so I kept it to myself. We'll see.

Vicky wasn't finished, though. 'Are you going to tell Mina about Immy?'

'No. Yes. Probably. You're not going to wear me down, you know.'

She concentrated on joining the motorway, and didn't speak until we passed a sign saying *Cardiff 130 miles*. 'I'm just trying to take your mind off things, Conrad. I'd have been there with you in the Old Network. You didn't have to do what you did for Mr Mole on your own.'

'Yes I did. Not for your sake, for his. At the end, he knew exactly what he'd become, and the shame of you seeing it would have been unbearable for him, and that would have made it unbearable for me.'

'Was it really that bad?'

'Yes. It was awful, Vic. I'll just say this: it's a good job Mina hasn't got into Jane Austen. I'll never be able to watch, read or listen to *Pride and Prejudice* again. Talking of Surwen's victims, how were the twins?'

'Poor bairns. Gwen doesn't quite grasp what's wrong with her, and her sister's furious but has no one to lash out at. I was glad I could walk away, to be honest.'

'Can the Lunar Sisters do anything?'

'Short-term, yes. Medium-term, yes. Long-term … who knows. Magick can't help the big problem, not legally or safely. They're going to start her on hormones and herbs, so at least she'll develop like a woman on the outside. The trouble is the school – Welsh is their first language, thanks to their parents, and they've been home-schooled for the last year. They'll probably stay at Lunar Hall until the summer, but after that…'

She went quiet. I could tell there was something else brewing, and when she didn't continue, I said, 'Spit it out, Vicky.'

'I was so focused on Guinevere that I didn't look properly at Elowen until Sunday. Her mother tinkered with her, too. It was subtle, complicated and she'd been doing it over a lot of years. I don't understand it, nor does Sister

Rose, the Healer. Despite her height, Elowen hasn't hit puberty either, and we think that Surwen was delaying it.'

I had a flashback to Moley's nest and his disintegrating body. A stab of pain on Elowen's behalf shot through me. 'Is she unstable? Will she end up like Moley?'

'No, thank the Goddess. Mother Julia said, "She's like a seed from an exotic country. We have no idea what she'll grow into."'

'That sounds alarming. What are they going to do?'

'Off the record, Julia says there may need to be a binding order that ties her to a Locus Lucis. Sort of like protective custody during her adolescence. She hopes it doesn't come to that.'

'So do I, Vic, so do I.' I paused for a moment, then went back to one of the many loose ends from the Battle of Lunar Hall. 'Do you know if the Sisters ever got hold of Keira's mother? Augusta, wasn't it?'

'No. And neither has Annelise. Not that she's tried very hard, I don't think. As soon as she got written confirmation that Augusta has no magick, she lost interest. You must be rubbing off on me, 'cos I don't like it either.'

'If you're getting more cautious, then I'm glad to be of service.'

We stopped at a service station just this side of the River Severn, and while we waited at the back of the car park for a rendezvous, I dug out the chain of Artefacts I'd removed from Surwen. I passed them to Vicky for a once-over while I had a fag break.

She joined me outside to stretch her legs and said, 'Surwen kept most of her Artefacts at the lab in the Nest. This is mostly storage gold – we'll get at least thirty ounces, I reckon. And then there's this.' She held up a Doodad in a heart shape. 'I don't want to look too closely, but I reckon it's got something to do with Elowen. This needs to go to Lunar Hall, and go soon.'

'Do you think she was using it to hold back Elowen's adolescence? Or worse?'

'Maybe. As I said, it's beyond me.'

I stared at the trees and passed her something else, not wanting to look at it myself. 'This is His Worship's chain of office. Is there anything I should know about it? There was a bit of an edge to his voice when he said I should take it.'

I felt the weight go off my fingers as she took it from me. Everything went quiet for a moment, and then she laughed. 'I don't think you'll be using this. I've never seen anything quite like it.'

I turned back and saw the fond smile on her face. 'Concentrate for a second, Conrad.'

She lifted the chain carefully over her head and patted the intricate medallion at the bottom. My magickal senses tingled, and I got a whiff of moleish halitosis followed by a booming, honking noise. And was that a passing lorry, or did the tarmac just tremble?

'Territory,' I said. 'Moles are nature's most territorial mammals, and this was his way of marking his territory. It's a shame he never got to use it on another mole.' I laughed. 'Only Moley could have come up with this.'

Vicky went to take off the chain, then stopped. She flicked the medallion round so that I could see the back. 'I think there was another reason he wanted you to take it.' Pinned to the back of the medallion was an SD card.

'Well I'll be. I wonder what on earth's on there.' I took the chain from Vicky and stared at the incongruous piece of silicon.

'Conrad. I think this is your Welsh buddy.'

Gareth rolled up in his MPV. There was no one with him, and he got out of the car carrying an A4 manila envelope. I made the introductions.

'Seeing Surwen's poncy car out here's like seeing a ghost.' He shivered, and handed over the envelope. 'Everything's in order,' he said. 'It nearly broke Harry's heart to sign this, but he did it.'

'How is the old devil?'

Gareth nodded. 'Bearing up. You did him a favour, dragging him up to the grove on Saturday. He took a good drink of power up there, and he's hanging a lot on you getting us out of this mess. Good luck.'

'Thanks.'

Gareth nodded to Vicky, climbed back into his car and headed off.

I brandished the envelope. 'The most powerful force known to mankind.'

'Known to *humanity*. Everyday sexism, Conrad.' She gave me her grin. 'Since I've known you, you've used a Kalashnikov, a pistol, a concussion grenade, a sword, a magickal pistol, and you've threatened to use nukes. What's the most powerful force known to humanity, 'cos I don't think there's a hydrogen bomb in that envelope.'

I put my coat in the back and took the driver's seat. 'Money, Vicky. Money is the most powerful force. You'll see.'

Back on the road, she asked if she could stick Moley's SD card in the Mercedes' system. 'At least we'll know what sort of files are on it.'

I passed her the chain and Vicky broke a nail trying to get the card off the back. There was a lot of swearing at that point. I concentrated on the road.

'Right. Let's see what the great bulldozer was up to,' she said, slamming home the card. 'There's a load of MP3 files. The most recent is called *Goodbye*. It looks like he wanted to pass stuff on. There's *The Worms of London, The Man in the Mask, The Red Witches, The Dwarf's Secret Client, The Nest of Spiders*. I hope these are fiction, Conrad, not memoirs. I really do.'

'Why? It sounds to me like he wanted us to know what he'd come across. I'll grant you the titles are a bit Gothic, but remember he didn't have much chance to develop his own literary style. What's the problem?'

'I really, really hate spiders. I'm not proud of it, but I do. The thought of giant spiders underground is gonna keep me awake for a long time.'

I looked over. She was sweating. 'We haven't got time now. I'll play them when we get back to civilisation.'

Back in the driving seat, I also had control of the radio and used my power to put on Classic FM Requests. Vicky whipped out a pair of headphones and stuck them in her tablet. What she was listening to, I don't know, but she seemed to be catching up on her emails while she listened to it.

As we drove through South Wales, I did a lot of thinking, not about our current mission but about the King's Watch in general. Rick James had been in touch this morning to say that he'd recovered Iestyn's body, that it was on its way to Machynlleth, and would I present the MC to Iestyn's parents at the funeral? Rick was overcompensating – presenting the medal was his job, not mine. I'd given a non-committal response, saying that the Dragon had to be top priority. Yesterday, I'd gone in search of the Honour Board for fallen Watch Captains, and couldn't find it anywhere accessible to me. All of this had generated the sort of deep unease I'd felt in Basra, just before it all went pear-shaped. I needed more information and I needed to work out the right questions.

As we approached the end of the M4, deep in Wales, nature treated us to a spectacular sunset, with frost promised tonight, but that wasn't the headline on the weather forecast. As Eleanor Noakes' efficient tones rattled off the news, the hairs on my arms were rising. The Pennaeth of MADOC had promised thunder for Surwen, and Storm Haley was going to deliver. An Atlantic weather front had picked up steam instead of decaying, and it was headed for the west of Britain tomorrow night. The Environment Agency was putting several valleys on the alert for flooding.

Coincidence? A Divine nudge? Was there any way of finding out?

We checked into the Premier Inn at Llanelli – it was only half an hour by car from Llandeilo and well away from prying Druids. We agreed to meet for food in the bar at half past seven, and I grabbed an hour's nap after a phone call to Maxine Lambert.

I ordered a steak pie rather than the actual steak. Tennille had been very clear about the limits of future expenses claims after our discussion on Monday; "nice" hotels were very much out of bounds unless I was willing to pay for them myself. Given our plans, I stuck to mineral water and wondered how to steer the conversation. While I was wondering, Vicky revealed what had been occupying her thoughts.

'Can we trust Rick? He can't have been happy with Hannah promoting you like that.'

'Of course he wasn't happy, but that doesn't mean he was *unhappy*. I trust him to do a stand-up job in Newport and not land us in the shit, if that's what you're asking. He's not a bad man, Vicky, he's just not a leader. I suppose that's the real reason he didn't go for the vacant Deputy's job.' I took a sip of water. 'I spoke to the Clerk earlier.'

'Oh. Did Maxine want you to bring some duty-free fags back from Wales? It certainly feels like a foreign country sometimes. D'you know she got in trouble for violation of duty-free rules in Gibraltar last year?'

'No, but I'm not surprised. I've been thinking, Vicky, and I asked her how many Watch Captains have died in the line of duty since 1945, and how many Mages have died at the hands of Watch Captains.'

Vicky put down her fork. 'Why in Nimue's name did you ask that? And why are you telling me? And why today, for goodness sake?'

'I was thinking about Iestyn on the way over here. We're the Law, Vicky. We should have support from every police force in the country 24/7, not just Ruth Kaplan during office hours.'

'That would be nice, Conrad, but it's not gonna happen, is it?'

'Perhaps it should. Maxine said that between 1945 and 2010, three Watch Captains and five Mages were killed. Since 2010, six Captains have lost their lives, seven with Iestyn. During that time, only one Mage died, plus Deborah and Surwen. Before I came along, that makes a change in ratio from 3:5 to 6:1.'

She took a drink. 'I've never thought of it like that.'

'No, but Hannah must have. Something's wrong, Vicky. That's a significant change in numbers, but I don't know what it means. Yet.'

Vicky stared at her rapidly cooling pasta and pushed the plate away; not only had I killed the conversation, I'd put paid to her appetite. We skipped dessert and went to get ready. By the time I'd changed, the confirmation had come through from Gareth. We were good to go.

'Does Dr Nicola know you've been raiding her gym bag?' I asked when Vicky appeared outside. Her outfit was too long in most places and too tight in others. At least it was black.

She blushed. 'Aye, well, there was dead lion all over me other stuff. I threw it out. And I got the car valeted – that was another fifty quid. You should give me half for what you just said.'

I opened the boot of the Mercedes and put in my new cricket bag – it was the only thing that would hold all the bits and pieces I was accumulating. I pushed the button to close the boot and said, 'There was dead lion, dead mole and dead Watch Captain on mine. That's what a washing machine is for.'

'Don't. You'll make me heave. Who's driving?'

'Me. When we get close to Nyth Eryr, I need you to watch out for Wards.'

We got in and I punched the code into the Satnav. Nyth Eryr means *Eagle's Nest* in Welsh. Apparently.

'I still don't see why you made me dress up when the plan is to talk to her,' said Vicky. 'It's alright for you, Mr Outdoor Man.'

'Remember what happened at the Dragon's Nest. We went in without gathering all the intelligence, and look what happened.'

'You don't think being led by a turncoat was the problem?'

'If I'd pushed Iestyn harder before we went into the Nest, he'd have given himself away. I want to know all about Adaryn's hideaway before we drive up to the front door. Besides, I need to test my new dowsing rod.'

We drove up to Llandeilo, through the little town and out to the north-east. I stopped half a mile from Nyth Eryr, up a country lane and just past a dairy farm.

'There's a public footpath over there,' I said, pointing to the right. 'It'll take us out of sight of the house.'

'How do you know that?'

'I checked the contours on the map. There's a ridge that'll hide us.' I might as well have been speaking Welsh for all that she understood what I'd said. 'I'm sure there will be a 3D map rendering App in the near future, so why should you learn now when you've got me to do it for you?'

She leaned across and punched my left thigh, because my left shin was out of reach. 'If it wasn't for you, I wouldn't need to go outside at all. Let's get on with it.'

I packed my rucksack and put it on my back. Vicky made sure she had the manila envelope and her Lightstick. 'Are you not taking the AK47?' she asked innocently.

'If anything looks dangerous, I intend to run. I've also invested in a close quarter option.'

'I can't wait.'

I led us across the road to the stile, and it became abundantly clear that my natural night vision is much, much better than Vicky's, because she slipped into the ditch.

'Eurgh. Me shoes are all icky and squelchy. Bugger this.'

'Doesn't matter now, does it? Let me hand you over the stile.' Once on the footpath, she powered up her Lightstick, and I walked in front until it was time to get out the dowsing rod and cut across the field towards a wood.

There were no Ley lines before the wood, and I had to lift her over the dry-stone wall.

'We'll never get through them brambles,' she moaned. I got out my close-quarter option. 'My god, Conrad. Is that a machete? That cannot be legal.'

'It is. The blade is less than 50cm, so it's legal to buy and sell. Carrying it is another matter. I'll cut a path then come back for you and the dowsing rod. Don't worry, the brambles will only be at the edge of the wood.'

I hacked through the undergrowth, and even I had to use a torch after the first few feet. The wood spread all over the hillside about Nyth Eryr, and slap in the middle, my new dowsing rod twitched like a phone on vibrate. 'Eureka! Brilliant! I've found it, Vic.'

'I'm glad one of us is happy with their new toys.'

'I bet Li Cheng's never taken you on a date like this.'

She took a swing at my bad leg, missed, and kicked a substantial beech tree. 'Ow! Me foot! I swear, if I thought for one nano-second that this was a date, you would so be history by now. For the love of the gods, Conrad, does Mina have any idea what she's letting herself in for?'

'I hope not. Let's keep quiet, now, shall we, and kill the light? I'm going to follow the Ley line downhill to the boundary of Adaryn's property.'

If Chris Kelly had been wielding the yew rod, he'd no doubt have told me the capacity, design and age of the Ley line. All I could do was follow it to a low wall topped with a wire fence. Beyond it, I could sense the land drop away. I stowed the dowsing rod and got out an image-enhancing mono-optic. I stood up and looked down on Nyth Eryr.

Adaryn hadn't skimped on landscaping. The natural slope beyond the wall had been terraced into ... terraces. With seats. I passed the scope to Vicky.

'What the fuck's all this?' she whispered.

'A natural amphitheatre. I reckon she's planning to unveil it as her personal concert venue and – if it's possible – create a new Locus Lucis.'

'It's possible, alright. What's that by the house?'

'Concrete footings. I reckon that's where the stage will be and maybe a green room or something.'

'Talk about blowing your own trumpet.'

We turned our attention to the house: a brand new, two storey farmhouse-style building in slate. We breathed a sigh of relief when we saw lights on downstairs.

'Are there any Wards?'

Vicky returned the optic and used her magickal Sight. 'Only a faint one. It would keep out the Ungifted, and trigger a warning, but no more.'

'Good. Let's get back to the car – we can follow this wall down to the road. It won't take long.'

Ve were back at the car in no time, then Vicky insisted on changing her shoes and socks. I'm surprised that the dairy farmer didn't come looking for us with a shotgun. I wonder how he would feel about his lane becoming an access road to Adaryn's personal Eisteddfod. Probably quite happy if he thought there was money to be made in parking on his fields…

'Ready, Vicky?'

'Ready. Let's go.'

There were big iron gates at the entrance to Nyth Eryr, and they were wide open. On top of the pillars were stone eagles. I could hear my mother sniffing her disapproval all the way from Spain, and in the background I could hear my father rubbing his hands at the thought of all the tat he could sell to someone who thought stone eagles were a tasteful addition to their home.

'Impressive,' said Vicky.

'If you ever become rich, I'm going to introduce you to my father.'

'Eh?'

'Because you're his ideal customer. Are there any Wards, or is this really wide open?'

'Just the tripwire and general discouragement, like at the wall.'

We passed through the gates without even registering the magick. The drive wound round the hill and opened to reveal the house and, out of sight behind some trees, a levelled-off area with portable toilets, a portakabin and other signs of building work. I parked the Mercedes facing the drive for a quick exit and activated my Ancile. I left the machete behind.

As we approached the front door, floodlights blazed on, and I flinched instinctively. When no assault came, we continued walking. I noticed that Vicky moved away from me, ever so slightly. Just enough to make two targets, not one. She's a quick learner, all right.

The door opened, and a figure was silhouetted against the light.

'Conrad Clarke, as I live and breathe,' came the lilting, husky Welsh voice. Her accent had grown a lot stronger (or reverted) since we'd last met.

I cleared my throat and did something I rarely do when not part of a crowd: I broke into song.

Oh is there not one maiden breast,
Which does not feel the moral beauty
Of making worldly interest,
Subordinate to sense of duty?

Adaryn roared with laughter. Vicky snorted with suppressed wonder and sheer incomprehension. I think.

'That certainly broke the ice,' said the silhouette. 'I'm touched that you remembered. Come in and take your shoes off.'

She disappeared inside, rapidly vanishing into some inner room. I stepped over the threshold into an impressive double-height hallway with galleried landing and feature staircase. I lowered my voice. 'I went to a boys' school and Imogen went to a girls' school. Every year we did a joint production, and every year none of the boys were good enough to sing properly. We were more into sports.'

'I can believe that, but I cannot believe that you just burst into song. What on earth were you doing?'

'*The Pirates of Penzance*. Imogen played Frederick as a Principal Boy. She brought the house down, big time. I was the stunt co-ordinator. I taught her how to sword-fight.'

'Seriously?'

'Seriously. I had a crush on her from the previous year, and I thought I was in with a chance, but something had changed and she didn't fancy me any more. Looking back, it may have been the magick growing in her. Either way, when Immy didn't succumb to my charms, her friend soon did.'

'Every time, Conrad. Every time I think you can't get more outrageous, you do.'

'Glad to live up to your expectations. Come on, we're letting the cold in.'

I slipped off my boots, and Vicky did likewise. Without thinking, she leaned on me for balance as she hopped about. Without thinking, I put my hand on her shoulder. Adaryn chose that moment to return with a bottle, and her eyes narrowed when she saw us together. Vicky, her back to the room, didn't notice.

'Come through,' said Adaryn. 'Did you wait until I was alone?'

'Not as such. Who was here?'

'Just the staff. I've only got three at the moment.'

Vicky muttered something, and Adaryn noticed her muttering.

Now that she wasn't in shadow, I got a proper look at the real-life Bard of MADOC, not the mural, and not my imperfect recollections of a teenage girl. She wasn't built like a Valkyrie, but she did have a big chest. You couldn't miss it with the low-cut dress. Surely she couldn't have been lounging around in that, could she? It was a blue ball-gown, silk and full length, swishing on the floor because she wasn't wearing heels. It wasn't full-on opera, but it was definitely evening wear. Did she put it on when we triggered the Wards? The waist was perfectly fitted, her arms exposed, and her hair (black and lustrous) was long and loose. Her adult face was heart-shaped and lovely, and if I'd been the Pennaeth of MADOC, I'd have prostrated myself before her. Good job she's not my type.

The reception room beyond the slate-tiled hall had new oak boards for its floor and full height windows hidden behind curtains. The room was big enough to accommodate comfy seating for a dozen guests and the focus of the layout was neither a TV nor a fireplace. It was Adaryn's golden harp.

'Wow,' said Vicky. 'What a beautiful instrument.'

'Do you play? Anything?' It could have been a polite question, but Adaryn put an edge to it that had Vicky confused.

'Sorry, no. Not my thing, really. Conrad likes the classical stuff.'

Adaryn turned to me. 'You also like Islay malt whisky, I hear.'

Vicky was confused, and now I was, too. How did she know that? I certainly didn't like Islay malt when I was seventeen – we all drank cider. 'I think of you every year, Imogen, on the 19th of September.'

Adaryn joined us in confusion. 'Why? The show we did was in December.'

'International Talk Like a Pirate Day. I raise a glass to you every year.' Adaryn and Vicky both gave me strange looks. I don't blame them. 'Talking of raising a glass, how do you know about the Islay malt?'

At that moment, Adaryn made her first big mistake. 'Oh, Clara from the Usk View Hotel told me.'

I could hear a low rumble. A harmony of low rumbles. Both Vicky and I were sub-vocalising our outrage at the betrayal. Clara, proprietor of the hotel we'd stayed at on Friday had betrayed us. No wonder Iestyn had paid the bill. I tried to swallow my anger for now and said, 'No thanks.'

Vicky added, 'We won't be accepting your hospitality.'

'I thought you could have done better,' said Adaryn, pointing at Vicky. 'Someone should tell her that Lycra is not a good look with her figure.'

I said nothing. If there was going to be an apocalypse, it had to be of Vicky's making. Somehow, she managed to say nothing either.

When the moment passed, and when Adaryn had put down the scotch, I said, 'It's time to wrap this up, Imogen. We've come to offer you a deal.'

'No thanks.'

Eh? Either she had something up her non-existent sleeve or she was bonkers. Vicky was leaning towards the latter.

'You haven't heard it yet,' said Vicky.

'I'm not dealing. I've got a statement for you, though. It goes roughly like this: In light of what I've learnt about the actions of Surwen and Gwyddno, I dissociate myself completely from their project to raise a Dragon, and will lend my support to any search that may be undertaken to find the beast. How's that?'

'About 120 hours too late,' I said. 'If you'd said that when we went to see the Pennaeth, when Iestyn was still alive...'

'Still wouldn't have been enough,' said Vicky. 'Leastways, not for me.'

Ouch. Adaryn ignored her. Another mistake.

'We've got some news first,' I said. 'The Pennaeth called a full gathering of MADOC tonight. You won't have heard yet, but they've declared all six of you anathema. You are cast from the circle and barred from the Grove.

There's an emergency meeting of the Druid Council on Thursday to consider a total bar. The Archdruid will be calling the King's Watch to speak. My colleague will have to speak in English, since your friend killed the only Welsh speaker on the Watch.'

'No. He wouldn't,' said Adaryn. 'Harry wouldn't do that to me.'

'Yes, he would,' said Vicky. 'And he did. Do you want to see what he said in the grove? I've got the text message here.'

Adaryn swept across the room, as you can only sweep if you're wearing a silk ballgown. When the edge flicked up, I detected a pair of slippers. She had got changed to meet us, then. She picked up a phone from one of the sideboards and checked for messages from her remaining friends in MADOC. I savoured the look on her face as she read them.

'You bastard, Conrad. It won't stick.'

'Yes it will,' said Vicky. 'You're finished, unless you take this deal.'

She made her way back across the room. 'What deal?' she said to me. I said nothing, because Vicky needed to get this one out of her system. So far, she was doing well.

'Surrender,' said Vicky. 'The Pennaeth will allow you to petition for return if you tell us where the Dragon is, and if you make Atonement for what you've done.' She chose that moment to get out the manila envelope, and waved it in the air to make sure Adaryn had seen it. A bit dramatic, but fair enough.

'I don't know where the Dragon is. I can't help you. The whole operation was designed to work independently once the Dragon left the Nest. I have no idea where they are. As for Atonement, I suppose I could do that. It'll be up to Harry.'

'And you reckon you can wind him round your little finger, don't you?' said Vicky. 'A token act of Atonement and business as usual. Sorry, Immy, that's not on the table. We need the Dragon.'

Vicky was going well off the script, now, but I wasn't going to stop her. This was too much fun.

'It's Adaryn. You call me Adaryn Owain, in accordance.'

'You're Anathema. I can call you what I want, you blowsy tart, and no, this deal's off the table.'

Adaryn went red and blotchy all over her exposed arms and chest. She also surged forward and made a grab for the envelope. 'Give that here, you horse-faced pikey.'

It was important that Adaryn didn't actually seize the envelope, and I didn't want Vicky to lose a fight, so... 'Captain Robson! Enough!'

Both women backed off. Adaryn was wound up, yes, but Vicky was a coiled spring wound right to breaking point. If she didn't get the next bit right...

'Captain Robson, these are not our papers to give or withhold. We're only the messengers.'

'Sir!' That's my girl. Vicky performed the penultimate act of our plan by pulling the papers out of the envelope. They had to be accepted openly...

'Adaryn Owain,' she spat. 'Do you accept these documents?'

Adaryn's internal alarm bells *should* have rung loudly at that point. They didn't. She took the papers from Vicky with a disdainful, 'Yes.'

'Read them through,' I said. 'We'll be outside.'

We waited until we were in the hall before we high-fived, and waited until we were shod and lurking outside before we spoke.

'Well done, Vicky. I don't know how...'

Vicky was in tears. 'The bitch. The moon-faced fucking cow. Fuck her. Fuck all the Welsh sheep-shagging bitches.'

'Here. Have a cigarette.'

She breathed out and closed her eyes, then shook her head at my offer. I lit up anyway. The dinner at Usk View last Friday had been very pleasant: just us, two other guests and the hosts. At one point, Vicky had mentioned that her mother was a second generation settled traveller who had broken with her family when she left her husband to escape domestic violence. That tidbit had gone straight from Clara to Adaryn and been turned into an insult. I hoped I never got to see Vicky that upset again.

'How long shall we give her?' asked Vicky, forcing herself to get back on track.

'If she hasn't just dumped them on the couch, she should be coming back around now.'

The heavy door was open a fraction, and if Adaryn had worn the heels to go with her dress, we'd have heard her coming across the slate tiles. Instead, the door was flung back and the papers waved in our faces.

'What the fuck is this? Which one of you came up with this idea?'

'Him,' said Vicky. 'You should have slept with him when you had the chance. He's ever-so nice to his exes.'

'Conrad, come back here and explain this. Leave the poodle outside.'

I turned my back on the door. 'Fancy a coffee, Vic? I brought a flask.'

'Aye.'

'Fine. Both of you come in.'

We stepped back inside. 'I think coffee really is a good idea,' I said to Vicky. 'Would you mind finding the kitchen while I go through the legal niceties?'

'Just this once.'

I told Adaryn where Vicky was going. She gave a nod of assent and pointed to a pair of couches flanking a coffee table. I sat down and weighed her up: she wasn't ready to absorb the contents of those papers yet.

'Tell me. How did you end up at a girls' school in Gloucester rather than with the Druids?'

'Chapel,' she said, bitterly. She blinked at me and came to a decision: she was going to talk. Whether that was because I knew her as she was, or because she was going to turn on the charm again, I don't know. She kicked off her slippers and drew her feet on to the couch, settling the dress around herself.

'I never knew my Dad, and my Mam should never have been a mother, or not at that age. By the time I was five, I was with my Gran and Mam was off the rails completely.' She looked at a picture in the far corner of the room, looking into the past. 'It's a cliché, and all that, but it's still true. Apart from keeping me safe, Gran did me two favours. First, she put me in the only Welsh speaking school around, and second, she didn't take me to a psychiatrist when I started hearing the voices.'

'Oh? Is that common?'

She turned back to me and made scare quotes with her fingers. '"The link between schizophrenia and magick is tenuous, but it does exist." That's what the Minister said. Gran was the last of the fierce Chapel generation, which probably explains why my Mam turned out like she did. I was always musical, Conrad, and I was in all sorts of choirs. One day, I heard a different voice singing in my head, and I joined in. The next thing I know, I'm in front of the Minister and his friend, trying to explain myself. The Minister's friend thought I had a Gift, and both of them knew about the Druids. They also hated them.'

'You know I'm still the newbie in this game, don't you? I still don't even know what happens to Roman Catholics, never mind Methodists.'

'Baptists. Gran was a Baptist. They're all signed up with the Invisible College, have been since the 1820s. I was taken to Salomon's House, assessed, and offered a scholarship to that school in Gloucester. It was the nearest sanctuary school to Wales. Some fucking sanctuary.'

I cast my mind back to the summer after *Pirates of Penzance*. 'You left, didn't you? You didn't stay for sixth form.'

'No chance. Have you any idea what it was like to be the scholarship girl from Cardiff Docks? The one with no father and a tart for a mother? The only thing that stopped me topping myself was the music and magick teacher who arrived when I was fourteen. She was brilliant, and she was Welsh. Before she turned up, all I'd learnt was how to detect Lux and open locks.'

'That's just about all I've learnt, too.'

'Are you really that rubbish? You can't be that bad if they've made you a Witchfinder.'

'Yes I can, I just happen to have powerful friends, one of whom has one eye and lives in Asgard.'

'So I hear. Are you two still…?'

'Not at the moment, but we've got each other on speed-dial.'

She laughed. 'What a thought. Tread carefully with that one.'

'I will. Did you turn me down because I had no magick?' In the background, Vicky emerged from a door, carrying a tray. She stopped to listen.

'You weren't my type at the time,' said Adaryn. 'Margaret – the music teacher – was a raging lesbian. That's what she called herself, by the way: *raging lesbian. Lesbian in a rage*. I sort of followed her lead for a while. It kept me away from boys like you.'

My eyebrows furrowed. 'She didn't abuse you, did she?'

'Just because she was gay? You should know better than that, Conrad. She took me, in flagrant breach of the rules, to a Druid gathering that Christmas, just after *Pirates*. I never looked back from that moment. In the summer, I left school, changed my name and reinvented myself. The rest is history, mostly engraved on trophies at the Druidic Eisteddfod.'

Vicky took that as her cue to rattle the tray. She brought it over and passed out cups, pointedly not asking Adaryn if she wanted milk or sugar. The Bard took neither, and sat up again.

'Tell me this is a joke, Conrad. I didn't get far, but this looks like a writ for damages. What's going on?'

'That's exactly what it is: MADOC are suing you. Because you're Anathema, you can't be tried for embezzlement, but you're still liable for damages in court. They're suing you for all the Alchemical Gold you stole from MADOC, and they've petitioned the court to make over those debts with the Belfast clan to you as well. The Druid Council, despite the Welsh Petition, still recognises the Cloister Court. I said I'd arrange a special sitting, with a Welsh Judge, if necessary. You'll cop the lot, Adaryn. They'll hang every ounce round your neck.'

'It wasn't just me!'

'On paper, it was. If you want to sue Gwyddno and the others in their turn, you're more than welcome.'

Vicky spoke up. 'What did you know about Gwen?'

'You mean Guinevere, as in the twins? What are you on about? And where the hell are they? I can't find out a thing about them.'

'They're safe. What do you know about them?'

She looked genuinely confused. 'Gwen's a nice kid, lovely voice. I don't do lessons, but I made sure she had a good teacher, and I've brought her along to all my masterclasses. Obviously, we won't know if she's going to be a Bard until she matures.' Vicky and I breathed a sigh of relief. 'Why? What's the problem?'

We'd discussed this, and decided that if Adaryn was ignorant, she should stay that way. On the off-chance that the twins returned to Wales, they had a right to their biological privacy. It also made Adaryn much less complicit in Surwen's evil acts.

207

'Never mind,' I said. 'Back to business. You've done very well for yourself, Adaryn. I'm impressed, and I'd love to hear you play that harp one day, but...'

'We're here as officers of the Court, as well as of the Watch,' said Vicky. 'We can take you into custody if we think you might flee the jurisdiction.'

Her face turned down. 'Did you to rehearse this?'

'No. We're just partners, that's all, and your associate tried to kill us on Saturday.'

She looked from me to Vicky. 'Yet you're still sitting here. Why do I think this isn't over?'

'Because the fat lady hasn't sung, yet,' said Vicky.

'*Body confident*, Vicky, not *fat*. And she's neither, anyway.' I took a deep breath. 'First, Adaryn, I want to make it clear that any deal we do is dependent on you helping us find the Dragon. If I discover you've left anything out, the deal's off, and that goes retrospectively. Clear?'

'Abundantly.'

'Vicky? Show her the goods.'

My partner dug out the Egyptian Tube from her pocket. Adaryn recognised it straight away. 'We rescued this from the Lions,' said Vicky. 'And it's not in our report. If you co-operate, we'll say that it was yours, and that you surrendered it to the Court voluntarily, as security against your debts.'

Her eyes widened, and didn't leave the manuscript container. 'But that's worth a fortune. Why? Why haven't you handed it in? Or kept it?'

'Because I'm willing to bend the rules, not break them,' I responded. 'That scroll should be in the Esoteric Library, and if they have to pay for it, they can afford it. We'll get the Dragon, you won't be ruined for ever and the secret of the Lions can be guarded. All in all, a win-win-win, wouldn't you say?'

'I want it sealed now, before I say anything.'

'No dice, Adaryn. I said this was retrospective. If you deal fairly, we'll seal the deal when we've found the Dragon, not before. You'll just have to trust us.'

'Drink to it.'

I looked at Vicky; she nodded, then said, 'Not whisky. I'll have gin.'

Adaryn rose from the couch. 'You do have *some* taste then. I'll get the drinks.'

She paused to check her phone again. It looked like more bad news, and whatever it was, it made her determined to get on with it. She rapidly poured three neat drinks and thumped them on the table.

'A deal's a deal,' she said. We echoed her and drank off a measure.

'Tell me about the operation,' I said. 'Just tell the story and we'll ask questions.'

'All right. It was in three parts, and we're up to stage three. I found the manuscripts for dealing with the Lions of Carthage, for the location of the eggs and for summoning VOLAC. Surwen did that stupid thing with the mole, but it didn't work, so we got help de-coding the cipher. Once we'd got the egg, Surwen got into the Nest and penned up the Lions, Gwyddno summoned the Dæmon and Myfanwy looked after the egg until it hatched. We moved the Hatchling straight away, and that was the end of Surwen and Gwyddno's involvement. Surwen said that she had stuff she wanted to do in the Nest.'

Vicky and I exchanged glances. 'Carry on.'

'Iorwen – you know she's an artificer, right?' We nodded. 'She made a cage to transport the Hatchling, and she'd sorted a cave somewhere for it to grow. She and Myfanwy have been looking after it. Iorwen's also been making the spear and shield.'

We looked lost at that, and Adaryn knew that she'd come to the end of our knowledge. She took another drink. 'Three of us, me, Iorwen and Rhein, are the only ones who know the full plan, and we made sure it stayed that way. Myfanwy thinks we're going to let the bloody thing loose, you know. She wants Dragons to take their place in the "Original Ecosystem of Albion." It was her who gave it the name *Welshfire*. Bloody tree-hugger. Surwen and Gwyddno knew that it was going to die, but not how.'

It was a shock to hear one Druid calling another *Bloody tree-hugger*, but there you go. 'How is it going to die?'

'I wanted the Royal Commission set up, with me on it. It would have catapulted me on to the top table of the Druid Council in one move. That was my price. Iorwen was different, she did it for her son.'

'Her son? No one said anything about them being related.'

'Rhein. He doesn't call her Mummy, but she's his mother. She wanted him to be the first Dragonslayer in a hundred generations, and I was going to propose he be named Warleader of the Druids. We haven't had one since the Romans. To do that, Iorwen is making a Dragonspear and Dragonshield. You wouldn't take on the Dragon without them.'

Vicky smiled. 'Conrad wants to use a nuclear warhead.'

'God, man, are you insane?' said Adaryn. I said nothing. 'I suppose it would work... Anyway, Welshfire is in a nursery cave.'

'What's a nursery cave?' asked Vicky.

'What do you know about Dragons? Or more to the point, where did you get it from?'

Vicky named the compendium that Desirée had been studying. Adaryn shook her head. 'Barely scratches the surface. Not that I'm an expert, or anything, and the real expert is no longer with us. Everything I learnt, I learnt from Surwen. As did the others.'

A horrible thought struck me. 'She didn't interfere with Welshfire, did she?'

'No. Too dangerous, she said. In a way, I'm glad she's gone – I'm fairly certain she would have had a go with the next one.'

'Small mercies, I suppose. Go on.'

'A Dragon goes through three stages: Hatchling, Wyrm and mature. A Hatchling has no fire and a Wyrm has no wings. When it can fly, it's considered mature. You probably knew that.'

'We knew it had to spend time underground. We didn't know about the Wyrm part.'

'That's because it doesn't last long. You've seen the blocked up tunnel in the Nest? When an egg is quickened, that tunnel should be filled with specially prepared firewood. The Wyrm has to burn its way out. Once it's loose, it hunts around the area until its wings are fully formed. That's when they're hunted – before they can fly. That's what Rhein is going to do.'

'Tell me you're joking,' said Vicky.

'I agree with my partner: letting a fire-breathing monster loose on the countryside is the worst idea I've heard in years.'

Adaryn shrugged. 'Part of the deal. Put it this way, I wasn't planning to watch. You're a Chymist, Captain Robson. What do you know about Aristotelian elements in magick?'

'I know a fair bit. Conrad here knows nothing.' She spoke to me. 'It's all about Earth, Air, Fire and Water, but more than that: there's Hot, Cold, Dry and Wet, too. It's all been replaced by Quantum Magick these days, which is why it's in the history section of the Occult Curriculum.'

'Another small mercy,' I said. 'Please don't tell me we're in for a long explanation.'

'Dragons are ancient,' said Adaryn. 'Their very nature is bound up with the Elements. A Dragon is beyond heat – its nature is pure Fire, and that's its weakness. A shield or weapon of pure Cold will be immune to Dragonfire. Up to a point.'

'Those aren't the sort of odds I'd go into battle with,' I said. 'I normally prefer better than *up to a point*.'

'The Wyrmhunt is as much a rite of passage for the Dragon as the hunters. In history, a whole group of young Druids would take part in the hunt. They'd give the Wyrm time to escape and to feed. The hunt could last for days, and it was common for the Dragon to survive and for most of the Druids to die. Dragons would be extinct if they didn't have a chance – and they're intelligent. They wouldn't play along if the odds were stacked against them.'

Vicky was bug-eyed. 'That's tantamount to suicide for the hunters.'

'Yet they still find volunteers for suicide bombings,' I chipped in. 'In most of history in most of the world, the life of young men has been cheap. In some places, it still is.'

'He's right,' said Adaryn. 'Iorwen doesn't feel that way, though, especially when it comes to her son. She's going to stack the odds against Welshfire. According to Surwen, that is. Rhein knows nothing about it. He thinks it's going to be a fair fight.'

Mothers and their magickal children. Again. 'What's she going to do?'

'Release it early, before it's fully grown. It should take days to burn through the stack of wood in the tunnel. According to Surwen, they've only ordered enough for a few hours.'

'*Ordered?*' I said. 'They've bought it?'

'Two trailer loads of fresh pine trunks.' There was an air of defeat about her now; she'd just given us the piece of intelligence she'd been squirreling away.

'Go on.'

'Iorwen made a joke of it. They bought the wood from Dragon Forestry Products.'

'Do you know anything else?'

She shook her head. I believed her and stood up. 'We're going to lodge the Julius manuscript with Rick James,' I said. 'In a sealed box, of course. He'll have instructions to give it to you if something happens to us. Here's the Keyway.' I placed a strip of metal on the table.

She nodded. 'Thank you. I did wonder how you'd keep your side of the deal if you'd been fried or kebabed.'

'I don't plan to be either, Adaryn. Could we use your bathroom before we go?'

'There's one off the hall.'

Vicky left without a word, and waited while I used the facilities. When it was her turn, I went back to Adaryn. She was crying.

'It was a lie, wasn't it? Harry isn't going to let me make an Atonement.'

'No. You should be able to clear your debts, though. I brought you this.' I handed over a screenprint from the Amazon bookstore.

She studied the printout. '*Teach yourself Irish Gaelic.* Kick a girl while she's down, won't you?'

'With my bad leg, I don't do so much kicking any more.'

'Yeah. I noticed that. Get in a fight with a Dwarf, did you?'

'The Taliban, actually. I was trying to say that where there's life, there's hope, Immy. You got out of that school. You can get out of this mess.'

'You're right, but it won't be Ireland though.' She found a tissue and dabbed her eyes. 'Brittany's the place for me. Welsh is related to Breton, and the scene is growing there. I don't even need to learn French – they all speak English. And don't call me *Immy* again, Conrad.'

'Sorry. And good luck. I will hear you play one day, Adaryn. I'll bring my girlfriend and leave Vicky at home.'

'Probably a good idea. Good luck with the Dragon, too.'

'Thanks. One last thing – where did you get the manuscripts from?'

'I picked them up here and there.'

211

'Don't lie to a liar. If the Bard of MADOC had found Dagda's Harp, I'd believe you, but I don't believe you stumbled across the complete *How to Find, Breed and Raise a Dragon*. Try again.'

She stood up and shivered. The temperature was dropping rapidly. She swished across to a cupboard and took out some sweats pulling on the hoodie over the ballgown. 'I'd rather die in Blackfriars Undercroft than tell you where I got those, and that's the truth. In fact, I'd rather drink bleach than tell you. Or anyone.'

That was a bit extreme. A shadow in the arched doorway told me that Vicky was back. I turned to go.

'Take the scotch, Conrad. I can't stand the stuff.'

I didn't turn round to respond. 'That's very generous, Adaryn, but no thanks. If you'd offered me a bottle of gin as well, I'd have taken them both.'

Vicky gave me an ear-to-ear grin from the doorway.

23 — An Amouse Bouche

Rick James was waiting for us in the hotel bar when we got back. I got two doubles, one for me and one for Vicky. Rick said he was on orange juice. While I stood at the bar, Vicky told him what we'd learnt, leaving out the part about the manuscript.

'So what's your plan?' he said at the end. To give him credit, he asked both of us, not just me.

'It's very simple,' I said. 'Tomorrow, we'll scope out the timber yard. Very, very carefully. Meanwhile, you continue to cause distraction while waiting for every Watch Captain that Hannah can spare to rendezvous at the Royal Hotel in Avonmouth. It's only half an hour from Newport, but very much *not* in Wales. When we've got the intel, we plan an assault on the nursery cave.'

'*Every* Watch Captain?'

'Every one that she can spare from life-or-death duties, and who can get there by five o'clock tomorrow. She also needs to have a word with the Prime Minister. Oh, and we want to bring one of the Druids on board.'

'What did she say?'

I looked blankly at him. 'Vicky told you what Adaryn said.'

'I mean Hannah. What did the Boss say when you told her your plan?'

'I haven't told her. I wanted to run it past you first, Rick.'

'Oh. Right. Which Druid?'

That's why he wasn't a leader: the least important part of the plan was the Druid.

'I rang Harry. MADOC are on good terms with the Order in Swansea, who have a member in South Wales Police CID. She'll pull out her warrant card at Dragon Forest Products and ask who's bought two loads of tree trunks. Harry doesn't know what I want her for.'

'Then it sounds like a plan. It's the Secretary of the Cobra Committee who deals with all magickal emergencies, not the PM.'

'Even ones that might require nuclear weapons?'

'Don't go there, Conrad. That's not going to happen.'

'I bloody well hope not, Rick, but if that Dragon matures… Do you want to tell the PM that we need to borrow a nuke, sharpish?'

'Borrow?'

'We don't have any small ones. Not since 1992. We'll have to borrow one off the Yanks.'

He shook his head. Vicky had reluctantly accepted the ultimate contingency plan. Rick, not so much. 'Do you want me there when you … take down the Dragon?'

I nodded to Vicky, and she brought out a box she'd borrowed from Salomon's House. The Julius manuscript was sealed inside.

I looked Rick in the eye. 'Yes and no. I need a witness, and I need someone to keep our side of the bargain with Adaryn if things go tits up. If anything happens to Vicky and me, ask yourself this question: did Adaryn hold anything back when we spoke to her? If the answer's no, give her this box. If the answer's yes, then kill her.'

'Eh?' That was Vicky. 'You didn't threaten her with that, Conrad. You just said that the deal would be off.'

'Then I'll leave that up to Rick. Come on, Vicky, let's go and Skype the Boss. If all goes to plan, Rick, we'll be meeting up tomorrow night, if we don't get flooded out. Have you seen the weather forecast?'

'Yeah. See you.'

We left Rick to finish his orange juice. He was staring at the box when we walked out of the bar.

The girl in the office went very quiet when we walked in. Our tame Druid didn't mess about: she flashed her ID badge and said, 'Detective Sergeant Helen Davies, South Wales Police CID. I need to ask someone a question about a delivery of raw logs.'

Dragon Forestry Products was bigger than I expected – the yard alone covered a couple of acres of the Neath valley, and there was a factory building, too. The offices, however, were small enough for everyone to share and share alike.

'Greg!' said the girl. 'It's the police.'

She scuttled off into the background, and a rather distracted man in his forties came to the front. Helen introduced herself again, and Greg woke up. He pointed to us and said, 'Who are these two?'

'MI5,' said Helen curtly. 'They're not big on real names. Just answer a question and we'll be gone.'

Greg's eyes widened until he realised he was staring at us. He went red and looked back at Helen. 'How can I help?'

'March last year, someone ordered two full trailer loads of raw tree trunks. A one-off order. You can't get many of them.'

'We don't. It was ordered by a building contractor, but someone paid cash in advance to guarantee delivery. Is this really a matter of national security? The woman who paid didn't look like a terrorist.'

'They never do,' I said sagely, in my poshest voice.

'Right. Hang on.' Greg commandeered the receptionist's computer and did a quick search. Ten seconds later, he handed over a Post-it note with the name of the contractor, delivery address and a vehicle registration number. 'Davey's in the yard, or should be. That's his lorry. He delivered it, if you want a word.'

Helen took the note. 'Thank you for your co-operation, sir. This has to remain completely confidential until you're told otherwise. Not even the rest of the office can know about it.'

'I understand.'

Helen scanned the note, passed it to me, and led us into the yard. She stopped to look at her phone. 'You guys find the driver, yeah? I'll catch you up.'

I read the delivery address: *Upper Tawe Valley. Ring for directions*. I shrugged and passed the note to Vicky. She shrugged, too. 'Over there. They look like wagons for transporting whole trees.'

We were bending down, checking number plates, when Helen strode over, coat flapping. There was a noticeably stronger breeze this morning, and potential gales forecast with the storm tonight. There was a stormy expression on Helen's face as well.

'What's going on?' she demanded, waving her phone. 'I've just heard that MADOC have declared Adaryn Owain and another five of their lot to be Anathema, for being complicit in the murder of Iestyn Pryce. I cannot believe Adaryn had anything to do with this – she's an artist, not a murderer. In Rhiannon's name, Clarke, what's going on?'

'We're trying to stop a Dragon,' I said. 'That's confidential, of course.'

She shook her head. 'I'm not stupid – there are no Dragons. You're just using me to track down the five Druids.'

'Find the Druid, find the Dragon,' I said. 'Ring Adaryn and ask her, if you don't believe me, and it's three we're after, not six: Surwen is with the Goddess, Gwyddno's in custody and we've dealt with Adaryn. As I said, the most important target is the Dragon.'

'You've dealt with Adaryn Owain? What happened? What have you done. Is she hurt?'

You can tell a lot about someone's priorities when they hear really bad news. Helen Davies was clearly a big fan of the Bard (unlike Vicky, who was rolling her eyes). 'Don't worry, Helen,' I said, 'Adaryn is fine. She'll sing again soon enough. And you're right – she had no direct involvement in Iestyn's murder. The Dragon, on the other hand…'

'Oh. Why didn't you tell me? And don't give me that *need to know* rubbish.'

'The deeper I get into Wales, the more I feel like I'm in enemy territory. Harry said I could trust you, but I'm getting paranoid. I'm sorry.'

She set her mouth in a grim line, pulled out her warrant card and tapped the back. 'I took an oath, too. We're on the same side, Clarke. Don't forget, Wales voted Leave; we've more in common with you than you realise. Neither of you are from London, are you?'

'Village near Cheltenham,' I said.

'Newcastle upon Tyne,' said Vicky. 'As if you hadn't guessed.'

'Then us three have got more in common with each other than we have with them in London. It's a fact.'

'It certainly feels that way,' I said, nodding. Vicky kept her own counsel.

'Then let's find this Dragon.' Helen pointed to the one truck we hadn't examined. 'I think that's Davey. Sir! Excuse me!'

The man stopped with his foot on the step to the cab. He looked over and saw us, then shut the door and walked to meet us half way. He looked an affable sort, mid-forties, sandy haired and stoop-shouldered. 'Are you after me?' he asked, somewhat surprised.

Helen announced herself, then told him it was a *very serious matter*. She passed him the Post-it note and asked if he remembered the delivery.

'Yes, officer, I do. Very unusual to have a one-off delivery of unfinished trunks.'

'Good. Where exactly did you drop them?'

'Right up the top of the Swansea Valley, in the National Park. I had to ring for directions.'

Vicky and I exchanged glances. The driver *thought* he'd answered our question, when he'd said exactly nothing. This is what happened when something was *Occulted*.

Helen hadn't got there yet. As most of her interviewees were mundane, she probably just thought he was thick. 'And where *exactly* did you go, sir? What directions did they give you?'

Poor Davey wanted to help. He really did. 'I stopped just before the National Showcaves Centre 'cos there was somewhere safe to pull in. I rang the number, and they gave me directions. I followed them to the site.'

Before Helen could lose patience, I stepped forward. 'Can you describe the site?'

'Sure. It was by a run of old cottages, probably built for a lime kiln, they were, in a little valley. Looked derelict now, but they had all sorts of construction plant at the back. I had ever such a job turning round. Ever so tight it was. They got me to drop the whole load by the side of the track.'

Helen was being patient with me, so I tested it a bit further. 'Did you speak to anyone? Did they say what was going on?'

'I only spoke to the site manager – woman, it was. Hard hat and everything. I remember that because you still don't get many women running construction jobs. She was pleasant enough, said they were going to move the logs on a little flat-bed, one at a time. Something to do with floating them on a marsh. The lads on the diggers must have been having their break. Or a day off. She was the only one around.'

'Can you remember what she looked like?'

'Attractive – sorry. That's not appropriate is it?'

Helen gave him a smile. 'If that's how you found her, sir, then who are we to judge? You should remember her, then.'

'Mmm. Quite young to be a site manager – no more than forty, I'd have said. She looked almost exotic, you know, dark skin, dark eyes, black hair, not like your average girl from the valleys. Didn't think much of her tea, though. Herbal stuff, it was.'

The penny finally dropped for Helen. 'Thank you, sir. This is a highly delicate matter. If you could keep it to yourself…'

'Of course.' He climbed into his cab, and we adjourned to the Mercedes.

'Gave the other builders the day off and slipped him a potion,' said Helen. 'I'm surprised he remembered the site.'

'It's hard to make someone forget something when they're standing there,' said Vicky. 'Making him forget the directions would have been a lot easier.'

Detective Sergeant Helen Davies, Druid of Swansea, was not a forgettable person. She was large, fair of skin and hair, and combined empathy with determination. If I had to sum her up, it would be *maternal powerhouse*.

'Caves,' I said. 'Davey mentioned the National Showcaves. Do you know the area?'

'A bit. The Western Beacons are riddled with caves. There's a huge one up there that my old station went down for a charity fundraiser. Not my cup of tea.'

'But exactly where you'd warehouse a Dragon.'

Helen moved her coat from underneath herself to get more comfortable. 'If they're using Occulting like that, it must be serious. What exactly's going on, Mr Clarke?'

'Conrad, please. Excuse me asking, but what's your involvement with the magickal side of the Order in Swansea?'

She laughed. 'You mean *How much Gift have you got?* If you need to ask, you can't have much yourself.'

'He hasn't,' said Vicky. 'And he's got great big feet. He loves to put them in things. He wouldn't have asked if it wasn't important, though.'

I gave an apologetic grin. 'Normally she hits my bad leg when I'm out of order, so I'll take that.'

Helen sighed. 'I'm just part of the chorus, that's all. I did a bit of Sorcery when I joined the Order, but I gave it up to join the police. That won't stop me coming with you, though.'

'I'm not sure…'

'…Sod that, Conrad. I'm not due on shift until two, and I can easily find an excuse to be late. Get driving and tell me what's going on.'

I looked at Vicky. She nodded her agreement. 'What about your car, Helen?'

'My useless son can pick it up, so let's get going.'

'Fine.' I took a quick look at the map and worked out a route. 'You tell her, Vicky. I'll drive.'

We were climbing the Inter-Valley Road, crossing from the Vale of Neath to the Swansea Valley, and it had gone very quiet in the car. The last thing Helen had said was, 'Lions? Real lions?' To fill the silence, I asked Vicky to call Rick and update him. He said in reply that six Watch Captains were on their way to the hotel. Helen went even quieter.

Vicky twisted round to face the back again. 'You don't have to come with us. I signed up for this – you didn't.'

There was a pause. 'You're not going to attack or nothing?'

'Why no, pet. This is just reconnaissance.'

'Then count me in. If I can help, I want to.'

'Good,' I said. 'Welcome to the Merlyn's Tower Irregulars.'

'You what?'

'Forgive my colleague,' said Vicky. 'He went to a boys' school and spent twenty years in the RAF. He likes to give things nicknames, and *Merlyn's Tower Irregulars* is just his name for everyone who helps us out.' She turned to face me. 'If he had any more magick, we wouldn't need them.'

'So I don't get a badge or nothing?' said Helen.

'Don't encourage him,' said Vicky, with some force. I actually thought that badges were a good idea. Maybe one day.

We crested the top of the road, and South Wales spread itself before us. The nearby fields were bathed in early spring sunshine, but now that we could see the horizon, we could also see Storm Haley on her way. The extra trip to Neath Retail Park for proper waterproofs was going to be a good investment. It was a shame that Helen wasn't so well equipped.

Something from last night had been bugging me. 'Vicky, you remember what Adaryn said about Aristotelian magick?'

'Aye. What about it?'

'How did that work? I presume that the Laws of Nature haven't changed since classical times.'

Vicky settled back in her seat. 'It was only a few lectures, just for background on the old texts. Your pal Chris Kelly taught it, so I can't say I was on the edge of me seat.'

'I won't have a word said against him.'

'I'm joking, man. He's not a bad lecturer, really, it's just that we have different views on the what makes an interesting subject. And by the way, the jury's still out on the Laws of Nature. Even some mundane scientists think they might have changed. A bit.'

'But the world has always been made of atoms and stuff, right?' That was Helen, from the back.

'Right. Chris said that the old magick is like old metal-working. People have been making steel for centuries, good steel, and they were able to vary the carbon content without ever knowing what carbon was, or even why they needed limestone and charcoal to make iron. They just got on with it. Once atomic theory came along, metallurgy became a proper subject, and that's when the Bessemer process was discovered, and all that stuff. And no, I haven't the foggiest idea what the Bessemer process is.'

'I do,' said Helen. 'My Dad worked at the plant in Port Talbot. Not that it's relevant.'

'Back to Aristotle...'

'Aye. Basically, it's all in the head. If you think in terms of Air and Fire, and you've got the Gift, the magick works. Most Circles outside the Invisible College still teach that way, am I right, Helen?'

'That's how I learnt. It was a long time ago, mind.'

'It gets more complicated at postgraduate level, and that's one reason I joined the King's Watch – I couldn't be bothered to get me head round the way the flow of Lux can be used to affect any other force – electromagnetic, strong, weak. Gravity, too, according to some. Never seen it meself. Anyway, it's mostly electromagnetic. A good Mage, no matter how they learnt their magick, can use Lux as a...' she waved her hands a bit. '... As a *meta-force*. Make opposites repel, change polarities. That sort of thing.'

'Wow,' said Helen. 'Is that really what they teach in Satan's House? Oops, ohmigod, I'm sorry. I didn't mean it.'

'Eh?' That was me.

Vicky went red. In the rearview mirror, I could see that Helen was even redder.

'Conrad's never heard that before,' said Vicky. 'It's what the Circles, especially the separatist ones, call Salomon's House. The radical protestants used to call it that, too, before they signed up.'

'Oh.'

The road dipped, we entered the Swansea Valley, and I pointed to a brown sign which said *National Showcaves / Dan-yr-Ogof, 10m*. It had a picture of a cup and saucer, too. 'Coffee. Map. Plan.'

'And fag,' added Vicky.

'If you insist.'

'Why are we doing this outside?' said Vicky, with a noticeable shiver.

'I thought you Geordie lasses were immune to the cold.' No, not me. That was Helen. Vicky gave her a dark look.

'I think we're done with the plotting,' I said, folding the map. 'We can finish our coffee inside, and I rather fancy one of those scones. Might be a long time before lunch. Could you do the honours, Vic?'

She held out her hand. Mutinously.

Helen had already taken the temperature of our working relationship, and instead of offering to pay herself, burst out laughing. I gave Vicky a twenty pound note and retreated to the lee of the visitor centre where I could smoke in peace.

I'd taken a quick look at the information display inside when we arrived, and had discovered that the caves were mostly in a strip of limestone that ran east-west on either side of the river Tawe. Assiduous Welsh cavers had mapped and tracked all the interesting ones, which left us looking for somewhere quiet, off the beaten track and which *might* have a cave. I'd noticed that the main road turned away from the valley, towards Brecon, leaving a tiny road to follow the river. I reckoned that we should start there, and as soon as we'd refreshed ourselves, that's exactly what we did.

In the lull before action, we discovered that Helen was married to a drummer turned plumber and had two children. The older, a boy, had neither Gift nor any form of intelligence whatsoever (according to his mother). In his defence, he was the one picking up her car from Dragon Timber, and also the one whose YouTube channel had paid for their last holiday. Her daughter was nine, and her potential for magick unknown. The whole family were nominally Druids.

Helen was about to explain what her useless layabout son got up to all day when I decided that the clouds coming over the hill were getting a little too dark, and ushered everyone back to the Mercedes.

We all got a bit nervous when we strapped ourselves into the car, though none of us wanted to show it. Vicky had her rugged tablet on her lap, and I passed the map to Helen, more to give her something to do than anything else. We passed a car park and sign to the Beacons Way long distance footpath. I knew exactly where it led, but asked the women anyway.

'Over the hills and far away,' said Helen.

'Avoids the Tawe Valley and climbs quickly,' added Vicky.

'Besides, our lorry driving friend didn't get his rig up there,' concluded Helen.

I drove on another quarter of a mile and took the left turn, leaving the A4067 behind. Away from the junction, the new road quickly became a lane, just big enough to fit the milk tanker.

'Losing signal,' said Vicky. 'And I don't think we'll get it back while we're in the valley.'

'Damn.' I drove another hundred metres and started to turn around in a field gateway.

'What are you doing?' said Helen.

When the car was pointing the right way, I twisted round to face the back. 'I'm going back to the main road and dropping you off.' Her face told me this was not being received well. 'Sorry, Helen, but I've got no choice. We need someone back there to update Rick James, and to keep an eye on traffic going up and down this lane.'

'You're just getting rid of me.'

'Up to a point, yes. You haven't got the gear for being outside in this storm. Be honest, Helen, do you even wear a Persona?'

'I… No. I don't. It would be too much to wear all the time, and I don't deal with magickal criminals. That's what we have the King's Watch for.' She thumbed the well-padded door handle. 'You're right, you're right. Take me back.'

'You should get a car brought up to you,' said Vicky. 'There's nowhere to shelter down there. You might have an hour before the rain comes.'

I drove down to the junction, discovered that the Mercedes' turning circle was bigger than a Hercules Transport, and finally came to rest. A last thought struck me as Helen said her goodbyes. I slipped out and tried to open the boot while she wasn't looking, but DS Davies is too good a copper.

I picked up my spare waterproof to give her, and found her looking over my shoulder.

'The last time I saw so many weapons in a car, we'd just busted the biggest drugs ring in Swansea. Why, Conrad? Why?'

The Hammer was at the side. I picked it up, showed her the Badge of Office and said, 'It's because they won't let me carry magickal rounds. Yet. And because people keep trying to kill me. If you know the Druid rep on the Occult Council, tell them to vote to arm the Watch. On St David's Day. Here. You can have this.'

Her own coat was good enough for winter in the city, but wouldn't last five minutes in a storm. She accepted my offer, and fiddled with the neoprene shoulder belt that held her police issue kit. From under her arm, she extracted a bright yellow plastic pistol – the X26 Taser. 'I'll do you a swap,' she said. 'This is totally non-magickal and dead easy to use. Just click off the safety and fire.'

Why hadn't I thought of a Taser?

'Are you sure? I promise not to use it unless I have to.'

'Go on. Hop it, Conrad. I'll be here.'

'Thanks.'

Having seen the narrowness of the road, I got Vicky to drive. Half a mile up, we passed a farm, and the hedges closed in even further. I told her to stop.

'Why? There's nothing here, man.'

'Bear with me.'

I took a good look at the verges on both sides. The delivery of logs had been made last summer, just before the end of the growing season, and there would have been lots of heavy plant to move out afterwards (assuming it was hired). Sure enough, although the winter had filled it in a little, there was lots of scarring from HGV wheels.

We were still close to the river, but I could see the road climbing ahead, hedges soon to be replaced by stone walls. At that moment, Haley drew a curtain over the sun. The leading edge of the storm would be with us very shortly. I got back into the car and said, 'We're definitely on the right road, and not too much further. Still no signal?'

She checked her tablet. 'No.'

'Then take it as slow as you can.'

She put the car in Drive and took her foot off the accelerator. We moved forward at a steady 4mph, both of us opening our Sight.

'There,' we chorused to each other

'Gotcha,' added Vicky, pointing to the left. The road curved right, quite sharply, and a chevron sign was placed to point this out.

The sign was an illusion, and the road actually divided, carrying straight on as well as bending right. Ahead, it became a track heading down to the valley.

'Let me get out, then shove the car in the hedge and let's take a look.'

Vicky took me literally, destroying half a hawthorn bush and ruining the Mercedes' paintwork. There was just enough room for another vehicle to get past, not that we'd seen a single one. I took the map and stood just outside the magick.

'Someone's been planning something for an awfully long time,' I said. 'You can use Occulting to change the Internet, but this map is at least ten years' old. See? There's nothing here, no tracks, no buildings, no abandoned workings. Nothing.'

Vicky examined the map. She examined it again when I pointed out where we were (she'd been looking at the wrong place).

'Wards?'

'None. Not here,' she said. 'This is a very effective Glamour because it fits with the road. I'm guessing the real action is away from here, which would make a Ward too difficult to sustain.' She looked hopefully back at the car. 'We're not going to walk, are we?'

'Not yet. If nothing else, I want to be equipped for a quick getaway. That's assuming our transport can actually go off-road. I'll drive from here.' I paused to look over the valley. Most of it was wooded near the river, and there were no buildings in sight. 'This is an awfully big target, Vicky, and I somehow get the feeling we're missing the big picture.'

'Isn't a Dragon a big enough picture for you?'

'You're probably right.'

The Mercedes nosed through the Glamour with a tingle, and we were suddenly invisible to anyone coming behind. I crossed a cattle grid into an open pasture, then alarmed Vicky by driving off the track and sweeping round. 'I'm going to reverse. All the way to the target, if necessary.'

Long-distance reversing is a knack. The first rule is never look over your shoulder – that's what wing mirrors are for, and the Mercedes came with a pair of TV sized beauties. After two hundred metres, the track swung west, down the hill and into a wood.

'I hope there's a bridge in there,' said Vicky.

'There will be.'

And there was. There was also another Glamour, hiding the bridge and making the river Tawe look twice as wide as it really was. 'No Ward?'

'No.'

I nodded. 'We'll risk another quarter of a mile, then head back. That should give us a small enough target to deploy the troops when they get here.'

Beyond the bridge, the track twisted a couple of times, then opened out at the edge of the wood. I stopped the car, pulling it slightly off the track. 'On foot from here. I think there might be buildings ahead.'

The trees had been sheltering us from the first raindrops. By the time I'd opened the boot to get my rucksack, we were pulling up our hoods and grabbing our waterproof trousers. It was going to get dark very early in the valleys today. At least no one would have heard us coming.

We moved apart and walked slowly to the edge of the trees. There was a ruined cottage on the right, a stream on the left, and behind the cottage was a green Volkswagen Golf. I touched Vicky's arm and pointed. 'Look familiar?'

'No. Should it?'

'I reckon it belongs to Myfanwy. It was parked outside the Old Chapel when we met with Harry Evans. When we came out, it had gone.'

Now that we could see beyond the wood, I cast my eyes around. The stream had cut a large but shallow cleft in the hills, and the road disappeared ahead. It was definitely wide enough for a delivery of logs.

'Hey, Conrad. There's something moving in the car.'

'Eh?' I peered at the vehicle. Vicky was right. In the front seat was a figure. I couldn't make out any face, but it was rocking and shaking. The passenger window was open a crack, and the figure was on that side. 'I think we need to take a look,' I said. 'You go round the back of the old cottage, I'll go up the front. If you see anything suspicious, shout loudly and run for the car.'

'Right.'

I gave her a few seconds to move off, then approached the car, keeping close to the ruined cottage, scuttling under windows (as much as I could scuttle with my leg), and jumping past the gaping door.

As I got closer to the car, I could see that the figure in the passenger seat was humanoid, and had a hood over its head. The rocking motion appeared to be an attempt to get the hood off by rubbing it on the central pillar. I saw the whole thing as a dumb-show, because the rain was bouncing off the roof, the road and every flat surface in sight.

Vicky appeared from round the back. I motioned her to take the driver's door, and moved round to the passenger side. It was only when I saw the hands, tied and bound, that I realised what was happening.

'Vicky! It's a goat! Run!'

Maybe it wasn't the best choice of warning. Vicky looked up, frightened but not understanding that this person had been tied up to lure us into a tiger trap, just like the goats in India. Before I could shout *Trap!* she was blindsided by a blur of movement, like a lorry hitting a pedestrian. She didn't even have time to scream before she hit the dirt.

I backed away from the car and the building, trying to get a sight of Vicky without getting too close. I heard a scream over the rain, then I saw what had flown out of the cottage and smacked into her: a man.

Vicky was face down in the mud. From her back rose a mad vision in blue. Rhein, son of Iorwen, had painted sigils all over his body with woad, the ancient blue dye, but these weren't just body art, they were Runes and Charms. His chest was crossed by an X-shaped leather harness but was otherwise bare. The twenty-first century intruded itself below his waist, with black running tights and fell-running shoes.

All that I saw in a glance, then I looked at his hands. The right was empty, the left was wrapped in some sort of cloth, and from his fingers dangled the chain from Vicky's neck. He had knocked her down and taken all her magickal Artefacts. I did the only thing I could do: I ran like fuck.

24 — A Tasting Menu

Why did I run? Because my only usable weapon was in the Mercedes, because I didn't have my Ancile active, because I was exposed in the open and above all because Vicky was still alive. It would have been far easier for Rhein to have killed her, but he'd chosen to capture her, and he'd chosen her not me. I'd have attacked me first. I looked over my shoulder. He wasn't following. Yet.

I reached the car and grabbed the machete and the large torch, leaving the Taser in my pocket for now. I didn't bother with the AK47. The only other thing I needed was the black balaclava.

I activated my Ancile, then worked round through the trees to approach the cottage from a different angle. This time I really did scuttle, keeping low and checking the building constantly. When the corner of the car appeared in view, I dropped to a crawl. I needn't have bothered.

From around the corner, Rhein pushed Vicky, her hands bound behind her. He was prodding her in the shoulder blades with a spear. *A spear! In Odin's name, what the fuck is he doing with a spear?* There was also a round shield on his left arm that practically glowed with Lux.

'Come out, Clarke!' he shouted. To add to his message, he prodded Vicky again. She jerked forwards and fell. Her back shone white where the spear had ripped through her waterproofs, and I could make out red lines. The bastard had already cut her.

I stood up, showing myself clearly, and walked slowly towards them. Rhein stopped prodding Vicky with the spear (which was why I'd shown myself), but he kicked her down with his foot when she tried to stand up. From the way she looked around, Rhein had put a Silence on her, a fact that became clear when she saw me approaching and screamed something, her mouth moving but the words disappearing into the magick around her. I came to a stop with six metres between us. I peeled back the balaclava so that he could see my face clearly.

'Put down the machete and unhook your Artefacts,' said Rhein. 'Then lie face down.' His voice was as lyrical and powerful as his body. It was a good job that Vicky couldn't see and hear him or she'd have fallen down in a swoon at his feet. Even I was a little bit in awe.

'No.'

That threw him. He curled his lip and prodded the spear toward, but not into, Vicky. 'Do it.'

'No. You were under orders to capture her, and until Mummy turns up, you won't kill her. Let's wait until the grown-ups arrive, then we can have an adult conversation.'

Rhein was about twenty-one, we'd thought. He had a confidence that was born of power, self-belief and hard training: this boy was faster, stronger and fitter than I'd ever been in my life. He was also still a boy, and my jibe about *waiting for Mummy* had struck a nerve.

He bared his teeth in feral anger. A real psychopath, no matter what their orders, would take this opportunity to torture Vicky. Rhein didn't. I clung on to that thought.

'Who's in the car?' I asked.

He rested the end of the spear on the ground, and I noticed that there was mud on his trousers, and that it wasn't being washed away by the rain: a Charm to keep you dry. Very useful in Wales.

'I think we'll wait,' he said. Score one for the boy.

'Look, Rhein,' I said. 'No one's died here. Yet. The cavalry aren't round the corner, but they're on their way. They know where we've been looking, and I hate to say this, but the Druids won't help you. You're already Anathema in Newport, and soon every Druid in Wales will turn their back on you, and a lot of them will want to join the hunt.'

I'd hoped for fear. Instead, I got anger. 'You'll both pay for this,' he said. 'We'll deal with the Council afterwards.'

I saw rather than heard the others approaching. The wind and rain absorbed the sounds of vehicles, but their headlights cut through the storm-dark valley as they approached. Three quad bikes led the charge, followed by a Range Rover Sport. The car stopped behind the cottage. The bikes swept across the grass and drew up next to the Volkswagen behind Rhein and Vicky.

The quad bike riders dismounted. The one at the back, the only one wearing a helmet, abandoned his bike and walked over to get into the Range Rover. From the other two bikes came a brace of female Druids, complete with (dry) white robes. They stood in a line with their Hunter. I was definitely going to have to explore that anti-rain Charm. On Rhein's left was a short, slight woman with dark hair and dark eyes, last heard of as the site manager when Davey delivered his logs. It was his mother, Iorwen.

Her I was expecting, the other one I'd hoped not to see again. On Rhein's right were the unmistakable curves of Adaryn Owain. At least she wasn't smiling.

'I'm sorry, Conrad,' she said. She touched Vicky with her boot. My partner flinched, cut off as she was in Silence. 'This one, I don't care about,' continued Adaryn, 'but you need to know that there was only one thing I wanted to do less than kill you.'

'Oh? What's that? Break a nail? Get laryngitis?'

She looked upset. 'You tried to help me, Conrad. Thank you for that. The only thing that's making me kill you is that the alternative was to gargle in bleach. I'm not doing that, not even for you.'

So that was it – whatever situation she'd gotten into to acquire the Dragon and Lion material was scarier than me, and if we were dead, the Julius manuscript would clear her debts. The image of a sad-faced Rick James handing over the Egyptian Tube at my funeral was a kick in the soul.

None of this had meant anything to Iorwen or Rhein, who clearly had a very different agenda. It was as thin as a cigarette paper, but if I could widen that gap between them...

'Which one of you bastards killed Surwen?' said Iorwen. Her looks were exotic, yes. Her voice less so: it had a screechy edge to it that didn't go with the Welsh accent.

'Iestyn killed her. They died together,' I said.

'Liar. Iestyn wouldn't have turned on one of his own,' she hissed.

I was furious on Iestyn's behalf, and I spat on the ground in front of Iorwen, something I've never done to a woman before. 'He was one of *ours*. He died a Watch Captain, at the hands of your mad friend, Lady Frankenstein. Do you even know what she did to her son?'

'What son?' said Adaryn.

'Guinevere.'

'Hey?'

'Come on,' said Iorwen, looking down. 'We've got dinner to prepare.' *She knew. She knew what Surwen had done.* The gap between the Druids had just gotten a little bit wider. Everyone jumped when the landscape was lit up by a huge flash of lightning, and everyone except Vicky jumped again when the thunder crashed down.

Iorwen bent down and grabbed Vicky, hauling her to her feet and patting her waterproofs. When she'd found Vicky's phone, Iorwen pushed her towards the bikes. Adaryn followed, and Rhein stood his ground.

I moved to the right, trying to circle round. This forced Rhein to give ground until they were clustered by the bikes and the Volkswagen. One of the quad bikes had an attached trailer, the sort of thing you see Border Collies sitting in on a working farm. Or bales of hay. Iorwen shoved Vicky into the trailer, heaving her legs up and squashing them down. With the quick hands of a master crafter, she tied Vicky down with bungee cords like a sick ewe.

Iorwen then jogged to the Range Rover. I saw her hand Vicky's phone through the window and bang on the roof. The 4x4 shot off. Of course – if anyone looked for Vicky's mobile signal, it would now show up moving away from the Tawe Valley. I hoped that Helen Davies got a good look at the car and its number plate.

Meanwhile, Adaryn had opened the passenger door of the Volkswagen and pulled the hood off the human goat, revealing the woman we'd identified as Myfanwy from Surwen's pictures. She did not look happy.

'Thanks for that,' said Adaryn to Myfanwy. 'We've got them. It'll be over soon.'

Myfanwy had been crying under the hood, and she was crying now, her pale blue eyes ringed with red. 'Stop it. Stop it, Adaryn. Stop it before it's too late. Enough people have died already.' Adaryn ignored her completely.

Someone had ripped the fascia off the passenger door and bound Myfanwy's hands to the bare metal. Adaryn checked the bindings and said, 'Here's your magick, in case you get out on your own.' She chucked a chain of Artefacts on to the back seat. 'And I'll put the key in the ignition. We'll be back before you die of hypothermia.'

With that, she slammed the door shut and turned her back on the car, joining Iorwen in walking back to Rhein. Another bolt of lightning struck the hill behind them, and the rain came down even harder.

I couldn't risk getting any closer, so I didn't hear what Iorwen said to her son. I saw her place her arm on his woad-painted shoulder, and I saw her lean up to kiss his cheek. His eyes never left me. She kissed his arm and backed off, climbing on the quad bike that had Vicky prisoner, then driving off into the storm.

I heard what Adaryn said clearly enough. She waited until Iorwen had gone, then turned to look at Rhein. 'Kill him,' she said, pointing at me. 'Hunt him down and kill him. It'll get you ready for when Welshfire is released.'

She turned and got on her own machine without looking back. And then there was just me, Rhein and the rain.

He lifted his spear and advanced. I retreated. He advanced faster, I retreated as fast as my bad leg would let me. He ran, I turned and ran as fast as I could.

It wasn't going to be a fair fight: he had youth, health, Charms and Enchanted weapons. I had a gammy leg and a machete. Oh, and something else – I'd fought for my life before. Several times. He hadn't, and he'd missed his chance to kill me when I got to the trees alive.

I crashed through the shrubs and picked the biggest tree to dodge behind. When I turned round, Rhein had slowed down. His shield was suddenly an encumbrance, and a seven foot spear is only deadly when you have a ten foot circle round you. As I'd guessed, all his training had been to face a Dragon in the open, not a desperate man in a forest. He was still quicker than me, though.

I only dodged the thrust at the last moment, and couldn't bring up my machete fast enough to strike back. It was time for my secret weapon. I retreated further, running the risk of falling over a root, but getting deeper into the dark recesses of the wood. That was the moment I switched on my torch.

Rhein closed into a defensive stance, bringing up his shield much faster than I could have closed in to attack. We dodged a bit more, but he knew it was a stalemate. With that light in his eyes, he could never risk a thrust, because he couldn't see me, and if he missed, I'd get a clear shot at whichever part of his body wasn't covered by the shield.

If you're wondering where the dialogue was, I'd tried that earlier. He would have ignored me, so I was saving my breath. I backed off a few paces and tried to work out if I could get the Taser out before he realised what I was doing.

And then it was him retreating, not me. I moved my position, keeping the light on him in case he tried to creep behind me, but no, he retreated to the edge of the woods, then turned and ran, loping easily over the grass. I didn't chase him.

When he got to the cottage, he planted his spear in a custom holder on the third quad bike and roared off. Only when he was over the hill did I emerge from the trees. If he'd given up the hunt that quickly, the timescales for tonight must be very, very tight, and I had only one hope – Myfanwy.

She was still staring at the hill where Rhein had disappeared when I got to her, and nearly jumped out of her skin when she saw me. She looked very, very frightened. I didn't shine the torch in her eyes, but I did lift the machete, just to make sure she'd seen it.

'What are they doing with my partner?' I said.

'Ruining everything. Everything.'

She was the youngest female Druid I'd met, even accounting for their age-defying abilities (I still couldn't believe that Surwen was older than my mother. Scary). Her hair was soaked, her robe smeared with mud and green stuff, and her limbs had been tied so tightly that I feared for her circulation. Give her credit, though: she was working steadily through the rope, using the sharp edge of the metal struts in the door. There was a long way to go.

'Too late for riddles, Myfanwy.' I lowered the machete, so that it was out of her sight line. 'I know you're not happy with what they're up to, so help me to stop them. I certainly wouldn't feel any loyalty to someone who tied me up in a car when there was a mad axeman on the loose. Never mind a Dragon.'

'I heard you, you know. Talking to the Pennaeth. I heard everything. He was right about one thing.'

I was going to give her two more chances to co-operate before I got aggressive, and she'd just used one of them. 'Right about what?'

'That you stink of the Old Enemy.'

I looked over my shoulder – a little divine intervention would be useful right now, but there were no hooded figures, no ravens and no one-eyed saviours waiting in the wings.

'I think I'm a long way from the Allfather right now, Myfanwy. I'm not his servant, you know.'

'I know. That makes it worse, because you think you're doing the right thing.'

'Surely the right thing is saving lives, Myfanwy.' She'd just used up her last chance, and I think she knew it.

'They're doing the *Blasu Diwethaf.* The Last Tasting.'

That did not sound good for Vicky. 'They're not going to eat her, surely?'

She looked at me as if I were mad. 'Not them. Welshfire. They're going to feed her to Welshfire, because Dragons only feed on what they know in the cave. Feeding them humans is a perversion – they're carnivores, yes, but they're only killers if you make them that way.'

'How long before they stick the knife in?'

'Alive. She has to be lowered into the chamber alive, so Welshfire can see her Imprint and know her for what she is. She also has to be anointed as food.'

'Who's going to be up there?'

'Doesn't matter. You'll never stop them.'

'If you don't help me try, you'll have a lot of deaths on your conscience. Who's going to be up there?'

'Adaryn and Iorwen. They sent the others off in that Range Rover.'

Others? Surwen hadn't any record of anyone else in her phone. Never mind, that was for later. 'What about Rhein?'

'He'll be going underneath, to the chamber entrance. Once the *Diwethaf* is complete, he's going to remove the cap from the tunnel. That will allow a circulation of air. Once the stones are gone, Welshfire can burn through the logs and absorb the magick.' For the first time, she looked upset. 'She won't stand a chance. She's not nearly strong enough.'

'Vicky is stronger than you think.'

'Not her. Welshfire. The Dragon's too young – we should have waited another month, at least.'

So much for sisterly solidarity. 'Where's the top of the chimney? I assume that's where it's going to happen.'

She nodded up the valley, slightly to the right. 'Somewhere up on the moor. I've never been. You'll never find it in time. Iorwen's too good an Occulter for you.'

'We'll see. What about the mouth of the tunnel?'

'Follow the road. There's some cottages and a small quarry behind them. The entrance is there.'

'Thank you. Is there anything else I should know?'

She shook her head. 'I won't help you hurt them.'

'Fair enough. I won't release you in that case, and you'll have to hope you're not in the path of a man-eating Dragon.'

'It would serve me right if I was. Can you do one little thing?'

I shut the door. 'If it takes less than ten seconds.'

'Pass me the water from the back. I'm not thirsty, but I do need to pee. Funny what goes through your mind.'

I took four seconds to check the water for magick, then chucked the bottle in her lap and jogged back to the Mercedes. I stowed the machete in my rucksack and picked up the dowsing rod. This makeshift Dragon nursery had been lashed together in a hurry, relatively speaking, and that meant the Ley lines would be close to the surface. I picked a course that would take me anti-clockwise of the moor, and headed off into the rain.

It's not bedtime reading, but *The Conduit of Lux* is a good general introduction to the transmission of Lux, dowsing and the construction of Ley lines. Chris Kelly had lent me a copy, and I even understood some of it. He'd also let me peek at his map of Wales.

A new Ley line is like a new motorway – not something to be undertaken lightly. I knew that the only line through the Brecon Beacons roughly followed the A4067, the road we'd turned off, the road where Helen Davies was waiting. To get Lux to the Dragon chamber, Iorwen must have tapped that line.

A Ley line can't go through running water, in the same way that you can't have a ford on a motorway, so either they'd tunnelled *under* the Tawe, or they'd put up a quick bridge. The storm wasn't helping my dowsing skills, but I had Harry's gift – the yew rod. I gripped the branch and mapped a course parallel to the Tawe in my head, then closed my eyes as much as I could and stumbled forwards, leaving Myfanwy, her car and the cottage behind. I was also putting distance between me and my worst failure as a CO.

If I hadn't become overconfident, Vicky wouldn't have been ambushed, and we'd be waiting in a dry car with Helen for the cavalry to arrive. I'd have to be my own cavalry. Again. At least the new waterproofs were still doing their job. I didn't panic when nothing showed up. It had to be there. Sooner or later, I'd find it. That would be the easy bit. I'd get there.

I stopped when I got to a dry stone wall and tried to look back through the rain. The cottage was already out of sight. Ice water trickled down my wrists (you can't dowse in gloves), and my shoulders slumped. *I'm so sorry, Vic. So sorry...*

I took a deep breath and looked right. The wood was still there, still following the river. There was still time for a quick bridge to be hidden by that wood. *Come on, Clarke, don't fucking give up yet.* I tossed the yew rod over the wall and heaved myself up. As I swung my leg over, I caught a whiff of barbecue. *Not Vicky. Not her. Not yet.*

I scrambled down and picked up the rod, yelping with fright when the Lux pulsed through my arm. Iorwen had run her temporary Ley line along the wall. I could almost hear Chris Kelly sniffing with disapproval at her laziness.

The power was strong, vibrant, ragged and very close to the surface. Even the densest Welsh farmer would notice something here. Had the Brotherhood of the Dragon leased all the surrounding fields, too? I squared my shoulders and followed the twitching rod along the wall, climbing steadily towards the moor. Rain lashed in from the left, and more lightning struck the hill behind me. My foot sank into bog, and that just spurred me on. Vicky was up there.

I'd felt power before, but never running like this. With the yew rod in my hands, I felt like I was water-skiing on Lux, and then the Lux leapt up from the ground and flowed into the rod, and from the rod it flowed into me, and I finally understood what it meant.

All the Works and Artefacts I'd learnt and acquired were conjuring tricks and tools compared to the feeling of the magick itself. With this inside me, I could do anything with reality – like turning the air over my head into a cone. I wove a magnetically charged cone that deflected the rain like an umbrella. Suddenly, I was not getting soaked any more, or not after I angled the top of the cone properly into the wind.

Hunh. Where had that idea come from? I had absolutely no idea, but that knack of twisting the forces into a cone of air had come from the flow of Lux under my feet, and the same thing was happening on a big scale just ahead of me. Somehow the Work/Charm was being echoed back down the Ley line, just beyond the edges of my consciousness. Was this how Vicky experienced the Sympathetic Echo when she was doing her Sorcerer bit?

I stopped thinking about the direction the Ley line was flowing and concentrated a bit closer on how it worked, closing my eyes. My Sight wasn't good enough to understand the structure of the Ley, but I did get two smells: one was sulphur, the other was a sweet pipe smoke, the sort of smell I'd always associate with Grandpa Enderby.

On top of the moor, they would be anointing Vicky for the *Diwethaf.* I had to press on, moving a little slower and trying to capture something I'd experienced before: the Earth's geomagnetic field.

Could you describe how you move your left hand, and explain how you feel touch? It's hard, and it's even harder to explain how I knew that the leaky, badly contained stream of Lux flowing up this hill was dragging electricity in its wake like dust in the slipstream of a lorry on the motorway. Other Ley lines were insulated, but this one was creating an electric current strong enough to deflect a compass needle. This was all very good, but could I use any of it to save Vicky's life?

The slope steepened, my breath flagged, then the wall veered right across my path. I didn't slow down because Iorwen had flattened the stones before she laid the line, blowing them into a heap like Keira had done in Wray when I tried to run her over.

I was on the open moor now, even more exposed and even more determined. I crouched down and shielded my eyes from the wind. The Ley line had run straight, so far, so I just gazed ahead. Was that a glow? Yes. About three hundred metres ahead, something was glowing in the dusk. I swept the area for other signs of life and found none. I stowed the yew rod in my rucksack and took out the machete.

The Ley line was my guide and friend up here. If I left its track, I'd lose everything, because Iorwen's Occulting would take over, and I might find myself walking off a cliff in short order. The closer I got, the more power leaked up through my boots, and there they were: three women in white. And two of them were fighting.

I broke into a jog. There was no stone rim round this chimney, just the soil scraped back to bare rock and Lightsticks planted in the peat around a hole. Iorwen was struggling to tie a rope round a female Druid while Adaryn stood off, holding something to her chest. Another fifty metres and I could see that the Druid was Vicky – they'd stripped her and shoved her into one of their robes. The back was already stained red with blood from the spear wounds.

To do that, they'd had to release her hands, and now she was fighting for her life. The Silence was gone, too, and I heard Vicky screaming defiance. And then I heard something else. The bump under Adaryn's cloak was a harp. She began strumming it and singing, a piercingly beautiful song of power. In Welsh.

Was it the song or bad luck? Vicky's bare feet slipped on the wet rock, and Iorwen pinned her down, pulling a cable tie around her hands. Iorwen was smaller than Vicky, but Vicky had no magick and Iorwen had clearly trained in martial arts. Vicky struggled for a second, then Iorwen punched her head down into the rock and Vicky went limp. It was time to close in.

I kept my eye on the women, and didn't see the bog leading up to the improvised chimney. I staggered and fell forwards just as Iorwen grabbed a carabiner at the end of a climbing rope. Vicky had recovered enough to get to her knees, but couldn't stop Iorwen clipping the carabiner to a climbing harness fastened roughly round her waist.

I levered myself out of the bog, and Adaryn saw me. She stopped singing long enough to shout a warning. Iorwen turned to look at me, and that was Vicky's chance. She'd picked up a rock when she was knocked down, and swung it in her bound hands into Iorwen's face with a crunch that felled the Druid. I'd have finished her off, but Vicky took a step back, allowing Iorwen to sweep Vicky's legs from under her.

In two more steps I was with them. Adaryn started singing again, a different song, and one I'd heard before, at Lunar Hall. Not a song, a sonic assault, an unbearable pain that drilled through your brain. I stumbled, Vicky clapped her hands to her ears, sinking back to the ground, and Iorwen moved away to where the rope was coiled, next to a great iron spike that anchored it to the rock. Iorwen clipped herself to the rope and fiddled with a belay brake – the device that would allow her to lower Vicky into the Dragon's chamber without killing her. With no Ancile to protect her, Vicky could be blasted into the chimney like clearing your patio with leaf blower.

The pain got worse, and I almost wished my ear drums would burst to stop it hurting, even as I took another useless step. Then Iorwen panicked, moved too quickly and the rope jammed in the belay brake. I had a few more seconds of agony to go before it was over.

Or a few more seconds to tap into that Lux and do something about it. Yesterday, I'd put a Silence on Gwyddno. I had no idea how it worked: I'd just summoned the magick from the Badge on my gun. But it was in there somewhere. I staggered left, to where the Lux was flowing like a brook over the edge of the chimney, and fumbled the Hammer out of its holster. I focused on the patterns under the magick and touched the Badge.

I tasted Nimue's Well. Under the sweet water was the peace of the lake, and under the peace was a protective … Silence. I wove the peace around me and Adaryn's Song was snuffed out.

Vicky was rolling in agony, only feet from the chimney, and Iorwen had nearly got the belay brake fixed. I took two of my biggest strides, and dived forward like I was trying to make the crease and score the winning run in a cup match. Instead of bringing my bat down, I stretched out to slam the machete into the rope. Sparks flew when the metal hit the rock, and the impact jarred up my arm. I must have put something extra into the strike, because the rope both severed and burst into flames. Vicky was safe. For now.

'Run!' I shouted, turning my head to see if she was OK.

Duh. She couldn't hear me, of course. Silence cuts all ways. The Work had spread to her, and she was no longer in agony. When she looked up, I pointed left, jabbing for her to move. She nodded, and I started to get to my feet. With no noise to distract me, my sense of smell kicked in. The wind wafted some air from the chimney, and I smelled the Dragon for the first time – a throat-gagging combination of burnt meat and more sulphur.

Adaryn was still making the Song, and it seemed to absorb all her attention. Iorwen, under her own Silence, had been concentrating on the belay rope, and only looked up when she was ready to blast Vicky down the hole. Instead of a powerless Mage, she saw me.

Iorwen stepped back quickly, and her Silence brushed against Adaryn. There was a flash of light and the two Druids flew apart like opposing magnets, both collapsing into the mire. The pain behind my eyes was so intense, I could barely open them.

I stopped focusing on the Silence and brought up my machete in defence, slashing the air in front of me while my eyes recovered. I stopped waving it when I heard voices.

'Come on, let's go,' said Adaryn.

'No. The *Diwethaf* isn't finished,' said Iorwen.

Adaryn and I both heard the sound of the fanatic in Iorwen's words. One of the spots in front of my eyes resolved itself into a white shape – Adaryn was picking up her harp and getting ready to scarper on her own. Iorwen was getting undressed.

What? No – she was taking off her harness, with the belay brake still jammed in the rope. When she'd freed it, she threw the harness overarm, above my Ancile, and used a blast of magick to push it in an arc that ended at the chimney. The harness plunged down the chimney, pulling the rope behind it. The cord unravelled until it was stopped by the metal anchor.

I took two paces forward, and Iorwen pulled out a short dagger that pulsed with magick. She was a master Artificer. She had made her son's shield and spear. I did not want to get stabbed by that dagger.

She circled left, trying to get a line on Vicky, so I moved to block her. She moved left again and swapped the dagger to her left hand. I'd clocked that she was right-handed, so what was she up to?

She feinted with the dagger, then bent down to pick up a bowl that was hidden behind a pile of Vicky's clothes. She tipped the bowl down her chest, covering herself with a viscous yellow goo that soaked her Druid's robe like a stain of insect blood. I got an immediate hit of sulphur.

She swapped hands with the dagger, then threw it straight at my heart. I ducked.

One day, I won't duck, when I've practised a bit more. My Ancile deflected the blade, because it was a missile, and I'd been in no danger. My bad leg spasmed, and I couldn't get up before Iorwen reached the chimney. She grabbed the climbing rope and jumped down, using her bare hands as a brake.

I winced in sympathy. If she held on to that rope there would be no flesh left on her hands when she got to the bottom... but there would be a Dragon. Welshfire would get her anointed *Diwethaf.* Iorwen was no longer a problem for me.

Where was Adaryn? Over there, crouched over Vicky, with a knife to her throat. I took a deep breath and walked towards them.

'You've over-played your hand, Imogen,' I said. 'You said that only both Vicky's death and mine would keep you out of the shit, so I'm not going to surrender.'

Vicky's eyes were closed. I knew she wasn't faking it.

Adaryn gave me a game grin, the sort you give someone before a hand of poker. 'You'd let me slit your bitch's throat? Not very chivalrous, Sir Conrad.

Don't you fancy her enough to save her life? Are you frightened your "girlfriend" might find out you've been mooning after the little pikey? Unless your "girlfriend" is just a figment…'

'Don't bother, Imogen.' I interrupted her bile, and took another step towards them.

Adaryn sliced the robe and revealed Vicky's naked breasts. She gripped one of them in her left hand and held the knife to it. 'Another step and I'll slice it off. Not fatal, but…' She saw the look on my face. 'You've never seen her tits before, have you? Dragons don't like artificial fibres, so we cut her bra off.'

I held my hands up and theatrically took a step backwards. 'I'll answer your question, Immy. It might help you understand your position.'

'My position?'

'Yes. Yours. For your information, if it was a choice of saving Vicky or my future wife and unborn children, I'd save Vicky. Every time.'

She relaxed her knife hand a fraction. 'Why?'

'Because I'm Vicky's Commanding Officer. I wouldn't follow a CO who wouldn't give their life for mine, so why should anyone follow me unless I set the same standard? The trouble is, you can't let either of us live, so you haven't gained anything.'

She let go of Vicky's breast. 'How did you do it? Yesterday, you couldn't light your own farts, so how did you pull that off just now?'

'Blame Iorwen. That Ley line she created up the hill was so crude I could almost drink the Lux. That and the gift of a branch from MADOC's Grove.'

'Harry gave you a cutting?'

I nodded.

'*Et tu, Pennaeth?* It wasn't Iorwen who made the Ley line. She's a perfectionist. Was.'

I took a moment to look round the hillside. We were in the middle of the lambing season, yet all this grass was far too long, and there wasn't a Black Welsh Mountain sheep in sight. Or a Texel Cross.

Adaryn wasn't looking at me any more. Maybe the isolation of her position was sinking in. I tried to engage her a bit more. 'Have you fed all the sheep to the Dragon?'

She laughed. 'Not personally. Rhein did that. And a cow, and some deer. Mostly sheep, though. You wouldn't believe how much a Dragon can eat.'

It was time to get back to business. 'You've got two choices, Imogen. Either three people come off this moor alive with one of them in custody, or you die. Look at it that way, if it helps.'

She reached under her robe, the knife never moving from Vicky's throat. She pulled out a walkie-talkie and pressed Send. 'Adaryn to Rhein. Over.'

'Go ahead.'

'…'

She'd switched to Welsh. I think I heard *Blasu Diwethaf* at one point. I definitely heard the note of triumph in Rhein's reply. Adaryn clicked off the handset and dropped it on the ground. 'Creative talents are seriously underestimated, don't you think? You did well at school. I didn't, because they don't like creative types. I didn't fit in their neat little boxes. Here's a third option.'

She began singing a gentle song, still holding the knife in a threatening position. Something was happening, and I had to stop her. I started to jog forward just as Adaryn dropped the knife and laid her hand on Vicky's chest. My partner's muscles spasmed, and then she flopped back. Adaryn stood up.

'I've stopped her heart, Conrad. You can chase me or try to save her. I kind of hope you do save her. And that the Dragon eats both of you.'

She lifted her robe and ran.

I ran, too, and the first thing I did was use the machete to free Vicky's hands, then cut off the Druid robes they'd put on her. I dragged her to a boggy pool and dumped her in it. Then I looked at my watch. She was cold before and the icy bog would quickly lower her core temperature, helping to slow decomposition. All in all, I might have another nine minutes before massive brain damage occurred.

A roar came from down the hill. Of course. Quadbikes.

I wasted three seconds collecting things, then scooped up Vicky's body. Sometimes you can't unsee things that your eye thrusts into your brain, and I would never unsee the tattoo just to the right of Vicky's Brazilian Strip. Ouch.

Iorwen's bike was just below the crest of the moor, less than thirty seconds away. As I placed Vicky in the trailer, I noticed that it had stopped raining. The key in the ignition saved me another minute.

Adaryn had followed one set of tracks, north west. A second set led south west, and those were the ones I took. Vicky's best hope was tied to the door of a green Golf.

25 — A Palate Cleanser

There were five minutes left on the clock when I roared up to Myfanwy's car. I left the bike's engine running and pulled open the door. The terrified Druid shrank as far back as she could with her arms nearly pulled out of their sockets.

'Adaryn stopped Vicky's heart. Can you restart it?'

'I … I don't think I can. I don't have the power.'

'I can get you the power. Don't move a muscle.'

I slid the machete carefully between her hands, hoping the blue in her fingers wasn't a sign of incipient gangrene. The rope and gaffer tape parted, and I swung her legs out of the car to release her feet. Four minutes.

She gave a cry of pain when the blood rushed back and she fumbled to rub life into her extremities. I jerked open the back door and grabbed her chain of Artefacts. 'Here. Don't try to stand. I'll lift you on to the bike.'

I rolled her out of the car in a fireman's lift and swung her on to the bike seat. There was just enough room for me to fit in front. I put the bike in gear and turned to the path I'd taken to find the Ley line.

'Where are you going?'

'Ley line up there.'

'There's another one to the mouth of the chamber. Follow the track.'

Three and a half minutes left. It was a gamble. I swung the machine round and roared on to the track, straight into the path of a red sports car.

Adaryn was getting away, and I swerved to avoid her, just as she swerved to avoid me. We passed in a shower of mud, and I was round the corner. The track only ran another hundred metres before the valley levelled out in an opening, and Myfanwy grabbed my shoulder. 'To the left. There.'

I glanced to the right, and got an impression of buildings and a bite taken out of the hillside. I turned left and stopped when an inbreath gave me a waft of sulphur.

With two minutes left, I handed Myfanwy off the bike. She'd torn the tape off her wrists, taking skin with it. There was blood, and it was red. Good. I left Vicky where she was, and took out my dowsing rod. It took me another thirty seconds to find the exact run of the Ley line because this branch was much better crafted and better hidden. It also had even more power running through it.

Vicky's naked body nearly broke my heart when I laid it on the gravel. Dirt would be pressing into those open wounds on her back. She'd need a visit to the hairdresser as well. 'You make a start. I'll tap the line.'

Myfanwy knelt by Vicky, placing her hands by the right shoulder and the bottom left of the ribcage. 'She's still in there, Clarke, but she's wavering at the edge. I need enough Lux to create an electric current.'

I held the rod and tried to draw up the power like I had on the moor, but all I got was another waft of sulphur. Damn.

'Now would be good,' said Myfanwy.

I had one shot left. One choice. My left foot sank into a boggy puddle, and I knew what that shot would be. I shuffled so that my left hand was on Myfanwy's shoulder, holding one end of the yew rod in my right. With a prayer to Odin, I jammed the rod into the puddle, down towards the power line.

Lightning flashed up my arm, scattered over my body and down into Myfanwy. Blue sparks flew off her hands as she jerked them away from Vicky, whose chest spasmed and lifted off the ground.

'Stop,' said Myfanwy.

I let go of the dowsing rod and dropped to Vicky's side. Where the Druid had touched her, bright red burns were blossoming. Myfanwy stroked Vicky's forehead gently as I reached for her wrist. I let out a sigh when a faint pulse kicked against my fingers.

'She's here. She's back,' said Myfanwy.

'And she needs to get to hospital,' I said. I went to pick out my rod, and felt a huge puddle of electricity gathering around it. I removed the rod gingerly, and the accumulated electrons flowed to earth through the pools of water.

I took it more slowly going back to the ruined cottage, and told Myfanwy to stay on the bike while I searched her battered VW. Myfanwy was wearing her street clothes, which meant her Druid robes must be nearby. I found the warm, dry garment in the boot and shoved it under my arm, then drove on to the Mercedes. I placed Vicky in the back, covered her with the robe and started the engine, turning the heat up to maximum. The cold on the moor had saved Vicky's life, but it would kill her soon. Only when I'd shut the doors did I turn to Myfanwy.

'Thank you. That was well done.'

She looked down. 'I'm sorry it was necessary.'

'So am I. Not only that, she's going to die again very soon if we don't act. DS Helen Davies is waiting at the main road, and you're going to take Vicky to her in this car. After that you've got a choice. You can take the Mercedes and run, or you can go to the hospital with Vicky and hand yourself in. If you run, I'll make sure no one chases you until tomorrow. Free and clear until then. If you surrender, I'll put in a good word. I'll do more than that, if I can.'

She rubbed at the sticky residue on her hands, reopening a wound. Her fingers weren't burned, and she wasn't even that wet. I got ready to count to twenty before taking action.

'I won't do more than my twenty-eight days in Blackfriars Undercroft.'

'You've lost me, Myfanwy, but don't take all day explaining it.'

Her cornflower blue eyes widened. 'Adaryn said you were wet behind the ears, but you must know about the Undercroft.'

'It's a prison. So what?'

'It's more than a prison. It's a sentence of death or madness to a Mage. I can do my month on remand, but any sentence has to be Seclusion under house arrest.'

'Don't ask for the impossible. You must know that I have no say in sentencing.'

'Adaryn also said your motto was *A Clarke's word is Binding.*'

I nodded.

'Then give me your word that if I'm sentenced to the Undercroft, you'll break in and release me.'

Vicky was dying. She needed me. 'Very well, but the bond only covers the offences I know about. Anything else and it's void. Deal?'

'Deal.'

'Get your phone out and video me. Make sure the sound is working. Quickly.'

She did what I asked with raised eyebrows, but she did it. I wiped my face and stared into the lens.

'Helen, listen carefully. Vicky needs to get to an ICU urgently. She's suffered cardiac arrest and may have hypothermia. Myfanwy will go with the ambulance or drive her in the Mercedes. Whatever you think is quicker. After that, Myfanwy needs to be taken into custody. When you've sorted Vicky, put out an alert for that Range Rover and the red Audi, if they passed your way. The occupants are not to be approached by the mundane police. Call Rick and tell him what's happened. I'll see you when it's over. Do not attempt to come up here.'

I signalled for her to stop recording. 'What *has* happened?' she asked. 'I've been locked in the car, don't forget.'

'Welshfire got her banquet of human flesh, but it was Iorwen on the menu. If she was your friend, I'm afraid I'm not sorry. Adaryn's buggered off. Rhein's going to release the Dragon.'

She looked up the track, not the hill. I'm guessing she wasn't a fan of Iorwen. 'It should never have come to this.'

'Get in and adjust the seat. I'm going to empty the boot.'

With the bags in a heap, I opened the driver's door and said, 'Hand over your Artefacts. I'll look after them.'

She hesitated, then hooped them off her neck. 'What are you going to do?' she said.

'What I always do. Try not to get killed.'

'Don't let Rhein do anything stupid. Help him if you can.'

Aah. It made sense now. As well as a passion for Dragons, the Druid with the cornflower eyes had a passion for the Hunter. I put my hand on the door. 'I got in a mess once. I was given a second chance. Don't blow yours. Now, hurry up.'

I slammed the door, and she pulled away, down the track and into the woods. I watched the brake lights until she disappeared around the bend, then I picked up the bags and trudged back to the Volkswagen.

When I emerged from the trees, sunshine bathed the clearing and the old cottage. The storm had passed over, and there would be an hour's light before night descended on the valley. The Watch Captains would be gathering in Bristol at this very minute.

I stowed the gear in the Volkswagen and took the keys. My bones ached, I was soaked from the knees down, and tired in every muscle, but Vicky was alive and on her way to hospital. I'd take that for now.

I lit a cigarette and turned to follow the track of the storm as it moved east towards the MADOC Grove and the wake they were holding for Surwen. The cumulonimbus rain clouds were thick and black over the hills, and towering above them was the cirrus anvil. Lightning flared from the bottom, and a light winked on the anvil above. Very end of the world. I dropped my cigarette and got back on the bike.

My plan was very simple, and consisted mostly of staying out of sight until I knew the cavalry were on their way, then retreating. I'll call that Plan A. With a bit of luck, it would take hours for Rhein to clear the stones from Welshfire's prison and release the Dragon.

There was plenty of gas in the quad bike, so I opted to explore first. I took a middle way, avoiding the paths to both the chimney and the buildings. Less vulnerable to surprise attack, but much more precarious – I was driving along the shoulder of a hill that had just been soaked by a month's rain. The bike's fat tyres held, just, with one alarming near slide as I crested the ridge. I dismounted with some relief.

Perhaps my luck was changing. A dry stone wall appeared and gave me the perfect cover to survey the target area. From left to right, I observed the stream, the spot where we'd resuscitated Vicky, the track, and then the buildings. A row of three cottages hunkered down against the wind. My eye was going to move on until I realised that they weren't derelict.

I raised the binoculars for a closer look and saw that they were in a good state of repair, even sporting curtains at the windows. Work had been done on the structure as well, and two of the three front doors had been bricked up to create a single building. I lowered my binoculars and the sense of unease I'd felt ever since we'd left the public road reasserted itself.

These cottages couldn't be newer than the 1920s, surely? Yet they were missing on the paper maps, as was the substantial track and bridge over the

Tawe. This whole property had been Occulted, and it had been hidden for years. Decades. Who by? What for?

Surwen's phone, Gwyddno's statement and Harry's actions all pointed to six members of the Brotherhood of the Dragon, so who was in that Range Rover? And who had constructed the Ley lines? I don't like loose ends, especially when I'm dealing with people who have crossed the line to admit lethal violence to their operations. I rubbed my chin and filed it for later.

Behind and to the right of the cottages was a complex of features and structures that took me a while to decode. Right at the back was the bite I'd seen taken out of the hillside where Welshmen had gouged the rock for limestone. Closer to the cottages was a disused lime kiln, and then some old buildings where the slaked lime was stored and which were now dedicated to farming. There were two empty pens in front of what would have been the lambing shed, if the lambs and their mothers hadn't been fed to a hungry Dragon.

There were several signs of the Brotherhood at work. First, the area in front of the lime kiln had been flattened and bedded to become a construction site. The heavy plant was gone, but two trailers were parked neatly to the side. Then there was the black Volvo XC90. What is it with Mages and their 4x4s? What I couldn't see was a quad bike or the bottom of the quarry. Time to move uphill.

Another few metres to the north east and I could see everything. From my reading and conversations, I knew that the main entrance to a Dragon's nest always slopes down from the surface, and with Myfanwy's information, I knew why. When Welshfire started burning her way through the logs blocking the tunnel, the heat and smoke would need to rise up, and the main chimney would switch to being the vent supplying the oxygen. Putting an airtight seal on the tunnel was a good way of keeping the Dragon penned in.

I had expected a pile of rocks, and that's what the ancient Druids had no doubt used. The modern Druids had built a short brick extension to the tunnel, then brought in a load of ready mixed concrete and cast a huge rectangular plug. Rhein wouldn't be getting through that in a hurry. Right on cue, he appeared from one of the buildings on his bike, pulling a trailer with a compressor and a pneumatic drill. If he used that to attack the concrete barrier, he'd be there for a month.

He dropped the trailer by the mouth of the tunnel and drove the bike away a short distance. There was a big sack on the back of the bike, incongruously pink. Incongruous because it contained ANFO – Ammonium Nitrate / Fuel Oil, the world's most commonly used industrial explosive. Oh. That would make his job easier. Nevertheless...

Even with the explosives, it would take a long time to drill the block. I focused on the concrete plug. It was already drilled. He must have brought the drill to clear out any blockages. Things could move a lot faster than I'd planned for. I took a close look at Rhein as he bent over the compressor. His woad sigils were covered by a boiler suit, and around his waist was a toolbelt. I lowered the binoculars, took in the overall layout of the site and revised my Plan A, adding a Plan B just in case. Plan A was risky, but not too risky, and all in a day's work for a Captain of the King's Watch. Plan B was another matter.

I drove down, round and stopped while the hillside still hid me from the buildings. I walked from there, slowly, until I could observe the targets from a safe distance. There was no sign of life anywhere except in the quarry, where Rhein was attaching the air hose to the pneumatic drill. When he stuck on a pair of ear defenders, I jogged round the cottages to the back door, the main door on any farm that I've ever visited.

I'd seen no smoke from the chimneys, and the range inside the farmhouse kitchen was cold and empty. There was, however, a fan heater and kettle, and plenty of signs of recent habitation. I was sorely tempted by the thought of hot tea. I closed my eyes, and I could feel the heat of the mug against my icicle fingers. Surely there would be time for that? I dug my fingernails into my palms and opened my eyes to stare at the table. Neatly piled up were the Druids' street clothes, bags and bits. I lifted the keys to the Volvo, snagged a bottle of water from the fridge and dodged outside.

I may not have any magickal bullets, but I still carried my mundane Sig handgun. I got as close to the quad bike as I dared, and waited for Rhein to get his compressor going. When he put the drill into the first hole, I fired three shots into his bike. The first two took out a tyre each. The third went into the instrument panel. It might hit something electric, it might not. There was no point shooting the explosives because you need a primary *and* a secondary detonator to set that stuff off.

I ducked back behind the shed when the drill stopped. I watched him giving about twenty seconds attention to each hole, and when he started up again, I jogged back to my own vehicle and took a good look at the surrounding countryside.

The stream had swollen quickly after the rains, and was now quite a torrent. A small path led to where the stream broadened and became more shallow. I took a closer look and saw why. Someone, probably with help from a JCB, had dug out the bank and laid slate blocks in the stream bed, making a useful fording point. Even with today's rain, the quad bike should get across quite happily.

Beyond the ford, the land rose more gently. It would finish by meeting the main moor up top, and presumably re-join the mundane world of long distance footpaths at some point. Down here, down in the Occulted valley, there was a mixture of marshy leas and stands of trees, and wouldn't you know it, there was a Ley line running under the ford, the continuation of the one that I'd tapped to help Myfanwy save Vicky. The oddest thing was that instead of running towards the National line across the Tawe, it came down from somewhere up that hill.

The compressor was still running in the quarry, so I got out my yew rod and tried to dowse while driving the bike. It wasn't easy, and twice I lost the run of the line before I rounded a knoll and came to a slope too steep to risk the bike. I killed the engine and dowsed my way up the bank. Over the lip, my dowsing rod went crackers, and I flinched away from the Lux up there.

On top of the mini-hill was a stone circle, or what you'd get if you told a mad Victorian landscape gardener to make you a stone circle. The twelve standing stones were a hazy green in colour, veined and stippled in bronze, and as alien to this valley as the slate bed of the ford. In the centre was not an altar but a pillar of polished anthracite, and it was gently smoking.

Beyond the circle, the land dipped again, and only then did I realise that this was not a natural feature. This stone circle had been planted on a man-made hill, and that pillar of anthracite had been driven into it to tap a primary source of magickal power.

I approached the ring of stones carefully, spreading my senses to check for Wards. I don't know why: I've never seen one myself, and I wouldn't know what one was like until I triggered it. I passed the line of the stones, and the distant sound of the compressor stopped suddenly, not with a cough and splutter, but like someone pressing the mute button. That was weird, but weirder still was the song which replaced it. Through the soles of my boots, I heard a male voice singing in Welsh, accompanied by a graceful harp.

The words were beyond me, but I know lamentation when I hear it, and when I closed my eyes, I could even hear the acoustics of where the song had been sung. It wasn't a siren-song, it wasn't rooting me to the spot with magick, so I decided to take a closer look at the anthracite pillar and put down my yew rod.

I picked it straight up when my jacket and all my clothes started to smolder and the song was replaced by a warcry: *Die, you Saxon bastard.*

I bowed low towards the pillar and stepped smartly backwards and out of the circle before the blessing inherent in Harry's yew branch stopped working. I checked my garments for combustion (especially down below. Certain areas had got *way* too hot). Satisfied that I wasn't on fire, I turned back towards the farm because I couldn't hear the compressor any more.

The mound was a good vantage point, and there was a nice grass ledge outside the circle where I could sit down and check on Rhein's progress. The binoculars revealed that he had finished his drilling, and that he was packing away the compressor. When he slipped off the ear defenders, I took out the radio that Adaryn had left on the hillside and pressed Send.

'Clarke to Rhein. Clarke to Rhein. Over.'

Through the binoculars, I saw him duck behind the compressor and take a good look round the quarry before picking up his walkie talkie to respond.

'Adaryn said you'd run away.'

I waited a second to give him time to follow protocol, then continued. 'Exactly what did she tell you, Rhein? Over.'

He laughed. 'She said that the *Blasu Diwethaf* was complete, that your sidekick was dead and that they were getting out of there. She said you'd run off and left Vicky to die.' He paused. 'Over, Captain Clarke.'

'Some of that was true. Adaryn did stop Vicky's heart, but she was the one who ran away. Myfanwy resuscitated Vicky and she's surrendered in exchange for a reduced sentence. They're both in Swansea by now, I should think. Did you honestly think I'd abandon my partner? And it's Squadron Leader Clarke, if you're being formal. Over.'

'I'd believe anything of a neo-Nazi thug. I don't care what happened to Meadowknickers or your pikey pal, if I'm honest. The *Blasu Diwethaf* has been completed, and soon the hunt will start. If you stick around, I'll hunt you down, too. Over.'

I had been planning to be gentle with him until his crack about Myfanwy and Vicky. That was out of order. 'If I'm telling the truth about Vicky, Rhein, who do you think completed the human part of the *Blasu Diwethaf*? When you confront that Dragon, do you think it will smell of your mother's perfume? Over.'

The radio stayed mute for a moment, then burst into Welsh. Twice, he said something that sounded like a plea for Iorwen to contact him. I still didn't feel sorry for him.

'You're going to die slowly for that, Clarke. My mother is safely out of the way with Adaryn, and she'll be glad to hear what I'm going to do to you. Over.'

'Two things, Rhein. First, a question: did Adaryn say *We're leaving* or did she say *I'm leaving*? Secondly, I've got the keys to your Volvo, and your bike's a goner. This is your last chance to surrender. Over.'

'The last thing you hear will be in Welsh, Clarke, just before I kill you. Over and out.'

I watched him toss the radio away and jog to his bike. When he saw the deflated tyres, he sprinted across the yard to the farmhouse. He emerged a few seconds later, craning his neck in circles to try and spot me. With the setting sun at my back, there would be no reflections from the binocular lenses, so I carried on watching as he dragged the sack of ANFO pellets to the concrete block.

The ground below me was perfect for what I had in mind for Plan B, if it came to it, and the extent of my preparation for Plan A was to move the quad bike beyond the Druid's mound so that my escape route was open. After that, it was just a question of waiting for the fun to start. I took the chance for a smoke while he rammed home the pellets and sealed the blasting caps. It didn't take long.

The rumble through the ground was faint. The sound of the blast was huge. When the dust had settled, I could see what the brick extension was for – to stop the rubble blocking the mouth of the tunnel. You don't want to be clearing up when there's a Dragon on the way.

Rhein marched out of the compound with his spear held high as wisps of smoke emerged from the tunnel. I did wonder at his strategy at first, because a bright blue Druid with a seven foot spear is quite easy to spot against the winter landscape. And then he cleared the buildings, squatted down and rubbed the sigils on his arm. The blue designs swirled, and he was gone, completely concealed, like a cartoon chameleon. I lowered the binoculars. No wonder he'd been able to ambush us by the old cottage – I might have walked right past him and not noticed.

I stared at the spot where he'd disappeared, and tried to use my Sight to detect his magick. Useless. Then he moved, and for a second his black pants were visible against the grey hillside. With his powers, I'd have hunted naked. Perhaps he didn't want his mother to see him.

The smoke from the tunnel was dense now, and I weighed up my options. I'd hoped to keep track of Rhein, and his ability to fade away like that was a complicating factor. Would he come looking for me and abandon the Wyrm hunt? Given that those radios had a range of over a mile and I could be hiding anywhere, he probably wouldn't risk it.

Adaryn had said there was enough wood in that tunnel to keep Welshfire busy for several hours. Good. My Plan A was to scoot over the hill at six o'clock, when the cavalry would be well on their way to rendezvous with Helen Davies.

I was reaching for my fags when Plan A went up in smoke: with a roar I could hear across the valley, Welshfire emerged from the tunnel and took her first look at the world. Shit.

First she squeezed her head out of the tunnel, then she used her chest to push the rock aside, and finally her back legs and tail emerged. The Wyrm *Welshfire* was as black as the anthracite pillar behind me, as keen to sniff the air as a hunting dog, and looked nothing like any dragon you've seen on telly.

I scanned the beast carefully, and I saw what Surwen had tried and failed to achieve with Moley. At some point in the past, long long ago in the past, some god, some Mage or some Spirit had created the race of Dragons, but they hadn't started with a blank piece of parchment: they'd started with a large reptile, probably a relative of the alligator. Mother Nature can be twisted and shaped, but she's very hard to replace.

Welshfire's head was slightly tapered, but there was no long sinuous neck behind it, and no sleek body either. Her chest was bulbous and broad, because this creature was going to fly, and to fly you need muscles to power your wings. Reptiles have four legs, and the front two had been stretched to thin remnants of limbs to act as the framework for leathery skin. Once clear of the rubble, she stretched her wing-arms to give herself some balance, and I saw that there simply wasn't enough surface area on her wing membranes for flight. Yet. Then she stood up.

In their Wyrm stage, a Dragon moves on its back legs, using its tail for balance, as I saw when she lifted herself to her full height and jogged forwards. I scrambled my brain, trying to get a handle on her size, and I did so when she passed the Volvo. Four metres at the shoulder. That's huge. Think African elephant. Think slow and lumbering, then add magick. Welshfire was as fast on her two legs as a T-Rex must have been, and no doubt twice as graceful.

She emerged from the compound, head swinging, and I thought she was looking for Rhein. I half expected the Druid to emerge from his hiding place and bring down the Wyrm where she stood, but no, he left her alone for now.

She flapped her wing-arms again and moved forward more slowly until she came to the stream. Can Dragons cross water? Is it damaging to them? No. She dropped her head into the stream and drank. She drank deeply, lifting her head a few times to shake water off her eyes then returning to the water. When she'd finally finished, she sat back on her haunches and folded her little arms on her chest. She was looking, sniffing and listening, but she was doing something else, too, and the answer came to me a moment before she proved me right.

Her abdomen had been pulsating while she sat still. Something had been going on inside her. Something that involved a lot of water. I thought of the night I'd snared Vicky into working for me at Club Justine, the night she'd given me my first lesson in magick. She'd taken a lighter filled with water and made it flame *by loosening the covalent bonds in the water molecules.*

Welshfire was doing the same, but on an industrial scale, and when she'd finished, she reared up on her back legs and used those chest muscles to blow a stream of fire that scorched the opposite bank black in seconds. Liquid hydrogen and liquid oxygen are what they use to power rockets.

The sweat running down my back went colder than the valley stream. Rhein was going to let Welshfire escape from this occulted valley and start eating any sheep, cow or farmer that got in her way. *Then* he was going to hunt her. Suddenly, in the absence of a thermonuclear warhead, Plan B was the only option.

Satisfied with her jets of fire, the Wyrm sniffed the air again, and started to move up the valley, towards the moors. Once she left the valley, there would be plenty of sheep to feed on up there, as she could no doubt smell.

I struggled out of my waterproof coat, jumped down the Druid's Mound and jogged along the Ley line until I got to the marshy depression. I splashed my way through the boggy puddles to where grass reasserted itself and looked up the valley. Welshfire was already almost out of sight.

I gripped my dowsing rod and tried to tease some Lux out of the line. I didn't want to plant it yet, but I needed a boost. As the Wyrm's tail disappeared round a bend in the hill, I got enough juice to amplify the signal and I activated Moley's Badge of Office.

The whole valley was suddenly filled with the essence of Mole, the gagging smell and the thump of paws under the ground, the feel of rock and the sheer Moleish arrogance that says *This is mine. Stay away.*

Welshfire is not mature. She's a teenager, and no teenage Dragon with attitude is going to put up with a direct challenge like the one Moley had just issued from beyond the grave. I held my breath for an age, until the Wyrm came running back down the valley, moving her head from side to side and trying to get a bead on Mr Mole.

More Lux flowed and I used Moley's badge again. Welshfire changed course and vaulted the swollen stream, heading straight for me. A blue and black figure detached itself from the rock behind her and gave chase. Good.

I drove my yew rod into the soft grass, right through the Ley line. I kept pushing until only an inch of wood remained above ground, and I put all my magick into making my dowsing rod a dam, as well as roughing up the Ley line to make it leak around the edges. When I stepped back, Lux and electricity were both starting to pool in the water around me.

Welshfire was nearly on me, and raising her head to roast my sorry carcase. I had one chance to save my life.

'*Croeso mewn heddwch,*' I shouted, sticking both arms high in the air. It was the only thing I'd learnt from Harry – *Welcome in Peace*. Somehow, I didn't think Myfanwy would have spoken to the Hatchling in English.

The Wyrm slowed her pace and held her fire. I kept backing away, stumbling and tripping over the rush-bearing tussocks. She moved beyond the buried yew rod, and little blue sparks shot from her claws. Welshfire was now far too close to me, and I was far too far from the Druid's Mound for this to end happily. The great jaws opened, the chest flexed and a jet of flame shot out. I cringed. I curled myself into a ball and dropped. Wouldn't you?

The flame had been aimed well over my head, a warning shot for me to stop moving. I stood up, soaked through now that I had no coat to protect me. The Wyrm looked at me and sucked in its cheeks, then the mighty lungs spoke with the power of a cathedral organ and her words echoed round the valley. '*BLE MAE'R FERCH!*'

I cringed again, and used the cringe as a cover to take a couple more paces back. Welshfire stepped forwards. 'I speak no Welsh!' I tried.

She lowered her head towards me, and I saw the intelligence in her eyes. '*Ble mae Gwenhwfar?*'

That sounded like ... 'Guinevere?' I said.

She rumbled, down in her chest. *Yes.* What did Welshfire want with Surwen's daughter/son?

A blue light licked up from the marsh to her wing-arms. If I stood here, I wouldn't have long to live – it was just a question of whether death came from above or from the Dragon.

Or from the spear.

A flash of blue to my left, and I dropped flat. Rhein launched himself at where I'd been standing and the Dragonspear flashed through empty air. Before I could move, he went for the killing thrust.

Welshfire roared. She smelled the Dragonspear and blew fire down on Rhein. And me.

He raised his shield, and the flames parted round it. When the flames had stopped, his shield was smoking gently. If it continued, this might not be such a one sided fight after all. I took my chance to stagger away from Rhein and get another metre closer to the Druid's Mound.

The Dragon had seen Rhein try to kill me, and she knew that Rhein was her enemy. For the moment, I was reclassified as *neutral* to Welshfire, so I escaped a personal scorching. What I hadn't anticipated was her resources, or lack of them. She plunged her snout into the biggest puddle and sucked up water. Oh.

Rhein was not so easily distracted. He held his shield to deflect any flames, and came for me with the spear. I had no machete this time, and no trees to hide behind. I glanced over my shoulder and memorised the driest routes to the Mound, then turned to face him.

'What does Welshfire want with Gwen?' I shouted.

'She was promised. We were going to use Gwen for the *Blasu Diwethaf* until you kidnapped her.'

'Did Surwen know about that?'

'She'd have come round after we'd done it. She could have concentrated on worthwhile stuff with that freak out of the way.' He grinned at me, and said something very smooth in Welsh.

'Was that supposed to be the last thing I heard?' I replied. 'Well, tough shit. I'm not going to be killed by a fucking gay Smurf. I'd rather get roasted. Watch your back, blue boy.'

I dodged to the left, and Rhein would have had to turn his back on Welshfire to attack me. He glanced over his shoulder and saw that the Dragon was ready to burn again. He spun round to face his enemy, and I spun round to run for my life.

I put everything into that run. Every ounce of willpower, energy and hope. At this point it was mostly hope and willpower. Behind me, I heard flames and I heard Welsh. A waft of hot air washed over me. I got to the bottom of the Mound, and was only six paces from safety when Rhein raised his spear and completed the circuit.

From a clear blue sky came death. The cirrus anvil that had topped the storm was over twenty miles away, but its hugely positive roiling mass of charged particles sniffed out the negative pool of electricity behind me. When Rhein raised his spear, a streamer of electrons rose up to welcome the positive leader poking down from the cloud. Boom.

A few hundred million volts flew between them. I was saved from the strike because the Druid's Mound had become positively charged after I'd stuck my yew rod in the ground. I was saved from the strike, but nothing could save me from Welshfire.

The Dragon exploded. All those gases inside her were ignited by the lightning, and the strike added its own blast. Together, they lifted me up the rise and into the circle. If I'd hit a stone, I'd have been Conrad paste. Instead, I burst into flames.

Harry's blessing saved me. In the wash after the blast, I heard the blessing he'd pronounced over the yew branch, and the stones held their peace. I was no longer being cooked from the inside out, but my clothes were still burning. I found the last bit of oxygen in my thigh muscles, crossed the ring in three strides, and launched myself off the other side.

I flopped on to the slope and rolled the last two metres into a puddle. The flames were snuffed out and cold bog water soothed my skin.

It was over. I was alive. Vicky was alive. The sheep of Brecon could safely graze on their hills, and their shepherds could sleep easily in their beds.

I stood up and checked myself for damage. There were some ugly red patches where blazing fabric had touched my skin, but eyes, ears and head seemed in working order. I touched my scalp. *Ouch.* All my hair had burnt off. Ah well.

I squelched round the Mound, giving the stones a wide berth and making a quick dash to grab my coat and rucksack. I dumped them on the quad bike and surveyed the scene of battle. In the centre, lightning had scarred and burnt the grass over a wide area. Scattered bits of white and brown might be Rhein or his weapons. The energy in that strike had boiled him like a microwave and blown bits of him everywhere.

Welshfire was gone. Completely gone as if she'd never existed. I peered in the long grass, looking for evidence. I found a claw and was bending to pick it up when the (scorched) back of my neck prickled. *Not safe.* I don't know why, but I left the claw where it was and drove back down the track of the Ley line.

The final casualty of the strike had been my yew rod, and Lux now flowed slowly towards the farmhouse.

I made it to the kitchen, put on the fan heater, boiled the kettle and stripped off my soaked, singed and stinking clothes. Rhein was shorter than me, but until I could be bothered to get down to Myfanwy's car and retrieve my overnight bag, his jeans and sweater would do just fine.

Reluctantly, I put my own boots back on and pottered with a proper tea tray. I'd seen a small bench outside the farmhouse that would capture the last five minutes of sunshine, and I was going to have a moment. I didn't notice that I'd put two mugs on the tray until a cloaked figure came walking up the path.

I struggled to my feet. 'Allfather. An honour.' I bowed and paused. 'Do you drink tea?'

He lowered his hood. Today, Odin was channelling a US Army general. I think. He was beardless, his pure white hair razored short and his one blue eye had a flinty edge to it. 'Thank you. May I sit?'

I put the tray on the flags and poured two teas. He declined sugar with a shake of his head. I was acutely conscious that he was bestowing a great favour on me by doing this, and waited nervously to see what he wanted. If I'd had any more energy, I'd have got up off that bench and put a respectful distance between us.

He took a sip and put down the mug. 'There's a vacancy for God of Thunder, if you're interested.'

'Erm…'

He smiled with one side of his mouth. The same side as the eye patch. 'Perhaps not. You're a bit too old.' He turned his head to the north. I couldn't see his face, but I could feel the currents of memory stirring around him. 'My son went into legend as an idiot, all arm and no brain. He was young, that's all. He never got a proper chance to grow up.' He turned back to me. 'What happened over there, beyond the stream.'

'Don't you…?'

He shook his head. 'Where there is no perch for the raven, he sees nothing. I saw you, a Wyrm and the Hunter go in. I saw the lightning and I saw you come out.'

I rubbed my chin. 'Is that because of the Druid's Mound?'

'Is that the name you gave it? It's as good as any, but the true name – in Germanic – is Bardsholm. It's been there for millennia but fell out of use until I saw Adaryn lead the funeral procession for Owain the Bard across that stream. This settlement was his home.'

I mulled that over. Like all the Creatures of Light (including Vicky), the Allfather was stingy when it came to information. He was letting me know something important, and expected knowledge in return. 'Do you mind?' I asked, flashing my nearly empty cigarette packet. He shook his head, and I told him the story from the moment we'd crossed the Tawe until I landed in the pool. He asked more questions about the Bardsholm than anything else, and at the end I had one question of my own.

'Did you have a hand in the lightning?'

'Still worried about free will, Conrad?'

'Isn't everyone?'

'Not me. What you did in there was legendary. Literally. There will be stories told about that encounter for a long time. Such a struggle sends waves all through the Sympathetic Echo, as they call it in Salomon's House. I would say that it shakes the roots of Yggdrasil.'

He picked up the stone cold mug of tea and blew on it. Steam rose up. Neat. He took a deep swallow and adjusted his cloak. 'The aftershock has given me a tiny window to visit you here, and to take on flesh to share your hospitality. It took me a generation to get an opening to visit you at Elvenham so that I could Enhance your powers last Yuletide. My scope to engage in the material world is very, very limited. Your will is as free as mine.'

He smiled on the last line, and I understood his ambiguity. 'Thank you, Allfather.'

'There are gods,' he said, 'who would have punished you for hubris. Calling down a positive lightning strike, they would say, is not for mortals. I say well done. In fact, I don't think I could have done it better myself.' He replaced his mug prior to taking his leave.

Before he could stand up, I said, 'Forgive me, but could I ask you advice on a matter of ... justice? Protocol?'

He stood up and swept his cloak out of the way. 'Of course you can ask.'

I told him about the Usk View Hotel, and the owner's betrayal of us to Adaryn.

He nodded, and his brow furrowed for a second. 'You are right. Such a breach of hospitality cannot be left unpunished.' His mouth twitched. 'Would roasting her over her own fire and serving slices to her children be too much?'

'A tad disproportionate, possibly.'

He bent down to whisper something in my ear. When he'd said his piece, he put his hand on my shoulder. 'I may be with you again soon. If Victoria Robson consents.'

Victoria? Oh. Vicky. The touch of his hand on my shoulder spread warmth down my back, running all the way to my left leg. When he pulled up his hood, all the pain from the burn down there was gone.

'Farewell and thank you,' I said.

'You honour me. Go well, Conrad.'

I bowed low, and when I looked up, he was gone. I touched the back of my head. *Ouch.* For one fleeting moment, I thought he might have cured my bald patch. Oh well.

The last rays of the sun had disappeared behind the distant Black Mountain when I drove the Volvo down to Myfanwy's car and got changed properly. It was weird knowing that no one was around for miles, and I wanted to get a move on, so I just stripped naked outside the old cottage and put on lots of warm layers.

The drive back to the main road was a slow one, just in case of ambush. When I came to the junction, I found Surwen's white Mercedes facing me. I stuck my hand out of the window and waved, then pulled up next to it, driver's window to driver's window.

'Thank all the gods you're OK,' said Helen.

'Battered but alive. See?' I lowered my head for her to see the burns. 'That's the worst, thank goodness. How's Vicky?'

'Serious but stable, according to the last update. I got a patrol car to come up here and wait with me, and when Myfanwy appeared with Vicky in tow, I put them both in Jonesy's car and he didn't need me to tell him to put the blues and twos on. Vicky's heart stopped again, just outside A&E, apparently. She'd have been dead for sure if we'd waited for an ambulance.'

I let out the drop of breath I'd been holding since Adaryn had pulled the cardiac arrest stunt. 'Thank you, Helen. I owe you.'

'Do you want directions to the hospital?'

I shook my head. 'She's in the best place. My role is to finish the job here. Do we have an ETA on the Watch Captains?'

'Forty five minutes. Do you want to come in here? I've got food.' She waggled a wide mouth Thermos and Tupperware.

'Helen Davies, why are you married to someone else?'

'That's what all the boys say. Come on over.'

27 — *Eat, Drink and be Merry*

I didn't get to see my partner until Friday afternoon, what with one thing and another. Helen pulled rank on the hospital to get constant updates, and with Vicky being in the ICU until Friday lunchtime, and her parents arriving, I judged it best to wait. I was also quite busy myself.

The first hurdle to seeing Vicky was the locked door of the Coronary Care Ward. I pressed the buzzer and said that I was there to see Vicky Robson.

'Police and designated family only,' said a tired Welsh voice.

I took a wild guess and said, 'I'm Uncle Conrad.'

'Oh. Okay. You're on the list. Hang on.'

She buzzed me in and told me that Vicky was in the isolation room at the end of the corridor. 'She's not infectious nor nothing,' said the nurse. 'It's just that the armed officer is rather distressing to the other patients. I think the consultant is with her just now, if you want to wait in the family room with…' She looked at me properly for the first time, and couldn't see how I could be related to any of the Robsons. '…with Vicky's parents,' she finished, rather lamely. 'Just over there.'

I'm fourteen years older than Vicky, yet her parents are older than mine. They stood up when I entered the family room, clearly expecting the consultant, and clearly disappointed when I wasn't him.

'Mr and Mrs Robson? I'm…'

'You're Conrad Clarke, aren't you?' said Mr Robson

You could tell he was an ex-miner: big, beefy and bald. His face told the story of his life with a scar on his cheek, damage from his years of drinking and a wariness from thirty years' sober. He didn't look happy to see me.

'Are you gonna tell us what the fuck's been gan'on with our girl?'

'Jack! Language! I'm sorry, Mr Clarke. I'm Erica, and this is John.'

Vicky's mother was nothing like her husband to look at, and you could see which side of the family Vicky favoured. Mrs Robson — Erica — was more delicate, more reserved and had dressed formally for her visiting. She offered me her hand, and when I bent down to shake, I could see the lines round her eyes, and the guarded look in them. She'd had her pain, you could see, and most of the time she hid it well.

I offered to shake hands with her husband, and he complied with some reluctance. 'I'm called Jack, not John,' was his concession to social niceties.

Erica sat down, leaving the men stranded until I took a chair across from them and Jack joined his wife. 'He's got a point,' she said. 'The police are lovely and all, but they won't say nothing about what happened, and Vicky's pretending to have amnesia.'

'She is a bad liar,' I said.

'She gets that from her father.'

'How is she?'

'A lot better, thanks. She's young, thank goodness, but she's been through a lot. Please tell us what happened, Mr Clarke.'

'Conrad. Please. Your daughter's a very special young woman, and so is the work she does. What has she told you about her life in London?'

It was tiny, but it was there. Erica's eyes flicked to her husband, then back to me. She understood; he didn't. Vicky's mother was from a family with magick in some degree, and she either knew instinctively about Vicky's gift, or she'd been told something. Erica folded her hands in her lap and waited for her husband to answer.

'She told us it was a desk job with the Ministry of Defence,' said Jack. 'Either it wasn't, or you have some very dangerous photocopiers in your line of work.'

'Vicky is a junior investigator,' I said, remembering the cover story she'd used with Dr Nicola. 'She's been assigned to me for field training and experience. I'm afraid I can't say any more than that there was a serious incident, that she acted with incredible courage and that she was injured in the line of duty.'

Jack half exploded out of his seat. 'She's only a bairn! What was she deein' out there in the forst place?'

Erica reached out a hand to still him. 'She's not a bairn any more, Jack. Do you remember how happy she was when she stayed with us the other week, when she was on her way to Alnwick? I asked if she'd got a boyfriend, but she said she'd got a new boss and that she was loving her work. Don't you remember that?'

'Aye, I do, but I'd rather she was bored than dead.'

Erica looked down, and her unspoken response hung in the air: *She'd rather do this than be bored.*

Jack sat back and rubbed his face with his hand. 'Were you there? Were you in danger as well?'

'Look at his head, Jack,' said Erica. 'He's got third degree burns up there, and you know the only thing Vicky said, don't you? She said that Conrad's first reaction was to get her to safety.'

'I owe Vicky my life. Several times over.'

'Aye, well, that's all very good, but...' Jack muttered something under his breath.

'Thank you,' said Erica. 'Thank you for bringing her back to life. In more ways than one.'

My blushes were saved by the entrance of the consultant. When I offered to leave them alone, Jack told me to stay. 'She insisted you were put on the list as family,' he said. 'It's obvious Vicky likes you and trusts you, but you know what hurts most?' I could see a smile lurking in his eyes.

'No?'

'She said that you could be my younger, better-looking adopted brother. She can be a cruel lass at times.'

'She also said you were spoken for,' added Erica, almost wistfully.

'If you've finished?' said the consultant.

We all sat down and the consultant said, 'She's making very good progress. There have been no further abnormalities in over twenty-four hours, and she's responded very well to treatment. She needs monitoring over the weekend, but I've scheduled a full work-up on Sunday afternoon.' He flashed us a bitter smile. 'We do work weekends, despite what the government would have you believe. If she gets the all-clear, she can be discharged on Sunday evening, but she'll need rest for a few days after that.'

'Oh,' said Erica.

The consultant ploughed on regardless. 'She also said you have a full-time job, Mrs Robson, and that she'd prefer to recuperate at a private medical facility called …' He checked his notes. 'Elvenham House Convalescent Centre. In Gloucestershire. She said it was covered by her work insurance.'

I had the sense to keep quiet. If Vicky didn't want her parents knowing that she was volunteering my house as a nursing home and my services as nursemaid, I wasn't going to disillusion them.

Erica gave an involuntary sigh of relief.

'We'll stay until she's had the tests,' said Jack, 'then I'll drive us home on Sunday evening. Traffic should be quiet then. She's a lot better, love, you said so yourself, and you've got enough on your plate with your mother.'

'Aye, well. We'll see.'

The consultant was on his feet and shaking hands before anyone could ask more questions.

When he'd left, Erica said, 'You see her first, Conrad. She's seen enough of us. Do you want a cup of tea?'

'That would be most kind. No sugar, thanks.'

I showed my ID to the armed officer on duty and knocked on the door. The policeman was more for show than anything else. While Vicky was still unconscious, Rick James had rigged Wards around her room to discourage Druidic interference and linked them to a bell. If anyone with magick (except me) crossed the Ward boundary, the bell would ring and the officer was supposed to get on the radio. One of the Watch Captains had also stood guard for the first twelve hours.

Oh, the recuperative powers of youth. Apart from lots of machines and wires running under her gown, Vicky looked no worse than the last time I'd seen her without makeup. She'd even washed her hair this morning. She was sitting up in bed, and opened her arms for a hug when I appeared.

'Not too hard,' she said. 'You'll knock off the sensors and trigger the alarms.'

I gathered her in my arms and kissed her cheek.

'Oh my life, Conrad, what's happened to your head? The officer outside said you weren't injured.'

'It's just awkward, that's all. It looks worse than it is because I don't want to wear a dressing and I can't wear a hat. It'll heal.' She was still reaching up to my shoulders, something that wasn't helping my back. I disengaged gently. 'You've no idea how glad I am to see you.'

'Why? Were you afraid I'd ruin your record by dying?'

I stood back. 'Something like that. Just because your heart stopped, it doesn't give you the right to make me your nurse.'

'Twice. Me heart stopped twice, Conrad, and I've got you to thank for this.' She pulled down the neck of her gown and showed me a dressing above her right breast. 'That's gonna scar, you clumsy bastard, and I've got a matching one here.' She prodded her abdomen and winced. 'And then there's the spear cuts on me back. More scars. You owe me big time, Uncle Conrad.'

'Well at least there'll be no awkwardness when I give you a blanket bath. After all, I've seen your tattoo.'

'You what! Why?'

I shrugged. 'You were dead. I had to dump you in freezing water to lower your core temperature. Myfanwy's seen it, too. And technically it was her who gave you the burns, not me.'

'Aye, well. I'm not gonna thank you, Conrad. That would be too awkward. I'm just glad to see you, too. Now sit down and tell us what happened. All I know is that all our side got out alive and that there's no need for nuclear bombs.'

I got the visitor's chair and sat down. 'What can you remember?'

'The last thing I remember is smashing that rock into Iorwen's face.' Suddenly she looked down. I'd thought the jokes and bravado were because she'd been scared of dying. I was wrong: she thought she'd killed someone.

I took a deep breath and took a big risk with our relationship. 'Why didn't you finish her off, Vic?'

'I was gonna. I tried to draw some magick, but I hadn't got any. If I'd just dived on top of her, it would have made your life a lot easier. I'm sorry. I'm really sorry.'

Wrong again, Clarke. She thought she'd let me down.

'Here. This might help. I found them in Rhein's quad bike.' I took a package out of my bag and passed over her chain of Doodads.

'Thank you. You may never know how good that feels.'

'I've got your tablet computer, too, but the battery's flat.' I scanned the room. All the available power sockets were running the monitoring machines that surrounded her bed.

'Leave it over there,' said Vicky, pointing to a tall, thin wardrobe.

A knock on the door announced Erica and tea. 'Are youse two gonna be a while?' she asked.

'Probably,' said Vicky.

'Then we'll go to the retail park and buy you a new phone, then nip back to the hotel. See you later, pet.'

She kissed her daughter and left us to it.

'Talking of hotels,' said Vicky, 'where've you been staying? Not the Usk View, I take it.'

I snorted. 'No chance, but I am going back to have a word with them tonight. I've been living it up in Nyth Eryr, drinking Adaryn's whisky and raiding her freezer. I did have supper with Helen's family last night.'

'Did she take pity on you, pet? Aah.'

'Do you want to know what happened or not?'

She shifted in the bed, lowering herself down and turning on her side. She winced when one of the burns got pressed down by the sheets. 'Go on then.'

I started with the end, with the news I'd had on the way to the hospital. 'Hannah's got the St David's Day meeting of the Occult Council postponed for ten days. She said they need to hear our testimony. Apparently the various Circles are abuzz with it all.' I hesitated. 'I had a long talk with her about risk. She agrees with me – something's going on out there. There's too much crawling out of the woodwork.'

'Aye. You're right. One of me tutors once said that there's a reason why old magick got forgotten: too bloody dangerous. And then people forget why it was forgotten in the first place. I should be back at work by the end of next week, and if you can't look after me, it's not a problem.'

'A week in Elvenham is just what we both need. Where was I? Oh yes, I was saving your tattooed arse…'

I took a break after telling her about the Allfather's visit, and went for more tea and a fag to give her a rest. I also left her with a box of Adaryn's hand-made Belgian chocolates. She'd eaten half the box by the time I got back.

When the cavalry had finally arrived at what I now called Bardsholm Farm, we'd split into teams. Rick and Helen had gone in search of Adaryn and the Range Rover crew, while the Watch Captains and I cleaned up at the farm. One of the many mysteries we might never solve was the identity of the farmer. Helen had come up yesterday and taken fingerprints from the agricultural equipment, but their owner wasn't on the system. With Harry Evans' help, we'd discovered that the farm was originally owned by the great Bard Owain's aunt, and her family before her. It had been a secret Druid refuge for generations, and Owain had worked to restore some of the magickal legacy, as well as modernising the farmhouse. Adaryn had quietly inherited it and what she'd done to the actual Bardsholm mound was being investigated. At my suggestion, Hannah had declared the farm forfeit to the Crown, then promptly gifted it to MADOC in trust for the use of all Druids.

The Range Rover turned out to have been registered to Adaryn, and we found it abandoned at Nyth Eryr along with her Audi. The engine was still warm when Rick arrived, but Adaryn, her giant harp and all her magick were gone. I'd tried to get Hannah to put out an alert with the Border Force, but she refused. 'One day, Conrad,' she'd said, 'but not today. Too dangerous.'

When we finally tracked down Iorwen's base of operations (thanks to Myfanwy), that, too, had been emptied of magick.

'Do you think Adaryn's still in the UK?' said Vicky.

'No. Ruth Kaplan rang me to say that Adaryn took the 07:30 Eurostar to Paris this morning. She'll be back, Vic, but not for a long while.'

'So that's it? All over?'

'Not quite. When I got to Nyth Eryr, I opened the door to that Range Rover, and it reeked of pipe smoke. You're the only one who knows this, but I'm going to make discreet enquiries through Chris Kelly when we get back. We've got the phantom Geomancer's fingerprints, too, both mundane and magickal.'

'Good.'

I could see that she was getting very tired. It was time to cheer her up and leave.

'Now for the fun part. Ready?' She gave me a weak nod, and I took a fat brown envelope out of my bag and held it up. 'Nyth Eryr is going to MADOC, as are all the Brotherhood's properties, but these are ours.'

I tipped a bunch of keys on the bed. 'Take your pick. We've got a Range Rover Sport, a Volvo XC90, the scabby Golf, Surwen's Mercedes and this.' I held up an Audi keyring. 'Adaryn's Audi TTRS Convertible. Happy birthday, Vic.'

She took the keys from me and leaned forward with a huge effort to wrap her arm round my shoulder. 'Thanks, Conrad. You're definitely me favourite uncle now. I don't know how you'll top that in September when me real birthday comes round.'

She flopped back on the bed, exhausted, but gripping the TT keys in her hand.

'Is it OK to give Helen the Range Rover? We couldn't have done that without her.'

'Hell, aye. Of course.'

I scooped up the remaining keys. 'One last thing. I'm also giving Helen one of these. You need one, too.' I passed her a small object and she forced her eyes open. 'Helen's lad knocked them up yesterday. He's a whizz at this sort of thing.'

She peered at the metal disk. It was a pin-on badge with a drawing of a castle on a hill, and the words *Merlyn's Tower Irregulars* around the outside.

She groaned. 'I can't leave you alone for five minutes, can I? Get out before I throw it at you.'

She was asleep before I got to the door.

The coach carrying the East Valley RUFC Veterans team bounced towards me down the access road. The driver had a pained look on his face which was explained when he killed the engine and I heard them singing. I sincerely hoped that their voices improved with alcohol.

Gareth climbed down the steps and joined me at the back of the car. My own car, not one of the fleet of expensive 4x4s I'd acquired recently. The journey to the Usk valley had put him in a good mood, and he gave me a big grin as he shook my hand, then patted the red jersey stretched tight over his ample waist. 'I'm starving, Conrad. Are you sure about this?'

We turned to look at the firmly locked oak doors of the Usk View Hotel. 'Tell the driver to park down by that fallen tree. We don't want any witnesses or awkward questions.'

While Gareth passed on the message, I opened the tailgate and moved the blanket. I hefted the felling axe on to my shoulder and waited for Gareth to rejoin me. He shook his head when he saw the axe, but kept his peace.

I walked slowly up to the front of the hotel and used the head of the axe to beat three times on the doors, then counted to ten. The fallen tree where I'd sent the coach had been standing when I arrived half an hour ago. It was dead and due for felling anyway, so I'd taken the chance for some practice with the axe and with a little Enhancement. Half way through my exertions, two cars with French number plates had left the hotel, a look of bewildered fury on the two families' faces. Good.

The Usk View Hotel is not a castle. The wooden doors – never normally closed – were solid enough to deter your average bailiff or burglar, but they were no match for a mad axeman. I stroked the blade of the axe and gave it the little magickal tweak that Rick James had shown me last night.

'Stand back, Gareth,' I said, and swung the axe round over my head. It struck the wood with a crack, cleaving the timbers and striking the metal bar that was keeping them closed. I brought it round for another swing, and this time it broke the bar right off. I balanced on my bad leg and kicked the doors open. Clara and her husband were cowering at the other end of the hall.

She was gripping her man and, to give him credit, he was putting himself between me and Clara. I walked slowly towards them and, ignoring the husband, I pointed the axe at Clara. 'You betrayed us. We were your guests, and you sold us out to Adaryn.'

'I've called the police,' said the husband.

'I know. They rang Inspector Williams, who's on the bus, to see if everything was OK. He said it was, and the control room marked it No Action Required. It's not you I have a problem with, old chum, it's her.'

'What are you going to do?'

I rested the axe on the floor and put my hands on the end of the haft. 'Grovel, Clara. On your knees.'

'What? You're mad!' said the husband.

Clara blinked and let go of him. Very slowly, she pushed him aside and knelt down. 'Forgive me, Mr Clarke.'

'I can't forgive you. What you did was literally unforgivable, and I'm not a Christian. Try asking for mercy.'

She lowered her head. 'In the name of the Goddess, have mercy.' She dropped to all fours and kissed the blade of the axe.

The husband was appalled. His eyes bulged and his mouth opened. He looked down at his wife, and what he'd thought was a bit of New Age nonsense and girlie bonding became the brutal reality of magick.

'Open your kitchens and cellars to my friends,' I said. 'Show some true hospitality and I will consider the debt paid.'

'Thank you,' she muttered.

Voices could be heard approaching the hotel. 'Get up,' I said. 'You'd better get a shift on, Clara. You're going to be busy, and I hope for your sake that you didn't send the staff away.'

The husband shook himself and helped his wife get to her feet just as the first of the team wandered through the entrance. He led her quickly through a door to the back of the hotel.

Gareth had stood back from my encounter with the proprietors, and now came forward. 'I can see why you did it, Conrad, but why get the lads involved? We're grateful for the night out, and all that, but you didn't owe us anything.'

'You're wrong. I invited the team precisely because the Usk View hurt them as much – if not more – than they hurt me and Vicky.'

'How do you figure that?'

'Clara offended against Welsh hospitality. She needs to make reparations to her countrymen as well.'

Gareth pulled his lip. 'You could say that. You could also say that you're making us complicit in an act of imperial domination, using us to keep the natives in line.'

The lads were mingling in the entrance, unsure where to go and looking to Gareth for guidance.

'There's the exit, there's the bar,' I whispered. 'You choose, Gareth.'

He leaned in to whisper back. 'This is my land and my people. I'll not have it said we betrayed a guest.' He straightened up and stepped forward. 'Right, lads, listen up. The proprietor foolishly made a bet with Conrad here that we'd beat the Nigels in the Six Nations.'

Translation: Wales would beat England at rugby. A voice from the back piped up, 'Not so foolish. We did it two years ago.'

'Well, we didn't do it this year, did we? The bet was that the loser paid the bill tonight, so enjoy yourselves, lads, but don't go daft. No ordering the most expensive wine just because it's free, and you can leave a tip at the end if you want. The bar's through there, and mine's a pint.'

I made polite conversation for half an hour, drank a symbolic glass and ate a symbolic steak sandwich. When I'd been for a smoke, I asked for silence and raised my glass. 'Gentlemen, the Queen.'

'The Queen!' they responded with gusto.

'And the Prince of Wales,' added Gareth.

I joined in the response, then slipped out before they started singing again.

The hospital in Swansea was as good as its word and Vicky was discharged into my care just as the sun was setting on Sunday afternoon.

'Why've you brought the skanky auld Volvo and not the Merc?' she asked as I loaded her gear into the back.

'Because you died in the Mercedes and because I sold it yesterday. Here – Happy St David's Day. I didn't get you a daffodil.' I passed her a brown envelope stuffed with twenty pound notes. It was well over half what I'd been given.

'Wow. I've never seen so much cash before in me life. I'll pass on the daffodil, thanks. Do I have to pay tax on this?'

'Only if you declare it. The Audi's being delivered to Clerkswell on Wednesday. Now get in before you catch your death.'

She stopped staring at the cash and gave me a grin. 'Yes, Uncle C. It's a good job I'm not on medication. You'd be a terrible nurse.'

The consultant had taken a lot of persuading that Vicky's *cardiac event* was a result of trauma rather than a genetic defect requiring surgery or lifelong treatment with drugs. After many tests, he'd concluded that a week's rest was all she needed to make a full recovery.

We were soon on the M4 and heading for England. 'I can't believe I'm gonna stay in your house,' she said idly. 'I bet it's really just a four bed semi on a little estate. I reckon you're not posh at all.'

'I'm not. I'm like you, Vic, just a tradesman. You'll see the house soon enough. Listen. I've had a wild idea.'

She groaned. 'No. Stop it. I'm convalescing. No more wild ideas for a bit, OK?'

'How about we propose Helen Davies as the next Watch Captain of Wales.'

'Don't be daft. She's got even less magick than you, and you need me to hold your hand. She wouldn't last five minutes.'

'It was something the Allfather said – the demise of the Brotherhood has left a window. A moment when things can be different. What if some of their loot was used to create an Artefact, a special Artefact for Wales. As well as

262

allowing Helen to do the job, it would be a symbol of commitment to Welsh magick.'

She looked impressed, and so she should. It was one of my better ideas. She nodded her head in approval, then fiddled in her bag and pulled out her tablet and her new phone. 'D'you mind? I couldn't get any sort of signal in that hospital room, what with all them machines around us. There's a lot of folks who need to know what's going on.'

'Go ahead, so long as you don't mind me having the radio on.'

'Fine.'

I listened to the Classic FM chart and she started texting and emailing. Suddenly she jerked upright. 'What the hell? Conrad, pull over. Quick.'

We were nowhere near a junction, so I pulled on to the hard shoulder and as far up the verge as I could. 'What is it, Vic?'

She tapped the screen and moved the tablet between us. I saw a shaky video of a corridor being filmed through the narrow crack of an open door. The angle changed and I could see the backs of two women, one in the blue uniform of a prison officer, the other pushing a trolley.

'Mina!' I blurted out, and though the woman with the trolley was definitely *not* Mina, she was familiar. 'That's Sonia,' I added for Vicky's benefit.

The video had scratchy sound, but it was clear enough when Sonia knocked at a door across the corridor. The PO unlocked it with one of her many keys and stepped back because prison doors all open outward. The door swung back and Mina herself stepped into the corridor, and my heart nearly stopped.

She was wearing a red tunic and black leggings from the stash I'd bought in Primark, and she'd spent time on her makeup. It was almost as if ... yes. She moved to the side, forcing Sonia to turn in profile. Mina knew she was being filmed, and wanted the camera to capture as much detail as possible.

'I've only met Mina when she was sitting down,' said Vicky. 'She really is tiny, isn't she?'

Before I could think of a sensible answer to that, Sonia dragged our attention back to the screen.

'Dinner,' said Sonia, lifting a covered tray off the trolley. 'It's your favourite, Mina. Beef.'

'Oh. Shit,' I said. 'This isn't going to end well.'

We watched Mina turn to the prison officer. 'Everyone in here knows that I'm on a Hindu diet,' she said with far more reasonableness than I'd have been able to muster.

The officer put her thumbs in her belt. 'Sonia? Do you have an alternative to suit our foreign guests?'

''Fraid not, Kathy.'

'Then take it or leave it,' said the officer.

Before Mina could say anything, Sonia took the cover off the tray and hurled it through the open door into Mina's cell. 'That's no way to treat your food,' said Sonia.

The officer took her keys in one hand and pushed Mina through the door with a great shove. 'If you're going to start a dirty protest, you can spend the evening locked up, Mina.' She slammed the door closed and locked it with a snap of the key. The video wobbled and stopped.

Sweat was pouring off my forehead and I was gripping the steering wheel as if we were at Silverstone and not on the hard shoulder. I stared at the blank screen until Vicky moved it away.

'Hang on,' she said. 'There's a message, too.' She offered me the tablet, but I found I couldn't let go of the steering wheel.

'You read it,' I said.

Vicky glanced at my face, then turned back to the screen. '*Hi Vicky*, it says. *I've sent this to you because he won't use a smartphone and I know he can't always get to his laptop when you're out saving the world. Tell him that Mr Joshi has the video, too, and he'll be contacting the Home Office first thing tomorrow. Tell him I'm OK. I'm really OK, but I might have a debt to pay later. Hope you're both safe and enjoying Wales.*' She swiped the screen. 'There's another one straight after. *And tell him that I love him, and that Desais push back.*'

I breathed out and peeled my fingers off the steering wheel. 'We'd better get going before the police turn up to see if we're okay. I don't fancy explaining the arsenal in the boot.'

'Are *you* OK?' said Vicky. 'Can you drive?'

'Yes. I know when I'm not safe.' I drove carefully down to the hard shoulder, then accelerated until I could rejoin the motorway. 'Do you mind if we stop? I'm fine to drive, but I could do with getting out of the car for a bit.'

'Aye. Of course.'

Vicky gave me time to think in the ten minutes it took us to reach the services. Of course I was worried about Mina, and not being able to do anything made it worse, but at the same time I was thrilled. Mina had been a victim of other people's wars for years, and to see her pull a stroke like that was amazing. If she could survive the next twenty-four hours…

Vicky had to keep as warm as possible, so I installed her near a radiator deep within the Costa Coffee franchise and got us some drinks.

'I can't believe what we saw,' she said, shaking her head. 'I've seen some bad stuff in pubs on a Saturday night, but never anything like that. She is one brave woman, Conrad.' She smiled. 'And you're a lucky man.'

'Don't I know it. Do you mind if I take a walk around the car park?'

'Course not.'

I marched round the floodlit wasteland of the service station, smoking and letting my nerves calm down with the movement and the chill air. In the end, the only way I could clear the last knot of stress was to send a text to Mr Joshi: *Let me know if there's anything I can do.*

His reply came back as quickly as he could type it: *Be there for her, Conrad. I have already made an appointment with an old friend from the chess club who's at the MOJ (not the Home Office). He's seeing me at ten tomorrow and Ganesh will look after her until you can take over. You've been very patient. It will work out.*

I showed Vicky the messages when we got back in the car. 'Hmm, invoking Ganesh could be a can of worms, right enough, but the main thing is that she's got you and Mr Joshi on her side.'

She stowed her laptop away and settled back in her seat. Vicky had the recuperative powers of the young, but it would take a while to rebuild her energy levels. When we got to the Severn Bridge, I glanced over. She wasn't asleep.

I pointed to the sign saying *Welcome to England*. 'We're home. It shouldn't feel like that, but it does.'

'It helps that this is your home county,' she replied grumpily. 'I don't feel very much at home here.'

'You'll love Clerkswell. Especially the pub.' I put on a casual tone. 'By the way, did you open Hannah's email? The one headed *Despatches*?'

'Nah. I thought she wanted me to write a report. That can wait.'

'Do you remember saying that you might have to kill me if I won a medal? Have a look at that email.'

She picked up her phone and scanned through the text. 'Oh my god! We've both got one! A Military Cross! Mam and Dad will be over the moon.'

'Nothing less than you deserve. She rang me about it yesterday – after sunset, of course – and said she didn't know whether to recommend us for the Bishop's Cross.'

'I've heard of that. I think. Wasn't it abolished?'

'Technically, no, and technically it's a higher honour than the MC, but it has to remain secret. Only Watch Captains and the Constable get to know about it. I told her I wanted it to be as public as possible because it makes a statement about what we do. Your parents deserve to know how brave you were, and the crew at Salomon's House need to appreciate the risks we take to keep them safe. Besides, there's another reason for having it presented formally.'

She looked at me suspiciously. 'Oh, aye?'

'I do love to see a girl in uniform.'

'Hah! You wait. You just wait, Uncle Conrad. I'll get me own back for that, you'll see.'

I let her have the last word because I'd met two sets of parents recently. Mr and Mrs Pryce would get their son's MC at his funeral, and I hope it helps them come to terms with their loss.

John and Erica Robson will get to see their daughter pick up her award in person. You can't ask for more than that.

Conrad and Vicky's story continues in The Eleventh Hour, Third Book of the King's Watch, available now from Paw Press. Turn over to find out more.

The Eleventh Hour
The Third Book of the King's Watch
By Mark Hayden

Another Day, Another Scar...

Conrad needs a rest. The Universe has other ideas...

Conrad had planned the perfect weekend in the English Lake District – tie up some loose ends and spend the night with Mina. Simple. What could possibly go wrong?

Everything is the answer. An innocent man is murdered to cover up magickal misdeeds, and before they can draw breath, Conrad and Vicky are on the trail of a Mage who hides behind dark magick to kill at a distance.

In the third book of Mark Hayden's highly praised King's Watch sequence, Conrad and Vicky take on the ancient families of the Lakeland Particular to unmask a killer with an agenda of vengeance. A Killer who doesn't care who dies on the way.

Available in Ebook and paperback.

www.pawpress.co.uk

Author's Note

Thank you for reading this book; I hope you enjoyed it. The King's Watch books are a radical departure from my previous five novels, all of which are crime or thrillers, though very much set in the same universe, including the **Operation Jigsaw** Trilogy that Conrad himself refers to as part of his history.

If you've only just met Conrad in this book, you might like to go back the Jigsaw trilogy and discover how he came to the Allfather's attention. As I was writing those books, I knew that one day Conrad would have special adventures of his own, and that's why the Phantom makes a couple of guest appearances in them.

A book should speak for itself, especially a work of fiction. Other than that, it only remains to be said that all the characters in this book are fictional, as are some of the places. Merlyn's Tower, the Dragon's Nest and Hledjolf's Hall are, of course, all real places, it's just that you can only see them if you have the Gift…

And Thanks…

This book would not have been written without love, support, encouragement and sacrifices from my wife, Anne. It just goes to show how much she loves me that she let me write this book even though she hates fantasy novels.

Although Chris Tyler didn't get to see the draft this time, his friendship is a big part of my continued desire to.

Finally, thanks to my wonderful cover designer, Rachel Lawston. She put up with a lot on the way to getting here, and I am eternally grateful.

Printed in Great Britain
by Amazon